continued ...

"Robert Gandt has done more than write a book about the people who fly . . . he has provided an unvarnished and intimate inside peek inside their hearts and minds."
—*Pacific Flyer*

"Informative, compelling, and thought provoking, [Gandt] offers an insider's perspective on what it takes to make the grade, and a number of interesting insights on key events and trends in today's Navy." —*Sea Power*

"Gandt may be the best unknown aviation writer around."
—*Air & Space*

"A former pilot who also happens to have the pen of a poet."
—*The Christian Science Monitor*

"Gandt manages to evoke both awe at and sympathy for aviators, so that readers will agonize over their defeats and cheer their triumphs." —*Publishers Weekly*

"A fascinating look into an arcane, risky, high-tech world."
—*Kirkus Reviews*

"Gandt expertly weaves human emotions onto the pages [and] tells a story that is not easy to forget."
—*Lake Worth Herald*

ACTS OF VENGEANCE

ROBERT GANDT

A SIGNET BOOK

SIGNET
Published by New American Library, a division of
Penguin Putnam Inc., 375 Hudson Street,
New York, New York 10014, U.S.A.
Penguin Books Ltd, 80 Strand,
London WC2R 0RL, England
Penguin Books Australia Ltd, Ringwood,
Victoria, Australia
Penguin Books Canada Ltd, 10 Alcorn Avenue,
Toronto, Ontario, Canada M4V 3B2
Penguin Books (N.Z.) Ltd, 182-190 Wairau Road,
Auckland 10, New Zealand

Penguin Books Ltd, Registered Offices:
Harmondsworth, Middlesex, England

First published by Signet, an imprint of New American Library,
a division of Penguin Putnam Inc.

First Printing, October 2002
10 9 8 7 6 5 4 3 2 1

PUBLISHER'S NOTE
This is a work of fiction. Names, characters, places, and incidents either are the
product of the author's imagination or are used fictitiously, and any resemblance
to actual persons, living or dead, business establishments, events, or locales is
entirely coincidental. .

For my son, Robert Gandt, Jr.,
with love and amazement

ACKNOWLEDGMENTS

Huge thanks to friend and fellow writer Lt. Cmdr. Allen "Zoomie" Baker, USN (ret). His mastery of tactical air combat and the F/A-18 Hornet fighter have again steered Brick Maxwell—and the author—out of harm's way.

A salute to 1st Lt. Chris Parente, USMC, for his help with matters of infantry tactics, weapons, and Marine Corps arcana. For their guidance through the murky waters of undersea warfare, another salute to Submarine Group 10 Command Master Chief Terry Byerly and Chief Petty Officer R. J. Hoon, USN.

Again a "well done" to Doug Grad, my editor at New American Library, for his clear eye and steady hand. To my literary agent, Alice Martell, another bouquet and big thanks.

To the real-life heroes who are holding the line against our nation's enemies, my admiration and profound respect. You're the best of the best.

"Never do your enemy a small injury."
Niccolò Machiavelli

"Vengeance is mine; I will repay, saith the Lord."
Romans 12:19

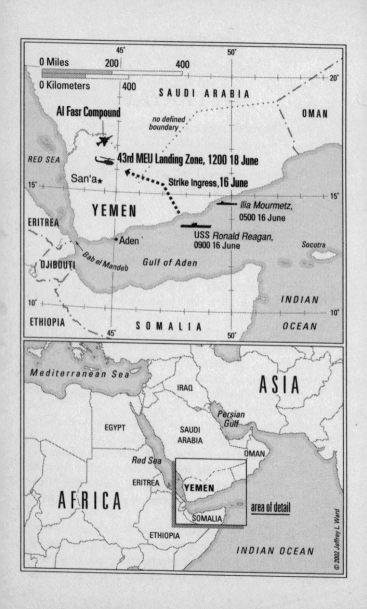

CHAPTER ONE

BETRAYAL

Abu Dhayed, United Arab Emirates
0710, Thursday, 20 May, three years ago

It sounded like a distant storm.

Colonel Jamal Al-Fasr pulled the Land Rover over to the soft shoulder of the highway. He rolled the window down and cocked his head, listening.

There it was again. A familiar rumble. An alarm sounded in Al-Fasr's mind.

Shakeeb, in the opposite seat, looked over in surprise. "Why are we stopping, Colonel?"

Al-Fasr ignored the sergeant. He opened the door and stepped out on the sand. He peered eastward, in the direction of the sea. Heat waves shimmered from the surface of the desert. The barren landscape seemed devoid of any sign of life.

Then he saw them. A wave of dread swept over Al-Fasr.

They were low, no more than two thousand feet above the desert. They looked like killer angels, flying in a loose combat spread. Al-Fasr tried to count them. A dozen, perhaps more. He recognized the sleek profiles, the canted vertical stabilizers: F/A-18 Hornets. Their long gray noses were pointed toward Abu Dhayed.

Al-Fasr felt his heart beating like a hammer. He squinted against the glare of the low morning sun, scanning the horizon. They wouldn't send fighters in low unless—

There. In the distance, just crossing the shoreline. He could pick them out, dark blobs pulsating like apparitions in the heat waves. He could hear the faraway beat of the whirling blades reverberating over the sand hummocks.

CH-53s, he guessed, and they would be filled with battle-ready marines. He stared in disbelief. Where had they come from? How did they know?

He glanced at his watch. Ten minutes past seven in the morning, exactly fifty minutes before the overthrow of the Emir's government. Al-Fasr had planned each minute detail, orchestrated every movement, assigned each duty of his clandestine force. It would be a lightning-quick transition from a feudal administration to a modern Arab state.

Something was wrong. The coup had been compromised. The Americans were in Abu Dhayed, and it could be for only one reason—to save the Emir.

He reached inside the Land Rover and yanked the cell phone out of its cradle. After several rings he heard the voice of his younger brother, Akhmed. In the background he heard the crackle of small-arms fire.

"They have the building surrounded," said Akhmed.

Al-Fasr muttered a curse. His brother's forty-man garrison was stationed in a downtown warehouse, poised to move out.

"Who?"

"The Royal Guard. Armored cars, tanks, at least a hundred troops." Akhmed's voice sounded desolate. "How did they know?"

"I don't know. But you must hold out. Naguib will be there soon with his brigade." There was no point in telling Akhmed the truth—that American troops were in Abu Dhayed. Naguib and his brigade were probably trapped.

For several seconds Akhmed didn't reply. Al-Fasr heard the sound of his brother's raspy breathing and, in the background, more gunfire.

Then a succession of explosions. "They're using grenades," said Akhmed. "I must go."

"Fight the bastards. We are on the side of the people."

"It looks bad, Jamal."

"You must hold out."

"*Inshallah.* If God wills it. Good-bye, brother."

"Good-bye, Akhmed."

Al-Fasr stood for a moment beside the Land Rover, stunned by the turn of events. His eyes remained focused on the incoming helicopters. The sound of the beating blades rolled across the desert like drumbeats from hell.

His main force, commanded by his Air Force colleague, Maj. Naguib Shauqi, was bivouacked at the Bu Hasa armory, five kilometers from the downtown headquarters. With armored cars, they were poised to race down the main highway to Abu Dhayed, where they would seize the radio station and the military command headquarters. At the same time the secondary force, led by Akhmed, would smash through the gates of the royal palace and take the Emir and his family into custody. The plan depended on the emirate's regular army troops perceiving that their position was untenable. They would lay down their arms and offer no resistance. Like most of the populace, the common soldiers had no love for the Emir.

Al-Fasr tried to imagine what had gone wrong. There could be only one possibility. Someone had betrayed them. He had no doubt that Naguib's brigade at the armory, like

Akhmed's downtown garrison, was surrounded by the Emir's soldiers.

He called Naguib's cell phone. After a dozen rings went unanswered, he replaced the phone in its cradle. Grimly he peered again at the warbirds swooping down on Abu Dhayed. If Naguib and his brigade were cornered or captured, the coup was doomed.

Akhmed was doomed.

They were all doomed.

Al-Fasr wondered how his brother would be treated by the Emir's soldiers. He shoved the image from his mind. It would be better if Akhmed were killed in battle. The Emir's Royal Guard was legendary for its viciousness.

Suddenly Al-Fasr remembered his parents.

His father disapproved of his sons' political activities, but he had not interfered. Al-Fasr's father had a special loyalty to the Emir, with whom he had gone to school and under whose protective umbrella the Al-Fasr family had accumulated great wealth.

Which was why Al-Fasr had kept his father ignorant of the approaching coup. Though the family would be exposed to a brief danger, the coup would be a fait accompli before any retribution could be taken against the family.

He cursed himself for his misjudgment.

Al-Fasr jumped back inside the Land Rover. In a flurry of sand he wheeled the vehicle around and sped back down the highway.

He kept the Jet Ranger low, skimming the floor of the desert.

Perched in the left seat, Shakeeb had the AR-15 pointed out the open hatch. For over twenty kilometers they hugged the ground, avoiding the roads that radiated like veins from the center of Abu Dhayed.

The Al-Fasr family compound lay to the west of the city, in an irrigated glade with grass and a palm-covered hillside that sloped behind the main building. Instead of using the helo pad next to the compound, Al-Fasr set the Jet Ranger down on a flat stretch of desert that was shielded from the compound by the hill.

Moving a few steps at a time, they approached the back entrance of the main building. Al-Fasr drew the SIG Sauer semiautomatic from its holster. With a nod of his head, he motioned for Shakeeb to follow. Holding the pistol in front of him, he entered the large hall that extended through the center of the house. The hall was strewn with debris—smashed furniture, paintings torn from the walls, shards of broken vases. The only untouched object in the room was a framed photograph of the Emir, smiling down on the room.

They had already been here. Al-Fasr took a deep breath and forced himself to remain calm. He had long ago forsaken his religious upbringing, but now he wished that he could summon help. *Allah, I beseech you . . .*

He opened the door to the family sitting room.

More debris. Carpets, smashed sculptures, broken lamps lay like rubble from an earthquake. His eyes swept the ruins, as he prayed that he wouldn't find what he most dreaded.

He saw something on the floor—a hand protruding from behind the slashed leather sofa. Al-Fasr scrambled through the rubble, around the sofa. He gazed down on the woman's body. Her lifeless eyes stared straight upward.

"Mother!" He knelt beside her body. Blood oozed from a single purple hole in her forehead. Her hand was still warm, her fingers clenched in a fist. For nearly a minute he remained with her, his chest heaving in sobs.

He felt Shakeeb's hand on his shoulder. "They may still be here, Colonel. We must leave."

He nodded and rose. Shakeeb was right. He could not help her, but the others—his father, his sister Aliyah. Perhaps . . .

He didn't have far to look. In the doorway to the kitchen, he nearly stumbled over a body. It was his sister. Like her mother, the young woman had been executed, killed by a single shot to the forehead.

Al-Fasr dropped to his knees, overcome by his grief. He kissed his sister's dead cheek. He clutched her body, rocking her as if she were a sleeping child.

As through a fog, Shakeeb's voice came in a low whisper. "I heard something. Someone is in the hall."

He rose and picked his way through the debris. Around the edge of the kitchen door he saw a man in a camouflage army uniform. He wore the black beret of an officer in the Emir's Royal Guard. His back was turned, and he seemed to be studying an object on the tiled floor.

The officer sensed their presence behind him. He whirled around.

In a crouch, Al-Fasr held the SIG Sauer in both hands, the sights superimposed over the officer's chest. He waited. He wanted the man to recognize him.

An expression of alarm spread over the officer's face, and his hand went for his holstered sidearm.

Al-Fasr waited.

The officer's pistol was clear of his holster, coming upward—

The nine-millimeter Parabellum round struck the officer in the middle of his chest. He reeled backward, then dropped. His weapon clattered to the floor beside him. Spraddle-legged, he braced himself with one hand, clutching his chest with the other.

Al-Fasr strode over to him. He knelt and picked up the officer's pistol. The man stared back up at him, his face contorted with pain.

As Al-Fasr rose, he noticed for the first time the object on the floor, three feet away, that had captured the officer's attention. Around it spread a crimson pool of blood. Al-Fasr's breath left him in a single gasp.

He was looking into the eyes of his father's severed head.

In the next instant, Jamal Al-Fasr, the Yale-educated eldest son of a cultured Abu Dhayed family, was transformed into a madman. His lungs filled with a burning fury. A primal scream erupted from him.

He seized the AR-15 assault rifle from the petrified Shakeeb. With his thumb he slid the fire selector to automatic. He shoved the muzzle into the wounded officer's face.

The man's eyes widened. "Please, have mercy . . ."

Al-Fasr held the trigger down. The officer's head exploded in a gelatinous spray of bone and brain matter. Al-Fasr kept the trigger depressed. He continued firing until the magazine was empty.

Smoke spewed from the heated barrel. Al-Fasr's chest heaved up and down, his breath coming in hoarse gasps. His trousers and boots were splattered with blood and bits of flesh. On the floor the Royal Guard officer's body jerked and twitched. The remains of his skull looked like a shattered melon.

Gently, Shakeeb removed the weapon from Al-Fasr's hands. He extracted the empty magazine and shoved in a fresh one. "They heard the gunfire, Colonel. We must leave."

Al-Fasr remained for another moment, staring at his father's head. The sightless eyes gazed back at him.

The Jet Ranger dipped its nose and skimmed over the hill behind the compound. Al-Fasr saw a vehicle coming—a desert-camouflaged four-wheeler, not a Rover like those used by the Emirate Defense Force. This was a larger vehicle, wider and lower to the ground.

An HMMWV—a Hummer—not more than fifty meters away.

Americans. Too late to avoid them. Would they open fire?

Al-Fasr hunched in his seat, braced for a burst of machine-gun fire.

None came. As the helo swept past the Hummer, Al-Fasr locked gazes with the occupant of the right seat. The man wore full battle gear, including the *Wehrmacht*-looking helmet and a sidearm. He was an officer, Al-Fasr guessed, probably Marine Corps. They had come not to lead the assault, just to support the Emir's cowardly Royal Guard troops.

Al-Fasr felt a wave of hate overcome him. *They helped kill my family.* For an instant he considered swinging back, ordering Shakeeb to open fire with the AR-15.

No, the helicopter was too easy a target. He would take his revenge at another time. Another way.

He pointed the nose of the Jet Ranger southeastward, toward the coast. They would remain inland from the shoreline and fly over the mountainous southern border of the emirate. During his planning he had established a contingency base in the high country of Yemen. That was where he and the *Sherji*—his militia of freedom fighters—would go if the coup somehow failed.

Now the coup had failed.

As the Jet Ranger sped across the low plateau, Al-Fasr tried to assemble the pieces of his shattered plan. One persistent thought burned in his mind like an ember. Someone had betrayed them. No matter how long it took, he would find the traitors. When he did, he would know how to deal with them.

Someone had summoned the Americans. Who? It had to be the Emir himself. Sheik Al-Fatiyah, the fat old Emir, was a man of meager intelligence whose appointed successor, his son, was even fatter and more unintelligent. Though the emirate possessed vast oil reserves, the Al-Fatiyah family's idea of governance had been consistent. Squander every *dinar* on family palaces in Abu Dhayed, villas in Switzerland, yachts in Cannes. And ignore the discontented masses who hated them.

As an Air Force officer, Al-Fasr felt a burning desire to restore the emirate's military. Under the Emir, the defense force had become flabby and obsolete, dependent on the benevolent shield of the American military. He intended to devote some of the nation's wealth to modern weapons, freeing the country from the onerous patronage of the United States.

The Americans. Where had they come from? Saudi Arabia? Oman? How had they entered the emirate without his intelligence sources reporting their presence?

As he thought about it, he realized it should be no surprise that the Americans would support the Emir. They were addicted to cheap gasoline. Stupid and corrupt as the Emir was, he could be counted on to maintain the flow of oil.

Five miles from the shoreline, Al-Fasr banked the Jet Ranger to the west and headed for the high mountainous ridge that defined the emirate's southern border. The vegetation became more sparse. The moonlike mountainscape showed only sprigs of sage, an occasional scrawny shrub.

The turbine engine of the helicopter labored as they ascended the barren ridge. At the summit, fifteen hundred meters above sea level, they had a view that extended a hundred kilometers into the sprawling desert plateau of Yemen. To the left, far below, the rocky salient of the Arabian peninsula jutted into the sea.

Out in the Gulf, an object caught his eye.

Thirty miles distant. There was no mistaking the distinctive gray flat-topped silhouette.

An aircraft carrier.

In a flash, it came to him. The helicopters, the marines, the Hornet fighters. He knew where they had come from.

He stared at the great death ship on the horizon. He thought of his father, beheaded for no reason except that his son was the Emir's enemy. His mother and sister, slaughtered like cattle.

A hatred more profound than anything he had ever felt took possession of Jamal Al-Fasr. He gazed at the ghostly form of the warship. In a voice too low to be heard over the thrum of the helicopter, he said, "I promise, Father. I will kill them."

CHAPTER TWO

INCIDENT IN DUBAI

USS Ronald Reagan
Dubai, United Arab Emirates
1045, Saturday, 15 June, the present

Incoming fighters.

Josh Dunn looked up from the flight deck and saw them—sleek gray shapes, low on the water, almost invisible in the morning haze. He could make out the long pointed noses, the missiles mounted on each stubby wing tip. They were aimed directly at the carrier's six-story island superstructure.

Dunn said nothing.

He kept his eyes on the fighters as they flashed across the harbor. The sun glinted from their wings. As the jets approached, the combined thunder of their engines rolled over the water, gathering momentum like a summer storm.

The timing was perfect. As the four F/A-18 Super Hornets swept down the length of the flight deck, the band swung into a spirited rendition of "Anchors Aweigh." Every head in the crowd, even the assembled air wing officers standing at parade rest, turned to follow the low-flying formation.

Vice Adm. Joshua Chamberlain Dunn nodded in approval. In his long career, he had endured dozens of these change-of-command ceremonies, including several of his own. This one was special. The young Navy commander standing at the podium in his service dress white uniform, though not Dunn's own son, might as well have been.

Prior to the official change of command, it had been his honor to pin on Sam Maxwell—Dunn had never gotten used to his Navy call sign, "Brick"—the Distinguished Flying Cross. In a coordinated air strike against targets in Iraq, Maxwell was credited with destroying a major weapons assembly plant at Latifiyah. On the same mission he shot down a MiG-29 flown by a legendary Iraqi squadron commander.

Now Commander Maxwell was taking command of a strike fighter squadron, the VFA-36 Roadrunners, based aboard USS *Ronald Reagan*. The ceremony was brief, deliberately so because the outgoing skipper, Cmdr. John "Killer" DeLancey, was absent. DeLancey was listed as killed in action during the same strike over Iraq.

A crowd of nearly two hundred occupied seats on the flight deck, facing the podium. On a raised dais were the guests of honor—Vice Admiral Dunn, Rear Adm. Tom Mellon, who commanded the *Reagan* battle group, and the ambassador to the United Arab Emirates, an ebullient Californian named Wayne Halaby.

Maxwell took the podium and greeted the guests. Out of respect for the deceased former commanding officer, he omitted the customary speech new skippers usually delivered. In keeping with naval tradition, he read the orders giving him command of Strike Fighter Squadron Thirty-six. Then he turned to the *Reagan*'s Air Wing Commander, Capt. Red Boyce. "Sir, I am ready to assume command."

He and Boyce exchanged salutes. The officers then turned to the two admirals, Dunn and Mellon, who stood at the edge of the dais. Again they saluted, and the admirals returned the gesture.

The ritual was complete.

A cluster of officers and guests gathered around the new squadron skipper, shaking his hand and clapping his shoulder. Josh Dunn watched from the edge of the group, thinking again how proud he had always been of young Maxwell. He had always been a good-looking kid, Dunn remembered, but now that he was nearly forty, he had a more mature look—that dark mustache, tall, rangy build, piercing blue eyes. He was the kind of son Harlan Maxwell ought to be immensely proud of—if he had any sense.

Dunn walked over to Maxwell and clasped the younger man's hand. "You're going to be a great skipper, Sam."

"I'm flattered that you came, Admiral." That was the protocol between them. In public, it was Admiral. In private, he had always been Josh.

"Wild horses couldn't have kept me away," said Dunn. "I just wish your old man were here to see this."

Maxwell nodded. "He could have been."

"You two have got to patch this up."

"Maybe someday. We don't seem to be ready for that yet."

Dunn shook his head. Adm. Harlan Maxwell was his best friend, academy classmate, and naval colleague of nearly forty years. He was also a pigheaded fool, thought Dunn.

He didn't even remember the exact cause of the rift between the elder Maxwell and his son, and he doubted that they did either. It was one of many such clashes the father and son had had over the years. They were two bulls in a pasture. For some reason, they couldn't acknowledge the underlying love and respect each had for the other.

Dunn reminded himself to talk to Sam about that.

"How about joining us for lunch in Dubai?" said Dunn. "The ambassador and Admiral Mellon and I are going to the Carlton."

Maxwell nodded across the deck to where a tall, chestnut-haired girl stood watching them. She was wearing a summer dress, a silk scarf at her throat. With the breeze ruffling the light dress, Dunn could see that she had a smashing figure.

She saw him and smiled.

"Thanks, Admiral, but I promised the lady I'd spend the day with her. We have some catching up to do."

Dunn grinned. So that was the girl he had heard about. Claire Phillips. She was a network television reporter assigned in the Middle East. According to the scuttlebutt, she and Maxwell were on their way to being an item.

"You're released on one condition." He took Maxwell by the arm and steered him across the deck. "You have to introduce me to the lady."

Hassan Fayez and Yousef Mudrun watched in astonishment as the four jet fighters swooped over them. For a terrifying instant, Hassan thought that the warplanes were coming for *them*.

Not until the jets were gone did he realize that it must be some sort of demonstration. Another American show of power.

The two men looked like any of the hundreds of boat people afloat that morning. Their ancient lateen-rigged dhow, with its large triangular sail, drifted in the outer harbor. To all appearances, the two sailors were fishing or perhaps diving on one of the sunken wrecks at the bottom of the channel.

Through his binoculars, Hassan studied the great gray mass of the American ship three kilometers in the distance. They were close enough. He had been told the American

Navy maintained a screen of surveillance boats around their flagship. He was sure, too, that they deployed sensors and weapons to discourage underwater intruders. It would not be easy to attack the *Reagan,* even though the vessel lay at anchor.

Looking at the immense size of the aircraft carrier, noting the array of guns and missiles and the massive deck filled with warplanes, Hassan felt a wave of fear pass through him. Why had he volunteered for this mission? The answer came to him immediately. He hadn't. The Leader himself had given him this assignment. There was no alternative. To refuse the Leader's order meant an abrupt departure from this life.

"Is it time yet?" asked Yousef. He, too, was a new recruit. Like Hassan, he had been assigned by the Leader.

Hassan trained the glasses on the blunt aft end of the ship. A stairway descended from the fantail to a boarding platform, where a boat was moored. "Yes," he said. "They're leaving."

He laid down the binoculars. "Rig the sail."

Yousef scrambled across the deck, swinging the suspended mast around so that it blocked any view of the dhow's deck from the ship across the harbor. The triangular sail hung like a curtain in the windless air. That was the way Hassan wanted it. He would be concealed behind the sail. "Bring up the launcher," he said.

Yousef ducked into the open hatch, then came back up with the Chinese-made weapon. Hassan busied himself affixing the launcher tube to the shoulder mount. Then he attached the reel of guidance wire to the base plate of the weapon. He tried to screw the threaded end of the wire to its connector on the missile but he was unable. His fingers were trembling.

"Be careful," said Yousef. "You'll blow us up."

"Shut up. I know what I'm doing." Hassan had performed

this task only once before, practicing with an inert round while the Leader observed his performance. It had been easy then.

Now it wasn't easy. The live round weighed several kilos more than the inert dummy. He drew a deep breath, clenched and unclenched his fist, then tried again. This time he succeeded. The threads caught, and the wire was attached to the connector. "There. It's done."

He peered across the channel. He had assembled the weapon just in time. Raising the launcher to his shoulder, he braced the tube across the lowered mast. He aimed the weapon toward his target.

From the fantail, Brick and Claire watched the admiral's gig pull away from its mooring. At the helm of the polished wooden boat stood a boatswain's mate in white uniform. Standing on the aft deck were Dunn, Halaby, the ambassador, and the soon-to-be-relieved *Reagan* Battle Group Commander, Tom Mellon.

Dunn waved from the deck as the polished wooden boat turned and pointed its bow toward the Dubai shoreline. Brick and Claire watched the boat churn across the Dubai channel. By the time it was a mile away, they could still see the tiny figure of Dunn standing on the aft deck next to the coxswain.

"He tries to act gruff," said Claire, "but that old sailor loves you."

"Josh is like a father to me."

"What about your real father? Why isn't he here?"

Brick didn't answer right away. He continued watching the boat as it headed into the choppy waters of the channel.

The reporter in Claire wanted to know more. She was about to ask another question; then she stopped. She saw something in Brick's face. He was staring at the harbor.

Squinting against the morning sun, she followed his gaze out over the water.

Then she saw it.

It looked like a fast-moving bird, zigzagging low over the water, gathering speed as if it were seeking something. The object, whatever it was, seemed to be trailing a plume of fire.

"Oh, no!" she heard Brick say.

Claire didn't know what it was, but her instinct told her it was something bad. In the next three seconds, she knew she was right.

The low-flying object struck the gig amidships. The main fuel tank exploded, and the boat erupted in an orange ball of flame. Fragments of teak and mahogany and brass and human bodies cascaded into the morning sky.

Several seconds after the flash, the sound of the explosion reached the *Reagan*.

Stunned, Claire stared at the cataclysm. Pieces from the ruined boat were raining like shrapnel back into the water. "My God, what happened?"

As a journalist she had seen only the aftermath of war and terrorism. Never had she witnessed such violence close-up, while it occurred.

Maxwell was shaking his head. His hands clenched the steel rail. "No idea. Some kind of missile."

A klaxon horn was going off. From the ship's public address loudspeakers, a voice boomed: "General quarters! General quarters! This is not a drill! All hands man your battle stations!"

"What does that mean?" Claire asked.

"We're going to combat readiness. Whoever fired that missile may be shooting at the *Reagan*. He grabbed her arm and hauled her away from the rail. "We're going belowdecks, down to the ready room."

From across the water they heard a siren wailing. On the

Reagan's flight deck, the blades of the SAR helicopter, a turbine-powered HH-60 Seahawk, began to rotate. Sailors ran across the deck, donning helmets and vests.

Before they ducked through the door that led onto the enclosed hangar deck, Maxwell stopped to peer out at the harbor. An oily slick was spreading out from where the gig had exploded. Flotsam littered the surface of the channel.

"I can't believe it," he murmured. "They're gone. Josh, the ambassador, the boat crew, Admiral Mellon."

Claire began to shake uncontrollably. "We could have gone with them."

Even before the debris had finished splashing back into the water, Hassan Fayez was dragging the launcher back toward the open hatch. On the deck lay the three extra missiles that he had not needed. Not yet.

"Move!" he yelled at Yousef. "Get the motor running! We'll run for the fishing wharf."

They had lied to him. They had assured him that the wire-guided missile was invisible. They said no one would know where it had come from. Their escape would be easy because it would be hours before anyone understood how the gig had been destroyed.

The instant he launched the missile, he knew they had lied. The ungodly thing looked like a signal flare. Any idiot who happened to be watching the harbor would have seen it, and he would deduce that it had come from the dhow out there in the channel.

Yousef had the diesel motor popping and growling. Even at full throttle the puny engine pushed the dhow through the water like a barge.

The fishing village was their only haven. Once they reached the wharf, they could melt into the throng of boat people. Their dhow looked just like any of a hundred other such vessels. They could abandon it and scramble across the cluttered decks of the boats that were moored to each other. The inhabitants of the floating village could be counted on to feign ignorance when they were questioned. The only loyalty the ancient cult of Gulf sailors had was to each other.

The harbor was buzzing with new traffic. Hassan saw a helicopter lifting from the deck of the aircraft carrier. It was headed toward them. He wished now that he had not been so quick to stow the launcher and the extra rounds. The helicopter would be an easy target.

The helicopter was keeping its distance from the dhow. That was bad, Hassan thought. It meant they had already concluded that he was a threat. They would be summoning help on the radio.

He tried waving to the crew of the helo. They didn't respond. The helicopter maintained its distance, hovering a hundred yards from the dhow.

"What will they do?" asked Yousef, standing at the tiller.

"Nothing," Hassan lied. "They don't know who we are. We are just fishermen."

It was then that Hassan saw the boat coming from the shore. A police boat, moving fast, trailing a high rooster tail in its wake. As the boat drew nearer, Hassan saw the machine gun mounted on the bow. A helmeted crewman crouched behind it.

Yousef saw it too. His face went pale. "They have us trapped, Hassan. We must surrender. We will go to prison."

Hassan knew about Dubai's criminal justice system. He and Yousef would never reach the barbed wire of prison. Their crime, by Islamic custom, had earned them a public beheading.

Hassan pulled the launcher back up through the hatch. He picked up one of the unused missiles and quickly affixed the guidance wire.

"No, Hassan! We must surrender."

Hassan ignored him. He slid the missile into the launcher tube. Bracing the tube on the lowered mast, he pointed the muzzle toward the police boat.

"Hassan! It's too late. We must—"

Whooom! The missile left the tube, trailing a torch of flame and smoke. With the guidance stick, Hassan steered the missile, trying to keep it superimposed over the police boat.

The boat was turning. The police crew saw the missile coming, and they were trying to elude it.

Hassan struggled to keep the missile directed toward the boat. This was more difficult than shooting the gig, which had been a steady target, moving away from him at a quartering angle. The police boat was dodging.

The missile missed the boat.

Hassan's heart sank. Yousef dropped to his knees, praying. Hassan struggled to affix the guidance wire to another missile. Glancing up, he saw the boat bearing down on them. A voice boomed over a megaphone, giving them an order Hassan didn't understand.

He finished affixing the wire, and he fumbled with the missile, getting it into the tube.

Bullets were already splintering the deck before he heard the staccato burp of the machine gun.

He saw something red spraying the deck.

It took Hassan a full second to realize that he had been hit, that his torso was ripped open, that it was his blood gushing over the ancient wood of the dhow's deck. His vision blurred and he toppled backward into the water.

Claire watched the port of Dubai slip into the distance.

"What's happening, Sam?" She nodded toward the captain's bridge high above them in the island superstructure. "Where are we going?"

"Back to sea. Captain Stickney is the acting Battle Group Commander, and he's getting out of Dodge."

Forty-five minutes had passed since the admiral's gig was destroyed. They stood inside a door in the island structure that led to the open flight deck. Claire and her camera crew and four other reporters were the only civilians left aboard.

She looked out to the harbor. "Do they know who blew up the admiral's boat?"

Maxwell shook his head. "Not yet. There have been other attacks. Someone gunned down four of our sailors in a bar in town. Another guy tossed a bomb into the entrance of the embassy. Must have been a bungler. He wounded a marine sentry, but no one else was hurt. They caught him, and they also captured one of the shooters from the boat that fired the missile."

"Was it some kind of reprisal action against Americans?"

Maxwell shrugged. "Who knows?"

Claire tried to read his expression. She was sure that he knew more than he was telling her. They both knew the rules—that she could report what he told her, but she was not to read anything between the lines. Just the facts, ma'am.

That was what was odd about their relationship. With her many other sources inside the military establishment, anything she picked up was free game. Journalism was a cutthroat business. Claire Phillips was masterful at piecing together stories from the tiny snippets of information gleaned in innocent conversation.

With Sam Maxwell, it was different. She had never violated their rule, not once, and she concluded that there could be only one reasonable explanation for this behavior—she was in love with the guy.

After a moment, she said, "I'm sorry about Josh."

Maxwell kept his eyes on the harbor. "Thanks."

"You'll miss him, won't you?"

He nodded.

"Was he a friend of your father?"

"Best buddies. Academy classmates, then squadron mates. Josh was my godfather . . ." His voice trailed off.

Claire tried to read his expression. His face was a mask, his eyes burning like coals. He seemed to be staring off into the desert. "You're thinking about who did this, aren't you?"

He nodded.

"Do you think there will be a retaliatory attack from the *Reagan*?" She knew the question veered outside the lines of their protocol. But she had seen that look on his face.

He didn't answer for a moment. His eyes were focused somewhere off in the Arabian peninsula. "There'd better be."

CHAPTER THREE

FACE OF THE ENEMY

USS Ronald Reagan
Southern Persian Gulf
1450, Saturday, 15 June

"Why did they do it?"

Cmdr. Spook Morse, the flag staff intelligence officer, peered at the questioner, a pilot from one of the Hornet squadrons, as if the guy had just landed from Uranus. Like most air intelligence officers, Morse had a low regard for the cognitive abilities of fighter pilots. Pilots were like single-purpose gladiators. They were dangerous if they knew too much.

"For the same reason they destroyed the World Trade Center. Because they could. In case you haven't noticed, that's what terrorists do—kill Americans."

The pilot wasn't satisfied. "Are you saying that these ass-holes get to take a shot at us whenever they feel like it?"

"No." Morse gave the pilot a glacial smile. "Listen up, and you'll hear what I'm saying."

The ready room was filled with the senior officers of the

air wing—squadron commanding officers, executive officers, designated strike leaders. A few, like the Tomcat squadron skipper Burner Crump and his beer-hoisting buddy, Rico Flores, who commanded a Hornet squadron, were nursing world-class hangovers. In the recall of personnel ashore, they had managed to jump on the helicopter from the fleet landing before the *Reagan* hauled anchor and headed to sea.

Maxwell sat in the row behind Boyce and his staff. He could feel the motion of the ship. The *Reagan* and its battle group were steaming southward in the Persian Gulf. He could only guess where. The Strait of Hormuz? Into the Indian Ocean?

In the front row sat Capt. Red Boyce, the Air Wing Commander. Boyce's honorific title was CAG—the extinct but still-used label for Commander, Air Group. Boyce was gnawing on an unlit Cohiba as he listened to Spook Morse's briefing.

Morse turned to the map projected on the screen before him. It was a topographic depiction of the southern half of the Arabian peninsula. He tapped the screen with his pointer. "Here's what you need to know," he said, leaving the clear implication—there's a hell of a lot more that you pilots don't need to know.

Listening to Morse's briefing, Maxwell couldn't help thinking about the strangeness of his situation. His life seemed to be punctuated by the loss of someone close to him. His mother passed away while he was still in high school and his absentee father was commanding a fleet. Debbie, his astronaut wife, had been lost forever in a burst of flame one morning at Cape Canaveral. Her death caused him to leave NASA and come back to the fleet. Then when it seemed that his career as a fighter pilot was washed up, his commanding officer, Killer DeLancey, died in a dogfight over Iraq. Maxwell took his place.

Of course, that could change. He had no illusions about how the Navy worked. To most of the men in this briefing room, he would always be an outsider—an ex-astronaut and test pilot. A carpetbagger who hadn't paid his dues like they had.

It was not the way he had expected to spend his first day as a squadron commanding officer. The USS *Reagan* had been scheduled for another week in Dubai. He had already booked a room in a small guest hotel on the outskirts of the city, where he intended to spend most of the week with Claire Phillips.

Claire. Though it was still too soon to trust his own feelings in these matters, he knew that he felt the stirrings of something very much like love. If his own instincts were correct, he was sure that she felt the same way.

Morse was pointing to a spot on the map. It was in the northwestern part of Yemen. "We don't have an op plan yet. Our guys nailed three of the operatives in the terrorist group, and they've provided enough intel data to give us a good ID of the group. They're exiles from a failed coup attempt in Abu Dhayed three years ago.

"We have good recon and intel data about the group's headquarters. They've got a few high-tech weapons, including some SA missiles appropriated from their own military in Abu Dhayed. We assume, too, that they've got some high tech communications and a certain level of intelligence-gathering capability, because the guy who runs the outfit has plenty of assets and a military education."

A lieutenant commander from the Bluetails spoke up. "Is this bunch connected with Al-Qaeda and Osama bin Laden's gang?"

"Yes, they're connected. But they're not part of the Islamic jihad movement. The leader of this group has a different agenda."

With this, he switched the picture on the screen. The portrait of a handsome Arab man in a military flight suit flashed into view. He had a neat black mustache. On his flight suit was embroidered a set of silver wings, and beneath his collar he wore a checkered scarf.

Maxwell felt a shock of recognition. *That face.* From somewhere back in time. He stared at the image, scratching his memory. *Where? What was his name . . . ?*

Morse supplied the answer. "Gentlemen, meet Col. Jamal Al-Fasr."

"I know him," said Maxwell.

Morse stopped. "Excuse me?"

"From the Red Flag exercise," said Maxwell. It was coming back to him now. "At Nellis about ten years ago. He was an F-16 pilot from one of the emirate air forces."

Morse was nodding his head. "That's correct. I was there too, and met this guy. The fact is, he was an impressive character. He'd gone through flight training with the U.S. Air Force. He did the fighter weapons course at Nellis, then came back with his home team to compete at Red Flag."

Maxwell stared at the face on the screen. Yes, it was definitely Al-Fasr. He was hard to forget.

Boyce turned around in his seat. "Was the guy any good?"

"The best they had. Very aggressive, but he had a problem. He broke the rules. He'd violate the hard deck altitude, take shots outside the box, whatever it took to win engagements. One day in a one-vee-one, he took it all the way down to the deck and scraped one of our guys off on a ridge in the Sierra."

"I remember that incident," said Boyce. "They kicked the sonofabitch out of the country and sent him back to the emirate."

"That's Al-Fasr," said Morse.

Boyce peered at the smiling face on the screen. "Spook, you're telling us that's the terrorist who took out Admiral Mellon and Admiral Dunn and the ambassador?"

"We have evidence that he planned it and gave the order."

"When do I get the chance to put a Sidewinder up his ass?"

"Not soon. According to the intel on this guy, he doesn't have any tactical aircraft. Certainly no fighters. You'll have to settle for a laser-guided bomb on his hooch in Yemen."

A strike leader from VFA-34 spoke up. "Does that mean we're launching a strike?"

"The new Battle Group Commander's on his way out, along with some honcho from the National Security Council. We'll know in a few hours."

The room became quiet, each pilot thinking about a possible air strike. From the projection screen, the face of Jamal Al-Fasr smiled down at them.

The high desert landscape looked like the surface of an asteroid. The entire valley was barren except for the terraced fields on the hillside where peasants tended a few scraggly sheep and tried to raise miserable crops of sorghum and millet.

Al-Fasr kept the Marchetti SF260 in a steep turn while he peered down at the target area. It would have been expedient to perform the mission with a MiG-29, he reflected. As a ground-attack platform, the MiG was a terrifying vehicle. But today's mission was special. He didn't want the speed and devastating firepower of the big Russian-built fighter.

The single machine gun of the Marchetti, mounted in a pod beneath the left wing, and the relative slowness of the aircraft—only 350 kilometers per hour in its dive—were suitable for his purpose. Al-Fasr wanted the luxury of time. He needed to observe his target at close range.

He flipped the master armament switch to ON. The target was below his left wing. He shoved the throttle to full power and rolled the Marchetti nearly inverted, pulling the nose through the horizon.

The targets appeared in his windscreen. In the rock-strewn clearing they looked like stick figures, pitiful caricatures of human beings. Al-Fasr almost wished he had armed them with automatic weapons. It would be more sporting if they could shoot back.

No, he thought. It was better this way.

He felt the airframe hum and resonate as the propeller-driven fighter-trainer gathered speed. He liked the agile little Marchetti. This particular example had been acquired from the Libyan Air Force, where it had flown in Khadafi's Sudan and Chad campaigns.

Through the fixed gunsight on the glare shield, he studied the six targets. They knew what was happening, and they were trying to conceal themselves behind each other. Like rats hiding from a marauding cat.

Each wore green fatigues except for one, who was dressed in a white, shirtlike *gellebiah*. Each was tethered to a mast by a four-meter chain.

At a range of three hundred meters, he squeezed the trigger. The vibration of the pod-mounted machine gun rattled through the Marchetti's airframe all the way to the control stick in Al-Fasr's right hand.

He saw the tracers kicking up dirt three meters short of the tethered prisoners. His aim point was slightly low. The prisoners scattered, running to the end of their tethers like chained dogs.

Using the tracers like the tip of a brush, Al-Fasr walked the fusillade of bullets to the left, where two of the prisoners had scurried.

Machine-gun fire tore through their bodies. The figures rolled and flipped across the dirt, arms and legs splayed.

Al-Fasr released the trigger and pulled up in a high chandelle over the target site. Looking back over his right shoulder, he saw the bodies of the two executed prisoners spread-eagled on the ground. The remaining four stared up at him.

It was appropriate. Condemned prisoners should serve a useful function, he believed. Like strafing practice. No one should be surprised.

Least of all Naguib Shauqi.

His faithful lieutenant. His fellow freedom fighter and commander of the Bu Hasa brigade. Maj. Naguib Shauqi and his armor could have saved Akhmed when he was besieged by the Royal Guard.

It was Naguib, he finally determined, who had betrayed the coup.

As he identified each of the traitors, he had dealt with them. Twelve of Naguib's collaborators had been assassinated. Another half dozen—all military officers and close associates of Naguib—were taken from their homes or offices. Naguib was snatched from the sauna in his villa where he had been found with his German mistress. After being forced to watch while the woman's throat was slashed, he was bound and gagged, then transported to Yemen.

To become a target.

Another firing pass. The prisoners darted back and forth, trying to anticipate the bullets. Naguib, conspicuous in his white garb, tried to conceal himself behind the others.

Al-Fasr fired at the prisoners, walking the trail of bullets through the scampering bodies.

Naguib was the only one left standing.

Al-Fasr pulled up and circled for another pass. As he brought the nose of the Marchetti back toward the target area, he forced himself to remember. *My father's severed head . . . the bullet in my mother's forehead . . . my sister, executed like a dog.*

He waited until he was close enough to see the terror on Naguib's face. He squeezed the trigger, working the tracers toward the cringing figure.

Naguib tried to run, then fell. Al-Fasr trained the hail of bullets on the white shirt. He saw the body shred, pieces scattering, the white shirt turning crimson.

At the last instant, he released the trigger and hauled back on the stick. The Marchetti skimmed low over the target, barely clearing the mast.

Al-Fasr realized that he was perspiring. His breathing was heavy and rapid. A feeling of grim satisfaction came over him. *Al ain bel ain sen bel sen.* An eye for an eye, a tooth for a tooth.

Most of the officers had left the briefing room. Maxwell sat by himself in the front row, studying the visage of Al-Fasr on the screen.

Boyce walked over. "You know this character. What do you think? Is he gonna be a problem?"

Maxwell nodded. "If it's the same Al-Fasr, yes. A big problem."

"Let me share some news that will fill your heart with joy. Guess who the President is sending out to oversee the Yemen operation."

Maxwell shook his head.

"Does this name ring a bell? The honorable Whitney T. Babcock?"

Maxwell groaned. It rang a bell. Babcock was the meddlesome Undersecretary of the Navy who had inserted himself into Admiral Mellon's op planning for the preemptive strike on Iraq's munitions factory. After the strike had been declared a success, it was Babcock who took all the credit.

"For some reason, the President loves this guy," said Boyce. "Thinks he shits gold bricks. He promoted Babcock to chief staff officer of the National Security Council, and now the little dipshit is coming out to run another war for us."

"Who's going to command the battle group?"

"A two-star named Fletcher. Apparently Babcock picked Tom Mellon's replacement. Ever heard of him?"

Maxwell shook his head. "What's his aviation background?"

"None. He's a black shoe—surface warfare, cruiser-destroyer guy. Except he didn't do much of that either. Stickney, who doesn't usually bad-mouth senior officers, turned livid when he heard about Fletcher. Says he worked for him at OpNav, and the guy was a political animal who spent his whole career cruising the Pentagon and working for civilian bureaucrats. Sticks said they used to call Fletcher 'the Governor' because he politicked like he was always running for the office."

"Like Babcock."

"You get the picture." Boyce turned to regard the photograph of Al-Fasr again. He pointed his cigar at the screen. "There's something wrong with this scenario. If that guy's half as smart as we think, why would he do something so amateurish? Like killing the admirals, then letting his stooges get caught. And botching that bomb job on the embassy. Pretty dumb."

Maxwell didn't have an answer, but he had a clear recollection now of Jamal Al-Fasr. Whatever he was, he wasn't dumb.

Chuff. Chuff. Chuff.

She had a good eight-minute-mile pace going as she completed the fourth lap around the perimeter of the hangar deck. Passing the number two elevator, she stopped. A yellow tug was towing an F/A-18 Super Hornet toward the elevator.

The Hornet belonged to the VFA-36 Roadrunners—her squadron. Beneath the left canopy rail was the name of the pilot, Lt. B. J. Johnson. Under the name was a freshly painted kill symbol—the silhouette of a MiG-29 and a small Iraqi flag.

"Pretty cool, huh?"

Surprised, B.J. turned to see Leroi Jones standing beside her. Leroi was a muscular young man from Nebraska. He was a lieutenant and the only African-American pilot in her squadron.

"Cool? Yeah, I guess so."

"The squadron's pretty proud of you, you know."

B.J. didn't know how to respond. Jones was one of those guys who, until last week, had treated her as if she carried the Ebola virus. As the only surviving woman pilot in the squadron, she had felt the resentment—hate, even—from the men. She knew the not-so-secret name they had for women pilots—*aliens*. As an alien aboard the world's largest warship, she was ostracized by everyone. The wall of bias had become impenetrable.

All that had changed in a single blazing afternoon over Iraq.

She was Brick Maxwell's wingman when they engaged a MiG-29, a big Russian-built fighter with the code name Fulcrum. The MiG was on Maxwell's tail, but instead of countering the fighter with one-versus-one defensive tactic, Maxwell set the Fulcrum up and trusted B.J. to do the rest.

She did, and now she had a kill symbol beneath her name. And the guys were actually talking to her.

Well, it was too late. To hell with them. Aliens didn't need the approval of jerks like Leroi Jones.

An awkward moment passed. Jones was shuffling his feet, gazing out through the open elevator door. "Uh, B.J., I've been thinking about something . . ."

"That's a change."

"I mean, I wanted to tell you . . . I wanted to apologize for . . ."

He couldn't get it out. Like most male primitives, he was inarticulate. She decided to help him. "For being an asshole?"

"Yeah, okay. I *was* an asshole. I was wrong, really wrong, and I apologize for the way I treated you."

She gave it a moment, not sure that he meant it. This mea culpa stuff didn't impress her. She should tell Jones to go shit in his brain bucket.

But he seemed serious. Leroi, she remembered, was never one of the really obnoxious ones. Just too supercool to associate with aliens.

"It's history, Leroi. I'm over it. Let's just be buds, okay?"

Jones seemed relieved. "Works for me." He held up his hand. She looked at him for a second, then they touched fists.

She resumed her run. Six more laps and she'd have her four miles. Jogging on the hangar deck was risky—tie-down chains, tugs skittering back and forth—but it was the only area on the ship with space. She hated treadmills, pounding along with an unchanging view.

Sometimes the new skipper, Brick Maxwell, jogged with her, and that was fun. For an old guy—he was at least thirty-eight or forty—he did okay. In fact, for an old guy he was kind of cute, with that brushy mustache and lopsided grin.

She remembered the *really* bad times, the alien days, when Maxwell was her jogging partner—and only friend. On one of the especially bad days, she poured out her innermost fears and frustrations to him. She was ready to quit, turn in her wings. Maxwell had talked her out of it.

She liked to think that they had a bond, she and Maxwell. Maybe more than a bond.

She knew the realities of military protocol. He was a commander and she was a lieutenant. He was a friend. A mentor. Nothing more.

She picked up the pace to a seven-minute mile. Running hard kept her from thinking too much.

After landing on the hard-packed road, he let the Marchetti roll under the camouflage nets, into the open bay of the underground revetment.

Climbing down from the wing, he saw Shakeeb waiting for him.

"I was watching, Colonel. Naguib is dead. The killing is finished, no?"

"No." Al-Fasr pulled off his helmet and handed it to him. "The traitors are dead, but the killing is not finished."

Shakeeb nodded, his face revealing no change of expression.

The overhead fluorescent lights illuminated the spacious bunker. In the same revetment were two MiG-29 Fulcrums. In the adjoining bunkers were four other Fulcrums, as well as six attack-configured Dauphin turbine-powered helicopters.

In addition to the MiGs, the complex's air defenses consisted of a SA-6 anti-aircraft missile battery on a self-propelled launcher, a dozen SA-16 shoulder-launched missiles, and a battery each of fifty-seven- and thirty-seven-millimeter antiaircraft guns. All Russian-built, purchased in the underground arms market of the third world.

His eight hundred *Sherji*—freedom fighters—were bivouacked outside the compound. Technically they were mercenaries, but most were veterans of the Afghanistan war and had been trained in Osama bin Laden's Al Qaeda camps. Each possessed his own ingrained hatred for all non-Islamic adversaries.

Though Al-Fasr had no belief in a being more supreme than himself, he understood the power that Islam had over its faithful. The *Sherji* believed that if they died in battle, they would join Allah in the hereafter. Their willingness to become martyrs, as well as their skill in guerilla warfare, made them the most potent weapon in Al-Fasr's arsenal.

His tiny air force was another matter. It was neither skilled nor potent. Despite that, it possessed an advantage of incalculable value: The Americans didn't know they existed.

Or so his intelligence source assured him.

The arrival of the MiGs two weeks ago—flown in darkness across the Red Sea from Chad, where they had been delivered by the Libyan Air Force—was timed to avoid the scrutiny of the two American reconnaissance satellites that regularly spied on Yemen. The satellite-tracking technology was a purchase from China, stolen, Al-Fasr presumed, along with a plethora of secrets from the United States.

They walked outside the bunker to Shakeeb's Land Rover. As they drove to the command post, Al-Fasr peered around the complex. It had been constructed back in the 1950s, when British Petroleum was still drilling the Arabian peninsula for oil deposits. Declaring Yemen to be a dry hole, they abandoned the complex, leaving behind the tin-roofed buildings and hard-packed road.

And the airstrip.

The old BP road meandered out of the desert, running in a nearly straight line for the last three kilometers to the compound. Though the road was gravelly and potholed, it was suitable for the sturdy MiG-29, which had been designed for the unimproved runways of Russia. For takeoff and landing, a door in each of the two big air intakes closed to prevent foreign object ingestion, while intake air was ducted through louvers on the top of the wing roots.

Seen from the lens of a satellite camera or a low-flying reconnaissance jet, the old road was nearly invisible. It looked like just another of the primitive camel paths worn into the arid earth of Yemen. It was a trick the Soviets had long used—building lengthy, straight sections of highway that could be instantly converted to tactical jet runways.

The Land Rover pulled up to the tin-roofed building that served as Al-Fasr's headquarters. An array of antennae festooned the building. Inside, a dozen technicians worked at the rows of consoles, listening to encrypted message traffic, monitoring the movements of the U.S. Navy's Middle East fleets.

The operator at the SatComm station looked up and saw Al-Fasr. "You have a message, Colonel. From the *Reagan*."

"There's the answer to my question," said Claire, pointing to the land masses passing on either side of the *Reagan*. "Now we know where we're going."

"Not exactly," said Maxwell. "But we know where we're *not* going."

They stood on the viewing deck behind the island, six stories above the flight deck. The heat of the afternoon sun was tempered by the twenty-knot breeze that whipped over the open deck.

The *Reagan* was leaving the Persian Gulf. To starboard, jutting into the sea like a spearhead, was the long, pointed tip of Oman. On the opposite shore lay the hazy brown coastline of Iran.

The entire battle group was steaming southeastward through the Strait of Hormuz. In the lead was a pair of destroyers followed by the Aegis cruiser *Arkansas*. Behind the cruiser sailed *Reagan*, flanked by a destroyer on either side and trailed by the amphibious helicopter carrier *Saipan*. The ammunition ship *Baywater* brought up the rear, in company with two more destroyers.

On the *Saipan's* flight deck Maxwell could see a swarm of medium transport helos and Cobra gunships. The ship carried an entire Marine Expeditionary Unit—over a thousand battle-ready marines.

From the loudspeaker bellowed the voice of the *Reagan's* air boss. "Stand by to recover CODs!" COD stood for Carrier Onboard Delivery. CODs ferried everything from personnel to airplane parts to toilet paper. "Recover CODs in five minutes!"

The bow was swinging into the wind. On the flight deck, yellow-shirted crewmen in float coats and cranial protectors scurried to clear the landing zone. The rescue helicopter lifted from the flight deck and wheeled out over the water, taking up its alert station.

The first of the two blunt-nosed turbo-prop C-2A Greyhounds was already in the groove. Maxwell watched the COD sweep over the ramp and settle with a plop onto the number three wire. Seconds later, the twin-engined aircraft was clear of the wire and scuttling to the forward flight deck. The second COD arrived, snagging a two wire, then joined the first one on the forward deck. The howling of the turbine engines came to a stop.

Maxwell saw the clamshell doors open in the aft fuselage of each COD. At the same time a party of officers came out of the island onto the flight deck. He recognized one of them, a tall man in khakis. It was Sticks Stickney, captain of the *Reagan*.

Over the loudspeaker blared the bosun's pipe. Following naval custom, the bosun's mate's voice announced, "Commander, Task Force Eleven—arriving." Another screech of the whistle, then, "Deputy National Security Adviser—arriving."

A civilian wearing starched khakis and aviator sunglasses emerged from the COD. He was followed by an officer with two stars. Captain Stickney rendered a stiff salute, which both men returned.

"Good Lord," said Claire. "Who's that?"

"The new Battle Group Commander. Admiral Langhorne Fletcher."

"Who's the civilian? The one dressed up like MacArthur that they're all kowtowing to?"

"You're looking at the honorable Whitney T. Babcock, confidant and adviser to the President. Remember him?"

Claire nodded. "Uh-oh. Watch out, Sam."

"My thoughts exactly."

*   *   *

Boyce sat alone in the conference room. Spook Morse had removed the image of Jamal Al-Fasr. Now a map of Yemen covered the screen.

Here we go again, thought Boyce. Within a few hours his strike fighters would be on their way to another target in yet another godforsaken hostile country. There was no end to it. The world was crazy. Instead of a single, monolithic kick-ass opponent like the Soviet Union, now they had an enemy du jour. Little pissant wars were breaking out like anthills in a pasture.

Boyce had already ordered a practice load-out. On the hangar and flight decks, the ordnance divisions of the air wing's squadrons were scrambling to hang weapons—thousand- and two-thousand-pound bombs—beneath the wings of the Hornet strike fighters. Chief petty officers were yelling at the red shirts, hacking stop watches, exhorting them to move faster.

When they were finished, they would unload. Then they would do it all over again. It was a backbreaking job, but critical. When the strike order came down with specific weapon loads, Boyce wanted his jets armed and ready.

He hadn't yet designated a strike leader. He had already ruled himself out, much as he wanted to be in the front. Something about this one was giving him a bad feeling. If things went sour, the place for an Air Wing Commander was not in the cockpit but here aboard ship.

Who, then? To be fair, the nod should go to Rico Flores, who commanded the VFA-34 Bluetails. He was the senior squadron skipper and a competent strike leader. Or Burner Crump, who ran the Tomcat squadron. Crump had the most combat experience and was a steady leader.

Something in Boyce's gut was troubling him. When you had nutcase enemies like these Islamic terrorists, who had nothing to lose and believed that dying was a ticket to paradise, you never knew what to expect.

There wasn't a textbook solution for everything that could go wrong on a deep air strike. They had to keep learning that same damned lesson every time—Lebanon, Libya, Iraq, Bosnia, Kosovo, Iraq again, Afghanistan.

Now Yemen.

This operation could turn ugly. He needed a strike leader who could make decisions on the spot. Somebody who could change the game plan if necessary.

Brick Maxwell.

Boyce could already hear the outraged bitching from the other strike leaders. It would be the same old stuff about seniority and that carpetbagging ex-astronaut and what the hell does he know about tactical air combat?

Too bad. They'd get over it.

Maxwell was the right guy. Every eye in the Pentagon would be on the *Reagan* and its air wing these next few days. Maxwell knew when to shoot and when to hold his fire. In the No-Fly-Zone over Iraq, he had passed up a sure MiG shot when it wasn't necessary to kill him. Then he had not hesitated to kill an adversary when the bastard needed killing. Maxwell was a guy who didn't agonize over decisions.

Boyce looked at his unlit cigar. The conference room, like almost every other space on the ship, was a no-smoking area. The goddamn tree-hugging pure air freaks had ruined it for everyone.

He pulled out his ancient Zippo and applied the flame to the cigar. He got a nice ember going, then wafted a cloud of gray smoke across the room. Yeah, he would take flak about his choice of strike leader. Sometimes you just had to break a few rules.

CHAPTER FOUR

KILO

Gulf of Aden
0450, Sunday, 16 June

Lt. Cmdr. Pietr Ilychin entered the control room. "It's here, Captain. The updated point of intended movement."

Capt. Yevgeny Manilov took the message from Ilychin and turned back to his keyboard. He inserted the coordinates of the new position into the Andoga navigational computer.

When he was finished, he tilted back and studied the display for a moment. "Almost no change, three kilometers perhaps. The wind must be shifting. They will change course to launch aircraft." Manilov handed the message back to Ilychin. He glanced at his watch. "Ahead five knots, maintain ninety meters. Set course for the updated position."

"Aye, Captain."

This last message from Yemen, via satellite, had arrived just in time. It was almost sunrise. In daylight he could no longer risk raising the periscope-mounted antenna even for the few minutes it took to download messages.

Yevgeny Manilov was the commander of the *Ilia*

Mourmetz, a Project 636 Kilo-class diesel/electric submarine with a displacement of 2,400 tons. During the pre-dawn
hours he had sailed the *Mourmetz* on the darkened surface
into the Gulf of Aden. Now that they were within fifty kilometers of prying eyes along the shoreline, they would sub-
merge and enter the littoral waters off the Yemeni coast.

The old Kilo-class boats and their *Amur*-class derivatives
were the stealthiest undersea vessels yet constructed in Russia. Even better than the brutish nuclear-powered Oscar
subs, conventional boats like the *Mourmetz* could hide in
shallow water, lurk beneath thermal layers—and emit virtually no acoustical signal. With the addition of the anechoic
tile coating on the outer hull, the *Mourmetz* in a passive
mode could elude almost all magnetic anomaly and sonar
detection equipment.

Sitting at his table in the control room, Manilov considered his situation. Nineteen years it had taken him to get
here. Nineteen humiliating, ruble-begging, egg-sucking
years. Like every other uniformed member of the Russian
Navy, he had endured months without pay, eaten food unfit
for cattle, suffered the indignity of seeing their once-
magnificent submarine fleet moldering like derelicts in the
naval yards.

Manilov had remained in the Navy mainly because he had
no other options. Being the underpaid captain of a derelict
submarine was preferable to hammering nails or selling
shoes or shoveling shit in the streets of Moscow. The nation's economy was treading water. Mother Russia was at
the mercy of gangsters, its own inept leadership, and, worst
of all, her former enemy.

The thought of the United States and its overweening ar-
rogance was enough to fill Manilov with rage. For years he
had played Cold War games, tracking the profiles of American warships. He had yearned for the order to send a torpedo crashing into one of those gray hulls. In his mind's eye

he could see the crimson fireball, the gushing oil smoke, the specter of a bow tilting upward and sliding like a steel sarcophagus beneath the waves. It would have been wonderful.

The order never came. Instead, the Soviet Union had burst apart like a sledgehammered pumpkin.

Then the final indignity. Everything was for sale—space vehicles, medical research, military technology . . . submarines.

The *Ilia Mourmetz*, Manilov was informed one day, had been sold. It would be Manilov's duty to deliver his vessel to the Iranian naval base at Bandar Abbas. It would also be, he knew without doubt, his last voyage as a submarine commander. Russia's Navy was transforming into a maritime auction house.

Four weeks elapsed while the *Mourmetz* underwent modifications at the Vladivostok naval base. The old boat's navigational gear was retrofitted with the newer, state-of-the-art laser gyro inertial guidance units. The sonar and fire control systems were replaced with an MGK-400EM digital sonar and the MVU-110 combat information computer. An oxygen/hydrogen generator plant was installed that allowed the sub to operate for weeks beneath the surface without snorkeling to recharge batteries or replenish air supplies.

This only exacerbated Manilov's mounting anger. The Iranians were getting equipment that was vastly superior to anything Manilov had used aboard the old *Mourmetz*. All it took was money! They all had it—Americans, Iranians, Chinese, Japanese—everyone except the Russians.

The deathlike bleakness of the Russian winter had not yet released its grip on Vladivostok. While he waited for the *Mourmetz*'s renovations to be completed, Manilov spent his idle hours in a quayside bar frequented by naval officers and shipyard bureaucrats. Only with sufficient alcohol in his blood could he put aside the dismal thoughts of his final voyage.

One evening in the bar, Manilov found himself in conversation with a dark-skinned man in an ill-fitting suit. Manilov guessed from the accent that he came from one of the newly independent republics—Uzbekistan or Azerbaijan, perhaps—somewhere in the southern Caucasus.

After several vodkas the man surprised Manilov with his knowledge of the *Mourmetz* and its upcoming voyage. Then he surprised him even further by presenting him with a business proposition. For an amount of money that exceeded anything Manilov could imagine, would he consider taking the *Mourmetz* not to its new owner, but to a different destination?

Manilov wondered if he was hearing correctly. Was it the vodka? It couldn't be real.

There was more. Instead of turning over the *Mourmetz*'s weaponry to the Iranians, would he be interested in fulfilling his nineteen-year dream? Would he, perhaps, be interested in sinking an American warship?

Manilov felt his skin prickle.

The man—he identified himself only as Hakim—suggested that they meet again the next day. In the closed booth of a hotel restaurant, Hakim gave Manilov a glimpse of his briefcase. It contained what appeared to be millions of stacked Swiss francs. Manilov, if he accepted the terms, could live the rest of his life in unimaginable luxury.

"It is too incredible," Manilov murmured. "Who wants this to happen? He must be insane."

Hakim shook his head. "His name does not matter for now. He is not insane. He is a military leader who will change the balance of power in the Middle East."

"By sinking one American warship?"

"It will be just one blow in a coordinated battle."

It was too much for Manilov to comprehend. For the moment he had no more questions. He gazed out at the dreary shipyard and its ghost fleet. He let his imagination run, thinking of a life away from this miserable place.

After a minute had passed, Hakim said, "You have had time to consider. You must decide. Do you agree to what we discussed or not?"

For the first time Manilov noticed an edge to the man's voice. Gone was the breezy vodka talk, the affable business manner. The man's eyes had darkened, and his voice was clipped. Manilov understood that they had crossed a point of no return. He knew almost nothing, but even that was too much. Without realizing it, he had allowed himself to be drawn into a minefield.

Hakim's eyes bored into him. Manilov ignored him, thinking about his situation. Life as he knew it was over. He was childless, with a plump and indifferent wife who lived with her parents in Minsk, in Belarus. He had nothing of value in Russia. But at the depth of his being, Manilov knew he would forever be a Russian. Russians were dreamers. Woven indelibly into the Russian psyche was a gloomy belief in mysticism, fate, and an inescapable destiny.

Through the grimy window Manilov looked out at the sprawling remnants of Russia's once-proud Navy. *Yes,* he thought. *Some things were meant to be.* He was a Russian dreamer. He believed in destiny.

"I agree."

Hakim smiled. The men raised their vodka glasses in a toast. *You have made a pact with the devil,* Manilov thought. *So be it.* So long as the devil wanted to sink American ships.

Thereafter, his task was to select his crew. He would sail with only eight trusted officers instead of the usual fourteen. He handpicked a dozen warrants, all known to him and chosen for their loyalty. Only the officers were told of the *Mourmetz*'s true mission and, as Manilov anticipated, each had agreed. The warrants were not informed until after the *Mourmetz* departed Vladivostok. Only one, a torpedoman named Kalugin, had flatly refused to cooperate, even when informed about his share of the reward. Kalugin was placed under arrest and confined to the ship's dispensary.

Six enlisted sailors embarked on the *Mourmetz,* all recruits still in their teens or early twenties. They were wide-eyed and respectful. Manilov expected no trouble from them.

Captain Manilov would go to sea with half his normal crew complement for a combat patrol. What they lacked in manpower they would make up for in tactical surprise.

The *Ilia Mourmetz* completed its voyage to the Gulf of Aden in ten days.

"Am I interrupting?" said Claire.

Maxwell looked up from his seat at the wardroom table. She was wearing her working outfit—a blue jumpsuit with the silk scarf that he had given her in Dubai.

He scrambled to his feet and pulled out a chair. "No, ma'am. I've been waiting for you."

Claire sat next to him and squeezed his hand. A half dozen officers sat at tables in the wardroom. A white-coated steward shuttled trays of coffee. The gentle motion of the deck beneath was the only clue that the *Reagan* was under way.

She nodded across the wardroom to where Whitney Babcock was holding court with several reporters. She lowered her voice. "The honorable Mr. Babcock is a media hound. He really expects that we will make him out to be the grand pooh-bah of military affairs in the Middle East."

"Well, won't you?"

"I'm a good reporter, but not that good."

Maxwell nodded. He still hadn't adjusted to the notion of having the girl he was in love with being aboard his ship—headed to war. The world had changed. So had the Navy.

He felt another pair of eyes on them. Then he remembered B. J. Johnson, seated at the end of his table. She was watching them with a strange look on her face. "Excuse me," Maxwell said. "Claire Phillips, meet Lieutenant Johnson. Call sign B.J."

As the women shook hands, Maxwell detected an instant coolness. Claire put on a polite smile. B.J.'s face was frozen in a tight mask.

Claire tried to coax B.J. to talk about what it was like to be the only woman pilot in a squadron. B.J. wasn't having any of it. She replied in terse, wooden answers. Yes, she liked flying fighters. No, she didn't care if she was the only woman pilot. Yes, she was doing fine, thank you. And so on.

Maxwell watched the exchange with curiosity. He wondered what had come over B.J. Until Claire arrived she had been carrying on an animated discussion about the history and topography of Yemen. In the ship's library she had mined every bit of reading material and turned herself into an expert on the ancient country. He decided that B. J. Johnson was the one to give the in-country brief on Yemen to his squadron.

B.J. was now as talkative as a clam.

Claire had an idea. "B.J., would you consider doing a taped interview for the evening report?" She glanced at Maxwell. "With your commanding officer's approval, that is?"

"No," said B.J.

"But you'd be perfect. You're so . . . you're unique. Our viewers would love—"

"No interview." B.J. folded her arms across her chest.

Claire looked to Maxwell for help.

He shrugged. "I think she means no."

"What a shame," said Claire. "It would be a great human-interest piece."

A silence fell over the table. B.J. seemed to be focused on a spot on the far bulkhead. Claire drummed her fingers on the table, saying nothing. Maxwell tried to think of something cheery. He couldn't, so he summoned the steward to bring them more coffee.

Women. He had never understood them. Never would.

"Yes, sir, Mr. Secretary, you can count on it."

Whitney Babcock hung up the secure phone and tilted back in his chair. Before he went back into the conference room to inform the officers about his conversation with the Secretary of Defense, he wanted to indulge himself.

He gazed again at his image in the mirror over the desk. He was wearing his favorite shipboard outfit—starched khakis, aviator glasses, collar worn open in the MacArthur style. He tilted his chin and struck another pose. Yes, in fact, he definitely looked like a young MacArthur, with that flint-eyed, aristocratic gaze, the keenly intelligent eyes. It was a face that would grace an upcoming cover of *Time*. The caption, he expected, would read something like *Whitney Babcock: Warrior-Statesman*.

He rose and strode into the adjoining room. Seated at the conference table were the Battle Group Commander, Admiral Fletcher, his Group Operations Officer, Capt. Guido Vitale, and the Flag Intelligence Officer, Cmdr. Spook Morse. In a huddle by the coffee mess were the *Reagan*'s skipper, Capt. Sticks Stickney, and Capt. Red Boyce, the Air Wing Commander.

Everyone in the room looked up. Babcock waited a second, extracting the maximum dramatic effect. "It's a go," he said, enjoying the moment. "The President has authorized a strike on the terrorist base in Yemen."

Murmurs passed through the room. Fletcher nodded his head approvingly. Stickney and Boyce exchanged sober glances.

"The joint chiefs are signing off on the op plan, and we'll be getting it within the hour. The *Reagan* battle group gets to carry the ball on this one because of the political sensitivity. We can't launch strikes from bases in any other Arab country. There's a symbolic issue, also. The terrorists attacked the U.S. Navy, and it is appropriate that we carry out the reprisal."

"An eye for an eye," said Admiral Fletcher. "Something the Arabs understand."

Babcock gave the admiral an indulgent smile. Fletcher was full of banal little aphorisms like that one. Babcock had tapped him to be the replacement Battle Group Commander precisely for the reason that he *wasn't* one of those old Navy mossbacks who thought they knew more than their civilian commanders. At one time it was unheard of that the Carrier Battle Group Commander was not an aviator, but in the new Navy, that was changing. Fletcher was a pragmatist. He could be counted on to implement, not interpret, the policies of his civilian chiefs.

Babcock was less sure about the others. The Group Operations Officer, Vitale, was an aviator, and he seemed to be a team player. Captain Stickney, who commanded the *Reagan,* accorded him a cool respect, but nothing more. He had not welcomed Babcock onto his bridge or invited him to his table. Stickney was due for a lesson in deference.

Boyce, the cigar-chomping Air Wing Commander, was one of those dinosaurs from the old days when fighter pilots thought they ran the Navy. Babcock had already tagged Boyce for an early departure from his air wing command.

Morse, the Flag Intelligence Officer, was a wild card. Like all intel types, he had the maddening trait of hoarding critical information and then parceling it out in incremental pieces. He possessed that air of intellectual superiority that made everyone, Babcock included, want to smack him down.

But there was another side to Morse, one that intrigued Babcock. The man had a formidable knowledge of Middle East geopolitics. Unlike most of the others in this room, he actually cooperated with Babcock and his staff. With a little urging, Morse might be a useful player.

"How much time do we have to do the load out?" Stickney wanted to know.

"We steam into the Gulf of Aden tonight," said Admiral Fletcher. "By tomorrow morning we'll be at the launch point. The *Arkansas* will deliver a salvo of Tomahawks in coordination with the *Reagan* strike group. It will be a concentrated air strike, nothing more."

"No assault force?" asked Boyce. "Isn't the Marine Expeditionary Unit going to clean out the terrorist nest?"

"No," Babcock interjected from across the room. "Absolutely no American troops on Yemeni territory. The President has ruled that out."

Boyce shook his head. "You really think we're gonna put this Al-Fasr away with just a single air strike?"

"Certainly," said Fletcher. "When you see the reconnaissance data, you'll get the picture. Their shacks and storage buildings are out in the open. The bivouac areas will be easy targets for your laser-guided weapons."

"What if we have downed pilots? We gotta have SAR and gunships and covering troops."

Fletcher was getting annoyed. "That won't be a factor. Commander Morse has shown me the intel data, and I can assure you, our adversary does not have the assets to bring down any of our strike aircraft."

Boyce's eyes narrowed. He removed the cigar from his teeth. "Sir, with all due respect, I have to tell you we *always* run the risk of having pilots go down. Even in a peacetime exercise. If I'm gonna run this strike, I intend to inform my pilots exactly how we're gonna extract them if someone goes down in Indian country."

Fletcher had no answer. He looked to Morse for help.

"The admiral has already covered that," Morse said. "Let's not waste time going over the same subject. Anyway, the poststrike details will be handled by the flag intel department. You'll get the information in due time."

A thundercloud passed over Boyce's face. He glowered at Morse as if he wanted to seize his windpipe and throttle him. Air Wing Commanders didn't take rebukes from intelligence officers.

Morse ignored him while he scribbled a note on his yellow pad.

Watching from the head of the table, Babcock smiled his approval. This was going better than he expected. He liked it when a squarehead like Boyce was put in his place.

"I'm expecting a call from the Pentagon," said Babcock. "We will adjourn until Admiral Fletcher's staff has had a chance to review the op plan; then we'll schedule a full briefing."

Boyce was about to raise another troublesome question, but Babcock cut him off. "You're dismissed, gentlemen."

CHAPTER FIVE

FEET DRY

Gulf of Aden
0430, Monday, 17 June

He lay awake, the questions flowing through his mind in an endless stream.

What if they have SAMs that we don't know about?

Air defense radar?

MiGs?

A hundred what-ifs.

At half past four Maxwell gave up trying to sleep and went to the shower. Standing under the hot water, he thought about the mission. Why were air strikes always launched in the morning? It meant that pilots got to lay awake all night in darkened rooms thinking unthinkable thoughts.

After he'd showered and shaved, he donned the camouflage flight suit. Sitting on the bunk, he pulled on the steel-toed leather boots. Unlike the flight suits they normally wore, this one bore no squadron or air wing patches, no symbols of rank. The desert-colored camouflage scheme was intended to blend into the Middle East landscape if a pilot went down.

He was almost ready. One item to go. He unlocked the door of his desk safe and pulled out the leather gun case. He removed the Colt .45 and held it under the light, feeling the heft and density of the big pistol. The bluing was faded, and the pearl handle insets were yellowed and worn. It was a Model 1911 military issue. On the slide action was the inscription *Lt. Harlan Maxwell, USS* Oriskany, *1965.*

The Colt had been his father's sidearm during two combat tours in Vietnam. It was a gift on the day Brick won his Navy wings, delivered not by his father but by Josh Dunn. He'd worn it ever since.

He checked that a fresh magazine was loaded, then shoved it into the grip. When had he last fired it? He couldn't remember. Not for years, and he'd never been able to hit anything with it anyway.

It didn't matter. He'd gotten used to the heft of the gun, even though the Navy had long ago switched to the smaller and more accurate Beretta nine millimeter. He slipped the pistol into its leather shoulder holster and headed out.

By 0730, the ready room was filled with pilots. Maxwell stood up in the front and said, "Seats, gentlemen. Lieutenant Johnson has a briefing that might just keep you alive."

B.J. clomped up to the lectern that faced the rows of chairs. Like the others, she was dressed in a desert-camo flight suit, wearing a holstered sidearm. For today's strike, she was assigned as the skipper's wingman.

As she rolled down a map of Yemen, several pilots exchanged amused glances. *The alien.*

She began with a discussion of Yemen's history, from the Ottoman Empire to the creation of the Suez Canal and British rule, until the present.

"The Republic of Yemen was created in 1990 by unifying

the two warring countries of South Yemen and North Yemen. In 1994, fighting broke out again between government forces and southern secessionists. Since then the government has had to cut deals with different factions in order to stay in power."

"Al-Fasr being one of them?" asked Hozer Miller.

B.J. nodded. "Terrorism is to Yemen what drugs are to Colombia. It's their number one exportable product. It protects the government and provides a cottage industry for the peasants."

While B.J. went on, Maxwell watched the pilots' expressions. It had been his idea to have B.J. deliver the in-country briefing on Yemen. Since she had downed the MiG in Iraq, the squadron pilots had developed a grudging respect for her. Most had gotten over their entrenched bias against women fighters, but not all. To a few, the women would always be aliens.

Now they were wearing a new expression. They looked perplexed.

Bud Spencer raised his hand. "Excuse me, B.J., where did you learn all this stuff?"

"Ship's library. The Internet. The intel office. When I heard we were headed into the Arabian Sea, I dug up everything I could find about the place."

Maxwell could see what they were thinking now. *Maybe this chick knows what she's doing after all . . .*

She went on, talking about the prevailing weather, which at this time of year meant monsoon winds that howled in from the sea. Sometimes, at least along the coast, it even rained.

Then she got into the part nobody wanted to think about.

"The highlands of northern Yemen, where we're going, are rugged but habitable. There's plenty of vegetation, terraced fields cut into the hillsides, even stands of forest. If you go down, you'll find cover. Stay in the hills, hide in the brush. Don't approach the farmers or villagers. Most will be carrying a curved dagger called a *jambiyya*. They will probably be sympathetic to the terrorists, or at least be frightened enough to slice your throat just to save themselves."

At this, several aviators stirred in their chairs. A few felt compelled to check the magazines on their service pistols.

At 0800, Spook Morse's face appeared on the ready room television monitor. "Good morning, ladies and gentlemen. The *Reagan* is currently steaming ninety miles from the coast of Yemen, abeam the port of Ahwar. The coordinates of our launch and recovery positions for today's strike on Al-Fasr will be on the screen at the end of the brief. Now, here are your entry and exit routes."

The camera switched to a colored chart of Yemen. Large arrows defined the path over the Yemeni shoreline, northwestward to the Al-Fasr target in the highlands. Another arrow leading due southward described the exit route from the target.

"The strike package will be led by Commander Maxwell. It consists of four elements—an element of HARM shooters composed of sections from all three Hornet squadrons, an LGB-dropping element from VFA-36, another LGB element from VFA-34, a cluster bomb element provided by VFA-35.

"Tanking will be provided by four KS-3 Vikings, who will shuttle from a pair of Air Force KC-10s on station over the Gulf. Note that the only CAP assigned will be the Tomcats on MIGSWEEP, due to the remote likelihood of enemy air opposition.

"The surface-to-air missile threat is considered negligible. Any sites that light up will be taken out by the HARM element that precedes the strike package. You might get some small-bore antiaircraft fire. Respect your minimum release altitudes, and it shouldn't be a problem."

Morse then went over the fine points of the mission:

mode one and two transponder squawks, the avoidance of collateral damage to nearby villages, lost-communications procedures, bingo fuel requirements, bull's-eye navigation reference points, code words, weapon loads, search and rescue contingencies.

From the Roadrunner ready room, Maxwell watched Morse's briefing. A cut-and-dried operation, he thought. Almost like one of the scripted air wing exercises they ran monthly while the *Reagan* was at sea.

Something nagged at him. It was *too* cut-and-dried. The target was too accessible. He couldn't get over the uneasy feeling that something was missing. What the hell was it?

She caught him in the passageway to the flight deck escalator.

"Hey, sailor," Claire said. "Leaving without saying goodbye?"

"Just taking a little airplane ride."

"That's not what I hear. You're going off to bomb terrorists."

"How much *did* you hear?"

"Enough to figure out what you're doing. Your Mr. Babcock has been very cooperative. I think he likes me."

"He wants to be sure this glorious show of American power lands on every television screen. And for the record, he's not *my* Mr. Babcock."

"Okay, the President's Mr. Babcock. He let me watch the briefing and he promised that I could hear the poststrike reports." She put her hand on his sleeve. "I know, for instance, that Commander Maxwell is leading the strike." Her face turned serious. "You're not going to do anything crazy, are you, Sam?"

"Flying off carriers is crazy. Everything else I do is sane."

"I mean something *really* crazy. Like taking revenge on whoever killed Josh Dunn."

He almost said the truth, that he was going to kill that sonofabitch. Seeing the look on her face, he caught himself. "No, nothing that crazy."

She eyed him for a moment. She looked at his flight gear—the helmet he clutched under his arm, the oxygen mask snapped to the harness. She took a close look at the pearl-handled .45. "Good lord, what is that? It looks like something Patton would have carried."

"His was a revolver. Two of them, actually, but they were inlaid with ivory. Patton thought pearl handles were for brothel madams."

She touched the white inlay with her finger. "I can almost understand why men love these things. They're beautiful—in a deadly sort of way. Like the fighters you fly."

Maxwell thought of the week they almost spent together in Dubai. He remembered all the things he wanted to talk with her about. They were still strangers, still learning about each other.

The peculiarity of the situation struck him again. Here he was, ready for combat, about to launch from an aircraft carrier, saying good-bye to the woman he cared for most of all in the world. This ought to be a time to hold her close. To say good-bye, just in case.

But he was still a naval officer. Not here, not now.

"Do you love me, Sam?"

He looked at her in surprise. After an awkward silence, he said, "Yes."

"Why don't you ever say it?"

"I just did."

"No, you didn't. I supplied the question, and you filled in the blank."

She had a point. "As you may have noticed, I'm not very good at expressing how I feel."

"Or not willing."

"I'm willing. Just out of practice."

"Then you should practice."

He nodded. "Okay, how's this?" He cleared his throat and said, "I love you, Claire. Even when you don't hear it from me, it's true. I love you."

She smiled. "You're definitely getting better."

He glanced around, then gave her a quick kiss.

Not quick enough. He felt another pilot in flight gear shuffle past him, heading for the escalator. He glanced up at the moving stairway to the flight deck. B. J. Johnson was glowering back down at them.

"Contact, Captain."

Manilov was instantly alert. He looked over at the sonar operator, Borodin, a bespectacled young warrant. "Range and bearing?"

"Thirty-five kilometers, bearing zero-six-four. Speed fifteen knots. Frigate-size."

Manilov nodded. A frigate was an escort ship. It was the advance vessel of the main battle group.

Manilov felt his pulse rate accelerate. At least two, perhaps three hours remained before the battle group reached the scheduled point of intended movement. He could smell a change in the atmosphere inside the *Mourmetz*. Ilychin, his executive officer, was sweating profusely, his shirt stained beneath each sleeve. Borodin was hunched over his control station, breathing like a man who had just run several kilometers.

Everyone in the crew knew that they were in dangerous waters. They all trusted the *Mourmetz*'s captain to keep them safe, to correctly assess the risks and make the right commands. To succeed in his mission, Manilov knew he must keep their trust. He must not let them know the entire truth—that he was not afraid to die. He was a man in the grip of destiny.

No one in his crew, including Manilov, had ever seen

combat. Not in decades had a Russian naval vessel fired a shot in anger.

Today all that would change.

The first to launch were the Prowlers—EA-6B electronic warfare jets that would detect and jam any enemy radar. Then the KS-3 Viking tankers that would rendezvous with the Air Force KC-10s, top off their own fuel loads, then take their stations to refuel the strike group.

The HARM shooters—Super Hornets carrying high-speed anti-radiation missiles—went next. If an enemy air defense radar was foolish enough to target the inbound strike aircraft, the HARMs would lock like homing pigeons onto the emitted radar signal. Behind them went the F-14 Tomcats, climbing directly to the tankers, then heading north to their CAP stations.

Last to launch was the strike package—sixteen Super Hornets in all—led by Brick Maxwell. In rapid succession the jets sizzled down the *Reagan*'s four catapult tracks. Half the Hornets were loaded with thousand- and two-thousand-pound GBU-16 and GBU-24 laser-guided bombs. The other eight F/A-18s carried Mark 20 Rockeye cluster bombs, designed to decimate vehicle and ammo depots.

In addition to its bomb load, each strike fighter bristled with air-to-air missiles—an AIM-9 heat-seeking Sidewinder on each wingtip rail, and AIM-7 and AIM-120 radar-guided missiles on the wing and fuselage stations. Each carried a full magazine of twenty-millimeter ammunition for the nose-mounted Vulcan cannon.

Already on station was the Air Force E-3C Sentry AWACS ship, high in its orbit over the Arabian Sea. Though the strike into Yemen was to be a Navy show, the ACE—Airborne Command Element—aboard the AWACS would be coordinating the operation. The ACE not only maintained a datalink with the strike fighters and the *Reagan*'s Combat

Information Center, he had a direct line to the three-star Air Force general in Riyadh who had overall responsibility for U.S. Forces in the Middle East.

CAG Boyce settled into his padded chair in CIC. The Combat Information Center was the battle nerve center of the ship, located in the command spaces in the forward part of the ship. The room was dark as a cavern, eerily illuminated by the spectral glow of the monitors and the large situational displays on the bulkhead. Sitting at their terminals, controllers and special warfare officers wearing headsets and boom mikes peered into their screens.

As he always did when he came down to CIC, Boyce was wearing his battered old leather flight jacket with the squadron patches dating back to his nugget days. Not only was the jacket a talisman—he had worn it during every combat event of his career—it was his defense against the numbing cold. The electronics geeks insisted on keeping the place frigid as an icebox to keep their precious equipment from overheating.

Boyce let his eyes adjust to the darkness. He peered over his shoulder, toward the elevated platform behind the consoles where a row of chairs lined the bulkhead. Through the red-lighted gloom he saw several observers in their padded chairs, looking down at the control room.

Claire Phillips waved to him. She had followed his advice and was wearing a parka. Claire's press clearance, strictly speaking, would not get her through the door of CIC during a combat operation. Even her current patron, Whitney Babcock, had stopped short of authorizing her to observe the show.

So Boyce had gone to the source of almost all authority aboard the *Reagan*—the captain. He and Stickney had been contemporaries—and rivals—for twenty-five years. Though Stickney had an attack and fighter background, A-7s and F/A-18s, his career path had taken him to surface deep draft, culminating in command of the world's mightiest warship, the *Reagan*.

"Look at it this way, Sticks," Boyce said. "If the strike goes okay, she's gonna make us all look good. If, God forbid, it turns into a goat rope, the woman will be objective and not write a lot of military-bashing bullshit like those guys from the networks."

As Boyce expected, Stickney warmed up to the idea of getting fair treatment from the media. "Your call, Red. If you don't mind a news snoop peering over your shoulder, fine. I've got important stuff to worry about."

He put on the Telex headset and scanned the situational display on the bulkhead. The entire strike force was airborne now. Only one jet—a Tomcat from VF-32—had been a no-go. The pilot reported a hydraulic fault while he was still taxiing on deck. Boyce ordered the hot spare launched, and five minutes later the replacement F-14 was thundering down the number one catapult.

From the pocket of his flight jacket he produced a fresh Cohiba. Wetting the end of the cigar, he clamped it between his teeth, then peered again at the situational display. The data-linked symbols of the strike elements were merging off the coast of Yemen like flocks of geese.

So far, so good.

He called the strike leader. "Gipper Zero-one, Alpha Whiskey."

"Go, Alpha Whiskey," answered Maxwell.

"Geronimo is in place," said Boyce. It was the signal that the Tomcats of the CAP element and the HARM shooters were on station. "You're cleared feet dry."

"Gipper Zero-one copies. Cleared feet dry."

Showtime. The strike force was cleared into Yemen.

A milk run, Boyce thought to himself. No enemy air opposition. No SAMs lighting up. Not even any radar-tracking AA positions locking onto the inbound strikers. The only radar emissions were coming from the air traffic control facilities at the airports in Aden and San'a.

This strike was a walk in the park.

He saw light pouring through the open door of CIC. Whitney Babcock strolled into the room, trailed closely by Admiral Fletcher and Spook Morse. Boyce noticed that Babcock was wearing a leather flight jacket just like his. It even had an assortment of ship and squadron patches sewn onto it. Babcock was chatting with Fletcher, giving him a lecture on geopolitics.

In that instant, it came to him. Boyce knew why he had elected to be in CIC and not out there in the cockpit. These two—a pseudowarrior and a policy wonk who had never fought in a real war—had.no concept of what strike fighter pilots did. He didn't trust either of them.

Rittmann ran his hand over the leading edge of the swept-back wing. In the stark, artificial light of the underground revetment, the MiG-29 looked like a prehistoric creature. With its long beaklike nose, its sharply swept wings, it seemed poised to kill.

"Have you changed your mind?" asked Al-Fasr.

"No." The question irritated Rittmann. It was more of that same old condescension, that *verdammt* superiority. This brown-skinned Semite liked to pose as if he were some kind of aristocrat, removed by several degrees of breeding from the likes of Rittmann and the other mercenary fighter pilots.

Oberleutnant Wolf Rittmann, formerly of the German Democratic Republic Air Force, considered himself the equal of any fighter pilot in the world. Or so he had been before the union of the two Germanys and the dissolution of the Soviet Union.

Since then life had been uncertain. Unlike several of his colleagues, he had not been invited to join the new MiG-29 *Staffel* of the German Luftwaffe. He was forced to seek employment as a MiG instructor first in Bangladesh, then Libya, and most recently in Iraq. In each case they were shit jobs, low-paying and dangerous. Low-paying because the compensation was always in the worthless local currency. Dangerous because the incompetent peasants whom he attempted to train were not qualified to drive oxen.

"Are you frightened, Rittmann?" A half smile played across Al-Fasr's lips.

Rittmann felt like telling the Arab to go fornicate with sheep. No matter how long he stayed here, he would never shed his feelings about this inferior race of people. To him they would always be desert dwellers whose circumstances had changed only because vast oil deposits existed beneath their feet. Otherwise they would be huddling in their miserable tents, cooking over camel-turd fires.

"Frightened? No." Rittmann gazed over at the sleek shapes of the other MiG fighters. "Am I worried? *Ja, bestimmt.* With only three of us to counter an entire strike force, what do you think? Of course I am worried."

"It will proceed exactly as I planned it," said Al-Fasr. "Carry out your orders, and you will be a wealthy man."

Rittmann had no idea how it would feel to be a wealthy man. Very nice, he suspected, but it didn't matter. Wealth was not the reason he had come to Yemen. Fixed in Rittmann's mind all these years was a different motivation. He wanted to fly in combat against a Western adversary. Not in simulation, not in training as they had done for decades in the East Bloc. He wanted to witness at close range the fireball from an American fighter that he had shot down.

For over ten years his theater of operations had been East Germany and its Warsaw Pact neighbors. Never had he actually confronted a foreign adversary. Instead, he had skimmed the edges of the three air corridors into Berlin, tightening the sphincters of American and British airline pilots. Once he had roared across the rooftops of West Berlin at supersonic speed. According to the newspaper reports, he had shattered shop windows for three kilometers along the Kurfurstendamm, the city's main artery. It was the closest he had ever come to inflicting damage on an enemy.

Until now. Al-Fasr was giving him an opportunity. His compensation—if he lived to collect it—was on deposit in an account in Luxembourg. A hundred-thousand-franc retainer, with another thirty thousand for each combat mission flown, plus a fifty-thousand-franc bonus for each American aircraft downed. It exceeded the total of everything Rittmann had earned in his life.

The plan was deceptively simple. A strike force from an American aircraft carrier would be arriving to pound what they thought was Al-Fasr's base, but what in fact was a collection of empty tin-roofed structures that Al-Fasr had erected in the highlands. As the strike fighters were entering their weapons-delivery profiles—when they were most vulnerable—Al-Fasr, Rittmann, and the Czech pilot, Novotny, would come blasting out of underground revetments. Using the old British Petroleum access road as a runway, they would stay low and accelerate, pouncing on the Americans without warning. Three more MiGs would remain concealed in the revetments, to be committed in later battle.

Three against a force of forty or more. Al-Fasr, he suspected, might be crazy. If so, he was also brilliant. Despite Rittmann's deep-seated ethnic bias against Arabs in general, he had to admit that this one was a competent fighter pilot. In their initial training sorties in Sudan, Al-Fasr had impressed Rittmann and the other mercenaries in one-versus-one air combat.

Their survival today depended on the element of surprise. Al-Fasr had assured them that the presence of the MiGs had not been detected. Rittmann found this hard to believe, but since Al-Fasr himself was leading the mission, Rittmann tended to believe him. If nothing else, Al-Fasr's intelligence network was superb. He had timed the delivery of the MiGs from Libya, via Chad to the old BP complex here in north-west Yemen, precisely during the window in which the Americans' Big Bird surveillance satellite could not peer down on them.

Standing next to the MiG he would soon be flying, Rittmann ran his hand along the slick leading edge of the wing. For all its complexity, the MiG-29 was suited to primitive environments like this. Designed as a self-contained fighter, the big jet could be loaded, started, and launched with a minimum of ground equipment. Despite its outdated technology, the MiG-29, with its brutishly powerful Klimov engines, was faster than the Super Hornet, more agile than the F-14 Tomcat. Its weapons were dated but deadly. The AA-11 Archer heat-seeking missile, with its broad off-bore-sight capability, was superior to the American Sidewinder.

He noticed Al-Fasr looking at him. That condescending smile still played on the Arab's lips.

Rittmann bristled. "When the Americans learn about these bunkers, they'll blow your compound to hell."

The smile stayed frozen on Al-Fasr's face. "Do not concern yourself with matters beyond your responsibility. Your task is to kill enemy fighters. Nothing more."

Rittmann wasn't willing to drop it, but then he heard a pulsing beep. It came from the transceiver attached to Al-Fasr's flight suit.

Al-Fasr turned away and put the handset to his ear. He listened for a moment, his head nodding. "Very well," he said. "Inform all stations."

He turned back to Rittmann. "This discussion is ended. Go man your aircraft. It is time for you to earn your money."

CHAPTER SIX

DECEPTION

Al Hazir, Yemen
0845, Monday, 17 June

From twenty thousand feet, the complex looked just like the recon photos. Maxwell could pick out what Morse had assured them was the headquarters building, a sprawling, metal-roofed structure with two extended wings. Arranged around it were a half a dozen smaller buildings, reported to be barracks and weapons storage facilities.

The complex lay in a wide valley with terraced hillsides on either side, opening to a sprawling plateau. Only one item seemed to be missing. Maxwell saw no sign of a road, no other access to the complex. The faded landscape might have been the surface of Mars.

It was spooky. No sign of life, no vehicles moving, no troops running for cover. If Al-Fasr possessed antiaircraft batteries, they were eerily silent. No missile alerts were coming from the strike fighters' RWRs or from the AWACS.

The HARM shooters had preceded the strikers, launching

ADM-141 tactical decoys to trick the enemy into lighting up air defense radars. If a target-tracking radar came on-line, a HARM missile was poised to destroy it.

So far, no HARMs had been fired. What radar the enemy possessed was staying off-line.

Likewise, the four-man crews of the EA-6B Prowlers had been frustrated. Their job was to jam the enemy's air defense systems with their suite of airborne electronic warfare equipment. There was nothing to jam.

High overhead, the F-14s on TARCAP—target combat air patrol—waited to intercept inbound enemy fighters. The Tomcat crews assumed that such a threat, though unlikely, would have to come from the west, either Eritrea or Chad across the Red Sea.

No fighters had appeared.

"Ninety-nine Gippers, check switches," Maxwell transmitted, using the groupwide call sign. Glancing over his left shoulder, he saw that B. J. Johnson was in good position, a quarter mile abeam. Off his right wing was his second section, Flash Gordon and Leroi Jones, also in position.

Each strike fighter was carrying a Paveway laser-guided bomb. Smart bombs were life insurance for fighter pilots. Besides being accurate enough to park on a doorstep, they could be released with the standoff distance to keep the pilot out of antiaircraft gun range.

Today it didn't matter. There were no antiaircraft guns.

Behind Maxwell's flight were two more four-plane divisions from the Bluetail squadron armed with Mark 20 Rockeye cluster bombs. The Bluetails were the mop-up crew. After the Paveway bombs had dealt with the buildings, the Bluetails would scour what was left with the cluster bombs.

Overkill, Maxwell thought. The place looked like a ghost town.

"Gipper Zero-one is in hot." Maxwell rolled in on the target.

In quick succession, each of the other three members of his flight reported rolling in on the target.

Through the HUD, Maxwell saw the headquarters building, the largest structure in the complex. It was a big, hard-to-miss sitting duck.

With his left forefinger he slewed the laser designator over the target, stopping it on the gray tin roof. A couple of fine adjustments, positioning the designator exactly in the center . . . hold it a second . . . release.

He felt the jolt all the way through the airframe of the Super Hornet as the two-thousand-pound bomb kicked free of its station.

While the GBU-24 soared toward its target, Maxwell found himself wishing. It would be sweet justice if Al-Fasr was in the building. He had delivered the order that took Josh Dunn's life. And Tom Mellon's. Today was payback time. Eight tons of armor-piercing, high explosive bombs in exchange for one wire-guided missile.

This was the hard part: waiting, letting the laser designator illuminate the target. Each of the other Hornets in his flight was doing the same, each lasing on a different optical frequency.

The bombs were all in the air now, descending like a hail of death on the tin-roofed buildings. Anything left alive would be shredded by the Bluetails and their Rockeye cluster bombs.

He sensed the bomb impact without actually hearing it. The center of the roof opened like the lid of a can, sucking the building inward. An orange ball of flame roiled into the sky. The sides of the building burst apart.

A microsecond later, the adjacent building erupted. Then another. Each of the tin roofed buildings was mushrooming into the morning sky.

It was a lesson right out of Sun Tzu: *Taunt your enemy, lure him into your territory, reveal to him your apparent weakness.*

A dozen times Al-Fasr had read the classic on guerilla warfare. Now he was executing the principles, not in medieval China but here in the milky sky of Yemen. *When he commits to the attack, surprise him. And kill him.*

So it was happening.

The three MiGs came blasting out of the underground revetments, taking off from the makeshift runway at the old BP complex, one behind the other in full afterburner. Staying low and accelerating to supersonic speed, they spread out in a loose line-abreast formation, separated from each other by half a kilometer.

No radio transmissions, no air-to-air radar—not yet. No signal that would reveal their presence to the enemy's electronic surveillance gear.

Ahead, beyond a low ridge, Al-Fasr could see plumes of black smoke. It meant the first bombs were already landing on the decoy compound. Against the backdrop of pallid sky, he could see the specks of two fighters climbing steeply up from the target. At any moment they would be detecting the unexpected presence of the MiGs.

At this altitude, less than a hundred meters above the terrain, the earth was flashing by in a brownish blur. He glanced at the machmeter. The Cyrillic-lettered gauge was showing 1.06 mach, which at this altitude equated to thirteen hundred kilometers per hour. *Speed is life,* went the fighter pilot's mantra. The more the better.

He glanced over his left shoulder. It took him a second to pick out the mottled paint scheme of Rittmann's MiG, nearly invisible against the landscape. To the right was Novotny, the Czech pilot. Novotny was an able but unimaginative pilot, always waiting to be told what to do. He had no illusions about Novotny's life expectancy in the coming battle.

Rittmann was another matter. He was aggressive—too aggressive, perhaps. In their brief training exercises back in Chad, before deploying to Yemen, Rittmann had surprised Al-Fasr with his boldness, but it was an undisciplined boldness. The German would thrust himself into air-to-air engagements like a snarling attack dog. Rittmann needed a leash.

Al-Fasr knew that any second now the American pilots would be receiving urgent warnings from their AWACS. He wished he could eavesdrop on their tactical frequency. It would make him laugh. The invincible American Navy pilots would be squealing like pigs about to be slaughtered.

He checked the display on his inertial navigation system. Ten kilometers to go.

"Radars active," Al-Fasr called to his two wingmen, breaking their radio silence. "Acquire your targets."

He punched the mode control on his Sapfir radar display from standby to acquisition mode. Three sweeps later the display came alive, the screen filling with greenish, hash-marked target symbols.

There they were, the two he had acquired visually as they climbed off target. Another pair was just pulling up. Behind them, approaching from the next quadrant, four more Hornets. Al-Fasr counted twelve in all. As he expected.

The information from his source was accurate.

There would be more up high. The MiG's Sapfir Doppler radar had a gimbal limit of sixty degrees up, not enough to paint any high CAP fighters, but it didn't matter. If the assessment report continued to be accurate—and Al-Fasr was now sure of it—he knew exactly where they would be. He even knew how many—four F-14 Tomcats orbiting at twenty-four thousand feet. Exactly the wrong place to counter the threat of low-flying MiGs.

Another lesson from Sun Tzu: *Learn your enemy's strength; conceal your own.*

On his armament panel, Al-Fasr selected an AA-11 Archer missile. The low growl of the Archer's heat-seeking head filled his earphones.

Boyce's eyes were glued to the tactical display screen. He hated this role, sitting here in CIC like a goddamn spectator at a ball game, watching his team play and not being a part of it. *Shit!* It had been his own paranoid decision to stay back here aboard ship. Him and his gut feelings. He should have swallowed his doubts and done what an Air Wing Commander was supposed to do—lead his people.

Well, it was turning out okay. Better than okay, because Maxwell and his strikers were taking out the terrorist compound like it was an anthill. Best of all, the ants weren't shooting back.

He could see Admiral Fletcher peering at his own tac display, while a young lieutenant explained the symbology on the screen to him. Boyce wondered again why a flag officer who didn't know shit about tactical air operations was in command of this show.

Then he remembered. Sitting next to Fletcher was Babcock, his chin in his hands, staring at the display.

The only problem so far had been with the KS-3 Viking tankers. While on his refueling station, one of the tankers had called in with a hydraulic failure. Now Stickney and Cmdr. Williams, the air boss, were preoccupied with getting him back aboard. Up on the flight deck, yellow shirts were scrambling to respot parked jets.

Down in the darkened CIC space, everyone felt their weight shift in their seats as the carrier heeled to port. Stickney was heading the ship back into the wind so the Viking could recover.

Boyce studied his display. For the third time in fifteen minutes, he called the AWACS. "What's the picture, Sea Witch?"

A pause followed. Boyce knew the controller—an Air Force captain named Tracey Barnett. She was sorting her own array of contacts. "Picture still clear," she reported. "Yankees on second, Pirates headed for first, Dodgers up to bat."

Boyce acknowledged. It corroborated what he saw on his own display. "Picture clear" confirmed that nothing hostile was showing—no MiGs, no SAMs, no target-tracking radars. The baseball team code meant that Maxwell's flight—Yankee—was coming off target, while his second division—Pirate—was just rolling in. Behind them Dodger flight—the Bluetails—was smoking in low and fast.

Boyce knew from experience there was always a glitch. If the place was totally undefended, it meant that they had gotten inaccurate intel about the defenses. But what if the enemy had simply been caught with their pants down? It meant that any moment they would wake up to the fact that they were getting the shit bombed out of them. They would start shooting.

The only thing they couldn't immediately assess was bomb damage. Not until they'd gotten reconnaissance footage obtained by a low-flying Tomcat with a TARP package—Tactical Air Reconnaissance Pod—and from satellite imagery would they know for sure whether Al-Fasr had been put out of business.

The photo of the terrorist smiling back at him from the screen in the briefing room was still in Boyce's mind. He hoped the grinning bastard had been nailed in his headquarters taking a nap. Or sipping one of those thick Arab coffees while he was—

"Pop-up! Pop-up bogeys, north bull's-eye five miles!"

The controller's call pierced Boyce's thoughts like a knife. "Two targets! North bull's-eye, four miles, closing fast!"

Boyce could hear the controller trying to keep her voice calm. "No!" she called. "Make that three targets!"

Boyce could see them on his own display, which was datalinked with the AWACS. Sure as hell, out of nowhere, three blips were there that weren't there before. Converging with the strike fighters.

Pandemonium spilled out of the strike frequency. "Bandits, bandits, two o'clock low!"

"Who? Who's got bandits—"

"Yankee One, bandits four o'clock low."

"Dodger One, snap vector, two-six-zero, four miles."

"Confirm bandits! Who's got an ID?"

"Sea Witch confirms three bandits, north bull's-eye, three miles."

"Threat two-four-zero. Looks like Fulcrums."

"Yankee Two spiked at seven o'clock!"

Maxwell could hear the urgency in B. J. Johnson's voice. "Chaff!" he answered. He wanted her to dump a trail of radar-deflecting foil. "Break left now! Keep the chaff coming."

He was getting the same warning on his RWR. They were both spiked by an enemy fighter's radar. They were the targets. With their tails exposed to the low-flying bandits, radar-deflecting chaff was their only salvation.

Unless the guy was shooting infrared missiles. Heat seekers didn't need radar. They could home on the IR—infrared—signature of your engines, or even the friction of the air over your jet's skin.

Over his shoulder Maxwell could see the dark shape of the bandit down low, coming at them in a nearly vertical climb. He recognized the low-slung belly scoops, the twin vertical fins. A MiG-29. As he grunted under the strain of the six-G turn, he saw a flash beneath the MiG's port wing root.

A missile. IR or radar? No change in the RWR. Had to be a heat seeker.

"Flares!" he called, toggling his own flare dispenser. "B.J., break left. Bandit, seven o'clock low. Missile in the air."

Like chaff, the flares were decoys that were supposed to deceive the missile's guidance unit. If the weapon was a heat seeker—and if they were lucky—the missile would lock onto the flares. Sometimes it worked. Often it didn't. The Russian-built Archer missile was smart enough to distinguish flares from tailpipes.

Pulling maximum G, grunting to keep from graying out as he kept his eyes on the fast-climbing Fulcrum fighter, Maxwell wondered how they got caught like this. *Where did they come from?*

How many were there? Why didn't they get picked up by the AWACS?

This wasn't supposed to happen.

In the lead Tomcat, Cmdr. Burner Crump listened to the urgent radio calls.

"Dodger One spiked at three o'clock!"

"Snap Vector, Pirate One, tactical, one-five-zero, five miles."

"Yankee Two, no joy, no joy!"

The last call was a woman's voice. The Roadrunner pilot, B. J. Johnson, was reporting that she couldn't get a visual on the bandit that was targeting her.

Crump felt like pounding his fist in frustration. He and his Tomcats had been orbiting on their overhead CAP station waiting for nonexistent MiGs. The trouble was, the MiGs weren't nonexistent, and they had somehow gotten down there to hose the bombers. The goddamn fight would be over before Crump and his shooters could get to them.

Maybe not. "Felix One, Sea Witch," came the voice of the AWACS controller. "Snap vector one-three-five, fifteen miles, low. Buster."

"Felix One copies," Crump answered, shoving his throttles into the afterburner detent. "Buster."

Here we go, thought Crump. *Better late than never.* The AWACS controller had just decided that maybe the Tomcats ought to join the furball. She was issuing the bearing and range to the targets. "Buster" was brevity code for maximum speed, which was a good clue that the Hornets were in deep shit.

Crump rolled to the new heading and dumped the nose of the Tomcat. Under full thrust of the F110-GE engines, the big fighter was accelerating like a bullet. In combat spread on the right, his wingman, Gordo Gray, was staying with him. The brown expanse of the Yemeni wasteland swelled in Crump's windscreen.

"You got 'em sorted, Willie?" he asked the RIO in the backseat. He could hear Lt. Willie Martinez, the radar intercept officer, breathing heavily into his hot mike. Martinez was peering into his display, trying to separate cowboys from Indians.

"Hang on a sec. We got a customer . . . twelve o'clock . . . yeah, get ready, I'm getting a lock—" The sound of Martinez's breathing abruptly stopped. "Shit, we're spiked! He's taking a shot!"

Al-Fasr grunted against the seven-G pull-up. The nose of his MiG-29 was pointed nearly vertical, climbing like a rocket from the energy of the supersonic dash over the surface. If his timing was correct, and if he was lucky . . .

Yes! They were directly above him. He flipped the radar to narrow scan and was rewarded with a target-acquisition

symbol. Not one but *two* targets, diving toward him, prob-
ing with their own radars.

It would be a snap shot. Only a marginal chance for a kill,
but he had no choice. They would merge in eight seconds,
and long before that the enemy fighters—they had to be F-
14s—would have their own missiles in the air.

He would have preferred a radar-guided Alamo missile,
but that meant he would have to remain locked on with his
radar while the missile tracked. That was suicide.

It had to be a fire-and-forget heat seeker. Al-Fasr punched
the fire control button on the stick. *Whoom!* An AA-11
Archer missile leaped from its rail beneath the right wing.

He punched again. *Whoom!* A second Archer streaked upward, both missiles trailing plumes of fire and gray smoke.

For an instant he wished he could wait and see the missiles do their work. But his life would then be measured in
seconds. He was a hunted animal surrounded by predators.

He flicked on the chaff dispenser and hauled the nose of
the MiG over the top of the loop, back down toward the
horizon. He punched his targeting radar off. No radar emissions, no electronic target.

His life lay in the effectiveness of his missiles. If the
Archers killed the F-14s before they could launch their own
missiles . . . if the chaff deflected the enemy's radar-guided
weapons . . . if he was not already targeted by other fighters . . .

The MiG was pointed in a vertical dive back to the earth,
back to the cover of the radar-scattering terrain.

The earth was expanding in his windscreen like a zoom
lens. *Don't fly into the ground,* Al-Fasr told himself. He
pulled hard again on the stick, coming out the dive within a
terraced valley. On either side the walls of the valley passed
in a brown-hued blur.

Through the clear glass in the top of the MiG's canopy, he
saw wreckage tumbling out of the sky: a dark shape, spew-

ing debris and orange flame and smoke. A Tomcat? Or one of his MiG-29s?

He saw pieces separate from the wreckage. A parachute canopy blossomed. Then a second. Two white chutes floating down to the Yemeni hills.

Al-Fasr felt a warm glow of satisfaction. The only multiple-crew fighters in this engagement were the Tomcats. One of his Archers had struck home. A face-to-face shot. He won; they lost.

He wondered how Rittmann and Novotny were doing. Had they scored kills? Or were they dead?

Rittmann cursed himself. Why did he take the shot? He should have waited.

In his great haste to kill the lead Hornet, he had fired the missile too soon. He, of all people! Even though he had a steady kill tone in his headset, he knew that the Archer's guidance unit was subject to false locks at this range, especially shooting upward into the sun.

The two Hornets were in a hard break to the left, spewing a trail of foil. The second section had broken to the right and were not a threat, at least not yet. Rittmann had a speed advantage, having converted his supersonic velocity over the surface into a vertical climb. He was closing on the first pair, who were in a high reversal turn to counter his attack.

Rittmann selected another Archer missile. The lead Hornet had gained enough angle off to be outside the Archer's off-boresight limit. It didn't matter. The wingman was still well within range.

He was getting a good acquisition tone from the seeker head. The IR rangefinder showed six thousand meters and closing—well within the envelope. This time he would do it right.

For another second Rittmann tracked the enemy fighter. He had a clear view of the Hornet's aft quarter—the twin afterburners torching flame, canted vertical stabilizers, the pilot's head visible through the back of the canopy. Wisps of vapor were coming off the wings, evidence of the heavy G-load the pilot was pulling.

Rittmann depressed the firing button. The AA-11 Archer missile rocketed ahead of the MiG, flying a curved track toward the hard-turning Hornet.

He saw what appeared to be—*Was ist das?*—balls of fire? No, he realized, flares. He had never seen them this close before. The Hornet pilot was ejecting flares to throw off the heat-seeking missile.

Too late.

Moving at three times the speed of sound, the Archer closed the distance between the fighters. For a second the missile veered toward the trail of flares. Then, like a trained hunting dog, the missile sensed the deception and swerved back to the real target.

The Hornet was in a vertical bank, making a maximum-G turn. With its tiny guidance fins, the stubby air-to-air missile was unable to match the tight turning radius. The Archer overshot, missing the Hornet's tail by twenty feet.

But it was close enough. The missile's proximity fuse detonated, and the metal-shredding shrapnel in the Archer's warhead ripped through the tail section of the Hornet.

Fascinated, Rittmann watched the Hornet go into a skid, then straighten itself, coming out of the hard turn. Part of the right vertical stabilizer was gone. Pieces were spitting out of the right engine, and flames licked around the outside of the fuselage. For a second Rittmann considered finishing the job with the thirty-millimeter gun in the MiG's left wing. Before the pilot could escape, Rittmann would convert him to chopped meat.

In the next instant, the Hornet erupted in a ball of fire. Instinctively, Rittmann threw the stick to the right and yanked hard, barely missing the fireball.

In clear sky, he took a deep breath. He had just killed his first real enemy. But the battle wasn't over. There were many more out there waiting to—

The *Sirena*. The urgent, warbling noise of his radar warning receiver filled his cockpit. He was targeted.

It would be a max angle off-boresight shot, but Maxwell didn't care. The MiG—this particular MiG—wasn't getting away. He would take this guy out any way he could. He'd use the nose-mounted Gatling gun if necessary.

Never in his career had Maxwell felt so frustrated. It had happened so suddenly. Just as he was reaching the apex of his defensive turn, he glanced over his shoulder in time to witness the disintegration of B. J. Johnson's Hornet.

That was when the MiG pilot made his mistake. He tarried too long behind the target after taking his shot. He was forced to make an evasive turn to the right, which gave Maxwell the opening he needed. Pirouetting his Hornet at the top of the arcing turn, he sliced the nose back downhill—toward the oncoming MiG.

Flash Gordon's voice came over the frequency: "Yankee Three and Four engaged. Bandit locked twelve o'clock low."

That explained what happened to his second section, Gordon and Jones. Coming off the target, they had made a hard break to the right to counter another low-flying MiG. That made two. Hadn't AWACS reported three bandits?

"B.J. is down," Maxwell said. "Anybody see a chute?"

"Yankee Three, negative," said Gordon. "We saw a fireball, Brick. No chute."

Maxwell struggled to control his emotions. *You lost your wingman.* If he had reacted quicker to the AWACS pop-up call . . . if he had made an immediate break into the threat sector . . .

He pushed the thoughts from his mind. *Focus. Kill this guy.*

The MiG was directly in front of him. The Sidewinder seeker circle in the HUD was superimposed on the sleek shape of the Fulcrum. The low growl of the missile's seeker unit swelled in his earphones, telling him it was tracking.

Without his second section and now missing his wingman, he knew he was vulnerable to attack by the third bandit. He should get the hell out of there and stay defensive.

No. Take this sonofabitch out.

The MiG was in a hard left turn into him. Maxwell could see the mottled paint scheme, the twin torches of flame from the afterburners.

He squeezed the trigger. From the right wing tip a Sidewinder air-to-air missile streaked out in front of the Hornet.

"Fox two!" he called, signaling the launch of an AIM-9 heat-seeking missile.

He watched the missile go into an arcing left turn, pursuing the MiG like a wolf chasing an antelope. He kept the MiG centered in his HUD. He rocked his air-to-air armament selector back to GUN. If the Sidewinder missed, he would do it the old-fashioned way.

It took exactly four and one-half seconds.

The tail section of the Fulcrum disintegrated in a shower of fragments. The fighter slewed into a rolling, yawing tumble to the right.

Maxwell saw something—the ejection seat?—separate from the cloud of wreckage. Behind the object trailed a stream of material, which then blossomed into the tan-colored canopy of a parachute.

"Splash one!" Maxwell called.

A few seconds later he heard Flash Gordon's exultant voice: "Splash one!"

Another MiG down.

He took his eyes off the tumbling wreckage of the MiG and scanned the sky around him. Two MiGs were out of the fight. That left one still alive.

Where?

No radar, no radio transmissions. Give them nothing with which they could track him.

His *Sirena* radar-warning receiver told him they were searching. With the sophisticated equipment aboard their AWACS ship, they probably detected him. But by his staying low, skimming the ground on the north slope of the massif that stretched to the Red Sea, his chances were decent. They improved with every kilometer he put between him and the enemy fighters.

Al-Fasr kept the MiG in full afterburner. It meant that he would be fuel critical within minutes. So be it. The only fighters that could threaten his escape were the Tomcats, and he was opening up enough lead to put him beyond their pursuit range. Within ten minutes he would be across the narrow Red Sea. Then he would put the fighter down on the strip in Eritrea.

The fight had gone as well as he could have expected. According to the reports from his battle observation monitors, stationed in a hundred-kilometer belt around the complex, at least two American fighters were down. He had lost two MiGs.

Two for two. It was a fair exchange, considering the odds.

Novotny was dead. He was sure of it. The blockheaded Czech had bored straight into a section of Hornets just as they were coming off their target. They had executed a nose-on attack before Novotny had even gotten a missile in the air.

So it went. Fools like Novotny were expendable.

Rittmann had remained in character. True to his word, he had not been afraid. He had thrust himself at the attacking

Hornets like a fearless—and stupid—German attack dog.
Kill and be killed. That was Rittmann's style. Now he was
either dead or lost in the vastness of the Yemeni highlands.
It didn't matter. Rittmann was more trouble than he was
worth.

His *Sirena* was chirping in the same mode it had been
since he left the battle. It meant their radars were scanning,
possibly even picking up a return from his low-flying jet.
From the display he could see that no threats were coming
his way. No missiles in the air, no fighters targeting him
from behind.

Ahead, the high ridge of the massif sloped toward the
horizon. He kept the MiG-29 low, skimming the boulders
and the scrub brush. Occasionally the blur of a terraced field
passed beneath him. He glimpsed huts, outbuildings, thin
wisps of wood smoke.

The brown landscape dropped away beneath him, and the
rocky shoreline came into view. Beyond lay the milky blue
haze of the Red Sea. He had been informed that the *Reagan*'s pilots, by their rules of engagement, were forbidden to
pursue targets beyond the coastal boundaries of Yemen.

The coastline flashed under the MiG's belly. Across the
narrow passage lay the shore of Eritrea.

Safety.

In the cockpit of the MiG-29, Al-Fasr let himself relax for
the first time since he'd left the revetment. He had survived
the first battle. The next was about to begin.

The red phone next to Boyce's chair rang. It was the direct line from the captain's station on the bridge.

"I'm afraid so," said Boyce, "two down, a Tomcat from
the TARCAP, and a Hornet from Yankee flight."

Boyce held the phone two inches away from his ear.
Stickney wanted to know where the MiGs had come from

and how come nobody saw them coming and why did this whole goddamn caper look like fucking amateur hour?

Boyce felt the eyes of Admiral Fletcher and Babcock on him while the *Reagan*'s captain roared over the phone. "I don't have the answers yet, Sticks, but I assure you we're gonna find out. My first priority is getting the RESCAP in place and snatching our people out of there."

He hung up and saw Claire Phillips standing beside him. Her face looked somber.

"It's not good, is it?" she asked in a low voice.

"I've seen better."

"Some of our pilots have been shot down. Who are they?"

"You know I can't tell you that."

"One of them is the woman pilot. The one they call B.J.?"

Boyce looked around the CIC compartment. Controllers were hunched over their consoles, coordinating the elements of the strike group. Fletcher and Babcock were staring at him again. "Look, Claire. This is a pretty volatile situation, and the media shouldn't be this close. I'm going to ask you to leave while we deal with this."

"Red, please, I won't interfere with—"

He took her elbow and steered her toward the door. "Listen to me, Claire. Not a word, not a hint of what you saw or heard in here will be reported without clearing it through me. Is that understood?"

Claire's eyes flashed. "Of course it's understood. Do you think I'm the enemy, Red?"

"No. Sorry, but you know what I mean."

On her way out the door she paused. "Just tell me. Is Sam okay?"

He glanced back at his tactical display. None of the symbols on the screen had changed in the past half minute. "Yeah. Sam's okay."

CHAPTER SEVEN

INDIAN COUNTRY

Al Hazir, Yemen
1045, Monday, 17 June

Stealth jogging.

Yes, she thought, that was it. It had a nice ring to it. Maybe she could use it someday in a paper or a lecture. It described what she was doing this very moment—hightailing it through the Yemeni hills like a hunted fugitive.

Which, of course, she was.

She wished she had her running shoes, the ones with the air soles that weighed eight ounces each. She'd be flying over the rocks instead of clumping along in these clodhopping boots.

B.J. jogged along the shaded slope of the ridgeline, stopping every minute or so to listen. She needed to put distance between her and the valley where the Tomcat crew was caught. *Keep moving, stop and listen for the bad guys, keep moving. Stay out of sight.*

If she got out of this place, she thought—and then instantly corrected herself. *Forget if. No more ifs. When you get out. You are getting out of this place. And after you do you will sit down and write one hell of an authoritative paper about escape and evasion. Maybe get it published in* Naval Institute Proceedings *or some such journal. Why not? Who else would know more about being on the lam in a garden spot like Yemen?*

It was luck that she hadn't been injured in the ejection. She'd punched out at high speed—something over four hundred knots, she guessed—barely beating the fireball when the Hornet blew up. She'd been in the chute only seconds, just long enough to smack down onto a rocky hillside, landing with an ungraceful thud and rolling twenty feet down the slope before she could disentangle herself from the shroud lines.

She was okay, just some bruises and cuts from the rocks. She could run, which was the most important item in her set of skills. Run like hell. The stuff she didn't want to carry—chute, helmet, raft, torso harness—she stashed beneath rocks and brush. She gathered the essential items into the survival rucksack and moved out.

Not until she'd gone a mile did she stop and try the radio. The emergency UHF transceiver was her ticket home. She could communicate with friendly aircraft, give her location, call in the SAR helo.

Overhead she could hear—and sometimes see—the multiplane furball that was still going on. At least one more fighter—she couldn't tell whose—had been shot down. A spiraling trail of black smoke marked its death dive.

Crouching beneath a shrub, she tried the transmit button on the transceiver. Nothing happened.

She turned the power button off, then on again. Still nothing.

. The radio didn't work.

She stared at it. No little red power light, no static, nothing. She wanted to scream. The goddamned emergency radio didn't work! Had it been damaged in the ejection? It looked okay, no dings or dents. Maybe the battery was kaput. For a long moment she stared at the black piece of inert hardware, suddenly hating it. All this goddamn useless technology. How could this happen? The most essential piece of survival gear in her kit didn't work. B. J. Johnson felt herself overwhelmed with a sense of hopelessness. She sank to the ground and wept.

After a minute, she began talking to herself. "Move it, girl. You're going to get out of here even if you have to walk. Go on, move your butt."

She moved.

Maxwell couldn't believe it.

He put both hands on the conference table and leaned forward. "Excuse me, Admiral, did I hear correctly? We're *not* sending in a search-and-rescue team?"

CAG Boyce, Admiral Fletcher, Whitney Babcock, and Spook Morse sat facing him at the long table. Half an hour ago Maxwell had landed back aboard the *Reagan*. He was still wearing his flight suit and torso harness, sweat-stained from the three-hour combat sortie.

"You heard the intel debrief," said Admiral Fletcher. "The RESCAP jets lost communications with the F-14 crew on the ground just before the SAR helos showed up. They came under fire and had to withdraw. Since then, nothing has been heard from any of the downed pilots. We have reasonable evidence that the F-14 pilot and RIO were captured."

"What about my downed pilot?" Maxwell said. "Are we giving up on her too?"

Fletcher gave him a baleful glare. "I'll overlook your choice of words, Commander. I know you've been under strain. For your information, we're not giving up on anybody. All the evidence we have indicates that the Hornet pilot was killed in action. As the Battle Group Commander, it's my responsibility not to sacrifice any more pilots and airplanes trying to rescue people who are already dead or captured."

Maxwell felt his temper flaring out of control. Before he could speak, Boyce cut him off. "Admiral, what Commander Maxwell and I don't understand is why we're letting this ragtag bunch of terrorists get away with this. Why don't we just go in there with an assault force—marines and plenty of air power—and take out the whole mess? Get our people back and exterminate those murderers."

Fletcher blinked, then looked to the end of the table. Whitney Babcock spoke up. "We can understand your sentiments, Captain Boyce, but you have to understand that more is at stake here than you probably understand. This is a national security consideration, not a simple tactical exercise."

It was Boyce's turn to seethe. He glared at Babcock. "If you mean decisions like that are above my pay grade, fine, I understand. But damn it, this is Yemen we're talking about, not North Korea or China. We could occupy that joint in half a day if we had the balls to do it."

Babcock gave him a patronizing smile. "I'm afraid that's out of the question. As the world's only superpower, we have a responsibility to demonstrate our restraint."

"So we're not going to do anything more? Just let them keep their MiGs and missiles and our captured pilots and wait for them to hit us again?"

"You can rest assured that it's being negotiated at the very highest levels. If any of our pilots are alive, they'll be returned. As for letting them keep their weapons, we've already made our point. Their complex, as you saw in the intel photos, has been destroyed."

Boyce had a retort, but he caught himself. He clamped his cigar in his jaw and turned to Spook Morse, sitting across the table. "Okay, intel officer. Where the hell did those MiGs come from? Why didn't you guys bother giving us that little morsel in our briefing?"

Morse shrugged. "Take it up with the CIA. Or the National Security Agency. They provide our intel data, and I just give you what they give us. Al-Fasr's group apparently managed to sneak the MiGs in between the flyover envelopes of our recon satellites. Nobody knew they were there. They have them concealed underground somewhere in the northwest quarter. They seem to be equipped with low-observable paint schemes and electronic countermeasures gear."

"Beautiful. Where'd they get them and who's flying them?"

"The MiGs came from Libya, according to our sources. The pilots were recruited from Russia's clients, probably Libya or the former East Germany. Al-Fasr himself may be one of the pilots."

"We nailed two of them, and one hightailed it. How many more are there?"

Morse shrugged again. "Very few, maybe none. If they have satellite tracking technology, which we suspect they do, then they know when we're not looking. It's going to be difficult to spot them."

Boyce looked disgusted. "Until they show up to bite us in the ass again." He fumed for a moment, then said, "Hard to believe, with all our advanced technology, those guys can catch us in the open like that. Almost like they knew we were coming."

"They did know," said Morse.

A heavy silence fell over the room. Boyce stared at Morse, not sure that he heard correctly. He removed his cigar. "Would you mind explaining that?"

"It's very obvious," Morse said, studying his fingernail. He looked up at all the expectant faces around the table. He let several seconds pass, the silence hanging heavy in the room. "They have an informer aboard the *Reagan*."

Brown.

The color du jour. It was exactly what she had told all those bored pilots in her prestrike briefing. Earth, trees, rocks, buildings—everything in Yemen bore the same monochromatic shade of brown.

And so would she.

At the base of a hill she found a stand of six-feet-tall scrub trees. She crawled into the shelter of the trees and unzipped her rucksack. Among her survival items was one she had added on her own: a tin of brown greasepaint. She smeared the stuff over her face, around her neck, on the backs of her hands. No white skin was left exposed.

Then, another extra item—the camo-colored bandanna. She pulled her hair into a bun and tied the bandanna tightly around her head.

When she was finished she checked herself in the signal mirror. She almost laughed out loud. *You look like a snake eater.* She resembled one of those action-movie heroes crawling on his belly behind enemy lines. Actually, she thought, it looked pretty cool.

She was still regarding herself in the mirror when she heard the vehicle.

She clambered to the top of a rock-strewn promontory that overlooked a valley. She peered in all directions, looking for the source of the engine noise.

Then she saw them.

They were coming down the valley, in full view from either side, two men in flight gear. One, the shorter of the two, was supporting the other. He seemed to be injured. He was walking with difficulty, dragging one foot.

The idiots were still wearing their helmets and torso harnesses! B.J. wanted to yell at them, *Get in the trees and hide, you meatheads!*

She knew what they were thinking. They would just call in the SAR, get in the open somewhere, get picked up. *No sweat, bubba.*

It was stupid. These two were strolling along like tourists on a nature walk. They should have attended her in-country briefing about escape and evasion. B.J. started down from the promontory to intercept them.

Then it was too late. In the next instant she saw an armored personnel carrier burst into the valley, kicking up a column of dirt as it came churning toward the two aviators.

The two pilots turned back in the direction they had come. The crippled airman tried to run, but he stumbled and fell. Kneeling, he turned and faced the oncoming vehicle. The other pilot ran several paces, then stopped and ran back to the side of his injured companion. Both had their pistols drawn.

Brrraaaaaappppp! A single long burst of automatic fire came from the machine gun mounted on the APC. The kneeling airman toppled end over end like a rag doll.

The second pilot stood motionless, yielding to the inevitable. He made a show of dropping the pistol and raising his hands.

Brrraaaaaapppp! The bullets caught him across the chest, hurling him backward. The pilot lay spread-eagled on the dirt, blood oozing in a pool around him.

B.J. felt sick to her stomach. From her vantage point two hundred yards away, she watched the APC pull up to where the two slain airmen lay. Half a dozen troops, each wearing desert-colored fatigues and carrying automatic weapons, climbed out the back hatch. They examined the bodies, rolling them over, removing the pistols and survival items. B.J. saw them studying the pilots' equipment, talking among themselves.

They have the radios, B.J. realized. If they knew how, the bastards could listen in on the SAR frequency.

After they dragged the bodies into the APC, two of the troops stood gazing around the valley with binoculars.

She knew what they were doing. They were searching. They knew another pilot was out there. She hunched down behind the cluster of rocks.

"You want a drink?" said Boyce.

Maxwell shook his head. "No."

"Too bad. You sure as hell need one." Boyce flopped down in one of the two desk chairs in his stateroom and motioned for Maxwell to take the other.

Boyce didn't mind breaking the Navy's traditional ban on alcohol aboard ship, just as he didn't mind firing up a cigar. Too much moderation was bad for you, he always said. He considered a highball after a hairy night of carrier ops to be good therapy.

But not tonight. Boyce busied himself scribbling notes on a yellow pad. Maxwell kept his silence, waiting for the boss to unload whatever it was on his mind.

He noticed that Boyce had aged in the past week. The wisps of red hair on his pate seemed to have grown thinner and grayer. He guessed that it was the stress of commanding the *Reagan's* air wing. Or the pressure of dealing with the likes of Fletcher and Babcock.

Boyce ripped off the yellow page and handed it to Maxwell. "That's the air plan for tomorrow. Starting at sunup, we're gonna keep jets over the area full-time. HARM shooters, EA-6 jammers, a rotating CAP. I'm putting a Tomcat with a TARPS package over the area once an hour." Each TARPS pod contained two cameras and an infrared scanner.

Maxwell studied the sheet. "Did the admiral sign off on this?"

"He doesn't have a choice. Fletcher is a political animal,

and he knows he can't appear to give up on missing pilots, especially when the word gets out that one of them is a woman. I'm gonna keep reminding him of that."

"What if Al-Fasr starts shooting again? What are the rules of engagement?"

"Anybody lights up—radar, SAM site, AA guns—we come down on them like the hammers of hell."

"Babcock is not going to like that. It wouldn't fit in with his negotiated settlement."

"Maybe not, but he's savvy enough to know how it will play on the evening news when America learns that one of our girl pilots might be held by a band of terrorists and we're not doing anything about it."

The thought of B. J. Johnson in the hands of Al-Fasr sent another surge of dread through Maxwell. "How long are we prepared to keep it up?"

A somber look came over Boyce's face. He leaned back in his chair and rolled a cigar between his fingers. "You and I came up believing that nobody got left behind. We don't give up on our people. We didn't do it in Vietnam, not in Desert Storm, not in Bosnia, not in Afghanistan, and as long as I'm running the air wing, we're not gonna do it in Yemen. If I send pilots into harm's way, then they have to believe that I'll come and get them if they get shot down. I'll stay until we find them."

"That may not be what they're thinking up on the flag bridge right now."

"Maybe not, but it's our duty to do what's right. Even if it means pushing the envelope a little." His eyes narrowed and he looked at Maxwell. "Maybe more than a little. Do you read me?"

Maxwell nodded. Boyce was an old warhorse from another era. He had risen through the ranks in a time when orders were clear, missions were specific, and the enemy was identifiable.

Well, times had changed. Red Boyce had not. Thank God for that.

"Yes, sir," he said. "Perfectly."

Spook Morse knew what was coming. He could see it in Fletcher's face, the way he sat there drumming his fingertips on the table surface.

Fletcher waited until the air wing officers, Boyce and Maxwell, had both left. The only ones left in the flag intel compartment were Fletcher and Babock, Captain Vitale, and Spook Morse.

"Explain yourself, Commander Morse," said Fletcher. "What the hell are you saying? Al-Fasr has an informer aboard the *Reagan*? You mean—"

"A spy? Yes, sir. I'm sure of it."

The admiral's face hardened. "May I ask why you haven't bothered to inform me, the Battle Group Commander, about such a matter?"

Morse took his time. He knew Fletcher. He was blustering, making a show of gruffness to impress the civilian, Babcock.

"Until now it was only a suspicion, Admiral. For that matter, I still have no proof, just some deductive reasoning and circumstantial evidence."

"Don't give me that intelligence community line about deductive reasoning. I'm your boss and I want some straight talk. Do you know who the informer is?"

"I can narrow it down to a dozen candidates."

"How would somebody get classified information off a carrier at sea without our knowing it?"

Morse wondered again how someone as clueless as Fletcher rose to flag rank. *Idiots.* "Lots of ways, Admiral. Using our own comm gear, if he knew what he was doing. Several million bytes of data get transmitted from the *Reagan* every day, and much of it is classified."

"Who are these suspects you have in mind?"

Morse didn't answer for several seconds. His eyes moved around the table, pausing on Vitale, then dwelling for several seconds on Whitney Babcock. Babcock returned his gaze while he played with a ballpoint pen.

"The list includes everyone who sits in on our top-secret briefings. That includes me, of course, and you, Admiral Fletcher, Mr. Babcock, Captain Vitale, Captain Boyce, and the strike leader, Commander Maxwell. Beyond us, there are half a dozen possible suspects who work in sensitive jobs."

He reached into his briefcase and pulled out a spiral notepad. He ripped off the top sheet and handed it to the admiral. "These are listed in order of likelihood. For your information, I've had each of their phones and their e-net lines monitored. Not that that will turn up anything unless our player turns out to be a total amateur."

Babcock spoke up from the end of the table. "I don't like the sound of this. Does this mean you're eavesdropping on us?"

"It's the system, Mr. Babcock. Nothing is exempt in counterespionage. I didn't say that any of us was a suspect, but no one should be off-limits."

"Including you, Commander Morse."

"Yes, sir, including me. I have more access to classified data than anyone aboard the ship."

At this, Babcock became silent. He sat at the end of the table, seemingly deep in thought.

Fletcher put on his reading glasses. After he perused the list, he said, "This is hard to believe. Why would any of these people be working for Al-Fasr?"

Morse shrugged. "If we figured out what turned people into agents and double agents, we could identify spies before they did us any damage. Some do it for money, obviously, but usually it's more than that. They see it as a romantic cause, or some sort of idealistic crusade. Sometimes they just get blackmailed into it."

Fletcher was still staring at the list. "What do we do about them?"

"Well, as a stopgap, we can reassign them while we keep monitoring their activities. Five work in sensitive intel and comm areas. Three officers, two senior enlisted, one warrant."

"What about the media people? Aren't they possible suspects?"

"We can't rule them out. None have access to discrete communications facilities that we know of, but one could have his own dedicated transmitter."

Babcock came out of his reverie and said, "They shouldn't be allowed this close to the operation. Even if they're not giving away secrets, they'll put their own spin on things, and we'll get smeared in the press just like they did to us in Somalia."

Vitale said, "We'll get smeared if we throw them off."

"It's the lesser of the evils."

"What do we tell them?" asked Fletcher.

"The truth. This is war and we're offloading all noncombatants."

Fletcher nodded and turned to Vitale. "You heard him. Do it."

Claire stepped onto the flight deck. Even through the padded cranial protector and the float coat, she could hear the thunder of the jet engines, feel the thirty-knot gale that swept over the bow. The C-2A Greyhound turboprop was parked beside the island, its back clamshell door open and waiting for her. The other reporters had already boarded.

"I've never been kicked off a carrier before," she said. "Was it Babcock?"

"Probably," said Maxwell. "The actual order came from

Admiral Fletcher. He says no more media coverage of the Yemen operation."

"Until something happens that makes him look good."

"You said it, not me."

"There'll be another strike, won't there?"

Maxwell put on his blank face. "I don't know."

She studied him for a moment. There was that hard look, his eyes glowing like coals. He was burning inside.

"You still want revenge," she said. "An eye for an eye."

His expression didn't change. "I do what I'm ordered to do."

She saw the crew chief waving to her from the back of the C-2A. "Sam, please get over it. You can't bring Josh back. Come back to me alive, promise?"

He looked at her, and for a moment the hard lines in his face seemed to soften. He smiled and said, "Okay. I promise."

She gave him a quick kiss, then trotted to the C-2A and climbed aboard.

It was nearly dark when she spotted him. Or when he spotted her. Each was taken by surprise.

B.J. was trotting along a path that traversed a cultivated hillside. Halfway down the hill she noticed rows of some sort of scrawny crop—sorghum, millet, something like that. She tried to remember from her homework what kind of subsistence farming they did up here in the highlands.

When she glanced up from the terraced hillside, back to the path ahead, there he was. Twenty yards away, he wore the ubiquitous kaffiyeh and a baggy shirt and trousers made of coarse sackcloth. Dangling from his belt was a scabbard, which she knew contained his *jambiyya,* the curved dagger Yemeni men carried in this part of the country.

He stood transfixed, staring as if he were seeing an extraterrestrial. She returned his gaze. For nearly a minute they

stood like that, neither moving, regarding each other warily.
He was a farmer, she guessed. Maybe a shepherd. One of
those dudes she had warned the other pilots about in her
briefing. *Don't expect the peasants to be friendly.* Their only
loyalty was to themselves and their families and to whatever
small-caliber sheik ran their local village.

She wondered if he had another weapon, a revolver or an
automatic pistol inside his baggy clothes. Guns were a way
of life here. That was in the briefing too. Peasants who
couldn't afford shoes here owned AK-47s.

She thought about the Beretta in her shoulder holster. He
could see the pistol. And he could figure by her costume
where she had come from. Everyone who lived in these hills
had seen and heard the air battle that raged over their heads
this afternoon.

Okay, let's break the stalemate.

She smiled at him.

He stared back, his face expressionless.

She took a step toward him, holding her hands in front of
her so he could see she meant no harm. She tried to recall
one of her Arabic expressions. Maybe she could persuade
him to—

He turned and ran.

Wait, she wanted to call out. Maybe she should run after
him. She would make the dumb sonofabitch understand that
she was friendly.

Forget it. What would she do if she caught him? Wherever this guy was running to, there would be others like him,
armed to the teeth. In any case, the word would spread like
wildfire about the woman snake eater running loose in the
hills. There might even be a reward for her.

She turned and trotted back down the path up which she
had come. She kept up a brisk pace, staying in the shadows,
pausing every few minutes to listen for pursuers. When she
came to a dry streambed, she turned and followed the twist-

ing, sand-filled bottom. After a mile, she left the streambed and began climbing the steep, brush-covered slope of a towering promontory. From such a high perch, she could survey the best routes out of this place.

Most of the hillside was in shadow now. The setting sun bathed the landscape in an orange-brown hue. The temperature had dropped by a good ten degrees. When darkness came, it would get cold.

When she was still a hundred yards from the summit of the promontory, she heard something. She stopped, crouching in the shadow of a rock formation. For half a minute she sat motionless, listening. At first she heard only the wind, the low buzz of insects in the brush. Then, something else.

The distant *whop-whop* of rotor blades. A helicopter.

Ours or theirs?

She pulled one of the colored smoke flares from her rucksack, checking it to make sure she could yank the ring when the time came. She would throw the flare, then run into an open area where the helo could land or hover while she got into the sling.

The *whop-whopping* grew more distinct, coming from the north.

B.J. was getting a bad feeling. North was not a good direction. The good guys would not come from the north.

Without warning the helicopter burst over the ridge, flying directly toward her. As she rolled into a fetal position, trying to meld herself into the rocks, she glimpsed the streamlined profile. It wasn't one of the big Sikorsky SAR helos. This was a French-built Dauphin.

She saw the gunner in the open hatch. He was wearing the same desert-colored fatigues as the troops who had killed the Tomcat crew. She prayed that her own camo flight suit, the glop she had daubed on her face, and the nylon scarf over her head would make her invisible.

The noise of the rotor blades became a throbbing pulse. The concussion hammered on her ears like giant drums.

She lay motionless. The scrub brush around her flapped in the downwash from the blades. Puffs of brown dirt kicked up like miniature dust devils.

She closed her eyes. The throbbing pulse changed in intensity.

The rotor noise lessened. The scrub brush stopped flapping.

Keep going, B.J. prayed. *Please go away.*

The sound didn't change. They weren't going away.

She forced herself to look. There it was, no more than fifty yards away, hovering over a flat clearing on the hillside. As she watched, men in camo fatigues jumped from the hovering helicopter onto the ground. One, two, three in all. Each carried an automatic weapon.

The leader peered around, checking his bearings, then looked in her direction. He barked an order at the other two; then they trotted single file away from the helicopter.

Toward her.

B.J. sprang from her hiding place. Down the hillside she bounded, taking great flying leaps, somehow keeping her feet beneath her as she landed, bounding again.

Behind her she heard the men pounding down the hill. The throb of the helicopter intensified again. They were coming after her.

CHAPTER EIGHT

PURSUIT

Gulf of Aden
1235, Monday, 17 June

"Depth?" Manilov demanded.

"Ninety meters, Captain," said the technician, his eyes riveted to the Fathometer. "Shallowing. Eighty-eight meters. Eighty-six now."

"Slow to two knots."

"Aye, sir."

They were inshore, gliding over the seabed of the shallow Yemeni coastline. Manilov wanted to stay close to the bottom, hiding beneath the thermal layer that lay like a shield between the submarine and the surface above. To scrape the bottom here could damage the *Mourmetz*'s hull, but the greater danger was the acoustic hell it would raise on the enemy's sonars. They would awake to the fact that a Kilo-class sub was lurking in their presence.

"One knot."

"Aye."

It was barely enough forward speed to keep the planes

working. The *Mourmetz* was almost motionless and, thus, undetectable. At least that was what Manilov had to believe. He had no choice except to place his faith in the submarine's ability to operate in nearly total silence. He knew that they still presented the tiniest of magnetic anomaly signatures, but unless the American sub hunters knew precisely where to search, there was only the remotest likelihood of being detected.

Last night had been their last opportunity to snorkel—to refresh the batteries and air. Now they would remain submerged until the conclusion of the operation. They could go for a week without snorkeling, and even longer if they went to extreme-conservation mode with the carbon dioxide scrubbers and the oxygen/hydrogen generator plant.

Such measures would be unnecessary, Manilov concluded. However the action ended, the last voyage of the *Mourmetz* would be over soon.

Perhaps this evening.

Darkness was coming, and with it his best opportunity to attack. Not until then would Manilov risk ascending to periscope depth. A quick look, then a decision. If he did not have a clear shot, he would drop the scope and immediately descend back below the thermal layer. If all parameters were correct, he would fire a salvo and then run.

What were their chances of escape?

He put the question out of his mind. The overwhelming magnitude of the enemy's antisubmarine warfare capability was enough to intimidate any boat captain. What counted to Manilov was getting off the first shot. Kill the enemy. Every minute they lived after that was an unexpected blessing.

Manilov waited, checking every two minutes with the sonar passive operator. "Bearing and range, primary target?"

"Zero-four-zero, seven thousand meters, moving northeast at fifteen knots."

Finally, sunset. Not completely dark, but it would do.

Manilov didn't want to wait any longer. Nineteen years was enough.

"Ascend to periscope depth."

"Aye, sir."

"Ready tubes one, two, three."

"Tubes one, two, three loaded, ready to fire."

The *Mourmetz* was carrying a load of ten elderly SET 16 torpedoes. It was all Manilov could requisition for the ferry trip to Iran. He would have been more comfortable going into battle with the normal complement of eighteen torpedoes as well as a battery of antiship missiles. The deal with the Iranian Navy included only enough armament for the *Mourmetz* to defend itself on the trip to Bandar Abbas.

It wouldn't matter. Ten torpedoes were more than enough. Long before he could expend all his weapons, this battle would be over.

As the *Mourmetz* slowly rose toward the darkened surface, Manilov gazed around the control room. He could sense the tension hanging like electricity in the stale air. Lieutenant Commander Ilychin, the executive officer, looked like he'd stepped from a shower. Perspiration streamed over the officer's face, dripping onto his console. Borodin, the young sonar operator, was moving his lips in some sort of prayer.

"Up scope," Manilov ordered.

"Up scope."

"Level . . . now." The *Mourmetz*'s periscope was protruding a few inches above the surface. The sea was almost calm. As he expected this close inshore, ripples still washed over the glass. Because they were motionless—zero forward speed—the planes were useless and the scope was not as steady as he would like it.

He first did a complete sweep with the attack scope, taking a 360-degree look at his surroundings. Whenever a wave splashed over the glass he made himself pause and wait until it cleared again. *Don't rush,* he commanded himself. The worst mistake you could make was to rush. Fear, adrenaline, the terrifying nearness of the enemy—all conspired to make you rush your shot and miss. *Be calm; be deliberate.*

He saw two ships, destroyers, both headed northeast away from them. Carefully working the scope he picked up what appeared to be an amphibious dock ship. Still rotating the periscope, he scanned eastward. Then to the south—

There it was! Manilov felt like shouting. Sliding into view was a silhouette, massive and foreboding. *My God!* He had never observed a vessel of such immensity through a periscope. Even in the gathering darkness he could make out the high, flat deck, the towering superstructure.

USS *Reagan.*

A wave splashed over the glass of the periscope, blurring his view. Manilov made himself wait while the image cleared. "Firing solution!"

At the MVU-110 combat information computer, the operator yelled out the data. "Primary target bears 155, range 8,640 meters, tracking 070, speed sixteen."

"Stand by tubes one and two."

"One and two standing by."

After all this waiting, Yevgeny Manilov's life had shrunk to this tiny speck in time. No past, no future. Just this moment.

He saw something. *What was that?* Another object, smaller, faster, directly aft of the carrier.

A destroyer?

Yes, damn it to everlasting hell, another destroyer! Pulling ahead, inserting itself between the *Mourmetz* and the *Reagan.*

Turning toward them.

He flipped the scope to aerial view and swept the sky over the ships. More trouble. A helicopter lifting from the fantail of the carrier. Swinging leftward, dipping its nose.

Coming toward them.

"Radar targeting," called out the electronic warfare specialist. "Upper-spectrum fire control radar, same bearing and range as the primary target."

"Down scope!"

He could still fire but it would be suicide. Even if they were lucky enough to score a hit, they would never live to see the *Reagan* sink.

"Descend to eighty meters, medium rate."

"Aye, sir," answered the engineer, his voice quavering.

"Ahead three knots."

Not too fast. Slow and easy. Just enough to give the planes effectiveness. At less than five knots, running on the electric motors, the Kilo class was virtually noiseless. He wanted nothing more than a silent descent back to the relative safety beneath the thermal layer.

As the *Mourmetz*'s bow tilted down, Manilov's mind raced through the possibilities. What had they detected? Just the tip of the periscope. A few sweeps of the radar, an imperceptible trace, then nothing. They would investigate, but if Manilov was quick and careful, they would detect nothing more.

He ordered the planesman to level the sub. The *Ilia Mourmetz* was running for its life.

Hurry, darkness.

B.J. ran, her heart pounding not so much from the exertion as from pure terror. *Keep running,* she commanded herself. *Keep them behind you.*

The sun was below the high ridgeline. In the dwindling light she was having trouble on the rough terrain. Twice she stumbled, once over a rock and then a low shrub, tumbling end over end. Her hands were bleeding. Her elbow ached, and her torn flight suit was flapping loose at the sleeve.

Keep running. Run out the daylight. The black of night was her only hope.

She could hear them crashing through the brush behind her. She heard them stop, bark at each other in Arabic, then come after her again. Overhead the helicopter was crisscrossing her path, losing her, picking up the trail again.

She zigzagged, taking abrupt turns, keeping to the darkened side of the hill. The light was fading, making it more difficult to keep her feet beneath her. She felt the terrain steepening. To her right, the hill dropped down into a murky gloom.

Her breath came in sharp gasps. She felt her heart pounding like a jackhammer. Her pursuers had to be locals. Mountain people. These guys spent their lives breathing thin air, navigating these rocky goat paths.

What would they do when they caught her?

You know.

The image of the F-14 crew flashed through her mind. She felt a new impetus. *Run!*

The chopper was above and to her left, the pilot apparently unwilling to descend into the darkness below the ridgeline. But the noises behind her seemed nearer. She could hear labored breathing, the steady clump of boots on rock, the metallic clink of weapons.

Thirty yards, she guessed. Maybe closer.

She wondered how they were catching her. Damn it, she was a marathoner, a fitness freak. She was losing the race to these goons in ratty fatigues.

It came to her. With every sharp turn she took, they were cutting across the angle, closing more distance on her. They didn't have to see her. They could follow the sound of her clunking boots.

She picked up the pace. More than ever she wished that she had her running shoes instead of these goddamn Clydesdale hooves. Her lungs ached. Her legs felt like rubber.

She fought back the panic rising in her. Being hunted by terrorists wasn't mentioned when she had signed up to be a naval aviator. Why had she thought being a fighter pilot was a great adventure? She would gladly change roles with any briefcase-toting woman professional in America. Let someone else run from these assholes.

Too late, girl. She reached down with her right hand and checked the Beretta. Still there.

Soon, within minutes, she would have to confront them. She could surrender, hope they let her live.

Or shoot it out. Try to kill them, all three—

She tripped.

Something—she never saw it, a stone or a branch—caught her toe, sending her headlong down the slope. She felt herself hurtling through space.

Whump. She hit on her side, rolling with the fall, airborne again.

She landed on her shoulder, ricocheting off the steeply sloping terrain.

End over end, glancing off the earth. Into space again. Tumbling, hitting something hard and gritty, hurting like hell, falling.

Then nothing. No pain, no falling, no awareness. Just the blackness.

In the flag plot compartment aboard the *Reagan,* one of the admiral's four phones jangled—the direct line from the duty officer in CIC.

"Fletcher."

"Admiral, the SPY-one radar operator on the *Arkansas* just reported a disappearing contact bearing 340 degrees, five miles. That puts it only two or three miles offshore."

"Disappearing? What kind of contact?"

"Two sweeps, he said, and it was gone. Their computer gave it a thirty percent probability of being a sub."

"What kind? Whose?"

"It would have to be a diesel/electric, either a Kilo or a Lada boat. In these waters it could be Iranian, maybe Libyan. Might even be Russian, but we don't show them having any operational Kilos deployed here. We've got a request in to SUBLANT for a status update on all Indian Ocean and Gulf fleets."

Fletcher considered for a moment. What would a Russian-built sub be doing in the Gulf of Aden? Nothing, probably, except being curious. "Thirty percent? What's the other seventy?"

"The usual stuff, sir. That close inshore they get a lot of those contacts. They give every one a track number and plot it whether it's real or not."

Fletcher had once commanded an Aegis cruiser, and he knew about such contacts. At least one of the array of SPY-1s was tweaked to pick out the return of a barely raised periscope. The trouble was, such a vague target could be mimicked by hundreds of natural and manmade objects—small boats, divers, all kinds of flotsam. Sub hunters spent their lives chasing phantoms.

"Okay, maintain a normal screen and have the *Arkansas* link all their contact plots over to us."

"Yes, sir, I've done that."

Fletcher went back to his plotting chart. Third-world submarine fleets were more of a nuisance than a threat. Backward countries like Libya and Iran and Iraq bought these obsolete Russian boats; then they went looking for games to play with them. Someday, Fletcher thought, one of those ragleg sub jockeys was going to push his luck and get blown out of the water.

A dull ache. That was all, just a remote pain, like the twinge of a forgotten injury. It wasn't even *her* pain, but somehow separate and detached from her body. She was someplace else, a space traveler in a dimensionless void. No gravity, no up, no down. Just this dreamy sensation, afloat in the universe.

Except there were no stars.

She thought for a moment that her eyes were still closed. No, that wasn't it. Had she lost her sight? She didn't think so. It was dark, dark as a thousand bungholes.

Then she tried to move. She nearly screamed as the pain seared through her legs, up through her torso, all to her arms. Everything hurt.

She wasn't a space traveler anymore. *What the hell happened?*

The details came back to her in fragments, like pieces of a dark mosaic. Running from the terrorists. The helicopter. They caught her—or did they?

She fell. That was the part that didn't come into focus. She went down the mountainside—and the rest became a blur. Was she hurt? Was she captured? Where was she?

Her legs and torso felt as though they were bound, immobile. Wherever she was, it was cold as hell.

She tried moving her right hand. It was okay. Fingers, wrist, elbow, all intact and functional. The other hand was okay too. She wiggled her toes. They all worked.

The problem was her legs. Her damned legs wouldn't move. Why?

Like a blind person feeling in the darkness, she explored her surroundings. On either side rose a rough, gritty surface, like a rock wall. Her hips and legs seemed to be wedged between the two vertical surfaces.

In short and painful movements she managed to sit up. After an agonizing effort, she managed to draw her knees toward her. She seemed to be at the base of some sort of crevice. In the darkness she couldn't determine how far up the walls of the crevice extended. Nor could she see in front or behind. For all she knew, she was perched at the lip of an abyss.

She was alone. That much she was sure of, and the thought made her rejoice. In the black stillness, she could hear nothing but the sound of her own breathing. When she tumbled down the mountainside, she must have dropped into this ravine. They lost her in the darkness.

They would wait until daylight, she guessed; then they would resume the search.

B.J. took an inventory. Bruises, abrasions, sprains, but nothing seemed to be broken. When she touched her head her fingers came away with a wet stickiness, which she traced to a nasty cut above her temple. Probably the blow that knocked her unconscious.

Her eyes were adapting to the darkness. She pulled out the water canteen. Still intact, thank God. Wetting her bandanna with water from the canteen, she dabbed at the wound on her head. The damp cloth on the open cut made her wince.

The signal mirror was in pieces, smashed during her tumble down the slope. Likewise the handheld GPS. When she flicked the power button, the little LCD screen remained lifeless. One of the pencil flares was broken in half.

Then she noticed the PRC-112 mobile radio. The most valuable escape-and-evasion item—and it had failed her. Why had she bothered to keep the useless device? It was deadweight. Now the radio's hard case was cracked open. The thing must have taken a hit during her plunge down the mountain.

Okay, no GPS, no radio. So much for the high-tech magic the Navy gave pilots who were shot down. She was down to old-fashioned compass and map. Kit Carson in Indian country.

Before throwing away the useless radio, just for the hell of it, she decided to try the power button one more time.

When she poked the button, she heard something. A hissing sound.

The tiny power light on the radio was glowing red. It was working.

"This is Runner Four-one on Magic channel. Anybody home?"

Leroi Jones listened for half a minute. It was his second attempt on the SAR frequency. He had tried calling the Tomcat crew and gotten nothing. Same thing with B. J. Johnson. Nobody home. No one down there was monitoring the frequency with their PRC-112 radio.

One more time. "Tomcat Five-one," he said, using the call sign of the F-14 crew. "Runner Four-one calling. Do you guys read me?"

Another half minute. Still nothing.

What the hell, thought Jones as he switched his primary UHF radio back to the AWACS frequency. It was worth a try.

He stifled a yawn as he squinted into the eastern sky. Even the hundred-percent oxygen flowing through his mask didn't make up for the lack of sleep. The emerging sun was just touching the horizon, framing the rim of the Gulf of Aden.

It had been a short night. At zero-three-hundred they'd been alerted for the mission. Blackness still covered the sea when he and his wingman, Flash Gordon, catapulted from the deck of the *Reagan.* Twenty minutes later they were established on the CAP station, twenty thousand feet over Yemen.

Jones could hear the other flights checking in with the AWACS.

"Rover Four-one, on station."

"Roger, Rover," came the voice of the controller in the AWACS. "Stand by for an update."

"Bluetail Five-one, confirm the picture for us again."

"Picture clear, Bluetail."

"Tomcat Four-oh is ready," reported the F-14 with the TARP package.

"You're cleared to enter the AOR, Tomcat. We show zero threats. You're good to go." AOR was for "area of responsibility," the target area of the previous day. The Tomcat would make a high-speed photo pass, hoping to pick up traces of the missing pilots.

Jones wondered why they were bothering. A thin morning fog veiled the valleys and plateaus. Peaks and ridges were protruding through the fog blanket, giving the landscape the appearance of a Jovian moon.

Not a sign of human existence.

Jones couldn't help thinking about B. J. Johnson. He liked her for the way she handled herself during the bad times when she was the only woman in the squadron and no one was giving her a break. Himself included, he recalled. He wished he had been a friend to her. Like the others, he had kept his distance from the alien.

Of all people, he should have known what it was like to be an alien. He was the only African-American pilot in the squadron, one of four in the entire air wing. Not a big deal in the Navy these days, but not so long ago it had been a very big deal. He knew what it was like to always have to prove yourself. To prove that you weren't there because you were getting special treatment.

You should have been her friend.

It was too late. If B.J. was still alive, she was either hiding or captured. Jones knew in his heart there was no way that she had survived. Someone would have seen the chute. She would have made contact with the emergency UHF radio. B.J. was scattered in the earth with the debris from her Hornet.

The Tomcat crew was another matter. Both chutes had

been spotted, and after the shoot-down they had made a brief transmission on the SAR frequency. Then nothing, which was a solid clue that they had been captured by the gomers. Short of an all-out invasion, there was nothing that could be done to get them back. It was in the hands of negotiators.

Yeah, B.J. was dead. But what the hell, one more shot. Just in case.

"Runner Five-two, stay with Sea Witch," he said to Gordon, a mile abeam in combat spread. "I'm gonna try the SAR channel one more time."

"Copy, Leroi. I've got Sea Witch covered."

He keyed the mike and used B. J. Johnson's call sign. "Yankee Two, this is Runner Four-one. Are you up?"

Silence. It filled his earphones like a stillness from the grave.

"B.J., damn it, this is Leroi. If you're alive, answer up!"

Seconds passed. Nothing.

It was a waste of time. Useless.

He was reaching for the channel selector to return to the tactical frequency when a voice came to him, distant and weak. "I hear you, Leroi. Please don't go away. I'm alive."

CHAPTER NINE

RULES OF ENGAGEMENT

USS Ronald Reagan
Gulf of Aden
0715, Tuesday, 18 June

Startled sailors jumped out of the way as the Navy captain in the battered leather flight jacket, cigar jutting from his teeth, stormed through their midst. Astonished, they watched him clamber up the ladder to the O-3 level, taking the steps two at a time.

At the top of the ladder Boyce swerved around a corner, nearly bowling over a female yeoman carrying a stack of files. He mumbled an apology and bolted on down the passageway.

At the flag intel compartment, he saw that Maxwell had beaten him there. He removed the cigar and stood gasping for breath. "She's alive."

Maxwell grinned back at him. "I heard."

Boyce barged on through the door to the intel compartment, hauling Maxwell along by the sleeve.

Admiral Fletcher, hunched over his desk, looked up as

they entered. On either side, peering over his shoulders, were Guido Vitale and Spook Morse. At the far end of the compartment, arms folded over his chest, stood Whitney Babcock.

Boyce's eyes went to the man standing across the desk from the admiral. He wore marine desert-colored BDUs—battle dress uniform. He had a bristly gray crew cut with an expanse of white on either side, a pair of round, steel-framed spectacles, and a ramrod-straight posture. On his collar he wore the insignia of a bird colonel.

"Gus Gritti!" said Boyce. "You bristleheaded sonofabitch, who let you aboard this ship?"

The marine regarded Boyce with icy brown eyes. "You've got a mouth like a megaphone, Boyce. When are you squids going to learn some manners?"

A huge grin split Boyce's face. He and the marine shook hands and clapped each other on the shoulder. Boyce knew Gritti from their academy years. Gritti was a paradox in the Marine Corps—a legendary, mud-crawling infantry warrior with a passion for the operas of Puccini and Verdi, and whose credentials included a master's in humanities from Stanford.

Ignoring the other officers in the room, Boyce turned to Maxwell. "You see this ugly jarhead? This is the toughest marine since Chesty Puller and absolutely the right guy to have on your side in a bar fight. He's also the right guy to get our pilots out of Yemen."

"Maybe," said Gritti. His eyes were fixed on Admiral Fletcher. "My team could snatch your people out of there, but you have to convince the Battle Group Commander that we need close air support while we're doing it."

"Close air support? Hell, yes, you need close air support." Boyce looked at Fletcher. "Sir? Aren't we going to—"

"Of course they'll get air support," said Fletcher. "But Colonel Gritti has a problem with the amended rules of engagement."

Boyce eyed the admiral warily. "What amended rules of engagement?"

"The altitude floor. By the new ROE, our close air support aircraft will be limited to a minimum release floor of twenty thousand feet."

"Twenty thousand feet!" Boyce sputtered. "You can't even see the gooks from there. Hell, Admiral, you can't support troops on the ground from four goddamn miles up."

A sour look was coming over Fletcher's face. Before he could respond, Babcock cleared his throat and walked over from the corner of the room. He gave Boyce and Gritti one of his patronizing smiles. "Believe me, it won't be a factor, gentlemen. The rescue of the downed pilots won't meet any opposition from ground forces. The altitude limit has been imposed because sensitive talks are now in progress between the U.S. and Yemeni governments. They've lodged a protest with the U.N. Security Council, and we have strict orders from the White House not to further provoke them."

Boyce's face was turning the color of fresh lava. "Are you telling me, sir, that those terrorists are just going to let us saunter into their country and pick up our people? That they're not going to shoot?"

"We have assurances to that effect."

"Assurances from murderers? You mean someone from our side is actually talking to those thugs?"

Babcock's smile was becoming strained. "I realize that these issues may be difficult for you to understand, Captain. You're a technician, not a diplomat. All you need to know is that this matter in Yemen will end with a diplomatic solution, not a military one."

Boyce's face darkened further. "What I really need to know is how I'm going to cover Colonel Gritti's marines while they're snatching our pilots out of Yemen. From twenty thousand goddamn feet—"

"That's enough, Captain," said Fletcher in a sharp voice.

"You're coming very close to impertinence, and I won't have it." He gazed around the room. "I'll remind everyone in this room that I'm still the Battle Group Commander, and that Mr. Babcock here represents the National Security Council and takes his orders directly from the President. He is the senior official in this theater."

Fletcher looked again at Boyce. "Is that clear enough for you, Captain Boyce?"

Boyce hesitated for a second, then felt Gritti's boot kicking his ankle. "Yes, sir," he said in a loud voice.

Claire sniffed the air and took an instant dislike to Aden. The reek of garbage, and something that reminded her of death, wafted in from the harbor. As the caravan of taxis drove the reporters to the Sheraton, hard-eyed Yemenis glowered at them from the roadside.

About forty reporters and cameramen were camped at the Sheraton, which was guarded at the entrance by a squad of surly Yemeni soldiers. No one wanted to venture into the city. Aden had the feel of an enemy camp. Still fresh in everyone's memory was the bomb attack on the American destroyer, the USS *Cole,* as it entered the port of Aden.

Mel Bloom, the chief of information for the U.S. mission in Aden, was standing at the lobby bar. He saw her coming and threw up his hands. "I don't know anything."

"C'mon, Mel. We know there are pilots down in Yemen, and another strike is in the works."

"Media brief at one o'clock. No updates before then."

"When will they let us go back out to the *Reagan*?"

"You gotta be joking."

Claire resisted the urge to seize Bloom's windpipe and choke the air out of him. He was a pompous bureaucrat, but she knew he was just doing his job. Anyway, he was probably telling the truth. He didn't know anything. Whatever happened in Yemen was still happening, and the military wouldn't disclose anything that might jeopardize the operation.

"Okay. Promise you'll tell me as soon as you know something about the pilots?"

"Sure, Claire. You'll hear."

At the bar she recognized one of the reporters, a stringer for Reuters. His name was Lester Crabtree and he was plastered. She took the seat next to him and ordered a vodka tonic.

"Hope you have a positive-space ticket," said Crabtree.

"To where?"

"Anywhere. This place is going to blow. When the Yemenis figure out we're bombing them, they're going to turn on us like a pack of jackals."

"Then why are you here?"

"Same as you. We're vultures. We circle around where we think the bodies will be."

She remembered now that Crabtree was a world-class jerk. "Do you think there'll be bodies in Aden?"

He shrugged and tossed down his drink. "Aden's on the coast, right? That means the Navy will have to evacuate us from here when the sticky stuff hits the fan. The real blood-bath will be up north, in San'a. That's the capital and it's where the rebels will go when they're ready to take over."

Claire sipped at her drink and watched their reflections in the mirror over the bar. Crabtree might be a jerk, but in this case he probably had it right. Yemen's shaky coalition government was hanging on by a thread. A well-armed rebel force could march into town and take over anytime they wanted.

She ordered another round for Crabtree, then paid the tab. "Thanks, Lester. See you at the press brief."

In her room on the third floor, she sat at the tiny desk and opened up her notebook computer. There was no direct Internet connection through the hotel's phone line. She drafted an e-mail message, which she would later take to the hotel's business center for uploading.

From: Claire.Phillips@mbs.com
To: SMaxwell.VFA36@USSRonaldReagan.Navy.mil
Subj: Love, etc.

Okay, sailor, you promised to tell me once a day how much you loved me, right? Well, maybe you didn't exactly say that, but you did say you would practice.

I'm frightened, Sam. I'm frightened for your safety and for everyone on the Reagan. But it's you I love, and I don't think I could bear losing you. I lost you once and it broke my heart.

Please don't let this war become personal, my darling. You lost Josh, but that is not a reason to throw your own life away chasing the animal who killed him. Nothing is worth that.

You must let me hear from you NOW so I'll know you're safe.

All my love,
C.
P.S. Yemen sucks.

When she was finished, she picked up the phone and asked the switchboard operator to connect her to the reservations office of Yemenia, the state-owned airline.

The agent spoke excellent English. She asked which flight Claire had in mind.

"San'a, the next available."

The voices crackled over the speaker.

"I hear you, Leroi. I'm alive. Please don't go away."

"B.J.! I can't believe it. You're down there. Are you okay?"

"I'm hungry, thirsty, tired, and I think I've got a broken rib. Maybe diarrhea. Other than that, I'm just fine."

"Sit tight, kid. We're gonna get you out of there."

Al-Fasr pushed the STOP button on the digital recorder. He advanced the recording to the next radio exchange. He listened again while the woman pilot authenticated her identity, then reported the grid coordinates of her hiding place.

Hearing the recorded voices, Al-Fasr found himself thinking about the woman pilot. What did she look like? Was she truly a female, with the softness and scent of a woman? Or was she one of those sinewy unisex creatures, like those in the American television shows?

Even with his background—his education and westernized attitudes—such a thing was anathema to Al-Fasr's Arab soul. Women! They had no place on the field of battle. It ran against the laws of nature. Tomorrow, when they had captured the woman, he would make an example of her.

For a moment he allowed himself to fantasize about the female pilot. The thought gave him an instant arousal. Yes, it would be appropriate to use her for his own pleasure. He would make her whimper and beg for mercy like the whore that she was.

When he was finished, he would throw her to his troops. The spoils of war.

He would transmit an image of the violated woman warrior back to the Americans. They would learn in the most basic fashion what it meant when they sent their daughters to war.

He forced himself to return his thoughts to the recorded radio exchange. Time was growing short. As he listened, he studied the captured grid map on his desk. It was still a puzzle. Instead of using the actual latitude and longitude of her position, the pilot seemed to be referencing the coordinates to the grid map. But the letters of the grid were based on some sort of key, which could be changed daily and which the pilots must have committed to memory.

It had been good fortune that they captured the handheld radios and the grid maps from the F-14 crew. But it was incredibly stupid, Al-Fasr thought as the anger rose in him, that the goat-brained platoon commander had allowed his gunner to kill the pilots. It was typical of these unthinking primitives. Not only could the captured pilots have revealed the key to the grid map, they could have been pumped for other secrets. Ultimately they could be used as bargaining tools.

Or bait.

Al-Fasr had ordered the platoon commander—a Yemeni named Arif, who came from the north country—and his gunner to be shot in full view of the assembled garrison. Not so much as punishment but as an example.

It had made the correct impression. An hour later the search squad in the Dauphin helicopter located the downed Hornet pilot. Instead of shooting to kill, they had pursued the pilot. Then they lost her in the darkness.

Which was just as well for now. So long as the Americans believed the woman pilot was alive and free on Yemeni soil, they would come for her.

Al-Fasr picked up one of the captured survival radios, turning it over in his hands, examining it from all sides. A useful piece of equipment, even more advanced than the older models he had carried when he flew F-16s in the emirate air force. And the handheld GPS. Such exotic technology in the hands of the Navy pilots. It had done them no good.

His MiG pilots, of course, didn't have such things. There was no need. Search and rescue was not a clause in their contract. He thought again of Novotny and Rittmann, his own downed airmen. Witnesses had observed Novotny's low-flying jet taking an air-to-air missile strike. It had gone instantly into the ground. There was no chance that Novotny had survived.

Rittmann was another matter. It would be convenient if he were also dead. The impertinent German had outlived his usefulness. The troops who found the wreckage of his MiG reported that the ejection seat was missing. Perhaps he had survived.

Too bad, mused Al-Fasr. If he turned up alive, he would have to be dealt with.

Boyce was the last to come into the briefing room. He slammed the door behind him, then barked an order. "Everyone sit down."

The air wing briefing compartment was only half the size of the flag intel space. Gritti squeezed into the end chair, while Maxwell, Guido Vitale, Spook Morse, and Gritti's executive officer, Lieutenant Colonel Hewlitt, assembled themselves in a semicircle around the illuminated map table.

Boyce looked grim and haggard. He perched on the edge of the steel admin desk and said, "We just got some bad news. About an hour ago the CAP leader had another radio exchange with Yankee Two. She reported that she had witnessed our two Tomcat crewmen being shot and killed."

A heavy silence fell over the room.

Maxwell could see that Boyce was taking it hard. Burner Crump, skipper of the Tomcatters and a much-decorated fighter pilot, was an old buddy of Boyce's. Crump's backseater was Willie Martinez, a wisecracking flight officer from southern California, one of the best RIOs in the business.

"What happened?" asked Maxwell. "Were they evading?"

"No details," said Boyce. "She verified it when he asked her again, and then the CAP lead told her to shut down and save her battery. She's going to need it for the SAR."

"How do we know she's for real?" asked Gritti. "Maybe they've got her radio."

"The first guy to talk to her, Leroi Jones on the CAP station, authenticated. She had the right password for the day. Leroi knows her pretty well, and he asked her some personal stuff, hometown, academy class, stuff like that. She's the real thing."

"Maybe she's being coerced," said Colonel Hewlitt. "What if it's a trap?"

"Low probability. It's part of our training that if you're being manipulated, you give bogus authentication. Leroi was convinced that she was in the clear."

"What's her condition? Is she injured?"

"Nothing serious. Scared shitless, but she says she can run and hide."

Gritti said, "That's a tough one about your pilots, gentlemen. I'm sorry. But that simplifies our recovery problem. I understand she has a GPS and a grid map?"

"She gave her coordinates, which are X-Y coded off the grid map," said Boyce. He leaned over the table and slid his finger in a circle over the illuminated map. "She's right in here. High, rugged terrain. We gave instructions for her to find a decent landing zone for the pickup. When we contact her again at oh-six-hundred tomorrow, she's supposed to pass the exact LZ location. If we can't communicate, we go to the original grid coordinates and look for her."

"What kind of team are we sending in?" asked Maxwell.

Gritti answered. "It's what the marines call a TRAP team—Tactical Recovery of Aircraft and Personnel. After you guys have your air defense suppression package on station, my team launches from the *Saipan* in a pair of CH-53 Super Stallions."

"How many marines are we talking about?"

"I'm planning a Delta-size TRAP package. Fifty, plus four corpsmen."

"The helos need escort," said Boyce. "What about the Harriers deployed on the *Saipan*?"

Gritti shook his head. "The kinder and gentler rules of engagement"—he paused and glared at Vitale—"prohibit using the Harriers. For the same reason we don't get low air support from the air wing. Too provocative, they think. The Sea Stallions will be escorted by four Whiskey Cobra gunships."

Vitale sat alone, looking like a kid ostracized from his playmates. The Group Operations Officer wasn't a bad guy, Maxwell reflected, just a guy in a bad job. Vitale had once been a patrol plane pilot, and as the only aviator on Fletcher's staff he was caught in the eternal friction between the battle group and the *Reagan*'s air wing. He received equal abuse from both sides. Even Spook Morse, who served under Vitale on the admiral's staff, was openly disrespectful of him.

Boyce broke the silence. "That's it, gentlemen. We play the hand we've been dealt. If anybody needs a refresher in the new rules of engagement, I have a copy you can read. Colonel Gritti and Colonel Hewlitt are heading back to the *Saipan* to do their own briefs. Commander Maxwell and I will stay in here and write the air plan. In three hours we do a full brief with the pilots. The SEAD package will launch thirty minutes ahead of the TRAP team." SEAD was the acronym for Suppression of Enemy Air Defenses—the mix of jammers, HARM shooters, and Super Hornet fighter-bombers.

At this, Vitale spoke up. "I need some information for the battle group tasking order. Who will be assigned as the flight leader in the SEAD package?"

"The best strike leader I've got," said Boyce.

Vitale looked at him expectantly. "And who would that be?"

"The guy sitting next to you. Commander Maxwell."

Vitale jotted the information on his pad. "And the TRAP team, Colonel Gritti? Who have you assigned to command the recovery package?"

"The toughest, meanest sonofabitch in the Marine Corps."

Vitale lowered his notebook and peered at Gritti. "I give up. Would you mind telling us who that would be?"

Gritti gave him a half smile. "You're looking at him."

"Vincent Maloney," said the bored voice on the phone.

"It's Claire Phillips. You're in luck, Vince. I'm in San'a."

Maloney's voice came to life. "Claire! The girl who spurned me in Bahrain. The one who broke my heart."

"I didn't spurn you. I just declined to go to bed with you."

"Same thing. Does this mean you've changed your mind?"

"No, it means I'm giving you another chance at being a gentleman."

"What do I have to do?"

"Take me to dinner."

"I know you. You want to interrogate me."

She laughed. "A little, maybe. That's my job. Where are we having dinner?"

Maloney declared that her hotel, the Al-Qasmy, had a restaurant as decent as any other in San'a, which didn't mean much. They were all god-awful, but what the hell, it beat walking the streets. San'a was a rough place these days.

Claire's flight from Aden, a 727 with a cabin that smelled of stale cigarette smoke, had taken forty-five minutes. San'a turned out to be even more polluted than Aden, located in a mountain bowl and lacking an ocean breeze to sweep away the smog.

She liked Vince Maloney, even if he was a dissolute character. He was a deputy political affairs officer who migrated from outpost to outpost in the state department, apparently never destined to rise above his present grade. She had met him at a consular party when she first arrived in the Middle East, and they went out on a few occasions.

Maloney was smitten by Claire. At regular intervals, she had to reexplain that their relationship was one of friendship, nothing more. Forget romance. Maloney accepted the situation with grudging good humor, but he never gave up.

They got together whenever they found themselves in the same port. He was good company, at least until he became too drunk to make sense. Sometimes he even told her things that were useful.

As she hoped he would this time.

Maloney appeared precisely at six o'clock in the lobby of the Al-Qasmy. He gave Claire a big sloppy kiss, and they took a table near the bar to catch up on the past months.

The place was busy, filled mostly with Arab businessmen and a few Europeans clustered by themselves at tables. Maloney ordered a double Scotch for himself and a vodka tonic for Claire.

He clinked his glass against hers. "You're more gorgeous than ever, Claire. Still married to that Australian journalist— what was his name—something Twit?"

"Tyrwhitt," she said. "That's history. We separated, and then he died."

"Too bad. But the silly ass never appreciated you. I, on the other hand, have always held you in the highest—"

"Too late, Vince. I'm spoken for."

"Aaagghh." He clutched his chest. "My heart. You're breaking it all over again."

"Have a drink. You'll get over it."

"Good idea." He chugged down his Scotch and signaled the bartender for another. After he'd tested the fresh drink, he said, "Who's the lucky guy?"

"I don't know about the lucky part. His name is Sam

Maxwell. He's a Navy pilot, a commander on the *Reagan*."

"Navy pilot, huh?" Maloney thought for a minute while he peered over the rim of his glass. "It's beginning to come to me. See if I'm getting this right. You're here because you want me to blab some information about the little military exercise this morning in Yemen. Am I close?"

"Try this one. I'm here because I'm a journalist."

Maloney didn't reply. He sipped at his drink while his eyes scanned the room. In a lowered voice he said, "This is a lousy place to be a journalist."

Claire waited a moment. "Listen, Vince, I know the terrorist is a character named Al-Fasr, and I know the Navy lost airplanes this morning trying to bomb him."

Maloney took another sip. "That's old news."

"And I know there's an operation under way to recover the pilot."

"So?"

"So what am I missing here? Why doesn't the United States just move in with massive force and squash this Al-Fasr character like a bug? If we can do it in Iraq, if we can do it in Afghanistan, it shouldn't be a problem in Yemen."

Maloney shrugged. "Decisions like that don't get made at my level."

"But you have an idea, don't you? You always have an idea, Vince."

He glanced around the dining room. Several other diners, mostly businessmen in Western clothing, were engaged in their own conversations. "You want the Maloney take on it? Off the record?"

"You know you don't have to ask that."

"The United States doesn't want to wipe out Al-Fasr because that would cost us our one great chance to control Yemen. Al-Fasr is the key. A quid pro quo. First we engage him, allow him to gain credibility in the Arab world by backing down the mighty United States. Then he seizes power in Yemen and becomes our new best friend. We protect his new government from all his resentful Arab neighbors, and Yemen becomes an American colony. Does that make sense?"

"No. He's a terrorist who murdered Americans. He's as bad as Osama bin Laden. How can he be our new best friend?"

"C'mon, Claire, grow up. 'Terrorist' is a removable label. It's a function of whether you're on the inside or outside. Our founding fathers were terrorists until they won the revolution; then they were patriots. Menachem Begin was a very nasty terrorist until he became prime minister of Israel. Then they gave him the Nobel peace prize. It's all bullshit."

"Okay, it's bullshit. So what do we care about Yemen anyway? What's in it for us?"

At this, Maloney peered around the room again, checking the other occupants. In a lowered voice he said, "I can't believe you're a reporter, being this naive. Or maybe it's just an act to get guys like me to run their mouths."

"I'm not naive and I'm not acting. Don't insult me, Vince."

"Sorry. You want to know why we care about Yemen? Guess what the most valuable commodity in the whole Middle East happens to be."

"Yemen doesn't have oil deposits. British Petroleum and several other companies bored all those dry holes years ago and gave up."

"Maybe they didn't bore in the right place. You know that vast reservoir that lies under Saudi Arabia? Well, it extends all the way south to somewhere around the northern border of Yemen, which, for your information, has always been disputed. No one wanted to get into a scrap with the Saudis over it—until now."

Claire put her fingertips together and reflected for a moment. "It all seems so cynical. Here we're losing airplanes, pilots dying in Yemen, and it's just for . . . oil. Nothing but economics."

"To us, maybe. Not to Al-Fasr."

"What does he get out of this?"

"Power, for one thing. Vengeance, for another. The story is that he's still bitter about his family being wiped out in a failed coup attempt in the emirates. He blames the U.S., which might explain all this thrust-and-parry stuff with the Navy. But the outcome is already agreed upon. A done deal."

"Deal? Who on our side would make such a deal?"

Maloney looked uncomfortable. He took a long pull on his drink, then looked at her. "Did you ever hear of someone named Whitney Babcock?"

By ten o'clock, Maloney was crocked. Claire steered him through the hotel lobby, past the desk and the gawking bellboys, out to the yellow-lighted sidewalk.

He looked at her blearily. "Whaddya say we go back to my place?"

She knew that was coming. Maloney never changed. "Is that another proposition?"

"Consider it an opportunity."

"Opportunity for what?"

"To make amends for breaking my heart."

She laughed. "We're buddies, Vince. Don't spoil it."

"Lemme give you a ride home."

"I'm already home. This is my hotel."

He looked around. "Oh, yeah, so it is."

"You're in no shape to drive. I'll get you a taxi."

"No way. I do this all the time. Got lots of practice at this stuff."

Claire knew she shouldn't let him drive, but arguing with Maloney was a waste of energy. Anyway, this was San'a.

Not much could happen to you in the twisting streets of the old city. You couldn't drive fast enough to do any real damage.

Maloney gave her a wet smooch. "Go on up to your room. Don't talk to anyone. These people hate you. They hate all of us."

After he had vanished down the sidewalk, she walked back through the lobby to the elevator. Again she sensed the hostile glares from the other guests watching her. Even the desk clerk gave her a baleful look.

When she reached her room, she locked the door, then fastened the clasp. For good measure, she slid the dresser away from the wall and braced it against the locked door. Just in case.

Maloney was right. *They hate all of us.*

Ping. Ping. Ping.

Slumped over his console, Manilov listened to the steady pinging that resonated through the *Mourmetz*. He forced himself to appear unruffled by the sounds. In front of the other crew members, he must not appear to be frightened. Or indecisive.

His executive officer, Lieutenant Commander Ilychin, seemed on the verge of an anxiety attack. Ilychin sat huddled at his own station, his arms wrapped around himself. His eyes darted around the control room with each new *ping* from the sonars.

Ilychin was a liability, Manilov decided. The executive officer's palpable fear could infect the rest of the crew. Already Manilov was hearing whispered grumbles from some of the young warrants. They had not signed up for a suicide mission. They thought this would be an easy patrol—a quick torpedo shot at an unsuspecting target, then a submerged run to safe waters. That was all. Once they'd finished the patrol, they'd be rewarded with money beyond their wildest dreams.

Manilov would have to reassure them. They had to have confidence in him. Ilychin's trepidation was poisoning them.

Ping. Ping. Ping.

Still searching. If they had the *Mourmetz* tagged, the underwater sound signals wouldn't be detonating in those random patterns and depths. The sound signals were dropped from a helicopter, and the fact that the pings were farther away now led Manilov to think they didn't have a positive fix on the *Mourmetz*.

What if they did?

He remembered what he had been taught as a young engineering officer on his first patrol aboard the old *Admiral Koblenko*: *Put yourself in the mind of your enemy.*

Manilov forced himself to detach from his present role. What would he do if he were the American antisubmarine commander?

Kill the unidentified submarine?

No. Not without knowing whose boat you were killing and not without first seeing some indication of hostile intent. You didn't risk starting a war because somebody's submarine was watching you.

What then?

Manilov thought for a moment. *You try to keep it locked up, of course. Make sure the sub commander knows he's tagged so he doesn't try anything adventurous. You might even drop some ordnance, not too close, just to generate some fear. To emphasize the seriousness of your intentions.*

But the American commander hadn't done any of those things. Why? It could mean only one thing: He was still fishing. He hadn't found the *Mourmetz*, or at least he didn't know within several kilometers where it was.

Manilov had chosen a good hiding place.

The Mourmetz lay motionless in the shelter of a protruding littoral shelf that dropped over three hundred meters to the ocean floor. It formed a natural blind from the enemy's underwater signals and magnetic anomaly detectors.

Ping. Ping.

Yes, he determined, the pinging was definitely moving farther away. All he had to do was wait. That was what submariners had always done—wait. You waited for the enemy to give up and move on. You waited for your opportunity to strike. You waited to die.

While he waited, Manilov scribbled on his notepad a personal assessment of his enemy's assets. By his own count the *Reagan* was escorted by four destroyers, and he had to assume there was one, possibly two more, screening the battle group from the south. He knew that antisubmarine helicopters were deployed not only aboard the giant carrier but also on the cruiser and maybe even on the amphibious assault ship with its complement of cargo and attack helicopters. Additionally, the *Reagan* carried in its air wing a detachment of S-3 Viking submarine-hunting jets.

Another chilling possibility nagged at him: The American Navy's anti-submarine forces were often augmented by nuclear attack submarines of their own. These were usually *Los Angeles*–class multipurpose boats that could haul commando teams, launch cruise missiles—and hunt enemy submarines. Killer submarines were a boat captain's most dreaded adversary.

American warships were not his only worry. The *Mourmetz* was now two days past its scheduled delivery to the Iranian naval base at Bandar Abbas, on the Strait of Hormuz. Since that time he had ignored the flow of increasingly urgent messages from the Pacific fleet command headquarters in Vladivostok. He had no doubt the Russian Navy was now at full alert, searching for its missing warship. He wondered if the Iranians had paid them yet for the submarine. He hoped so.

Manilov sat back in his metal chair and looked at his assessment sheet. The odds against him were staggering. One lone submarine against the two most powerful navies in the world.

He tossed the notebook onto the desk. *Fuck the odds.* When he took the *Ilia Mourmetz* into battle, none of that would matter. He was a Russian, and this was his destiny. Only fate mattered.

CHAPTER TEN

LIMA BRAVO

Gulf of Aden
1145, Tuesday, 18 June

Colonel Gritti felt the dank sea air blasting through the open hatch of the CH-53E Super Stallion. Next to him, eyes sweeping the horizon, the machine gunner hunched over his fifty-caliber gun.

A hundred yards in trail was the second Stallion. Bracketing the cargo helicopters were the AH-1W Whiskey Cobra gunships, one in the lead, one in trail. The formation skimmed the surface of the Arabian Sea at two hundred feet.

The southern shoreline of Yemen swept beneath them in a brown blur. Gritti keyed his boom mike: "Warlord, Boomer is feet dry."

"We see that, Boomer," answered Guido Vitale. "The SEAD package is on board. Your signal is Lima Bravo."

"Boomer copies. We have Lima Bravo."

Lima Bravo was the go signal. The TRAP team was cleared to proceed with its mission.

Gritti gazed aft in the crowded interior of the cargo helicopter. His marines were crammed into the rows of bench seats on either side of the cabin. Each wore full battle gear, carrying a hundred-pound pack. Every young face wore a rapt, tense expression.

Two and a half decades as a grunt, thought Gritti. That was how long it took him to rise through the commissioned ranks of the Corps to what he considered to be the best job in the world—Commander of the 43rd Marine Expeditionary Unit. It was one of only seven such elite outfits deployed around the world. For a marine, this was as good as it got.

As he always did just before going into action, Gritti felt the weight of his responsibility. *These kids expect me to get them in there—and back again.*

Well, by God, he would. To the best of his ability. This was what they had trained for, and he knew there was no other outfit on the planet that could do this job as well as the 43rd MEU.

Still, he couldn't get over a nagging feeling. What had they missed? Did they have enough firepower? Could they shoot their way in, pick up the downed pilot, and shoot their way out?

He had placed another entire rifle company on status sixty—a one-hour alert—ready to reinforce them. Just in case.

The formation of helicopters crested the high ridgeline that paralleled the southern coast of Yemen. Descending the far slope, they continued north into the great desert plateau of the Saudi peninsula. This was the ingress route that was supposed to keep them away from major settlements and clear of any identified threat sectors.

Gritti watched the monotonous landscape sweep beneath them. Thank God for global positioning satellites. Without GPS, how the hell did anyone find anything in this barren wilderness?

Out the open left hatch, he could see the range that extended into north Yemen, paralleling the Red Sea. When they were abeam the crossroads village of Al Hazm, the formation would turn westward and enter the rugged highlands.

But he still didn't know where they were going. Not exactly.

"Warlord, Boomer. Do we have LZ coordinates yet?"

"Negative, Boomer. Yankee Two hasn't checked in. Your target is still X ray."

Gritti peered out the hatch again. Damn it, this wasn't good. The downed pilot hadn't come up on the SAR frequency and given coordinates for a landing zone like she was supposed to. What did it mean? That her battery was dead. That she had been compromised.

That she was dead.

Well, it didn't change anything. They were committed. They would continue to X ray, the code name for the position she reported in her first contact.

Gritti tried to shove the worries from his mind. It would be okay. They had the best intelligence sources in the world. Every scrap of information indicated that Al-Fasr's forces were standing down, just as Babcock had assured them. The TRAP team would rescue the pilot. No sweat. They'd hit the ground, grab the pilot, get the hell out, go back to Dubai or wherever.

Then he would throw the biggest goddamn party these kids ever saw.

From the cockpit of his F/A-18E, Maxwell gazed down at the arid landscape. He shook his head in frustration. If he and his Hornets were ordered to deliver their loads of anti-personnel bombs from four miles up, they were as likely to hit friendly forces as the enemy.

It was stupid. Criminal, even. Wars were fought by warriors, he remembered hearing from Josh Dunn, but rules of engagement were written by politicians.

He tried the SAR frequency again. "Yankee Two, this is Runner One-one. Are you up on this channel?"

Nothing.

He tried again. "Yankee Two, do you copy Runner One-one?"

Still no answer. B.J. wasn't talking.

It could still be okay, he told himself. If the battery was dead on her radio, she would know to stay close to her original position. When she saw the TRAP team helos, she could mark her spot with a smoke flare, and they would make the pickup. The radio problem was a minor glitch.

Yeah, right.

Maxwell knew from experience that specialized military operations seldom went as planned. Something unexpected always popped up. There was always a glitch.

Like the MiGs. That had been a major kick-in-the-balls glitch. The fact that no one had foreseen the insertion of enemy fighters was enough to erase any confidence Maxwell had in their own intelligence resources.

That was one glitch that wouldn't happen again. This time they wouldn't be caught flatfooted. On CAP station was a flight of F-14s. The Tomcatters had lost their skipper to Al-Fasr's MiGs, and they were looking forward to a return match.

If the enemy turned on air defense radar, a section of two Bluetail Hornets was poised to launch HARM antiradar missiles. Included in the SEAD package were two EA-6B Prowlers with highly sophisticated electronic detection and jamming capabilities and two HARMs each. On its station high over the Arabian peninsula was the AWACS, with its ability to pick up any emission in this part of the Middle East.

Maxwell called the AWACS. "Magic, this is Runner One-one. What's the picture?"

"Picture clear, Runner One-one," came the voice of Capt. Tracey Barnett. "The only radar activity is at San'a airport. We're watching, but we don't think it's hostile."

"Runner One-one, copy."

No radars up except the air-traffic control facility in the capital of Yemen. For all they knew it might be relaying contacts for Al-Fasr. Even if it was, Maxwell doubted that Fletcher would permit a HARM attack on the site.

It didn't matter. With the assets in his SEAD package, they had the airborne threat covered.

That left the close air support mission. It was the task of Maxwell and his Super Hornets to handle any ground opposition the TRAP team ran into.

From twenty thousand feet. It was a joke.

Maybe Babcock was right, he thought. Now that Al-Fasr had flexed his muscles, maybe he just wanted to kiss and make up. Killing Josh Dunn and Tom Mellon and making war on the United States of America was nothing more than a political statement. Now that he had humiliated the Navy, he would allow them to recover their survivors and slink back out to their ships. Babcock and the guys in suits would take over and negotiate with Al-Fasr as if he were a legitimate diplomat.

The thought filled Maxwell with loathing. He felt himself torn between strict compliance with his orders and dealing with Al-Fasr and his terrorists.

Maybe, reflected Maxwell, he no longer belonged in the Navy. At one time he had thought commanding a strike fighter squadron was the highest calling in the world. That was before Whitney Babcock and Admiral Fletcher and Jamal Al-Fasr.

He peered down again at the unfertile brown landscape of Yemen. *Stay focused,* he told himself. *Get this job done; get*

*B.J. out of there. And while you're at it, maybe put a cluster
of bombs on Al-Fasr's head. Then think about what to do
with the rest of your life.*

"Warlord, this is Runner One-one," he said, calling Vitale
aboard the *Reagan*. "Any contact with Yankee Two?"

"Negative, Runner One-one. Nothing yet. Boomer is pro-
ceeding to X Ray, as briefed. He's fifteen minutes out."

Maxwell peered down again at the hostile brown landscape. It looked as forbidding as the back side of the moon.
In fifteen minutes he would see the column of helicopters
making its way across the terrain to Yankee Two's last reported position. Four miles below.

She held her breath, listening for the sound to repeat itself.

There. She heard it again, wafting through the hills, faint
but coming closer. The distant beat of helicopter blades.

It was coming from the east, which meant it could be either friend or foe. She didn't dare show herself. Not yet.
What a cruel joke if she dashed into the open, waving and
igniting smoke flares, only to confront another helicopter
full of *Sherji*.

The damned radio. As abruptly as it had begun working,
it quit again. Exasperated, she had poked the thing, shaken
it, banged on it with her fist. The little red power light remained dark. She couldn't communicate with the SAR helicopter, tell them where the landing zone ought to be.

Okay, she'd stay concealed, get a visual ID on whatever
was coming this way. If they were the good guys, they
would go to the last set of coordinates she had transmitted.
That was a quarter mile away from where she now crouched
in the shadow of a pair of large boulders.

She had selected this open space because it was close
enough to the original location that she could get their attention. Seeing the place in the light of dawn, she was filled

with doubt. It was a small clearing on the slope of the mountain, covered with large rocks and scraggly waist-high shrubs. The slope looked steeper than it had in the darkness.

It would have to do. Maybe they could snatch her up in the sling.

The whopping noise was coming nearer. Definitely the sound of a helicopter. More than one, judging by the pulsating throb, and that was another good sign. The SAR team would not come in-country with just one chopper. They'd have escorts. Gunships, probably.

Despite her fatigue, B.J. felt herself filled with new energy. She was getting the hell out of Yemen. She made a silent vow that she would never return to this evil place—unless she was delivering high explosives.

She checked her signaling equipment. The flare lay on a rock beside her, the toggle ready to yank. They were the same old day/night flares that pilots had carried for a half century. One end for day smoke, the other for a night flare. When she saw the helos she would get the smoke going. Then she would start firing off the pencil flares, and then—

Another sound.

B.J. held her breath. This wasn't the beat of helicopter blades. She was hearing engine noises, vehicle sounds, the clatter of a half-track.

Coming her way.

She snatched up her flares and survival satchel and scrambled up the slope, toward the high ridge that overlooked the clearing. Her heart was racing again.

Reaching the summit, she crouched and peeked over the ridgeline. Half a dozen armored personnel carriers were assembling in a line behind the crest of the ridge. She could see tracked vehicles with heavy gun mounts. *Sherji*—she guessed at least a hundred—were fanning out ahead of the APCs, taking up positions behind boulders and shrubs. They were spreading camouflage nets over the mobile guns.

She saw something else—movement on the slope directly below her.

Not all the *Sherji* were digging in. A platoon-sized group was scurrying up the slope of the ridge where she lay hidden.

B.J. fought back the panic that was seizing her. She wanted to jump up and run like a jackrabbit. Get the hell out of here. Flee, bolt down the hillside, race across the clearing.

Brilliant, she thought. *Really cool. They'll shoot you before you've gone a hundred yards.*

She stayed crouched while she scuttled down the back side of the ridge, away from the advancing *Sherji*. At the base of the ridge, she entered a narrow ravine, sheltered on each side by a growth of prickly shrubs.

Staying low, she put another quarter mile between herself and the concentration of *Sherji*.

The sound of the incoming helos was nearby, thrumming against the hills like the beat of a primitive instrument.

They were sitting ducks. Al-Fasr knew they were coming. And where.

She looked at the useless PRC-112 radio. She should have known. They had captured the radios and maps from the Tomcatters. The bastards knew everything the SAR team knew.

A wave of rage swept over her. *Technology! Brilliant fucking high-tech devices that don't work when you need them, and when they do work, they help the enemy more than us.*

In a fit of rage, she banged the dead radio—*whap*—against the edge of a boulder.

Instantly, she felt silly. It was childish, acting like a kid who lost her candy. But hell, it *did* make her feel better. Now she could just toss the thing and—

She heard a familiar noise.

Hissing. It was coming from the radio. The little red power light was on again.

"Go! Go! Go!" yelled the master sergeant.

One after the other the marines spilled out the aft cargo door of the Super Stallion. The last out was Colonel Gritti, with Master Sergeant Plunkett trotting along beside him. They kept running until they had reached the shelter of the trees at the edge of the clearing.

Gritti stopped and looked back. Across the clearing, he saw the other Super Stallion discharging its load of marines. Hauling their hundred-pound packs, the marines were fanning out around the landing zone. After they'd secured a perimeter, they would send out search patrols while the Cobras flew cover.

It was a hell of an LZ, Gritti observed. It happened to be the only open spot remotely close to the last position reported by Yankee Two. The clearing had enough rocks and shrubs to make it damned difficult for the pilots. The pilot of his own CH-53E had managed to settle directly over a bathtub-sized boulder, ripping a hole in the belly and inflicting God-knew-what damage to cables and plumbing.

At least they had landed, which permitted the marines to hit the ground quickly instead of fast-roping out of a hovering chopper. They could reboard and get the hell out just as quickly.

Overhead, he saw the Cobra gunships sweeping the area while the marines established the perimeter. Gritti signaled for the communications specialist, a corporal named Oberhof, to bring the PRC-117D Manpack transceiver.

Gritti barked into the mouthpiece of the radio, "Roscoe, this is Boomer. Any sign of our customer?"

"Roscoe One, nothing yet," came the voice of the lead Cobra pilot.

"No joy from Roscoe Two," called the second Cobra pilot.

Where the hell was Yankee Two? Gritti wondered. If she had popped smoke to mark her position, they could have been in and out in minutes, mission accomplished. Now they had to do it the hard way.

Gritti was getting an uneasy feeling. It was a bad sign that they'd gotten no more radio transmissions from the downed pilot. Now that they were in the pickup zone, they were seeing no smoke, no flares, no sign of Yankee Two.

"Boomer, Roscoe Two," called the second Cobra. "I'm gonna fly directly over Yankee Two's grid coordinates and check it out."

"Boomer copies." Gritti had just released the transmit button when he noticed something. "What the hell is that?"

He rose to his feet, staring at the apparition. Plunkett was staring too.

Something rising from behind the ridge—an erratic, wispy smoke trail, curling into the sky. Toward the Cobra gunship.

"Goddammit!" Gritti mashed hard on the transmit key again. "Roscoe Two, you're targeted. Flares! Flares!"

The Cobra pilot heard the warning. A luminescent stream of glowing fireballs appeared in the wake of the gunship. By now the pilot had seen the threat coming toward him. He banked the Cobra hard to the right, dropping the nose, diving for the ground.

Too late.

Whump! The missile hit the helicopter amidships.

Gritti watched, transfixed, as the Cobra buckled in the middle like a smashed beer can. It tumbled end over end to the earth, then exploded in a sheet of flame that covered the hillside.

Gritti had no time to react. In the next instant he heard the staccato rattle of automatic weapons fire. He whirled, trying to locate the source of the firing. It came from across the clearing, from the rocks and trees where his troops were setting up the perimeter.

A burst of automatic fire kicked up the dirt five feet from where he stood.

He dived for cover. Plunkett was doing his own version of the belly crawl toward the nearby boulders. The sound of gunfire was spreading, a mixed clatter of automatic weapons. He picked out the distinctive three-round bursts of the marines' M16A2 combat rifles. It was interspersed with an intermittent crackle—Kalashnikov AK-47s. Lots of them, judging by the sheer intensity of the gunfire.

The firefight was spreading, the gunfire becoming more intense. Rounds whined overhead, pinging into the rocks, shredding the skinny shrubs on the hillside. From just inside the tree line, thirty yards away, Gritti heard the angry *brrrrrrrrp* of a submachine gun—one of their own Heckler & Koch MP-5N nine-millimeters, a short-range weapon used for close-in fighting.

Gritti crawled over to where Plunkett was huddled. "Get an assessment, Master Sergeant. Where are they and how many? Have we secured the perimeter?"

Plunkett nodded and grabbed his own transceiver, calling the team's squad leaders.

A hundred yards away, the other Cobra was in a low-level run on a target behind the ridge. As Gritti watched, a torrent of LAU-68 rockets belched from the inboard pylon. With luck the Cobra could hold them off while they got the perimeter nailed down.

He called the pilot, a captain named MacKenzie. "Roscoe One, this is Boomer. What are we up against, Mac?"

"An old fashioned ambush, Boomer. At least a hundred gomers are dug in here on the two western quadrants. Maybe more. Looks like they got some light armor under nets, which I'm trying to— Whoops, hang on a sec. I've got a problem here."

While Gritti watched, the helo pulled up from its attack and veered back toward the clearing. A cloud of gray smoke streamed from the gunship's turbine exhaust.

"We just took hits," MacKenzie called. "Red lights are coming on all over the panel. We gotta get back inside the perimeter."

The Cobra wheeled, dipped its nose, and lurched toward the clearing. Bullets pinged into the fuselage as the stricken helicopter heaved itself up over a final clump of boulders. Losing power quickly, the gunship settled toward an open space in the clearing. As the Cobra's slowly rotating blades expended the last of their energy, the helicopter smacked down hard.

Gritti winced as the sound of the landing carried across the clearing. A geyser of dirt and smoke and broken metal cascaded into the air. The blades drooped like broken wings over the shattered fuselage. The skids splayed outward, nearly flattened from the hard landing.

While the cloud of debris was still settling, Gritti saw a cluster of marines pulling the crew out of the wrecked helicopter.

"MacKenzie's okay, just shook up from the landing," Plunkett reported. "The gunner, Sergeant Porter, was killed by an incoming round."

Gritti nodded. The Cobra gunships were not only his close air support, they were his tactical reconnaissance assets. Now he had lost them, with three of the four crewmen killed. The mission was turning into a disaster. What else could go to hell?

In the next few seconds, he knew.

Kabooom! An ugly brown mushroom exploded in the clearing, sending pieces of shrapnel whizzing over Gritti's head.

Another. *Kabooom!*

Mortars. Another round exploded, this one twenty yards from the nearest CH-53E.

They were finding the range.

"Launch the helos," Gritti barked at Plunkett. "Get the Stallions out of here."

The master sergeant stared at him for a second. "Colonel, those choppers are our only transport out of this place."

"They'll be dog meat in half a minute. Tell the pilots to get clear. Find a place to loiter until we get this thing stabilized."

Plunkett nodded unhappily, then turned back to his radio.

In seconds, the blades of the big cargo helicopters were kicking up minitornadoes of whirling dirt. The first one—the Super Stallion that Gritti had arrived in—lifted and tilted to a nose-down attitude. Free of its load of troops and equipment, the powerful chopper accelerated quickly across the open clearing and away from the firefight.

The second Stallion was lifting, still transitioning to forward flight, when the next mortar round arrived.

Ka-whoom! The incoming round took off the tail boom. Without its tail rotor, the machine whirled out of control. The nose tipped forward, and its long refueling probe dug into the earth. Slowly, majestically, the chopper pirouetted around the stuck boom, tail high, rotating until it came back down on its port side.

Another geyser of dirt and smoke and broken metal. Pieces of the shattered rotor blades slashed across the clearing like rapier blades. Black smoke and dirt billowed from the hulk of the destroyed helicopter. Fire gushed from the ruptured fuel tanks. Within seconds the Super Stallion was transformed to a fountain of orange flame.

From a hundred yards away, Gritti could feel the intense heat of the blaze. None of the crew—pilot, copilot, crew chief—emerged from the wreck. The big helicopter was a burning inferno.

Stunned, he stared at the calamity. It was a marine commander's worst nightmare. They were in Indian country, cut off and surrounded.

He toggled the channel selector on the UHF TACSAT radio back to the command frequency. "Warlord, do you read Boomer?"

"What's your status, Boomer?" answered Vitale aboard the *Reagan*. "We've lost datalink on your escort aircraft. Have you made contact with Yankee Two?"

"Three of my aircraft are destroyed. Negative contact with Yankee Two. For your information, we are engaged at close range. We need close air now. Do you copy that?"

A silence of several seconds passed. Gritti could hear the rattle of automatic fire coming from all sides of the clearing. He knew that Vitale was discussing the situation with the Battle Group Commander.

Another mortar round exploded in the clearing. Pieces of shrapnel zinged over Gritti's head.

"Negative, Boomer. Same rules of engagement. The Hornets will provide high cover only."

Gritti stared at the transceiver. He had heard wrong. He must have heard wrong, because not even the Navy could be that fucked up. "Warlord, for clarification, I repeat, we are defensive." Gritti heard the rage building in his voice, and he didn't care. He was losing marines while this idiotic conversation took place. "We are surrounded, and the enemy has armor and artillery. We need close air support, and I mean *very* fucking close. Do you copy that?"

Another silence. Gritti could visualize the scene in CIC. Vitale explaining the situation to Fletcher. Fletcher covering his ass, waiting for a decision from up the chain. Babcock, the thumb-up-his-ass civilian, presiding over the gathering like Lord Nelson.

While Gritti waited, he heard a burst of automatic fire not more than thirty yards away. It was the distinctive hollow crackle of a Kalashnikov. If the cavalry was ever to come charging to the rescue, he thought, this would be a hell of a good time.

"Sorry, Boomer," he heard Vitale say over the command channel. "The rules of engagement stand."

CHAPTER ELEVEN

GEOPOLITICS

USS Ronald Reagan
1245, Tuesday, 18 June

With his courtly manner and his avuncular voice, Langhorne Fletcher was a public affairs officer's dream. He was a tall man—six feet two—with a craggy, aristocratic nose and a full mane of prematurely white hair. A southerner by breeding and instinct, Fletcher could trace his roots back to Virginia plantation owners. His ancestors had signed the Declaration of Independence, served under Washington, distinguished themselves as commanders in Lee's Army of Virginia. Since 1874 an unbroken lineage of Fletchers had been officers in the U.S. Navy. Seven had risen to flag rank, including Langhorne Fletcher.

Fletcher's greatest asset, beyond his imposing looks and sonorous voice, was his ability to please his superiors. He knew how to make his bosses—civilian or military—look good, a precious talent that had propelled him upward through the hierarchy of the Navy. All the way to command of a carrier battle group.

Except, at this moment, he didn't feel in command. Fletcher felt like he was standing in quicksand. Thirty years in the Navy, waiting for a major fleet command. Now this. Disaster.

In the two years that he had served under Whitney Babcock, starting with the job as senior staff officer when Babcock was still the Undersecretary of the Navy, he had been unfailingly tactful.

Tactful to a fault, he thought. Perhaps it was time to be blunt.

He gazed around, making sure they were alone in the flag compartment. "What do you mean, Mr. Babcock? I've got a team in serious jeopardy on the ground, and you're telling me I can't use all the force available to me. How am I supposed to explain that to the other officers in my command?"

"This is not the time to panic," said Babcock. "The situation is not as bad as it seems."

"If I lose the recovery team on the ground, I'll be blamed for the biggest debacle since Somalia."

"You won't lose them. It's a communication problem. I've been on the line with our people in San'a, and they tell me that Al-Fasr is standing down."

"He'll be more inclined to stand down if I put an air strike on his camp."

"No!" The abrupt answer took Fletcher by surprise. "No bombing. No overt attacks, do you understand? That would compromise the negotiations that are going on at this moment."

"What negotiations? I have twelve hundred marines aboard the *Saipan* and enough aircraft and bombs to eradicate Al-Fasr. Why do we have to negotiate?"

"To avoid putting us at war with Yemen. Every peasant in those mountains is a potential guerilla. Is that what you want, Admiral?"

Fletcher hesitated. The truth was, he didn't know what he

wanted. At the moment he wanted nothing except for someone else to take responsibility for the debacle in Yemen. "We
have to do something," he said. "The media will know soon
enough that we've got people on the ground in Yemen. We
have to get them out of there."

"Not if it means sending more troops in. This has to be a
mediated settlement, Admiral." He gave Fletcher one of his
patronizing smiles. "Look at this as an opportunity. There is
much more to be gained here than the immediate safety of a
few marines and pilots."

Fletcher felt the quicksand deepening. "What, may I ask,
is to be gained?"

The smile again. "The security of our allies in the Middle
East. The vast oil wealth of the Saudi peninsula. But you
shouldn't concern yourself with geopolitics, Admiral. Your
job is to command the carrier battle group in what is nothing more than a routine military operation. Leave the bigger
issues to the strategists."

He glanced at his watch. "I'm due for a conference call
with the Secretary of State and our ambassador in San'a. I'll
brief you later on the status of the negotiations."

Fletcher was left standing in the flag intel space as Babcock strode back to his own private quarters. Babcock's
words still rang in his ears. *Leave the bigger issues to the
strategists.*

It was an insult, but he had become accustomed to such
insults. It went with the job.

Twenty thousand feet above the battle, Maxwell could see
the unmistakable black smoke billowing into the morning
sky. Helicopters were burning.

He and his strikers were on their own tactical frequency,
so he couldn't hear the communications between the TRAP
team leader and the Battle Group Commander. The situation
was going to hell on the ground.

CAG Boyce's voice came over the strike frequency. "Runner One-one, Battle-Ax."

"Go, Battle-Ax."

"Showtime. Boomer needs your services. You're cleared to expend ordnance. The TARCAP is in place and the picture is clear. Forward air control will come from Boomer on button four."

About time, thought Maxwell. "Runner One-one copies. Are we cleared all the way down, Battle-Ax?"

After a second's pause, Boyce replied. "Negative, Runner. Rules of engagement. Observe the specified altitude."

Maxwell could hear the disgust in Boyce's voice. Boyce despised the rules just as much as he did.

He called the other three pilots in his division. "Runner flight, check switches. We're in hot."

Hozer Miller, on his left wing, acknowledged. Leroi Jones and Flash Gordon, flying in combat spread to the right, also acknowledged. Master armament switches hot, bombs ready to release.

He could see dirty brown puffs erupting in the clearing. Mortars or light artillery. How the hell were they going to pick out the gunners from here? They needed a real forward air controller and a reference—

"Runner lead, do you read Yankee Two?"

The voice was weak and distant, breaking up as it reached his headset.

"Is that you, Yankee Two? Where've you been?"

"The taxpayers get a refund on this radio. It quit, and now it's back again, but I don't know for how long."

She sounded tired, Maxwell thought. Or scared. "What's your status? The recovery team is looking for you."

"I'm five hundred yards from them, but the *Sherji* are closing in. They've already knocked down the helos. They've got some kind of small missile—might be an SA-16—and they're bringing up track-mounted guns."

"How about you? Are you in a secure spot?"

"For the moment. Brick, I think Al-Fasr has been moni-toring the SAR frequency on a captured radio. He knows everything we're doing."

Maxwell digested this news for a second. It explained how Al-Fasr knew when the recovery team was landing. Why did they keep underestimating the sonofabitch?

"Copy that, Yankee Two. Stand by for a minute."

His four Hornets were armed with cluster bombs—CBU-59s and Mk 20 Rockeyes—designed for low-level release, to decimate personnel and equipment. Dropped from high altitude, they were as likely to hit the friendlies as the *Sherji*.

He considered. It wouldn't do any good to ask Battle-Ax again for clearance to go on down. It was Fletcher and Bab-cock's show. Boyce's hands were tied.

Orders were orders. That was what it meant to be a pro-fessional military officer. You took orders, then executed them to the best of your ability. That was the career he had chosen.

Well, it had been a nice career. At least he got to com-mand his own squadron for a while. *Kiss it good-bye.*

"Yankee Two, can you spot targets from your position?"

"Affirmative," she answered. "I've got a front-row seat."

"We're inbound. Give us an orange marker smoke. All targets referenced on the smoke, okay?"

"You've got it," B.J. answered. The weariness had left her voice. She sounded buoyant. "Here goes your smoke. Give 'em hell, guys."

"Nothing? What do you mean, nothing?" Babcock was al-most screaming into the handset. "We were supposed to have the accord from Al-Fasr in our hands this morning. In-stead, we have a bloodbath going on in Yemen!"

"Yes, sir," said Perkins, his aide in Washington. "Bankhead

has been waiting at the embassy in San'a all night. He says they're stonewalling. He doesn't know why."

Like all his SatComm communications from the *Reagan*, this phone call was digitally scrambled. Still, Babcock couldn't help worrying that someone—*anyone* other than Perkins and his two deputies, Triolo in Aden and Bankhead in San'a—might somehow decrypt the message.

It would be a public relations disaster. If the press or any of the howling jackals that inhabited the United States Congress learned of his agreement with Al-Fasr, not only would his own head roll, but the ensuing scandal could topple the administration.

Not that he was the first. Hadn't scores of security advisers and presidential deputies before him made clandestine deals with foreign operatives? The Iran-Contra affair was just the tip of the iceberg.

"Tell Bankhead to establish contact with Al-Fasr. I don't care how. Smoke signals or carrier pigeon, that's his problem. I need a SatComm hookup with him today, before this thing goes any further. Understand?"

Perkins understood.

Babcock hung up the secure phone and stewed for a minute. What was Al-Fasr up to? It didn't make sense that the Arab would double-cross him. Why would he? The man had just been handed the keys to Yemen. The existing government could be deposed in a matter of hours—with the full support of the United States. Al-Fasr would be transformed from a fugitive, like bin Laden, to a head of state and staunch ally of the most powerful country on the planet.

It was possible, he supposed, that Al-Fasr was crazy. But not likely. For nearly twenty years—since they were at Yale together—he had observed Al-Fasr's career, his rise in the military, his growing status as the scion of a powerful Arab family. The man had a formidable intellect mixed with a streak of iconoclasm. He could bring something new and modern to the feudal political system of the Middle East.

Not that he and Al-Fasr were friends. More like fellow visionaries. Al-Fasr was more of an idealist than Babcock, more romantic and impetuous. But never one of those Islamic extremists. He wasn't crazy.

Until now. Now Babcock wasn't sure.

It was glorious.

B.J. wanted to stand up and cheer. The first Hornet—Maxwell's, she presumed—was coming in from the east, skimming the edge of the long spinelike ridgeline. Against the glare of the low morning sun, the fighter was nearly invisible. The sound hadn't yet reached the plateau where B.J. huddled with her radio.

One of the *Sherji* moving up the slope spotted the jets. He stood and yelled something in Arabic, pointing at the oncoming fighters. Confused, they stopped, peering at the apparitions flashing toward them.

The bomblets were already dropping. The swarm of dark objects hurtled toward the ground.

Blam! Blam! Blam! Blam! A dozen *Sherji* who had remained standing were cut in half. The hillside erupted in a wave of exploding dirt and shrubs and flesh. In a fifty-yard-wide swath, the cluster bombs ripped up shrubs and rocks and running soldiers.

Those who survived the wave of cluster bombs were on their feet, running for the cover of the trees when the second Hornet arrived. The next swath sliced through them like a scythe.

"On target!" B.J. yelled over the radio. "That stopped the advance wave. Runner One-three and -four, move your aim point a hundred yards, three o'clock. I see a concentration of troops in those trees."

She saw the incoming Hornets bank to the right, adjusting their aim points. They skimmed down the ridgeline, bearing down on the target. The bomblets looked like blackbirds swarming to a nest.

The trees disintegrated in a geyser of foliage and dirt and shrapnel. B.J. could see panicked and wounded *Sherji* running for cover.

Somewhere nearby, a big gun belched fire. Then another. The guns were concealed beneath camouflage, but she saw the ringlets of smoke that followed each burst.

"I've got another target. A heavy gun emplacement, fifty-seven millimeter, maybe."

Maxwell answered. "We've each got one CBU canister left, and the cannons."

She gave him the bearing and distance of the gun emplacement from the smoke marker. As the Hornets rolled in on the new targets, B.J. could see tracers and hear small-caliber guns firing on the jets. *Good luck,* she thought. Hitting a jet moving at five hundred knots was a feat of marksmanship far beyond these hooligans.

The first load of bombs ripped through a stand of trees, exploding a vehicle but missing the gun emplacement. The gun belched another round into the air.

"Runner One-two, move your aim point thirty yards, three o'clock."

"Runner One-two, wilco."

The bombs cut through the camouflaged emplacement, shredding equipment and vehicles and bodies. A secondary explosion—an ammunition cache, she guessed—belched a mushroom of dirt and flame.

"On target! On target! Keep it up."

B.J. scanned the ridgeline and the plateau where the marines were dug in. On the far side, something glinted. She saw movement, dark shapes skulking through the bush.

"Bull's-eye one-five-zero degrees, a thousand yards," she

called. "Looks like another troop concentration. They're approaching the marine perimeter from that hillside on the west. Do you see them, Runner?"

Several seconds passed. "Runner One-one tallies the target."

B.J. watched Maxwell's Hornet roll into a shallow dive, aimed at the hillside where she had spotted the *Sherji*.

It sounded like a giant buzz saw. The Hornet's twenty-millimeter cannon spat fire at the horrific rate of six thousand rounds per minute. A swath of earth erupted on the hillside, decimating everything in its path. Troops leaped from concealment and fled toward the gully below them.

From the TRAP team's perimeter, another hail of machine-gun fire opened up, cutting down the retreating *Sherji*.

Maxwell's Hornet pulled off the target as the next was bearing down on the fleeing enemy. And the next. More swaths of dirt and fire.

The *Sherji* were in full rout. As they retreated down the slope, the marines lobbed mortar into their ranks.

"Yankee Two, do you read Boomer?"

It was a new voice on her radio. B.J. was instantly suspicious. The SAR frequency had become a party line. "Who is Boomer?" she asked.

"The marine whose butt you just saved. Great job of forward air control, Yankee. Can you make it to our perimeter?"

"It depends on how many— Uh-oh. Stand by, Boomer."

She lowered the radio and peered down the hillside.

Something down the slope moved—a glint of metal, a patch of the wrong color.

She waited, watching the bushes and boulders.

There it was again. Coming toward her. Taking their time, being stealthy, using the rocks and shrubs.

How many? How did they know she was here?

Easy, she realized, looking at the orange smoke that was

still gushing upward. They saw the smoke and heard her calling targets on the SAR frequency. A no-brainer.

Across the valley, Maxwell's Hornet was making another pass on the retreating *Sherji*. She considered calling a strafing pass on her own hillside. Forget it. The guys coming up the hill were already too close to her position.

"What's going on, Yankee?" came the marine commander's voice. "Are you in trouble?"

She didn't know whether to laugh or cry. "I've been in trouble for the last twenty-four hours, sir. This is just more of the same. Sorry, I've gotta go now."

She stuffed the radio back into her satchel and surveyed her escape routes. The *Sherji* owned most of the real estate on the hillside that sloped toward the marines' perimeter. Behind her lay an undulating series of gullies and then a terraced slope that someone had cultivated with rows of sorghum. At the far end of the gullies, about three hundred yards distant, rose another wooded hillside punctuated by craggy rock formations.

Throwing the satchel over her shoulder, she scuttled up the path toward the gullies. The *Sherji* might get a glimpse of her, perhaps even take a shot. So be it. She would do what she did best—run.

In a sprint she reached the shoulder of the hill, then dropped into one of the gullies and headed toward the woods. At the end of the gully she ducked behind a boulder and stopped to look back.

No *Sherji*. At least none on her heels. For a moment she stood still, listening. She didn't hear anything coming her way. Just the sound of her own raspy breathing—and the throaty whine of the jets overhead.

The Super Hornets were still shredding the Al-Fasr position. She saw a Hornet skimming in low over the ridgeline, flame spitting from the muzzle in the long slender nose. As the Hornet came off target, B.J. noticed something else.

A smoke trail, going straight up. It was the same squiggly, erratic kind of trail she had observed when the Cobra gunship was destroyed.

She fumbled for the radio in her satchel. While she punched the transmit button, her eyes followed the wispy column of smoke.

The Hornet was in a hard right bank. The smoke trail was following it.

"Flares, Runner!" she yelled in the radio. "Smoke in the air! You're targeted."

CHAPTER TWELVE

MERCENARY

Al Hazir, Yemen
1305, Tuesday, 18 June

He heard the warning at the same time he picked up the telltale smoke. It was coming from the grove of trees near where the guns had been concealed.

Maxwell's thumb went for the flares/chaff switch on the throttles as he yanked the Hornet into a seven-G turn. Speed and Gs were his best defenses down low. He was only five hundred feet above the terrain. A Hornet moving at four hundred knots was a hell of a lot tougher target than a hundred-mile-per-hour chopper. Hitting such a target with a shoulder-launched weapon was a nearly impossible task. Unless the shooter got lucky.

A sudden concussion passed through the airframe of the jet like a hammer blow. Maxwell felt a vibration that seemed to come from the tail of the fighter.

So the shooter got lucky.

The jet was still flying. Maxwell tensed, ready to pull the ejection lanyard. How badly was he hit? He rolled the Hornet out of its right bank. The fly-by-wire flight control system was still working. The damage seemed to be in the tail section, maybe the stabilators. If it wasn't too bad he could—

"Engine fire left!" It was the voice of Bitchin' Betty, the robotic aural warning. Her irritating monotone cut like a knife through the cockpit. "Engine fire left!"

He yanked the left throttle back, then punched the illuminated fire light, discharging the extinguisher.

The red light remained on. The vibration worsened, sending a tremor through the jet.

The jet was rolling to the left. He had the stick to the full right position—with no effect. The electronic inputs to the flight control system were gone.

The Hornet was slicing toward the brown hills below.

Like all fighter pilots, he had visualized this moment. During all the years he had flown fighters, he had never been forced to eject. Given a choice, this wasn't the way he'd do it—high speed, low altitude, hostile territory.

No choice.

He shoved his helmet back against the headrest. Closing his elbows tight to his sides, he gripped the ejection lanyard between his legs with both hands and yanked the handle.

The shock was greater than he expected. It felt as if he were being shot from a cannon. The wall of air hit him, blurred his vision, ripped at him like a beast. He was an unguided missile hurtling through the sky at half the speed of sound. Dimly he felt the drogue chute slowing him, sensed the automatic release from the seat.

With a violent jerk, the main chute opened.

He knew he was close to the ground, but he couldn't tell how close. He felt himself make one pendulum swing beneath the deployed chute, then sensed in his dimmed vision the earth rushing up to meet him. He crashed through the foliage, limbs snagging and snatching at him. He dropped in a heap at the base of a scraggly tree.

For nearly a minute he lay there gathering his senses. The parachute canopy was snarled in the tree. Something was jammed into his face. It hurt like hell. He realized it was his oxygen mask, skewed up over his nose from the wind blast.

Still dazed, he detached the mask, then unhooked the seat pack from his harness. His hands trembled as he worked the fasteners on the harness.

He did a quick assessment, moving each limb, one at a time. No broken bones, no major sprains, at least that he noticed yet. He was bleeding from a small gash in his forearm. There were some abrasions, probably from the plunge through the tree.

He tried pulling the parachute canopy down from the branches. The more he yanked, the more snarled the canopy became. *To hell with it.* He didn't like leaving the thing there, but he couldn't waste time getting it down.

He had to gather the essential equipment, then put some distance between him and the parachute, which was flapping in the breeze like an outdoor advertising sign. The *Sherji* would know exactly where to start looking. Maxwell had no illusions about the treatment he would get from those he had just finished strafing.

He checked his sidearm—the Colt .45. It had survived the ejection, still strapped inside the leather shoulder holster. He retracted the slide, then quietly eased it home, feeding a round into the chamber. He stuffed the pistol back into the holster. He shoved the helmet and mask beneath a shrub, along with the torso harness and life raft and other equipment he wouldn't need.

First he would find a hiding place, then break out the radio and make contact with the recovery team.

The terrain sloped upward to the west. That would be the

best course. Head that direction, put a few miles between him and the telltale parachute. Then he'd—

"Put your hands against the tree."

It was a guttural, thickly accented voice, coming from behind him. He turned to look at the speaker.

"Don't move. I'll shoot you where you stand."

Maxwell got a look at him. A stocky man with short brown hair and a stubble of beard. He wore a brown flight suit and held a semiautomatic pistol in his hand.

"Who are you?" Maxwell asked.

"My name is Rittmann. I'm here to kill you."

A gift from heaven.

When he saw the parachute descend into the trees only half a kilometer from him, Wolf Rittmann knew what it meant. He had been saved.

The American pilot was his passage out of Yemen.

Rittmann had no illusions about his status with Al-Fasr. Even before the disastrous air battle, Rittmann knew that Al-Fasr was finished with him. He was expendable, just like the worn-out MiG-29 he had been flying. He was certain that the *Sherji,* who were now in a ground battle with the Americans, had orders to kill him if he turned up alive. Or deliver him to Al-Fasr, who would dispose of him in one of his own imaginative ways.

Now he had something of value to offer Al-Fasr—a captured American pilot. He would be an immensely valuable bartering item. Al-Fasr would be persuaded not only to give Rittmann his liberty but he would even compensate him for having shot down one of the American jets.

Rittmann sized up his trophy. The man was half a head taller than he, fit-looking, with dark hair and a mustache, in his late thirties, maybe early forties. He seemed to have suffered no serious injuries from the ejection.

"Put your hands on the tree," Rittmann said again.

The American was regarding him with curiosity, his hands still at his sides. *Typical American insolence,* thought Rittmann. A bullet through the elbow would teach him some manners.

Not yet, he told himself. The pistol shot might reveal his position to the *Sherji* or to any Americans patrolling the area. *Later.*

He approached the pilot, keeping the Czech-made Parabellum pistol pointed toward him. The man watched him, still curious.

"Your name is Rittmann?" the American said. The blue eyes studied him. "You're German."

"My nationality doesn't matter."

"Former East German? You hired on to fly the MiG-29s."

Rittmann felt a flash of anger as he remembered the insults the East German military had endured from the Americans. He aimed the pistol in the man's face. "I ask the questions. Turn around and do as I say."

Slowly the man turned, his manner still imperious, insolent. Rittmann promised himself that he would change this man's attitude.

He removed the sidearm, a heavy, large-caliber automatic pistol. *Peculiar,* he thought, hefting the gun. How could the highly advanced American military issue such a useless weapon? A pistol like this one could not possibly be fired with any accuracy.

Keeping the muzzle of the Parabellum pressed into the man's back, he searched the pockets of his flight suit. He removed the survival knife, a dull-bladed tool with a serrated edge. Another odd weapon, as useless as the obsolete pistol. Americans were strange.

He dumped out the contents of the pilot's survival pack, including a handheld radio, various signaling flares and pyrotechnics, and a device that looked like a global positioning system. Rittmann was impressed. Unlike the silly gun and the knife, this was definitely *not* obsolete equipment.

When he was finished, Rittmann stepped back and said, "You will tell me your name and rank."

"Samuel Maxwell. Commander."

"To what flying unit are you assigned?"

"United States Navy."

Rittmann jabbed the pistol into his ribs. "*Geschwader!* I want to know your unit and base."

"Are you an interrogator? I thought you were a pilot."

"From an aircraft carrier you came, is that not correct? What flying unit?"

"None. Actually, I'm a tourist. Where did you learn to speak such bad English?"

Rittmann's anger burst out of control. In an overhand, chopping swing, he brought the butt of the Parabellum down on the back of the man's neck. The American grunted and dropped to his knees.

Rittmann delivered a kick to the man's ribs, causing him to double over. "On your feet. I give you one more opportunity to answer my questions."

The American raised himself up on a knee, then slowly stood. The blue eyes had narrowed to slits, fixed on Rittmann as if he were a specimen.

In truth, Rittmann had no interest in the man's answers. Al-Fasr's sources had already reported that the F/A-18s came from the aircraft carrier *Reagan,* cruising the Gulf of Aden. The only purpose of Rittmann's questions—and the subsequent punishment—was to make this American *Scheisskopf* beg for mercy.

"Your unit. Its designation and its commanding officer. Tell me now!"

The American returned his gaze.

Rittmann swung the pistol again, striking him in the face. The man reeled backward, his cheek spurting blood.

Rittmann's pent-up anger was taking control of him. He swung again, the blow glancing off the man's head.

Stunned, the American dropped to one knee. Again Rittmann considered using the Parabellum, blasting him in the elbow or the knee, inflicting some real pain.

No, not the gun. The knife.

He unsheathed the Denckler fighting knife. The twenty-centimeter, double-edged blade was honed to a razor sharpness. For years Rittmann had imagined actually using the Denckler in combat. The oldest and most basic of military weapons, it was beautiful in its pure simplicity. No weapon instilled such raw terror as the cold sharp steel of a knife.

He shifted the pistol to his left hand. With the handle of the knife nestled in his right palm, he stepped toward the kneeling American.

The first slash caught him across his raised forearm. The German was holding the knife at waist level, thrusting it like a fencer.

He slashed again, ripping through the sleeve of Maxwell's Nomex flight suit. Maxwell tried to dodge the thrusts, but he was slow, still dazed from the ejection and the blow on the head. Blood spurted from the wound on his right arm.

Rittmann seemed to be enjoying the one-sided duel. A smile flitted over his face as he shifted his weight from foot to foot, advancing one step at a time.

He thrust again. The point of the blade caught Maxwell's left shoulder, penetrating the fabric of the flight suit. Blood streamed down Maxwell's left arm.

He tried to fend off the knife thrusts, but the German was quick. Too quick. It occurred to Maxwell that the man could have killed him already. What did he want? Did he intend to carve him up first, then kill him? It was as if he were settling an old score.

Rittmann thrust again with the blade. Maxwell dodged the

slashing blade—and tripped. He tumbled backward, then rolled, trying to regain his feet.

Too late. The German lashed out with his boot, catching Maxwell in the chest. The German was on him before he could regain his feet. Light glinted from the polished blade as he thrust it toward Maxwell's throat.

"That's enough! Drop your weapons."

The voice came from behind. The German stopped in midthrust. The smile was gone, replaced by a look of confusion.

"Drop the gun and the knife on the ground."

It was a woman's voice.

Rittmann nodded. His lips parted in a knowing smile, and he turned to face her.

Blam! He felt the bullet sizzle past his ear.

The smile vanished, and he let the knife drop.

"The gun," said the woman. "Drop it or the next bullet goes into your head."

He released the pistol. It fell to the dirt with a plop.

Rittmann stared at the intruder. His eyes took in the blackened face, the flight suit, the diminutive size. She was holding an automatic pistol in both hands, ready to fire again. It was incredible. "You're a woman?"

"You better believe it," said Maxwell, rising to his feet. He gathered up Rittmann's pistol and the knife. He looked down at his bloody sleeve. "Lieutenant Johnson, for the record, I am very glad to see you. I don't suppose you could have gotten here a couple of minutes earlier?"

"Couldn't run any faster," said B.J. "You should have punched out closer to where I was."

"I should've dodged the SAM. Then I wouldn't be here."

She looked the German over. "Who is he? He doesn't seem like a very nice person."

"This is Herr Rittmann," said Maxwell. "Formerly of the East German Air Force. We're going to get to know him very well. But first, you'll have to excuse us while we finish some international business."

"Business?" B.J. looked at him questioningly.

"A reciprocal trade matter."

He tried not to telegraph what was coming, but at the last instant the German sensed it. The punch came straight from the shoulder, with all his strength behind it, augmented by anger and several gallons of adrenaline.

Rittmann tried to duck, but he was a microsecond too late. Maxwell's fist caught him just beneath the right jaw.

The German let out a whooshing sound as he flipped backward, arms and legs askew.

B.J. stared at the unconscious man. "Skipper, is that a civilized way to treat a prisoner of war?"

"Who said I was civilized?"

"Good point. I retract the question."

Maxwell retrieved his Colt from Rittmann's pocket. In the distance he could hear the rattle of automatic weapons. The marines were still shooting it out with the *Sherji*. The jets were no longer overhead.

CHAPTER THIRTEEN

COLT .45

San'a, Republic of Yemen
1745, Tuesday, 18 June

"It's Maloney," said the voice on the phone. "We need to talk."

Claire could tell that he'd been drinking. She was at her desk, working on a dispatch to her bureau chief in Bahrain.

"About what?"

"Not on the phone. I'll pick you up in front of your hotel in twenty minutes."

She groaned. Of all the ways she could choose to spend an evening in scenic San'a, going for a ride with a drunk was not one of them. "Is it urgent?"

"It has to do with the lucky guy you told me about."

Claire's heart froze. Something had happened to Sam. "I'll be waiting at the lobby door."

The relentless pinging stopped.

Three hours had elapsed since the *Ilia Mourmetz* settled into its hiding place beneath the littoral shelf. The

Mourmetz's passive listening equipment was hearing the steady passage of sub-hunting helicopters and S-3 Vikings.

Still searching.

Manilov had just returned to his command desk in the control room when they came to him. A dozen of them, mostly warrants, stood in a cluster behind Pietr Ilychin, the executive officer. Two lieutenants—Boris Antonin, the navigation officer, and Dimitri Popov, the engineering officer—were in the group. Each wore a sullen look.

"Captain," said Ilychin, clearing his throat, "the crew has taken a vote."

"A vote? About what?"

"About whether to continue this patrol."

Manilov gave him a piercing look, causing Ilychin to avert his eyes. *The time has finally come,* he thought. *Ilychin has contaminated the rest of the crew. Now I must deal with it.*

"I was not aware that the Russian Navy was a democracy. I am the captain, and I have the only vote."

"This is no longer the Russian Navy," said Ilychin. "We are private citizens. We have a right to decide our own fate."

"You are officers and crew of the *Ilia Mourmetz,* and I am your commanding officer. Until this boat docks in port, you will continue with your duties. I expect you to carry out my orders without question."

At this a murmur rose from the assembled crewmen. Ilychin took this as a sign of support, and a smile passed over his narrow face. "The men of the crew no longer recognize you as their commanding officer."

"And who do they recognize?" Manilov said, knowing the answer.

"They have elected me as the new captain."

"Did all the crew vote for this change?"

Ilychin hesitated. "A majority."

"And what do you propose to do as the captain of the *Ilia Mourmetz*?" Manilov's eyes bored into Ilychin.

"That depends," he said uncertainly.

"On what, Mr. Ilychin?"

"On whether we can escape this place. It is still possible to deliver the submarine to Iran. We can sail to the base at Bandar Abbas."

"That's brilliant, Ilychin. The Iranians will be most happy to receive the boat. Then they will arrest you and turn you over to Russia, who will line you up and execute each of you as a traitor."

Ilychin blinked, again uncertain. "We can surrender the vessel to the Americans. They will give us asylum."

At this Manilov felt a surge of anger sweep over him. Surrender to the Americans! He could still see the great mass of the *Reagan* floating like an apparition past the lens of his periscope. He had not waited this long to abandon the single defining mission of his life. It was unthinkable that he should become a vassal of the Americans. That was not his destiny. Fate had sent him here to sink the devil ship.

And so, by God, he would.

Manilov shifted his eyes from Ilychin to the others. They, too, looked frightened, uncertain. They were young men, most of them from the desolate provinces of Russia. They had families and dreams and hopes for the future. What they desperately needed now was leadership. It was his duty to provide it.

He still sat at his desk. During the exchange with Ilychin, Manilov had slid his right hand into the pocket of his uniform tunic. Now he drew it out. It was wrapped around the grip of his Simonov semiautomatic pistol.

He rose to his feet and aimed the pistol at the head of Pietr Ilychin. "You cowardly son of a bitch!"

Ilychin saw that he meant it. His eyes filled with terror. "Captain—"

The 7.62mm round caught him in the temple. Ilychin's head snapped back, and he toppled into the cluster of men behind him.

For several seconds the gunshot echoed in the confined space of the submarine.

"Who's next?" Manilov roared. He waved the pistol at the pack of frightened men. "Who wants to take command of this vessel from me?"

They stared back at him. No one answered.

Manilov assumed that some must have come to the meeting with weapons of their own. The clip of his Simonov held eight more rounds. He would use them all if necessary.

"Who else wants to surrender this boat to the Americans?"

Still no answer.

"Listen to me," said Manilov. "The *Ilia Mourmetz* will carry out the mission it has been assigned. You are still Russians, and you understand the meaning of honor and dignity. I ask you to remain steadfast in your duty. Serve with me and I promise you this one thing—we will cover ourselves with glory."

They had formed themselves in a semicircle around the sprawled body of Ilychin. Blood oozed from the purplish wound in the officer's temple. His eyes were wide open, staring blankly at the overhead.

"You two," Manilov said, pointing to the two men nearest the body. "Place him in a plastic bag and store him in the torpedo room. When we have completed our business here and have again reached the open sea, we will give Pietr Ilychin a proper service and a burial at sea."

"Aye." The two warrants hauled Ilychin's corpse toward the passageway.

"Lieutenant Popov," Manilov said to the engineering officer, whose eyes were fixed on the body being carried away. The officer looked up with alarm. "You will assume the duties of executive officer. Take charge of Ilychin's console and keep me informed about any changes in the status of our power plants and weapons systems."

Popov nodded his head cautiously. "Aye, Captain."

Manilov glowered at the remaining crewmen, his eyes moving from one to the next. None would return his stare. They stood in an awkward cluster, waiting for an order.

Manilov gave it to them. "Back to your stations. We will be moving into position to attack the enemy. I need the faithful service of every one of you. Do not disappoint me."

He stuffed the Simonov pistol back into his pocket and turned from them.

Back at his command desk, he watched the crewmen shuffle away to their respective work posts. The crisis had passed, but only for a while. He could not keep their fealty if they remained for long in the midst of an enemy armada.

As he reflected on what happened, he had to admit that Ilychin was right about one thing: This was *not* the Russian Navy. Not any longer. They had no allegiance to any country, not Russia, certainly not to Yemen or Al-Fasr. They were free agents, without rules or command oversight.

What did that make them? Mercenaries? Pirates?

For a career naval officer like Yevgeny Manilov, it was a discomforting thought. He decided not to think about it.

In the darkness Maxwell could hear the sounds of automatic fire around the marines' position.

"Boomer, this is Runner One-one," he said quietly into his PRC-112. "Do you read, Boomer?"

Several seconds elapsed; then the voice of Gus Gritti

crackled over the radio. "Nice to hear you're among the living, Runner. What's your status?"

"Operational. I've got company."

"Yankee Two? Have you joined with her?"

"Affirmative," said Maxwell. He decided not to pass the message that they had captured one of Al-Fasr's pilots. Not over the SAR channel.

"What's your position, Runner? Are you close to us?"

"Negative. No position reports in the open, Boomer. Be aware that this channel has been compromised."

"Okay, we sort of suspected that. Are you able to join our party?"

"Not in the darkness. Too many obstacles. What do you suggest?"

"Stay put. Warlord says they're negotiating something. They're gonna pick us up when the deal is made. In the meantime, keep your heads down and wait for the cavalry. When you see 'em, mark your position with smoke."

"Copy that. We're shutting down to save juice."

"Good luck, Runner."

The prisoner regarded them with a sullen stare. His face was swollen on the right side, and a residue of blood stained the corner of his mouth.

"I think you broke his jaw," said B.J.

"That was an accident. I was aiming for his nose."

Their eyes had adjusted to the darkness. The sounds of gunfire over the hill were less frequent now. They huddled in the shelter of a row of thorny trees.

Maxwell knelt before the German, who sat cross-legged at the base of a tree. His wrists were bound behind him. Rittmann's eyes looked like opaque beads in the darkness.

"The war's over for you," said Maxwell. "Your only chance to save your life is to cooperate."

"I am a prisoner of war. I have nothing to say to you."

"We've already been through that. You are a mercenary. And a terrorist. You have no rights."

"I am protected by the Geneva Convention."

For a moment Maxwell studied his own bandaged arm; then he looked at Rittmann again. "I don't recall you worrying about the Geneva Convention a couple of hours ago."

Rittmann gave him a sullen stare.

"Maybe you wouldn't mind telling us how Al-Fasr knew when the air strike was coming. What is his source of information?"

"I have nothing to tell you."

"You don't owe any loyalty to Al-Fasr. He left you for dead out here."

Rittmann didn't respond.

"He used you, then dumped you, right?"

No response.

Maxwell gave it a minute, then sighed, "You must understand, Herr Rittmann, this is a very bad situation for us. We have to keep moving, keep running from the *Sherji*. We can't do that and drag a prisoner with us. Especially a prisoner who has no value." He looked at B.J. "Isn't that correct, Lieutenant?"

She nodded, looking worried.

Maxwell pulled out his .45 pistol. He could see by Rittmann's eyes that he had his full attention.

"No hard feelings, chum. You, of all people, should understand how it is." He took a step toward him. "I'll try to make it painless."

"You won't kill a prisoner," Rittmann blurted. "Americans are not permitted to do that."

"Oh, sure they are. It's allowed under special circumstances, when our own lives are at stake."

Rittmann tried to scuttle away. Maxwell grabbed him by the collar of his flight suit and yanked him to his knees.

He jammed the muzzle of the pistol against Rittmann's temple.

B.J. was making a great show of clearing her throat. "Excuse me, sir. Could we have a private discussion?"

Maxwell stepped away from the prisoner. She leaned close to his ear and whispered, "Please tell me you're not going to do something crazy."

"How do you define crazy?"

"Killing this guy."

"The thought crossed my mind."

"No," she said, shaking her head. "You wouldn't do that." Then she saw his face. "Would you?"

Maxwell nodded toward the bound German. "Rittmann here is exercising his right to remain silent. We can't wait for the *Sherji* to come and pick us up, can we?"

B.J. stared, speechless.

With his thumb, he released the safety on left side of the pistol. It made an audible click.

"This is barbaric!" yelled Rittmann.

"Exactly my thoughts half an hour ago."

Holding the .45 with both hands, Maxwell aimed at the German's forehead.

"No!"

"No!"

The two voices—Rittmann's and B.J.'s—were simultaneous.

"Al-Fasr has intelligence sources," Rittmann blurted.

Maxwell kept the .45 trained on his forehead. "Tell me something I haven't already figured out. Who? Where?" He let Rittmann continue looking into the muzzle of the Colt.

"On your ship, the *Reagan*. I don't know the name—Al-Fasr has never said. Someone with access to operational secrets."

"How is the information passed?"

"The informer transmits the data by satellite, in some kind of encrypted form. In his underground base here in Yemen, Al-Fasr has very sophisticated communications equipment. He even knows the overflight schedules of your surveillance satellites."

Maxwell kept his expression blank. "Weapons," he said. "What sort of equipment does Al-Fasr have? How many MiGs?"

"He had six. I don't know how many are left."

"Where is your base? Where did you take off from?"

Rittmann kept his eyes focused on the pistol. "Eritrea. Across the Red Sea."

Maxwell watched his eyes. He knew Rittmann was lying. The MiGs couldn't have come across the Red Sea without being detected. He would revisit that subject in a minute.

"What else? Armor? Air defense?"

Rittmann paused; then his eyes focused again on the pistol. "Personnel carriers, I don't know how many. Ten, fifteen. Six helicopters, Dauphins. He has a supply of SA-16 antiaircraft missiles."

Maxwell nodded. So it had been a shoulder-launched SA-16 heat seeker that brought down his Hornet and, probably, one of the marine Cobras. The SA-16 was a deadly weapon at short range against low flyers. Another item they needed to know on the *Reagan*.

Maxwell looked at B.J., whose face was slowly regaining its color. "We have to get this guy back to the ship for interrogation."

At this, Rittmann became agitated. "Ship? What ship?"

"The aircraft carrier."

"No! Not the *Reagan*."

The urgency in the German's voice surprised Maxwell. "It's not as if you have a choice in the matter."

"The *Reagan* is . . . is not safe."

"Not safe? Explain, please."

"Al-Fasr—" He caught himself.

Maxwell tried not to sound too interested. "The *Reagan* is a hundred-thousand-ton warship. Nothing can happen to it."

Rittmann shook his head. "Something will happen."

Maxwell and B.J. exchanged glances.

"Keep talking," Maxwell said. "What will happen?"

"I don't know. Only that Al-Fasr hates the Americans, their Navy, their ships. This little war—it is all a charade. So he can spring a trap."

"What kind of trap? What's it got to do with the *Reagan*?"

"He has bragged about how he would sink the Americans' most powerful ship."

"And how did he say he would sink it?"

"He didn't explain, only that he had a way." With that, Rittmann seemed to realize that he had said more than he intended. He lapsed into another sulking silence.

Maxwell wondered how much the German was holding back. He considered threatening him with the pistol again. Or even the long-bladed knife. Perhaps he needed another near-death experience.

He pulled the knife out of his pocket and removed it from the scabbard. He looked at it for a moment, then put it down.

No more rough stuff, he decided. It was best that they deliver this creep to the intel debriefers. Let the professionals evaluate the information he was giving them.

B.J. said in a low voice, "Should we pass this information on the radio? They need to know that we have a prisoner."

He shook his head. "Al-Fasr monitors everything we transmit. If he learns we have Rittmann, he'll start a massive search for us."

"So what do we do?"

"Wait for the helos to pluck us out of here in the morning. Rittmann too."

In the darkness, the German seemed to be in a trance. He leaned against the tree with his chin on his chest.

"What about him?" she asked. "We can't keep him tied up like that all night."

Maxwell considered for a moment. "We'll give him a chance to eat and relieve himself." Maxwell lifted the .45. "Go ahead and untie his wrists."

B.J. nodded and went to the prisoner. She knelt beside him and untied the parachute cord that fastened his wrists.

It happened so quickly that Maxwell couldn't believe what he was seeing. Rittmann was on his feet. Holding B.J. from behind, he had an arm clamped around her neck.

Maxwell saw a flash of silver. Glinting in the darkness was the long slender blade of the fighting knife.

The damned knife! Thoughtlessly, he had put it down, forgotten it. Somehow Rittmann had managed to snag it and cut himself loose.

He was holding the blade against B. J. Johnson's throat.

For several seconds no one spoke. Maxwell stood with the Colt in his hand, feeling powerless, furious with himself. Rittmann studied him. He kept the knife poised beneath B.J.'s chin.

"Our positions reverse again," said Rittmann. "Stay where you are and drop the pistol."

"It's a standoff," said Maxwell. He gestured with the .45. "If you do any harm to her, I'll empty this pistol into you."

Rittmann stared back at him, desperation showing in his eyes. "Would you like to see her throat cut?"

"Would you like to die from seven gunshot wounds?"

Rittmann tightened his grip around B.J.'s neck. "You won't shoot while I have this knife."

"Release her. You don't have any options. You'll be treated decently by the U.S. Navy."

"You are a liar. I will be a prisoner."

"You don't have to be a prisoner. You can be a defector."

"I will never defect to the Americans."

"If Al-Fasr finds you, he'll dismember you and feed you to the vultures."

"He will be pleased to have a captured American pilot." He glanced down at B.J. "Especially a captured woman pilot."

Maxwell felt the situation slipping away from him. This was his fault. His own stupid bravado, roughing up the German, intimidating him into talking. It was payback time.

"Let her go." Maxwell forced himself to keep his voice calm. "I give you my word as an officer, if you release her, we will allow you to leave. You can go free."

He saw B.J. watching him, wondering whether he meant it.

Rittmann wasn't buying it. "She comes with me. Do not follow us or I cut her throat."

He began walking backward, forcing B.J. to match his steps.

Maxwell watched them move away. He felt B.J.'s eyes on him, waiting to see what he would do. They were nearly into the bushes, slipping away in the darkness.

He felt the weight of the Colt, more than two pounds, inert and useless as a stone. Another act of bravado, hauling around the clunky pistol that weighed twice as much as the more accurate Beretta. Even at close range, inside twenty yards, he was a lousy marksman with the .45. With any pistol, for that matter. He was a pilot, not a grunt.

They were vanishing in the trees. He raised the pistol, holding it in both hands. In the darkness he could see B.J.'s face, Rittmann's arm around her neck, his face peering from behind her.

Maxwell aimed. His hands were shaking.

It was impossible. The sights were nearly invisible in the darkness. He would hit B.J.

If he missed, Rittmann would kill her.

Impossible.

He drew in a single deep breath. His world shrank into a narrow, dimly lit tunnel. The passage of time slowed, then stopped.

Nothing existed. Nothing but the dull blur of the gunsight, the dark oval of her face . . .

His hands no longer shook.

Freeze the picture. Shut out the world. Squeeze . . .

It sounded like a cannon. He was momentarily blinded by the muzzle flash.

As his vision returned, he saw them in the darkness. B.J. was down, writhing on the ground. Rittmann was still standing. He held the knife in one hand while he clutched his neck with the other. Blood spurted from between his fingers.

Maxwell's eyes went from the girl on the ground back to the German.

An uncontrollable rage seized Maxwell. In a dreamlike state, he was transported back in time. *He tried to take her away.* He saw a red-haired girl. It was happening again. *You're losing her . . .*

Rittmann lurched toward her.

Maxwell fired again. The bullet caught the German in the chest. He was blown backward.

Maxwell fired again. And again. He kept firing until the trigger wouldn't pull anymore. The magazine was empty.

Stunned, he lowered the pistol. Gradually he became aware of B.J. staring at him. Her eyes were large and pale in the darkness.

He dropped the empty pistol and went to her. A dark wetness was spreading over the front of her flight suit.

"You know something? You're one hell of a lousy shot."

"What do you mean? I shot Rittmann."

"You weren't supposed to shoot *me*."

"What did you expect? This is government work. Hold still while I get this antiseptic on."

Dressing her wound, Maxwell realized again what a brutish weapon the .45 caliber was. Though the bullet hit only the muscle between her neck and her shoulder, just missing her collarbone, it left a two-inch-deep wound that was bleeding profusely.

In Rittmann's case, the damage was more dramatic. He had fired all seven rounds—the full magazine—into the German. Rittmann was a mess.

Gross overkill. Maxwell could still feel the dark emotions that had taken possession of him. It was the first time he had killed an enemy at close range. No bomb, missile, or cannon. He could still see the look on Rittmann's face.

"Owww, damn, that hurts!" B.J. said.

"It's supposed to hurt. That's how you know the stuff is working."

The wound was still bleeding. He made a compress from several layers of gauze and pressed it onto the wound.

She winced again, then began to shiver. "I'm cold, Brick."

"I'm almost finished. Don't move while I put the bandage on. Then we'll get you wrapped in the thermal blanket."

It had been close. He knew he could never duplicate that shot on the firing range—hitting Rittmann in the throat at twenty yards, while missing the body of his wingman. Practically in the dark.

Well, *nearly* missing. B. J. Johnson would always have an interesting scar to remind her of how close she had come to a fatal bullet. Or getting her throat cut.

The memory of what happened kept inserting itself back in his mind. He was shocked at the ferocity that had overcome him. Rittmann was dead as a post. What secrets he possessed had exited through the seven bullet holes in him.

A high overcast obscured the sky. The darkness filled in the shadows around them. B.J. complained again about the cold, and Maxwell wrapped her in the thermal blanket from his survival pack.

They huddled in a crevice beneath a large boulder to wait out the night.

"Do I get a Purple Heart for this?"

"No way. You have to be wounded by the enemy."

"But it was the enemy who caused me to be wounded. That, and your lousy aim."

"It won't help your case by making slurs about your commanding officer."

She lapsed into a silence, and after several minutes Maxwell realized that she was sleeping. She lay snuggled close to him, her head on his shoulder.

Tentatively, so as not to disturb her, he put his arm around her.

CHAPTER FOURTEEN

SAN'A

San'a, Republic of Yemen
1930, Tuesday, 18 June

Claire saw the battered white Toyota swinging around the corner. As Maloney rolled up to the front of the Al Qasmy, he reached over and opened the right door.

"I know a restaurant not far from here," he said. "Off the street and quiet." His face looked puffy, as if he hadn't gotten much sleep.

She kept her silence while he weaved along the cobbled streets. Maloney, she remembered, loved intrigue. Whatever he had to tell her, he was going to milk it for its full dramatic value.

The restaurant was a hole-in-the-wall called Al-Salah, in a narrow side street about eight blocks from her hotel. The windows were curtained, and an awning covered the sidewalk in front. Half a dozen Yemenis looked up from huddled conversations as they entered. Maloney led her to a back table.

He waited until the drinks came. He looked around, then said in a low voice, "There was another airborne operation today. A team of marines went in to pick up a downed pilot, but they came under fire and now they're on the ground too."

Claire listened, barely able to breathe. "You said something about the lucky guy."

"Another Hornet was shot down supporting the marines."

She took a deep breath and waited.

Maloney said, "What is your guy's name?"

"Maxwell. Sam Maxwell."

He hesitated, and she could tell by his expression what was coming. "Claire, I hate to be the one to tell you this, but that's the guy."

"Is he . . ."

"No details. They think he ejected okay, but no word yet about his situation."

Claire's mind raced through the possibilities. If he was alive, he may have joined the marines on the ground. Or he was captured.

Or killed.

As these thoughts played in her mind, the anger swelled up inside her. "What the hell's going on, Vince?" She knew she was speaking too loudly. The cluster of Yemeni men across the room looked up in surprise. They had probably never heard a woman raise her voice in anger. "Why are they letting this . . . this half-assed little bandit, Al-Fasr, get away with this? Why don't we—"

"Ssh-shh." Maloney was holding his finger to his lips, looking more nervous than ever. He nodded toward the Yemeni men. They had all halted their own conversations and were staring at them.

Claire turned and glowered back. "To hell with them," she said. She swung back to Maloney. "To hell with all of them. Since when does the United States have to bow and scrape to thugs who kill Americans?"

Maloney's nervousness ratcheted up another notch.

"Look, Claire, I know how you feel. This is a very danger-ous situation we're in—"

"Dangerous for who? Are you state department people afraid you might lose your precious little jobs if you speak up? What about those Americans out there in the hills get-ting shot at by"—she paused and glowered again at the gawking Yemenis—"a bunch of Stone Age ragheads?"

At this, Maloney winced. She knew she sounded hysteri-cal, but right now she didn't give a damn. Sam Maxwell was in trouble, and nobody was doing diddly about it.

Maloney had his notepad out, scribbling something on it. He ripped out the page and slid it to her. "This is the phone number of the embassy security office and the address of the front gate, written in Arabic. If this thing blows up—and I predict that it will—get yourself there immediately. Give this to a driver you can trust and go to the front gate. The sentries will know you by name. Don't tell anyone at the hotel where you're going; don't take luggage. If there's an air evacuation, you have to be inside the embassy compound to get on it."

"You really believe this place will blow?"

"If Al-Fasr comes to town, yes."

"And you think he will?"

"Yes."

"Then why don't you just get out now while you can?"

Despite his inebriation, Maloney seemed thoughtful. "You will find this hard to believe, but I still have a tiny sense of duty left in me. You know, the old death-before-dishonor thing. I intend to stay at my post."

Claire nodded and finished her drink in silence. She was sorry she had flared up at Maloney. He was still her best friend in this hostile country.

They pecked at dinner, neither of them hungry, and made small talk about everything except what was on their minds.

He paid the bill and they left. Passing the table of dark-eyed Yemeni men, Claire glowered again at them.

Outside, darkness had descended over the city. The air had turned chilly. She could see Maloney's white Toyota parked a couple hundred meters down the street.

Maloney said, "I think you should come with me to the embassy compound."

"What for? Is this another proposition?"

"You'll be safe there."

For a moment, she considered. Maloney meant well, even if he was potted. It wasn't his fault that she was distraught, worried sick about Maxwell.

"I need to be alone. I want to walk back to the hotel."

"No way, Claire. Too dangerous. C'mon, I'll drive you back."

"I'm okay, really. I just need to be alone. Don't worry about me."

Before he could argue any more, she gave him a peck on the cheek, then started walking down the street. She glanced over her shoulder once and saw Maloney watching her. He was leaning against the Toyota while he fumbled with the key. He gave her a wave, and she waved back.

She was half a block away when she heard it.

The sound of the explosion and the concussion arrived together, rocking her like a blast of wind. She whirled in time to see the Toyota's hood and other assorted pieces clanging off the building across the street.

The car was a fireball. The flaming pyre gushed thirty feet into the air, illuminating the cobbled street in an angry orange glare.

Her first instinct was to run to the burning automobile, try to help. Do something. Maybe Vince had somehow survived. Maybe . . .

She ran a few steps, then stopped. *He's dead, you idiot. And you're next.*

In the glare of the fire she saw figures, silhouettes. Heard voices yelling in Arabic.

She turned and ran. One of her high-heeled leather shoes caught on the cobblestones. She fell, banging her elbow and knee on the rough-surfaced street.

Behind her the voices were coming nearer. She heard running footsteps. Bystanders? Witnesses? Police?

Killers.

She yanked off her shoes and jumped to her feet. Ignoring the pain of the stones on her bare soles, she ran down the yellow-lighted street. She heard them running after her.

An image was floating through Gus Gritti's mind. In his fatigued imagination he could see his hands wrapped around the windpipe of the dumb sonofabitch who was responsible for putting him and his marines in Yemen.

The only problem was, there were multiple dumb sons of bitches. One was a two-star squid Battle Group Commander who didn't know an amphibious assault from a circle jerk. Another prime candidate was the pissant civilian tea sipper who thought marines were as expendable as Kleenex. Gritti would happily strangle either of them.

Another volley of AK-47 rounds pinged off the boulder where he hunched down next to Plunkett. The incoming fire had slackened, becoming more random. Darkness had come, and Gritti guessed that the *Sherji* would either make an all-out assault on the perimeter, or they would back off and wait for the next wave of helos.

"What's the count, Master Sergeant?"

"Seven wounded, three dead, not counting the chopper crews. Two on the first Cobra and one the second. Three wiped out in the Stallion."

"Where's Tillman?" Lieutenant Tillman was the weapons platoon commander.

"One of the wounded. Sergeant Gonzales reports that he has the north perimeter stabilized."

Gritti listened for a moment to the sporadic sounds of gunfire. He heard a single sharp crack of a heavy-caliber gun.

"Have the sniper teams deployed yet?"

"One in position with the Barrett," said Plunkett. "The second is getting set up now." The Barrett M82A1A sniper rifle was an extreme-range weapon. It was carried in several pieces by members of the team. The rifle's massive .50-caliber slug could spread terror by picking off unsuspecting targets—officers, vehicles, antennae—more than a mile away.

That was exactly what Gritti wanted now—some old-fashioned terror among the *Sherji* before they got their nerve up for another assault.

He still didn't know what they were up against. How many more did Al-Fasr have out there? Was another wave coming? He was getting assurances from *Rivet Joint*—the four-engined RC-135 intelligence-gathering jet in orbit offshore—that no heavy equipment was being deployed toward the marines.

Yeah, bullshit, thought Gritti. After this sucker trap, he had zero faith in the battle group's intelligence sources. At the moment he was willing to believe only what he could see, which included the knowledge that his marines had killed at least fifty *Sherji* during the initial assault. He also had seen the Hornets decimate another unknown number with their cluster bombs and twenty-millimeter cannon. Al-Fasr's artillery and most of his armor had gone silent after the bombing.

Now what? Warlord still wasn't saying whether the TRAP team was being lifted out, reinforced, or to be included in an all-out sweep through Al-Fasr's stronghold.

Gritti had never felt so frustrated. He didn't want to sit inside the perimeter waiting for the *Sherji* to make the next move, but he was too short on perimeter defenses to risk sending out patrols.

"Stay here," he said to Plunkett. "I'm going to check on the wounded."

There was a tiny lapse between transmissions. That was to be expected, Babcock assumed, when your call was scrambled, bounced off a satellite, and then unscrambled.

"You have not kept your word," he said.

"I gave my word that we would not retaliate after the air strike if you did not send in an assault force. But then you sent in an assault force."

"That was not an assault. You already know that the marine team was sent for no purpose except to retrieve the downed pilots. No other objective. Now the situation has become very complicated. The President has no choice except to order a strike."

For several seconds Babcock heard nothing on the secure telephone. He wondered if they had been disconnected. He heard only the tinny background hum of the satellite uplink.

"This can still be resolved," he heard Al-Fasr say. "My agents in San'a report that they are almost ready to initiate the coup. When they give the signal, my troops will seize the military headquarters and the government broadcasting station. We expect no resistance. I will control the Republic of Yemen."

"Fine. What about our marines on the ground? They have to be lifted out."

"It will be possible within a day or so."

"We don't have a day or so. I'm telling you, the United States will not tolerate letting its soldiers be trapped by an enemy. If you resist another recovery attempt, I cannot be responsible for what happens. A massive strike will follow."

Another silence of several seconds. "That would be a grave mistake, my friend."

Babcock was losing patience. "Why are you complicating

this? Why are you keeping our marines pinned down in Yemen?"

"To insure that your government keeps its word. We are at a crucial moment in this adventure, Whitney. I must be certain that the United States will not betray us at the last moment and install one of their puppets in San'a."

"You have to trust us. You have no choice."

"Choice? Oh, I have many choices. It is you who has no choice, not if you wish to have a presence in Yemen after I control the country."

"Just tell me that we can retrieve the marines. There must be no more ambushes, no resistance."

"Soon. I will inform you."

The tinny sound of the satellite phone abruptly ended. Al-Fasr was gone.

For a while Babcock stared at the silent phone in his compartment. More than ever, he had the feeling that he had made a pact with a terrorist. It was possible that someone would someday uncover a record of these negotiations with Al-Fasr. He would be judged by history as the visionary statesman who secured America's energy supply for the next decade. Or he would be pilloried as a traitor.

Which? It depended on what happened in the next four hours.

Al-Fasr emerged from the communications bunker, his eyes adjusting to the darkness. The temperature in the Yemeni highlands was balmy, the air dry and cool. He was wearing his usual working costume—tailored olive flight suit, polished boots, sunglasses. On his hip was the ever-present SatPhone and the nickel-plated SIG Sauer semiautomatic pistol.

He needed a walk in the night air to consider these recent developments. This last dialogue with Babcock was worrisome. The Americans would not wait much longer.

One part of Al-Fasr almost welcomed such a development. The U.S. Navy would execute one of their classic tactical air strikes, using all the wrong weapons and employing tactics used against adversaries like Iraq and Yugoslavia. It would be a pigeon shoot.

With his concealed air defense assets—the three remaining MiGs, an arsenal of SA-16 air-to-air missiles, and a battery of fifty-seven-millimeter AA guns—he would take a heavy toll on their strike fighters.

What if they also sent in an assault force?

He would be forced to yield territory, of course. But northern Yemen was perfect guerilla country, and the Americans had no stomach for close-in fighting in these hills. Nor would the citizens of the United States tolerate planeloads of their young men returning home in body bags. A ground war in Yemen was not on their list of options.

But he couldn't allow a strike. Not yet. Not until the long-standing business in the Gulf of Aden had been settled.

Where was Manilov?

His last communication from the submarine had been early yesterday. The Russian had signaled that he would be in a position to attack this morning.

And then nothing.

Who was this Manilov? Al-Fasr had never met him. Hakim, the agent who had secured the contract with the Russian, had been convinced that he was reliable. The submarine captain, according to Hakim, possessed a hatred of the Americans that nearly equaled Al-Fasr's.

Now Al-Fasr was not sure. In his experience, Russians were unreliable. They were temperamental romantics whose passions came and went like the tides. Today they hated Americans, tomorrow someone else. Vodka and corruption were the only constants in Russia.

Nothing had happened in the Gulf, according to his source aboard the *Reagan*. The radar operator on the guided missile cruiser *Arkansas* had reported a disappearing contact—a possible submarine—but the subsequent search had turned up nothing. For good reason, Al-Fasr had not solicited more information from his source about the contact. The source aboard the *Reagan* was uninformed about the Russian submarine and its mission.

Al-Fasr was concerned. Had the Russian captain been intimidated by the firepower arrayed against him and decided to run? Or were the American antisubmarine forces so effective as to thwart any attempted attack?

As he walked, he kicked at loose stones, thinking about the absent Russian submarine. Everything depended now on Manilov. Everything that Al-Fasr had planned for so long was waiting to come together, like electrons of an imploding atom.

He walked past the row of camouflaged bunkers that contained racks of missiles. Beneath a retractable screen, a huge dish antenna pointed at the sky and the constellation of satellites that served Al-Fasr's bank of communication devices. He could make an instant connection with any commercial telephone in the world, receive any televised newscast, conduct encrypted and scrambled conversations with anyone he chose.

Except Manilov. What the hell was happening?

She knew she was running away from the hotel, but she had no choice. She came again to the Al-Salah restaurant. For a second she considered dashing inside, asking for help. Then she saw the Yemenis come out—the same grim-faced men who had stared at her. They were watching, pointing, gesturing with their arms. One of them yelled.

Was he yelling at her, or giving directions to someone else?

The footsteps behind her were louder, closer.

A hundred yards away she saw a dimly-lighted T intersection. She sprinted toward the corner, then peered left and right. In either direction, the street narrowed and angled off into darkness.

Which way?

To the right. She rounded the corner and bolted down the narrowing lane.

She felt her heart pounding in her chest, her breath coming in short, heavy rasps. She wasn't a runner, never had been; hated it, in fact.

In a darkened doorway she heard something—a hissing noise. Cat? Rat? The spike of fear sent another surge of adrenaline through her. Her foot banged into an object, something metallic, a trash can, she guessed, sending it clattering into the darkness.

Behind her, the footsteps were louder, drawing nearer. She heard men's voices, heavy breathing. How many? Who were they? What did they want?

The narrow street meandered left, then right, twisting like a snake between the ancient buildings. She was lost, running without direction, plunging into the darkest heart of Yemen.

Another intersection of narrow lanes. To the left she saw a glimmer of light. She turned the corner, and saw a faint illumination somewhere ahead, around the bend in the lane.

She couldn't keep running. Her need for oxygen was critical, and her legs had become numb and wooden. It occurred to her that she should have asked Maloney for some sort of weapon. A gun, a knife even, to hell with legalities. She could have concealed it in the leather pouch she wore under her blouse where she kept ID cards and money and her passport.

Too late. The most lethal instrument in her kit was a tube of lipstick.

The dim light ahead was moving, casting a ray of light against the front of an ancient plaster wall. As she rounded the corner she saw that the yellow glow came from the headlights of a clattering automobile. It was stopped at the junction a hundred meters ahead. For what?

She slowed, suddenly more afraid of the car than of the running footsteps behind her. The car wasn't moving. It seemed to be waiting.

Drawing nearer she peered at the rickety vehicle. It was a rusty Peugeot, a diesel, judging by the clacking engine noise and the stench of exhaust. On its roof was an object, a dimly lit marker with Arabic lettering.

A taxi.

She saw the driver, a hawk-nosed man wearing a checkered kaffiyeh. As she ran to him, he regarded her with dark, interested eyes.

She reached inside her blouse, zipped open the leather pouch, and pulled out a folded piece of paper, the one Maloney had given her at the restaurant.

She thrust it at the driver. "American embassy," she said between gasps. "Please, please, take me there."

She heard the running footsteps in the lane behind her. The driver heard them too. He gazed at Claire, then he held the piece of paper up to the light.

The footsteps were loud, almost there. Wheezing voices, someone barking orders in Arabic.

"Please," she said. "They want to kill me."

The driver peered at the running figures coming toward them. He had dark, penetrating eyes, like the men in the restaurant.

Maloney's words came back to her. *They hate you. They hate us all.*

The driver looked at her. Abruptly he reached behind him and opened the passenger door.

There were four of them, running toward the taxi at full tilt. The first was reaching for the door handle just as the driver shoved the Peugeot into gear and floored it. In a shower of dust and dirt and diesel fumes, they sped down the street.

CHAPTER FIFTEEN

DELIVERANCE

Al Hazir, Yemen
0545, Wednesday, 19 June

The eastern ridgeline glowed orange in the approaching dawn. At exactly 0600, Gritti's voice crackled over the PRC-112 transceiver.

"Runner One-one, do you read Boomer?"

"Go, Boomer."

"Showtime, pal. Our train's coming in."

"Copy that. We've got our tickets ready."

As he put down the radio, Maxwell heard the faraway beat of inbound helos. He saw that B.J. was awake now. She lay under the thermal blanket, regarding him with large, somber eyes. Her face was still blackened, and her short, dark hair lay in a mat on her head.

She was a good-looking girl, he observed, even with all the glop on her face. Funny that he had never noticed before.

She caught him studying her. "I look like a witch, don't I?"

"More like a girl who's been chased by guerillas in Yemen."

She gave him a wan smile. "Are they going to pick us up?"

"They're on the way."

"Will the *Sherji* start shooting again?"

"I don't know. Maybe."

She slid the blanket aside and sat up. Her left arm was bound in the sling he had made for her. She winced when she tried to use the arm. "Owww, that *really* hurts."

"Are you able to move? We have to find a clear spot for the pickup."

"Don't worry. Nothing is going to stop me from getting into that chopper."

They gathered their equipment into the two satchels. With Maxwell in the lead, they started down the hillside. He didn't want to risk traveling far, only to an open area with enough clearance for the helo crew to pick them up.

It would have to be a quick snatch. The *Sherji* would know about the helos as soon as they did. He carried the .45 with a refilled magazine in his right hand, just in case.

On a terraced hillside he found a clearing that looked suitable. Not too steep, not so open that it would be a shooting gallery. He motioned for B.J. to take cover in the bushes above the clearing. "When they get close, we'll throw the smoke flare into the clearing. Don't wait for them to land. Just run out and let the crew haul you aboard."

She nodded. "Do you think it's gonna work?"

"We'll be okay."

She looked at him for a moment. "Well, just in case, I wanted you to know . . ." Her voice trailed off.

"Wanted me to know what?"

She swallowed, then finished. "I mean, you know, I wanted to say . . . thanks."

"You saved me first, remember?"

"Uh-huh." She kept her eyes focused somewhere over his

shoulder, avoiding his look. "That's not really what I meant. Look, I have to say this, just get it out and then drop it."

"I have no idea what you're talking about."

She blurted the rest. "I love you. That's all. It's crazy, I know, but I just had to say it and I promise I'll never bring it up again, okay?"

She turned away and began furiously retying her boot-lace.

Maxwell stared. He tried to think of something to say but nothing came out. He was still standing there, speechless, when the *Sherji* guns opened up.

The sounds of battle again spilled out of the hills.

The Whiskey Cobras came in low and fast, rockets blazing from their inboard pylons, streams of cannon fire spewing from the chin-mounted twenty millimeters. Behind them, approaching the marine perimeter, the big vulnerable CH-53E Super Stallions were already taking hits. The first cargo helicopter pulled up and made a hard turn away. Then the next. And the next. None were landing.

The *Sherji* gunners were getting the range on the helicopters.

"Abort, abort!" Maxwell heard Gritti calling on the SAR frequency. "Pull the Stallions back. It's another fucking ambush."

He heard the frustration in Gritti's voice. The Cobras were dueling with the *Sherji* gunners, concealed in a line of scrub trees south of the marines' perimeter. In the distance Maxwell heard the bullets pinging into the retreating Super Stallions.

Maxwell had already tossed his flare. Now a gush of orange smoke was wafting into the sky from the clearing where Maxwell and B.J. were huddled.

"Do you think the helicopters see us?" B.J. asked.

"I don't know, but the *Sherji* definitely can." He stashed the PRC-112 radio and yanked B.J. to her feet. "This is turning into another shooting gallery. We've gotta get out of here."

"Wait," she said. "They still might be able to—"

A nearby burst of gunfire cut her off. It was close, no more than a hundred yards. Without protest, she grabbed the satchel with her good arm and followed Maxwell down the hill.

Before they'd gone twenty yards, they heard the sudden racket of rotor blades. Maxwell turned to see a Cobra gunship pop over the ridgeline behind them. Directly behind the Cobra appeared a UH-1N Super Huey utility helicopter. While the Cobra flashed overhead, the Huey swept in over the clearing where Maxwell had thrown the smoke flare, kicking up a tornado of dirt and orange smoke.

A crewman in the three-man sling was descending from the hovering Huey. Maxwell and B.J. retraced their steps, running to where the crewman was just stepping to the ground.

He wore a cranial protector and goggles and a helmet-mounted radio. Blinking, coughing in the dirt and smoke, B.J. and Maxwell each slipped a loop of the sling around themselves as they had been trained. The crewman gave the sling a quick check, then flashed a thumbs-up to the man peering at them from the open hatch. With a lurch the sling yanked them off the ground, reeling them upward. While they were still clambering inside the cabin, the Huey's nose tilted forward and accelerated.

They sat facing each other in the drafty cabin of the helicopter as they sped back southward. Neither spoke. B.J., still black-faced and wearing her sling, huddled in the corner, avoiding Maxwell's eyes.

Out the open hatch he saw the column of Super Stallions following them. "How many did they pick up?" he asked the crewman, already knowing the answer.

He shook his head. "Just you, and that was blind-ass luck.

The Cobra gunner spotted your smoke. Nobody could get inside the perimeter."

B.J. gazed out the hatch at the empty cargo helicopters. "Al-Fasr knew they were coming, didn't he?"

Maxwell nodded. "Yeah, he knew."

"Surrender?" said Gritti. "He's gotta be kidding."

"No, sir," said Captain Baldwin, the compactly built young officer Gritti had sent over the wire. "The guy was dead serious. Says we have one hour. Then they come into the perimeter with tanks and artillery and a force of infantry. If jets or helicopters show up before that, they're gonna get shot down with missiles."

"And if we surrender?"

"He says we'll be fed and treated as guests, not prisoners."

Gritti snorted. "Hostages, he means."

Baldwin just nodded.

Gritti couldn't remember when he had felt so lousy. He had been in this goddamned hellhole for . . . how long now? Eighteen hours? No, longer.

At least the heavy firing had ceased. For the past three hours there had been just this eerie silence. No mortars, no sniper fire.

Then, this afternoon, a white flag. Three hundred yards away, from the tree line where the *Sherji* were concealed, an emissary in fatigues and a brown kaffiyeh walked out into the open. He carried a megaphone. He announced that he wanted to talk to the marine commander.

Gritti had dispatched Baldwin to talk to the emissary. After ten minutes of discussion, the young captain returned.

Now, through his fatigue, Gritti was trying to make sense of the situation. "Tell me what you think, Captain."

Baldwin glanced around, then said in a lowered voice, "I think it sucks. So do the rest of our marines. They want to know why we're stuck here without support. Where the hell are our reinforcements?"

Gritti nodded southward. "Out there. On the *Saipan* and the *Reagan.* Waiting for someone to give the order."

"Almost seems like they *want* us to be captured, doesn't it, sir?"

"The thought crossed my mind."

"Are we going to surrender, Colonel?"

Gritti didn't answer. For the third time that day, he called Warlord on the UHF/SAT channel. He had to speak quickly. The batteries were almost shot. Another shining example of America's high-tech hardware turning to inert shit when it was most needed. Here they were, surrounded by third-world guerillas—whose equipment was more sophisticated than their own.

Gritti gave Vitale a quick version of the surrender demand. *Let them chew on it,* he decided. *Let the brass earn their pay.*

"We copy that," said Vitale. "Stand by."

Gritti knew what that meant. Fletcher and his staff were wringing their hands over the problem. Maybe even running it past JTF or someone in the Pentagon. It also meant, he had no doubt, that the civilian pissant, Babcock, was making the call.

"Boomer," came Vitale's voice again. "We have reason to think that this channel—all the channels on your field radio—might be compromised."

"Good thinking. We figured that out yesterday." He knew the sarcasm was spilling out, but he didn't care. *Navy dip-shits.*

"Your orders are unchanged, Boomer. Maintain your perimeter while the situation gets resolved diplomatically."

"Listen!" Gritti exploded. "Before you people get the situation resolved diplomatically, the game will fucking be over. Do you understand that? When is someone going to get their thumb out of their ass and thump these guys?"

He laid down the microphone and took a deep breath. *Okay,* he thought, *you've gone over the edge. That takes care of your career. But what the hell? If you live through this, you get to go fishing.*

A long pause ensued. He thought maybe his batteries had finally expired.

The earphone crackled again. "Boomer, regarding the present situation, Warlord authorizes you to use your own discretion."

Gritti stared at the radio. He felt a wave of depression descend over him. *Use your own discretion.* They were telling him he could keep fighting or surrender. He was on his own.

Al-Fasr paced the hard dirt outside his command bunker. When he reached the end of the path, he turned and retraced his steps. As he paced, he kept glancing at the sky, listening for the sounds of incoming aircraft.

Nothing. An hour had passed since he had sent the ultimatum to the marine commander.

No response.

Al-Fasr had monitored the radio exchange between the marine colonel and his commanders. He had heard them, with typical American military ineptitude, tell the colonel to "use his own discretion." What did that mean? That he could surrender?

As if he had a choice.

Thinking about the incompetent commanders on the *Reagan* angered Al-Fasr. Why didn't they *order* the marine to surrender? Where was Babcock? Why wasn't he intervening? Babcock understood that the United States, more now than in recent times, had no stomach for casualties of war. They would vastly prefer seeing their soldiers held captive over being slaughtered like cattle.

Al-Fasr didn't think they would deliver more air support. He had demonstrated that he could shoot down helicopters as if they were guinea fowl. The fighters were deadlier, but they had shown no further interest in using them after losing three of the outrageously expensive craft in action.

Al-Fasr himself had no need for more dead Americans. What he needed now was fifty live prisoners. Holding the marines as hostages would discourage any further thoughts by the Americans about invading Yemen or assaulting his complex.

It would buy him the time to complete his mission.

Al-Fasr stopped his pacing and peered again at his watch. Perhaps he should go himself, engage in a personal discussion with the marine officer. If the man understood how hopeless his situation was, how pointless it would be to suffer more casualties, he would acquiesce.

What if he refused?

Al-Fasr considered for a moment. Time was running out, as well as his patience. With each hour the danger was increasing that the enemy—the United States and its evil leaders—would launch an assault on his complex in Yemen.

It would be the end.

He could not allow his mission to be thwarted because of the obstinance of one blockheaded foot soldier. If the marines did not lay down their arms and surrender peacefully, he would take the perimeter by force. Quickly and without regard for life. If any survived, they would become his prisoners.

"Are we going to surrender?" asked Baldwin.

Gritti looked at the young officer. He didn't have an answer. Not yet, anyway. He had been a marine for most of his adult life, but nothing had prepared him for this. Every fiber in his being told him to continue fighting, to tell Al-Fasr to go take a flying leap.

For what? So he and his young troops could prove that marines would rather die than surrender? What if they became hostages? If the military commanders running this operation were cynical enough to allow them to perish out here without throwing in massive quantities of firepower to support them, what the hell difference did it make? Better live hostages than dead marines.

The low point had come in the early morning, when the rescue helos had appeared—then turned back. He wondered what happened to the two downed Hornet pilots. They weren't coming up anymore on the SAR channel. It meant they were either picked up or captured.

Conspicuously, no jets had swept in low as they did yesterday to strafe and bomb the *Sherji.* It occurred to Gritti that maybe Baldwin had it right. Perhaps the guys on the command ship really expected them to surrender.

The thought caused the anger to rise in Gritti again. At this very moment, he knew twelve hundred marines were poised on the *Saipan* to swarm into Yemen. Within six hours' flying time, another two thousand could be on the ground here. In a day, an entire division could be airlifted from Europe.

Where the hell were they?

The fatigue was settling on him like a drug. Gritti let his mind wander for a moment. How would he be remembered after this episode? Marines had held their ground at Belleau Wood, at Iwo Jima, at Khe San. Of all the proud events marines celebrated in their long history, surrendering was not one of them.

He felt Baldwin's eyes on him. "Are we going to surrender?" he said, repeating the captain's question. "No, Captain, we are not."

Baldwin gave him a curt nod. "Roger that, Colonel. What do you want me to tell Al-Fasr's emissary?"

Gritti thought for a second. He didn't know much Arabic,

but he remembered something he'd learned in Riyadh. "Give him a little message from me. Tell him *Manyouk*."

"Which means . . . ?"

"Fuck you."

Baldwin's dirt-streaked face split in a grin. "Yes, sir. I'll tell him it's from all of us."

"What the hell are we waiting for?" Boyce demanded. "Why aren't we launching an alpha strike and a ground assault force now?"

Boyce's strident tone alarmed Fletcher. Navy captains weren't supposed to use that manner with admirals, particularly admirals who were their boss. The Air Wing Commander was coming close to insubordination.

"Because we follow orders in this battle group," said Fletcher. "I take mine from OpNav and the Joint Chiefs and the Commander of the Joint Task Force. I'll remind you that you take your orders from me. Lower your voice, Captain."

Boyce acknowledged with a short nod. He jammed his cigar back in his mouth and resumed pacing back and forth in the flag plot compartment.

Fletcher wished Boyce would leave the meeting, go busy himself with some air wing matter. He was becoming Fletcher's biggest headache.

Seated at the table in the flag conference compartment were Sticks Stickney, Guido Vitale, and Spook Morse. Watching from the far end of the room was Whitney Babcock, who had a telephone pressed to his ear.

Babcock hung up the phone and walked to the conference table. "That was the chairman of the Joint Chiefs," he said. "The President and the National Security Council are fully apprised of the situation. They have authorized an amphibious assault to retrieve the marines—"

"About damn time!" Boyce interjected.

"—subject to the Battle Group Commander's discretion,"

Babcock went on. "The on-scene commander—that's Admiral Fletcher—has been given a window of twenty-four hours to resolve the situation."

Boyce's eyes bulged. "Twenty-four hours? What for? We could launch the assault now—with full air cover."

"Absolutely not," said Babcock. "The marines are in no immediate danger. It is still possible that the situation can be resolved diplomatically. We don't want to start a war in Yemen."

At this Boyce exploded. "Excuse me, but this *is* a fucking war. What do you call it when you lose three jets and four helicopters and a dozen fighting men? We're supposed to negotiate with that sonofabitch?"

"That's enough, Captain!" snapped Fletcher, giving Boyce a fierce look.

"It's okay," said Babcock, his voice indulgent. He smiled at Boyce. "The President believes, as I do, that a diplomatic solution to this matter is preferable to a military one. We don't want to lose any more troops saving the ones who are already on the ground."

"This reminds me of Bosnia," said Boyce. "When the Serbs took the U.N. peacekeepers hostage and tied them to the targets they thought we might bomb. For a while we actually let them get away with it. Looks like we're doing it again."

"This isn't Bosnia," said Babcock. "There's much more at stake here than in Bosnia."

"More at stake than the lives of fifty marines?"

Fletcher was giving Boyce the look again.

"Gentlemen," said Babcock, "I suggest we adjourn while the admiral and his staff prepare the op plan. You'll be notified of any new development."

That was fine with Boyce. He crammed the stub of his cigar back into his face and stalked out of the compartment.

*   *   *

Farewell to Yemen, thought Claire. *And good riddance.*

From the window of the CH-53E Super Stallion, she watched the stuccoed buildings and the treeless landscape of San'a drop away. With her in the cabin of the big helo were two dozen other civilians, mostly wives and children of embassy staffers.

"Where are we going?" she had asked the loadmaster back at the landing pad. He was a marine gunnery sergeant, wearing full combat gear.

"Can't say, ma'am. Not until we're out of country."

The NEO—Noncombatant Evacuation Order—had come within two hours of her arrival at the embassy. The killing of Vince Maloney provided the final stimulus to remove the American presence from the troubled country.

She still had on the linen pantsuit she'd worn to the restaurant with Maloney. It was a mess—torn and soiled from falling in the street—but it was all she had. Everything she had brought to San'a—luggage, clothing, toiletries, notebook computer—was back in the Al Qasmy hotel.

Oh, well. The computer, of course, she would miss. All her working notes, e-mail, and contacts were stored in its memory. Still, she had only to remember the dark-eyed killers in the streets of San'a to be glad she was leaving, with or without a computer. She was alive, thanks to a Yemeni taxi driver whose name she never learned.

It took six CH-53Es, Marine aircraft from the *Saipan,* to retrieve the evacuees from San'a. Another half dozen, she was told, were fetching Americans out of Aden.

The column of helicopters threaded its way through the mountains east of San'a, then turned south and followed a valley to the sea. Claire was numb from fatigue and fear. She had dozed for no more than a couple of hours at the embassy, waking in a panic. Still vivid in her memory was the orange glare, the crackling heat from the funeral pyre of Vincent Maloney.

A wave of sadness passed over her again. *Poor Vince.* She had accused him of doing nothing, of protecting his job, and she was wrong. For all his sloppy habits and flawed character, he was a dedicated foreign service officer. Why did they kill him?

In a flash it came to her. It wasn't just him. She was supposed to die in the car with him. That was why they chased her through the streets. They wanted her dead.

They hate us all.

She drew her arms around herself and shivered in the drafty cabin of the Super Stallion. It was too much to comprehend in her exhausted condition. All she knew was that she hated Yemen. She wanted out of this god-awful place. She wanted Sam Maxwell. For all she knew, he was dead too.

She felt the helicopter bank, and she sensed that they were about to land. Through the open hatch the gray silhouette of a ship came into view. Behind it glistened a wide, white wake, sparkling in the morning sun.

The helicopter tilted back, slowing as it passed over the ramp of the flight deck. Claire felt the wheels clunk down on the steel deck. The whopping rotor noise hushed.

The hatch swung open, and in the backdrop Claire could see the distinctive, antennae-covered superstructure. Parked on the deck was a swarm of sleek, swept-wing jets.

A man wearing a cranial protector and a float coat over his yellow jersey appeared in the hatch. "Hope you had a nice ride, folks," he yelled over the engine noise. "Welcome to the USS *Ronald Reagan.*"

CHAPTER SIXTEEN

THE MOLE

Gulf of Aden
0800, Wednesday, 19 June

Lt. Dimitri Popov, the new executive officer, entered the control room and came to where Manilov was jotting on his notepad.

Manilov put down his pen. "Yes, Lieutenant?"

Popov looked nervous. "Captain, the men have requested that I . . ." His voice faltered.

"What is it, Popov? What do the men want?" *Here it comes again,* Manilov thought.

The officer swallowed hard and resumed. "They do not wish to seem disloyal. But they would very much like to know what will happen to them when we complete this mission. Where will we go, and what will we do with the *Mourmetz*?"

Manilov nodded. These were legitimate questions, ones that had nagged at him since they left the yard in Vladivostok. Whenever the problem drifted unbidden into his thoughts, he always came up with the same answer. He had no idea.

But that would not please the crew.

The truth was, Manilov did not want to think about it. He was approaching the single culminating moment of his life. All that had happened to him in the past nineteen years was a prelude to the events of the coming hour. He had no thought of living beyond today. To make plans for tomorrow, next week, to plot an escape to some balmy paradise would only undermine his resolve. He had to remain focused.

To carry out his mission, he needed the crew of the *Mourmetz*. They must believe that they would live through this day, that their lives would go on.

"You may tell them that we will escape with the *Mourmetz* and sail to a neutral port," Manilov said. "I have selected a place where the boat can eventually be reclaimed by its, ah, owners."

"And the crew, sir? What will become of them?"

"We will be met by representatives of Al-Fasr, who will deliver to us our remuneration for the mission. His agents will organize travel, clothing, new passports, that sort of thing. It has all been arranged."

Popov was nodding his head, pleased with the information. "This neutral port, Captain. May we know *which* neutral port? Capetown, perhaps? Mombasa?"

"It is best that we not divulge that information, since we are entering a combat situation."

Popov seemed satisfied with the answers, unaware that Manilov was inventing them on the spot. "I will tell the men. They will be greatly relieved to hear this."

"Thank you, Mr. Popov." He watched the executive officer stride out of the control room.

"Close the door," said Boyce.

Maxwell shoved the door closed, then sank into a chair at Boyce's conference table. He had been en route to the flag

intel compartment for debriefing when Boyce snatched hi
and pulled him into the office.

They were alone in the air wing office. Boyce clampe
down on his cigar and said, "I'm writing you a letter of re
rimand for violating the rules of engagement."

Maxwell looked at him, too tired to protest.

"You would have gotten a court-martial, but none of t
pussies on flag staff seems to comprehend what you actual
did. Fletcher won't make an issue of it because he wants a
other star. He knows he can kiss it good-bye if some report
digs up another Mogadishu story about him being respons
ble for GIs trapped in Yemen."

"So why am I getting a letter?"

"For the record. Off the record, I'm throwing it in the shi
can. Also off the record, what you did out there was exact
what I expected you to do. I'm pleased, and I'm su
Colonel Gritti is pleased. How're you feeling?"

"Terrific. Haven't felt so good since I had dysentery."

"Too bad. After they finish debriefing you upstairs, go g
yourself checked out by the flight surgeon. Then get son
rest and be ready to fly again. We're not finished with th
mess in Yemen, and I'm gonna need you. By the way, how
your wingman? I mean wingperson, or whatever the hell s
is. You know what I mean. I'll never get used to this gend
shit."

"B.J.'s okay. Except for the gunshot wound."

"The *what* wound? From . . . ?"

Maxwell hoisted his Colt .45. "From this."

Boyce was giving him a strange look. He shoved the cig
into his mouth and tilted back in his office chair. "Either I'
getting senile, or I'll swear you're gonna tell me you sh
your own wingman."

Maxwell poured himself a coffee. While Boyce gnawe
the end off his cigar, Maxwell told him about the SA-16 h
the ejection, then about the German mercenary pilot. He r

called for Boyce what Rittmann had said about the *Reagan* and about Al-Fasr having an informer aboard.

When he was finished, Boyce removed the cigar and said, "Un-fucking-believable. Then you had to go and shoot the sonofabitch."

"It was him or B.J."

"You got the daily double. Remind me to schedule you for remedial training on the shooting range."

With the other evacuees, Claire stepped onto the windswept deck, blinking in the bright daylight. It was the same surreal tableau she had left behind two days ago—howling engines, clouds of steam billowing from catapult tracks, men in colored jerseys and cranial protectors scurrying between airplanes, jets hurtling off the bow.

They were herded across the deck, through a door into the island structure. After they had removed their headgear and flotation vests, a chief petty officer led them to a briefing room. Another twenty civilians were there. Claire recognized several of the reporters from Aden, including Lester Crabtree.

They were still asking each other questions when the chief barked out, "Attention on deck!"

Into the compartment strode a tall man in khakis with an eagle on each collar. Claire recognized Sticks Stickney, captain of the *Reagan*. Stickney saw her and gave her a quick smile.

"Welcome to the USS *Reagan*," Stickney said to the group. "Chief Harkins will give you your berthing assignments. We're short of accommodations, I'm afraid. The women will be doubling up in staterooms, and the men will be billeted in temporary quarters we've set up on the O-3 level. For those who haven't been aboard a *Nimitz*-class carrier before, notice that there is a diagram with a map on how to get around. In the event I find it necessary to call the ship to general quarters, everyone aboard the ship—including guests—will go immediately to their battle stations. Yours happens to be right here. Please make it your business to know how to find this compartment."

The civilians all nodded, some grinning uncertainly.

"There is a list of areas that are off-limits. You will see these marked on the diagram in red. No one will be permitted to enter these areas without an escort."

More nods, a few more uncertain grins.

"For the media personnel, individual clearances have been issued for each of you. Note that there will be a mandatory press briefing at ten-hundred each morning in this compartment so long as you're aboard. Any of you who misses the briefing or is discovered in a restricted area without specific consent from me will be confined to your quarters, under guard, until you can be offloaded from the ship. Any questions?"

They stared back at the captain. No one was grinning now.

A man raised his hand. "Captain, that seems rather draconian. Does that mean we're at war?"

Stickney gave him a thin smile. "What it means, sir, is that we are on a heightened readiness status. Which is also why each of your dispatches must be cleared through our public affairs office."

The man rose to his feet. "That's censorship. We happen to represent the free press, and this is a breaking story. We have a right to report the news as we see it."

This time Stickney wasn't smiling. His eyes drilled into the reporter, trying to read his name tag. "Mr. . . . ?"

"Crabtree. Lester Crabtree, Reuters."

"Mr. Crabtree, you are a guest aboard this vessel because you've been evacuated from a hostile country, courtesy of the U.S. Navy. If you attempt to transmit one byte of information that has not been cleared by me, I will have you locked in the brig. If this conflicts with your sense of a free

press, I will make arrangements for your immediate return
to Yemen. Is that your wish, sir?"

A look of shock passed over the reporter's face. "No," he
muttered, and sat down.

Spook Morse, Maxwell couldn't help noticing, had eyes
like a ferret. The intelligence officer's tiny brown eyes were
darting from one person to the other at the conference table.

"I'll remind you that this is a debriefing, Commander
Maxwell," said Morse. "I get to ask the questions."

The combination of fatigue and frustration was catching
up with Maxwell. All he wanted to do now was reach across
the table and seize Morse by the neck.

As if reading his thoughts, Boyce spoke up. "Everyone
should bear in mind that Commander Maxwell has been
under considerable stress," he said. "Let's just get on with
the debriefing, Spook."

Morse flashed the briefest of smiles, then continued. "Beginning with when you ejected from your aircraft. How did
you happen to find this mercenary pilot, Rittmann?"

"I didn't. He found me. I was still putting my gear together, getting ready to move out. He showed up and held
me at gunpoint."

"What happened then?"

Maxwell related the story about Rittmann's interrogation
and the knife, and the timely appearance of B. J. Johnson.

Morse was making notes on a yellow pad. He looked up
and said, "After you and Lieutenant Johnson had Rittmann
in your custody, what did you do?"

"We asked some questions."

"I see," said Morse. "You consider yourself an intelligence specialist, do you?"

Maxwell felt his temper flaring again. He received a
nudge in the ribs from Boyce. He took a deep breath and
said, "I considered myself a downed pilot in serious trouble.

It seemed possible that Rittmann might have informatio
that would keep us alive."

"And what, exactly, did he tell you?"

At this Maxwell paused. He felt Boyce's eyes on him. I
his mind Maxwell could see Rittmann, bitter and cynic
glowering at him in the darkness.

"Go ahead, Commander Maxwell. What did Rittmann te
you?"

"He described the Al-Fasr order of battle. He thinks si
MiGs, maybe four left, ten or fifteen APCs, six Dauphi
choppers, and a large supply of SA-16 missiles."

Morse was scribbling furiously. "Did he say where th
MiGs came from?"

"Libya, via Chad."

"Did he say where the MiGs launched from when the
pounced our strikers?"

"He claimed they came from Eritrea. I was working o
that when he told me about the *Reagan*."

"What about the *Reagan*?"

"He said that Al-Fasr intended to sink it."

Morse looked up from his notepad. "He wasn't serious?

"Very serious. He said that Al-Fasr hates the U.S. Nav
and his ultimate goal is to sink a carrier."

This brought a chuckle from the intelligence office
"How did he say this feat would be accomplished?"

"He said he didn't know. I pressed him on it, but h
clammed up. Soon after that was when he grabbed Lieu
tenant Johnson, and I had to shoot him."

Morse's eyes were locked onto Maxwell. "Did it occur t
you that Rittmann was a valuable intelligence source? Wh
did you kill him?"

That exceeded Maxwell's limit. He glowered at Mors
and said, "Because he pissed me off."

Boyce intervened again. "That's enough. We've bee
over that. He already told you he shot the sonofabitch be

cause it was the only way to save Lieutenant Johnson. You have obviously run out of intelligent questions. It's time that Brick got some sleep."

Without waiting for Morse to object, Boyce rose from the table and Maxwell followed. They left the intel compartment, closing the door behind them.

In the passageway, Boyce glanced around, making sure they were alone. "Why didn't you tell him what Al-Fasr said about having intelligence sources aboard the *Reagan*?"

Maxwell shook his head. "I don't know. Something, a gut feeling maybe. You said Morse already suspects a spy on the *Reagan*?"

"Yeah. Are you saying you think it might be him?"

"No. But it's possible, isn't it? In any case, we can assume it's someone who knows what Morse is doing. If he's running a witch-hunt, the real mole will know it. If he hears what Rittmann said, he'll go deeper underground."

Boyce rubbed his chin. "Okay, here's how it's going down. Not exactly the approved routing, but I'll take the heat for it later. I'll relay the whole package of what we know directly to my old boss, Admiral Riley, at the National Security Agency, and let him deal with it. If he wants to handle it without getting our flag intel in the loop, that's his call. We're off the hook."

Maxwell nodded his head wearily. "Then can I hit Spook Morse?"

"No. You can hit the rack. That's an order."

"Aye, aye, sir."

Fletcher gazed through the thick-paned glass of the flag bridge compartment. The darkness over the Arabian Sea was almost total. No stars, no moon, not even lights along the Yemeni coast. To the south lay the horn of Africa, black and inscrutable beneath the invisible horizon.

Fletcher was in a contemplative mood. For once, briefly

at least, he was free of the troublesome presence of Whitney Babcock, who had retired to his stateroom to handle some classified message traffic. Traffic with whom? Chief of Naval Operations? The Joint Chiefs? The President, perhaps?

Or the terrorist, Al-Fasr?

It was a joke, he thought. He was the Carrier Battle Group Commander—the ultimate combat post for a naval officer—and here he was, subservient to a civilian with less military experience than most of his teenage sailors. Babcock conducted briefings with CNO, the Joint Chiefs, and the Joint Task Force Commander for Southwest Asia—without Fletcher's participation.

Most amazing, though, was how Babcock had maintained control of the operation. With the initial go-ahead from Washington to launch a strike against Al-Fasr, Babcock had insisted that it be a Navy show, with minimal participation by Air Force or Army units. Fletcher could imagine the bitching going on at the Air Force tactical fighter bases in Saudi, and inside the Army's elite Delta force. They had been excluded from the show.

Gazing out at the darkness, a feeling of dread passed over Fletcher. Against his judgment, he had let Babcock establish the rules of engagement. He had been in the Navy long enough to know what would happen next. Inevitably he would be summoned to account for the losses they suffered in Yemen. America hated body bags.

He had presented his concerns to Babcock. As usual, Babcock was dismissive. "The objective is worth the price."

"I've lost over a dozen American lives and six vastly expensive aircraft. May I ask what objective is worth that sacrifice?"

"A strategic objective, not a tactical one. It's not your job to devise strategy, Admiral, just implement tactics. All you need to know is that the southern Arabian peninsula is a region of far greater importance than you can appreciate. What we're accomplishing here will affect the future of America."

Fletcher had not been pleased with the answer. Nevertheless, he kept his silence.

"Excuse me, Admiral." Fletcher's thoughts returned to the present. He turned to look at Meyers, a lieutenant commander on his staff. "The new op plot that you ordered is ready."

Fletcher slid his half-frames down over his nose and gave the plot a quick scan. The plot included a depiction of the Arabian Sea and its surrounding coastlines. Symbols and arrows denoted the location and direction of each element of the battle group as well as their projected positions.

Fletcher traced with his finger the courses of the *Reagan* and the amphibious assault ship *Saipan,* the two leviathans of the battle group. At 0300 they would turn in place and cruise westward to a position near the mouth of the Red Sea, above the Greater Horn of Africa. Eight other warships, including the Aegis cruiser *Arkansas,* would assume new positions in the formation.

He noted the coordinates of the new position, then grunted his approval. It would be sent, as it was every day, by satellite UHF to the commanding officers of each ship in the battle group.

Fletcher scribbled his initials at the bottom of the op plot and handed it back to Meyers. "Transmit it encrypted to all elements. Copy Fifth Fleet and JTF."

"Aye, aye, sir."

The compartment allotted to the working press contained three steel chairs and a standard Navy gray desk. On the desk was a single military-issue ship's telephone.

When the other reporters had gone, Claire pulled up one of the chairs and telephoned the air wing office. A yeoman grilled her about who she was and why she wanted to speak with the Air Wing Commander.

She heard Red Boyce's booming voice. "Claire Phillips? How the hell did you get back aboard the *Reagan*? You're amazing."

"I'm a reporter. I get paid to be amazing." She told him about Aden and San'a and the noncombatant evacuation.

"What can I do for you?"

"Tell me what happened to Sam Maxwell. I know he was shot down."

There was a long silence, and Claire's anxieties started kicking in again. *Please, God, let him be okay.*

"Where are you now?"

She told him.

"I'll be right down." His voice seemed oddly casual, as if he were enjoying himself. "I have some news that may interest you."

In accordance with Admiral Fletcher's orders, the updated op plot was transmitted to all elements of the *Reagan* battle group.

Thirty minutes later, a figure emerged on the viewing deck, aft of the island superstructure on the *Reagan*. The carrier was slicing through the Gulf of Aden at a speed of fifteen knots, but the impression from high up on the island, 120 feet above the water, was one of motionlessness. The ship seemed suspended in a black void, swept by an invisible breeze.

For several minutes the man stood with his hand on the rail, letting his eyes adjust to the darkness. He wanted to be sure that he was alone. Sometimes at night he encountered strangers—sailors gazing at the stars or listening to music or, as he'd seen one night, sipping prohibited alcohol.

It was possible, he supposed, that he could be watched by observers using night-vision equipment. But all they would see would be a man using some sort of device—a tape or CD player, a radio, a stargazing scope. If danger was imminent, he could always throw the device over the rail.

Merely possessing the SatPhone, of course, did not implicate him in espionage. Even though the use of such a device was prohibited aboard Navy ships at sea, he could claim ignorance. The phone was a commercial product, manufactured in the United States. Ironically, it utilized the same constellation of satellites the U.S. Navy employed for the transmission of their own secret data. The only additional feature installed in his phone was the scrambling software, which was also a commercial product.

He extended the antenna and punched in a twelve-digit number. After fifteen seconds, he heard a sequence of beeps. He was connected.

From his inner pocket he retrieved the document. Using a red penlight, he read the data from the op plot into the phone. When he was finished, he waited until he received another series of beeps.

Received and acknowledged.

He tore up the document, then made balls of the shredded pieces and let the wind carry them into the blackness of the Gulf.

From the end of the table in the flag conference compartment, Fletcher glowered at Vitale and Morse. "This is unbelievable. Someone passing our op plots as soon as we write them? Explain to me how that can happen."

Morse said, "The technicians down in surface watch who monitor the emissions from the battle group just alerted us. Their RF scan was picking up stuff in a format that didn't come from us. The transmissions are scrambled, but there's no doubt they contain classified data about our movements."

"What ship is it coming from?"

"Right here. The *Reagan*."

"What kind of transmissions?"

"Some kind of commercial phone, they think. Iridium Global Star, SatPhone, one of those. We don't know which yet."

"How long has this been going on?"

"Longer than we'd like to think. It might explain how A Fasr has anticipated our operations at every turn."

Fletcher slammed a fist onto the table. "All this high-tec equipment we invent to protect our secrets, and someon can blab them to the enemy like they had their own go damn private line."

For a moment, the room was silent. It was not Fletcher style to use obscenities—he liked his image of a souther gentleman—but his anger was spilling over. "How ca someone transmit secrets from one of our ships without o knowing it?"

Vitale and Morse looked at each other, neither having a answer. Vitale said, "I've instructed the surface watch off cer to set up a scan that will alert us as soon as he transmit In the meantime Spook has narrowed our list down to handful of possibles—those with access to classified data– and we're running checks on them."

"That's what you said before. You still haven't caugh anybody. What did ONI say when you reported the intell gence leak?" ONI was the Office of Naval Intelligence, lc cated in Suitland, Virginia.

Vitale pulled a printout from the stack in front of hin "They passed it to NSA, and a counterespionage team is c its way to the *Reagan*. They should be aboard by tomorrow The NSA—National Security Agency—was the intelligenc unit responsible for cryptology and security of sensitive in formation.

"What kind of team?" asked Fletcher.

"FBI, CIA, probably. Might include a cryptologist, computer hacker, guys with special tools."

Fletcher turned to gaze out the window of the flag bridg

He saw only blackness. No horizon, no distinction between the overcast sky and the dark void of the ocean.

Spies. Moles. Agents. The whole thing was incomprehensible to him. People aboard his ship with telephones communicating via satellite? What the hell had naval warfare come to?

Gritti looked at his defenses and nodded in approval. He didn't have many advantages over the enemy, but at least the terrain was in his favor. The ground sloped away to the north, where the *Sherji* had their guns and armor concealed in a grove of trees. They were too far away to be reached with mortars, but he had a solution for that.

He guessed they had waited until nightfall, thinking the perimeter would be easier to breach. It was a blessing. Under cover of darkness he would deploy patrols outside the perimeter, including mortar teams. If the *Sherji* got to the perimeter, they could find themselves attacked from *behind* as well as frontally.

He finished his tour of the team's positions and hunkered down beneath the boulder where he had established a command post. Inside the makeshift shelter were Master Sergeant Plunkett and Captain Baldwin.

"Snipers?" Gritti asked.

"In place, covered the best they can be," answered Plunkett. "Two with M-forties and two Barrett teams."

"Keep 'em moving. Two rounds max; then change cover."

"Yes, sir," said Plunkett. "They know their job."

Gritti smiled at the mild rebuke. Plunkett was right. Marine snipers were not only professional marksmen, they were masters of camouflage and concealment. The snipers were essential to any chance they had of surviving another attack. If they could pick off the *Sherji*'s leaders and point men from a great distance, it might strike a little terror into them. Maybe change their minds about dying for Allah.

The M40A1 sniper rifle was a hellish weapon. The heavy-barreled gun could reach out a thousand yards and nail a ten-inch target. Even more hellish was the Barrett M82A1A fifty-caliber special-purpose rifle. In the hands of a trained marksman, the Barrett could stop targets as large as a truck.

Gritti saw that the wind, though light, was out of the south. Another advantage.

"Be ready with the smoke," he told Baldwin. "If they start shelling, we lay the smoke and get the fire teams deployed. Maybe we can surprise the sons of bitches with mortars and a couple of ambushes."

"Yes, sir."

If the *Sherji* waited until sunrise and began their attack in broad daylight, Gritti would put down a thick blanket of smoke. Under the smoke, the marine fire teams would move out.

Would it work? *Probably not,* Gritti thought. But it would be sweet. Since they'd landed in this shitty place, it had been Al-Fasr, time after time, who had delivered the surprises. Now it was their turn.

Waiting for the battle to begin, Gritti sensed the same old doubts nagging at him. He had fifty able marines. Against how many? Several hundred, perhaps more. The *Sherji* would whittle at them until the core of their fighting strength was nil.

Is it worth it?

It was not too late. He could still show a white flag.

No. The thought of surrender was unacceptable to him. Not while they could fight, not while they could inflict pain and death on the enemy.

Gritti checked his watch. Dawn was coming soon. He wondered what Al-Fasr was thinking. Would the *Sherji* wait for daylight?

Would *he*? *Hell, no.*

As if triggered by the thought, the first rumble from the

valley below reached him. It sounded like a thunderclap. A fifty-seven millimeter, he guessed.

Claire took a deep breath, then knocked on the stateroom door.

She had a cute little speech prepared, something to the effect that he ought to let her know before he went off on a hiking excursion in the Middle East. He ought to be more considerate than to leave a girl without telling her when he was coming back. It was supposed to be funny.

Then a panicky thought. *I look like utter hell.*

She should have taken the time to fix her hair, put on some makeup. She was still wearing the torn pantsuit that made her look like a refugee, which, of course, she was. After learning from Red Boyce that Sam was alive, she had run directly to—

The door opened.

He had been asleep, and judging by the lined face and reddened eyes, he needed it. He was wearing a white T-shirt and warmup shorts. His left arm was bandaged from something.

Maxwell's face broke into a happy grin. "Claire!"

The cute little speech vaporized. She threw herself into his arms. The words tumbled out. "Sam, Sam . . . I thought I'd lost you . . . I missed you so much . . ."

He held her until she'd run out of words, ignoring the curious officers walking past the doorway. Then he pulled her inside and closed the door. He took her face in his hands and kissed her.

She pressed herself against him. For a precious moment they were finally together. She was safe and Sam was safe and nothing—not Yemen, not the Navy, not Jamal Al-Fasr— mattered.

For a long while he continued holding her. He stroked her

as he nuzzled her neck. Her own numbing fatigue melted away. She held him tightly, wanting him.

He tilted her chin back and looked at her. "I believe we've reached the point where I'm supposed to tear your clothes off and take you to bed."

"I believe we're aboard a U.S. naval vessel, Commander."

She knew the Navy's position on the matter. Intimate relations aboard a naval ship were taboo. But they were alone, the door was closed, and she didn't give a damn about the Navy's taboos.

Maxwell seemed to be going through his own thought process. He kept his hands on her shoulders, regarding her with those icy blue eyes. "I'm the guy who tells his people not to do this."

"Is making love to me in your stateroom a bad thing?"

"It is if you're the squadron skipper."

Claire sighed. That was what was so contradictory about Sam Maxwell. He had no problem breaking rules, but he refused to be a hypocrite about it.

"Will we still spend a week together when this is over?"

"Anywhere you want."

"Doesn't matter as long as I'm with you. And it's not in Yemen." She shivered, the memories of her last night in San'a coming back to her. "Hold me, Sam. I'm afraid. Something bad is happening, and I don't know what it is."

He tousled her hair. "You're safe now."

"I don't know what safe means anymore."

While he held her, she blurted the whole story—San'a, Vince Maloney, his revelation about Al-Fasr and Whitney Babcock. And the car bomb.

Maxwell didn't speak. She wondered if he understood what she had told him.

Finally he said, "We have to tell this to someone. The part about Al-Fasr and Babcock."

"To whom? The intelligence officer? What's his name— Morse?"

He shook his head. "Not yet. I want you to tell this to Red Boyce, verbatim, exactly like you just told me."

"Do you think it could be true, the part about Babcock making a deal with Al-Fasr?"

A cloud passed over Maxwell's face. "It fits."

"Why is Babcock letting the press cover the story now? After kicking us off before?"

"Publicity. Self-glorification. He thinks the situation is almost wrapped up, and he wants to make sure you portray him as the brilliant leader who took command and made it happen. While you're aboard this ship, he can control whatever information is dispensed to you."

She nodded. "Then that's why we had that little briefing this morning. The message seemed to be that we had better give him plenty of camera time; otherwise we'd find ourselves back in a tent at the Aden airport."

She shivered again. The accumulated stress of the past two days was bearing down like a weight on her. She put her head on his chest. "Sam, I never thought I'd miss you so much."

He took her in his arms, stroking her hair . . .

Thunk. Thunk.

Maxwell glared at the door. "Damn."

"It's okay," Claire said. "It might be important."

He opened the door. Standing in the passageway, staring as if she were seeing an apparition, was B. J. Johnson. She saw Claire inside the room. For a long frozen moment the two women held eye contact. Volumes of unspoken communication passed between them.

Abruptly, B.J. whirled and bolted down the passageway.

Maxwell called after her: "B.J.! What was it you—"

She was gone. Maxwell stood in the passageway, shaking his head.

CHAPTER SEVENTEEN

BAITING THE TRAP

Southern coast of Yemen
0240, Thursday, 20 June

At a speed of three knots, the *Ilia Mourmetz* crept from its hiding place beneath the littoral shelf. Manilov was doing his best to keep the boat at a depth of seventy meters, where it was still concealed under the thermal layer. At this snail-like speed, the big bow planes of the *Mourmetz* were almost useless.

The risk was enormous. The Americans had displayed too keen an interest in the brief contact they had picked up when he last peeked with the *Mourmetz*'s periscope. For several hours they had bombarded the area with sound signals and sonobuoys, passing back and forth with their helicopters and S-3 Vikings equipped with magnetic anomaly detectors.

Finally they had given up the search.

Or had they? As he had done earlier, Manilov tried to place himself inside the mind of the American commander.

If you were unable to pinpoint the precise location of the enemy submarine, what would be your next course of action?

Elementary. You backed off and waited for the enemy submarine to emerge from hiding.

As he was doing now.

Of course, it was possible that the Americans had never confirmed a positive contact and were merely being cautious. That would be typical of the U.S. Navy, with their ridiculously overstuffed budgets, to waste tons of ordnance and fuel in such a stupid exercise.

Everything depended now on the Kilo class's legendary stealthiness. The special single-shaft, seven-bladed screw was driven by the nearly silent Elektrosila electric motor. Anechoic rubber antisonar tiles covered the *Mourmetz*'s hull. The submerged vessel was as indistinguishable in the sea as a mackerel.

At the large three-paneled control console of the MGK-400EM digital sonar, Warrant Officer Borodin tracked the enemy's ships. The MGK-400 was one of the retrofits the *Mourmetz* had received in the Vladivostok yard. The new sonar was working in passive mode now, emitting no acoustical signals while it absorbed and plotted the signatures of every moving vessel in a thirty-kilometer radius.

Peering over Borodin's shoulder, Manilov estimated that it would take two, perhaps three hours to reach the firing position he wanted. Each of the *Mourmetz*'s six torpedo tubes was loaded with a SET-16 torpedo containing a two-hundred-kilogram warhead. He had four more torpedoes in racks with the new fast-loader at the ready. More than he would ever need.

Manilov wished again he had the firepower of a Russian Navy submarine on routine patrol. He would have television-guided electronic homing torpedoes that he could manually switch to alternative targets if necessary. He'd be equipped with Novator antiship missiles in the event he was thwarted from firing his torpedoes. The Novators would deter the destroyers that would come racing like greyhounds to kill him.

Deterring aircraft was another matter. Before the voyage to Iran, he had insisted that the *Mourmetz* be armed with Igla SA-N-10 infrared-guided anti-aircraft missiles. Only after a bitter argument did the flotilla commander let him requisition three of the sophisticated missiles. Three! Nothing more than a flea bite against the overwhelming airpower of the Americans. Still, the presence of the missiles gave him a small comfort.

For two hours the *Mourmetz* crept southward, deeper into the Gulf of Aden. Manilov repeatedly checked the MVU-110 combat information computer for updates on the target.

At least the enemy was predictable. The great acoustic mass of the target ship—it had to be the *Reagan*—continued to move in a large northeast-southwest oval pattern. It was probably in accordance with the wind direction, launching and recovering aircraft, then returning to the original position to repeat the operation. Smaller warships—the destroyer screen—seemed to be following random patterns, crisscrossing the path of the carrier.

Judging by the benign activities of the destroyers and the absence of sonar-dipping helicopters, Manilov was sure that they had not been detected. He uttered a silent thanks to the *Mourmetz*'s designers—the Rubin Central Maritime Bureau in St. Petersburg.

Russians had proven themselves to be inept at so many things. But they knew how to build submarines.

"I'm Commander Morse," said Spook, forcing a smile on his face as he rose to shake hands with the members of the counterespionage team. "Welcome aboard the *Ronald Reagan.*"

The counterespionage team had landed aboard the *Reagan* on the 0700 COD—a C-2 Greyhound cargo hauler—

from Dubai. Carrying their equipment in padded bags, the four men were taken directly to the flag conference compartment and introduced to Admiral Fletcher and Spook Morse.

Two were from the FBI—the bureau's counterintelligence division—and two from the Central Intelligence Agency. Each was a civilian, wearing khakis with no insignia. Each had a guarded, suspicious manner about him.

As if they were investigating *him*.

Morse kept the smile frozen on his face. In truth, he despised these agents. As civilians, they operated outside the military chain of command. They were invariably abrasive, disrespectful of rank and authority.

These were no exception.

One of the FBI agents, an encryption specialist named Korchek, dropped his bag and looked at Morse. "What's your job here, pal?"

"Flag intelligence officer. You can call me Commander."

Korchek seemed to find this funny. "Yeah, sure thing."

Admiral Fletcher appeared not to notice the agent's manners. "Make yourselves at home, gentlemen. You can set up your equipment here, if you like. Commander Morse will see to it you have whatever you need."

More than ever, Morse was concerned about security. He had insisted that the briefing be restricted to those with an immediate need to know—himself, Vitale, and Morse. None of the air wing officers, especially the contentious Boyce, had been informed. Nor had Whitney Babcock, for reasons that Morse did not want to explain to Fletcher. Not yet.

"It will take us a while to get set up," said Korchek. He had a pockmarked face and oily, slicked-back hair. "In the meantime, this room is off-limits to everyone except me and my agents, unless we specifically invite you to come in."

"Now wait a minute," said Morse. "This happens to be the—"

"Never mind," said Fletcher. "We're going to cooperate with these gentlemen. Tell us what you want us to do."

The agents exchanged private nods. Korchek said, "First thing, I want the files on each of your suspects, plus the locations of their work and sleeping quarters."

Fletcher nodded, and Morse handed a stack of files to Korchek.

"Here's the way I see your situation," said Korchek. "You've got encrypted data leaving this ship in one of two ways, maybe both. Somebody is transmitting with a satellite comm device. That's an easy one to home in on, if we know when the guy is using it. Another way is over the intranet, which is a hell of a lot more complicated because there are so many goddamn computers on this boat."

"How can someone be sending classified data via the ship's intranet without our comm monitors reading it?" said Morse. "Everything that goes out is monitored."

"That's what you think. They could be using some kind of plain-language encryption. Like a how-are-you-I'm-fine note to their mom, but embedded in the language is another message."

"You mean, something that can be decoded with a key?"

"You got it. Old-fashioned shit, but very sophisticated in the short term, especially if they change the key every time they transmit. The problem is identifying whose computer it comes from."

Morse said, "Sorry, but that theory won't wash. I happen to know that we can trace any e-mail on this ship to the sender."

Korchek gave him a withering look. "What you happen to know happens to be flat-ass wrong, pal. There are tools out there—really magic shit—that can totally erase the origin of any Internet message. And there's even newer stuff available that can undo the erasure. And so on. It all depends on who owns the latest stuff."

"Do you people have the latest stuff?"

"Do you think we'd travel all the way out to this barge if we didn't?"

"There it is," said Korchek. Two hours had passed before he summoned Morse and Fletcher back to the flag conference room. "Anything in any bandwidth or medium that goes out from the *Reagan*—satellite phone, Internet connection, you name it—we should be able to identify and locate it."

He pointed to a device that looked like a laptop computer. Depicted on its color screen was a schematic view of the O-3 level of the carrier. He tabbed a key, and the screen flipped through a series of displays showing each separate deck and level on the ship.

"This is a CRC-91 integrated location processor. We feed it data from whichever homing monitor first picks up the transmission. In less than a minute after we've intercepted the transmission, we get a plot here on the screen. We can tell within twenty yards where on the ship the signal is coming from."

Fletcher peered into the screen. "This is amazing. Why don't we have this equipment running full-time on our ships?"

"This is cutting-edge stuff," said Korchek. "Still highly classified. The more exposure it gets, the sooner someone figures out a way to beat it. We don't want any more people than absolutely necessary to know this exists."

"Okay," said Morse. "That takes care of satellite communcations. What about Internet traffic?"

Korchek pointed to a notebook computer with a flickering blue screen. "See this? This box is running a software package that can detect embedded encryption. If we feed this program a normal e-mail message, then encrypt it and hide it in other normal message traffic, this little package can go after it and track it down like a bloodhound."

Fletcher was shaking his head. "You lost me. How is that going to help us?"

Korchek gave Fletcher one of his patronizing smiles. "Simple. We're going to send a plain language message, one that we know how to read. Then we're going to get your spy to send the same message, encrypted."

Fletcher was frowning. "And then . . . ?"

"And then this software—it's called Omnivore—performs a million or so content comparisons, runs some very fancy algorithms that one of our borderline nutcases invented, and looks for a match. When it finds one, it shows up right here on this screen."

"How will you know whose computer it came from?"

Korchek tapped the stack of files Morse had given him in the afternoon. "Every one of your suspects has a personal computer. Every one of them now conveniently contains an invisible command—a thing similar to the 'cookie' that on-line merchants sneak into your computers. It will respond to a query from our computer in this room. Then we'll know who sent the encrypted message."

"Amazing," said Fletcher.

"No," said Korchek. "Pure fucking magic."

TO: CVBG ELEVEN, ALL COMMANDERS
FROM: COMMANDER CARRIER BATTLE GROUP
ELEVEN
COPY: OPNAV, JOINT TASK FORCE, SOUTHWEST
ASIA, COMMANDER FIFTH FLEET
CLASSIFICATION: SECRET
SUBJECT: CVBG REVISED POINT OF INTENDED
MOVEMENT
REFERENCE: OP PLAN 04061830Z

UPDATE PIM USS REAGAN 0600Z 20 JUNE; AIR
OPS SCHEDULED 0630Z, LAUNCH AND
RECOVERY POSITION N1248W5105. CVBG
DISPOSITION DELTA.
NEGATIVE ACKNOWLEDGE.

Fletcher finished writing the message, then handed it to
Korchek. "There. The revised point of intended movement
amounts to about seventy miles. Normally, it would go to all
the escorting vessels in the battle group."

Sitting at his computer, Korchek quickly pecked the message onto the screen using two fingers. When he was finished, Fletcher gave the message to the flag office yeoman,
who delivered it to the ship's communications center for
transmission to the battle group.

The counterespionage team members had their remote
monitoring gear set up at three different stations—on either
side of the island and one on the fantail. Korchek waited in
the flag conference compartment to see if the spy took the
bait.

It took four hours. Korchek and one of the CIA agents,
Dick Mosely, were alone in the compartment.

"Gotcha!" yelled Korchek as the data began streaming
into his computer. Encoded, the message didn't make sense,
not without going through the laborious computer decryp-
tion process that sometimes worked quickly and sometimes
didn't. Korchek didn't care. The match was positive. Omnivore had detected an encrypted version of Fletcher's message.

It also identified the computer from which it was sent.

Korchek jotted down the information on a steno pad.
Then he reached into his briefcase and pulled out the holstered Glock semiautomatic. He shoved a full magazine into
the grip, then slipped the pistol into the holster in the small
of his back.

Korchek summoned the two marines who were stationed in the passageway. They wore BDUs, helmets, and flak jackets. Each carried an M16A2 combat rifle.

"Where we going, sir?" said one of the marines, a burly sergeant.

"Big-game hunting, Sergeant."

Cmdr. Lou Parsons had been in his stateroom for five minutes when he was startled by the pounding on the door. He replaced his spectacles and went to the door.

"Yes?" he said, peering into the passageway.

It was the last word he could utter. The door slammed into his face, knocking his spectacles off, sending him reeling backward into a steel locker.

Korchek went in first. He seized Parsons's arm, spun him around, slammed him against the locker. He bent Parsons's arm up into the middle of his back.

"Ahhhhh!" Parsons screamed in pain.

"Frisk him," Korchek ordered the marine sergeant.

"Goddammit!" Parsons yelled. "Who are you?"

The marine patted the officer down. "He's clean."

"What's this all about?" Parsons's voice was outraged.

"Cuff him," said Korchek. "Hands behind the back."

While the two marines put the plastic handcuffs on Parsons, Korchek pulled on a pair of latex gloves and began searching the stateroom. He went through each drawer, dumping the contents onto the deck. He found nothing.

Next he went through the locker, yanking clothes off the rack, going through the pockets of every garment.

"What are you doing?" Parsons demanded, wriggling against the firm grip of the two marines. "What the hell are you looking for?"

"Shut up," said Korchek.

He continued ransacking the officer's room. He lifted the mattress, looked under it, then yanked off the sheets and bedding. He pulled out the drawers beneath the bunk bed and hauled out the folded clothing, throwing it all onto the deck.

Nothing.

Korchek looked around. His gaze came to rest on the safe that was mounted on the steel desk. He turned to Parsons, who was staring at him myopically. "What's the safe combo?"

Parsons glowered back at him. "Go fuck yourself."

"Okay, smart-ass, have it your way. Watch how a professional does it." Korchek pulled up the steel work chair and sat in front of the safe. From his satchel he produced a stethoscope.

Parsons stared in dismay as Korchek went to work. Even the marines seemed awestruck. After he inserted the earpieces, Korchek held the rubber listening cup against the dial of the safe. His brow furrowed in concentration, he carefully rotated the dial, listening for the tumblers to click into place.

He nodded, hearing a faint click. He reversed direction with the dial.

Another click. Back the other way.

It took less than two minutes. "Kid stuff." He yanked off the stethoscope. "No challenge at all."

He twisted the handle of the safe and the foot-square door swung open. Korchek reached into the safe and came out with a manila envelope. He set it aside, then reached in again. This time he came out with a vinyl case.

Parsons stared. "What the hell is that?"

A knowing smile spread over Korchek's moonscaped face. He unsnapped the vinyl case and pulled out the device. He turned it over in his hand, studying the keys, the liquid crystal display, the retractable antenna.

The marine sergeant peered at the device. "What is that thing?"

"Evidence," said Korchek. "Enough to send some asshole to prison for the rest of his life."

"So we've got our man," said Morse.

Korchek's feet were propped up on the table in the conference compartment. He had a toothpick in his mouth. "Not unless he confesses."

"What do you mean? We have enough to send Parsons to Leavenworth for a hundred years."

"There's still a thing called 'due process,'" said Korchek. "The case against him so far is circumstantial."

"We caught him sending an encrypted classified message. We found the SatPhone in his safe. What's circumstantial about that?"

"All we know is that the message was on his computer. We don't know how it got there, or whether he sent it. As for the SatPhone, that's incriminating, but no one has actually proved that he owns the thing or that he used it for any purpose."

"Look, Mr. Korchek, you sound more like a lawyer than an investigator."

"I *am* a lawyer, pal. Don't presume to tell me how to do my job."

At this, Morse's eyes widened and his chin tilted upward.

Korchek recognized the look. It was the same look the military intelligence twits always wore when they had just lost a round with him.

Korchek was enjoying himself. Being a civilian, he made it a point not to take shit from officers, especially officers like this asshole Morse. Korchek was a Chicago cop before going to law school and being recruited by the FBI. He seized on the cryptology job when it came along because he loved messing with computers, and, besides, it got him out of the grunt work regular agents had to do.

Korchek said, "It isn't an airtight case. Maybe Parsons is your guy, maybe not."

"Parsons fits all the profiles," said Morse.

"What do you mean by that?" said Admiral Fletcher, watching the exchange from the end of the conference table.

Morse tossed a thick manila file folder onto the table. "This is his background file. Top of his NROTC class at Michigan. Ditto at the Navy postgrad school in Monterey. BS in electrical engineering, master's in industrial management. Served two previous shipboard tours as comm officer—one aboard the *South Carolina,* then a WestPac cruise on the *Lincoln.* Here's an interesting part: He put in a long tour—four and a half years—at NATO Forces South Command in Naples as a liaison officer. Had top-secret clearance and, according to this report, had contacts with foreign military counterparts all over southern Europe."

"Is that when you think he was compromised?" Fletcher asked.

"Nothing turned up in any of the security checks they ran on him—except one glaring susceptibility. He's subject to blackmail."

"Because of . . . ?"

"His sexual orientation."

Fletcher nodded. "He's gay, you mean?"

"It came to light back when he was at grad school. Seems he's always had a companion. Several, actually."

Fletcher shook his head. "How did he get a top-secret clearance? I thought homosexuals were considered a security risk."

"Not in the new military. There was a legal challenge to that one back in the last administration, and the Defense Department backed off. You can't yank someone's clearance for that specific reason."

Fletcher looked at Morse, then at Korchek. "That makes a pretty good case that Commander Parsons is our spy."

"I'm certain of it," said Morse.

Korchek lowered his feet to the floor. He spat his tooth-pick on the deck and left the room.

"Babcock?" said Boyce.

He sat at the small conference table in the air wing office, gnawing on a cigar. Claire had finished telling her story. "You mean that's what this circus in Yemen is all about? Whitney Babcock and Yemen's oil?"

"That was Vince Maloney's take on it. The same oil reser-voir that Saudi Arabia is tapping apparently extends some-where past Yemen's border, wherever that is. He said that no one has ever officially determined the border."

"But you're saying that someone will? Like Al-Fasr, if he takes over the country?"

"Not if. When. It's supposed to happen very soon."

"And it's supposed to happen with the collusion of . . ." He left the sentence unfinished.

She nodded.

He removed the cigar and stared at the bulkhead for a mo-ment. "I'm not saying that I believe it—not yet—but if it's true, it means our battle group is being used not to fight a terrorist, but to accommodate the sonofabitch."

"Worse than that," said Maxwell. "It means we're letting him keep our marines in Yemen just so he can have a bar-gaining chip."

Boyce thought for a second. "Claire, we have to get this guy Maloney out here and report this to—"

"Too late."

"He won't talk?"

"He was killed by a car bomb." As Boyce listened in amazement, she told him about the Toyota and the killers in the street.

"Holy shit." He shook his head. "You nearly went with him."

She nodded.

"You know, Claire, without your guy to give us testimony, all we have is conjecture, nothing more."

Maxwell spoke up for the first time. "We can pass it to Admiral Fletcher."

Boyce snorted. "You mean Babcock's lapdog."

"Maybe he doesn't know the real story about Babcock."

"There's no limit to what Fletcher doesn't know."

"He's still a naval officer. He's the guy who's supposed to be our boss."

"He's supposed to be a lot of things that he's not." Boyce couldn't contain the disgust in his voice. "Just what do you think Fletcher's going to do?"

Maxwell shrugged. "I don't know. It's possible that the man has a tiny speck of integrity left in him."

"I doubt it. But what the hell, I've been wrong about everything else in this operation." He picked up the phone on the yeoman's desk. He punched a number, listened for a moment, then said, "This is Captain Boyce. I need to speak with Admiral Fletcher."

Manilov hated moving at this slow speed. Even though they were ninety meters deep, the *Mourmetz* was swaying like an unsteady barge.

He stood behind the two technicians—Borodin, the sonar operator, and Keretzky, the combat information computer specialist. By the heavy acoustic mass in the sonarman's screen, Manilov knew he was seeing the passive return of the aircraft carrier. Cruising between the *Mourmetz* and the *Reagan* were two escort vessels. Frigates or destroyers? He couldn't tell. Beyond the carrier he saw the shape of another heavy ship. A supply ship? A cruiser?

Again Manilov wished that he had a full arsenal. With wake-homing torpedoes or, even better, the new video-guided weapons, he could steer the warhead around the interfering ships, select his target, punch the hull of the big carrier at any place or depth he chose.

Not today. Not with his complement of torpedoes. But even though the SET-16s were old, they possessed the same advantage as the aging submarine—stealth. For the first portion of their journey, the SET-16 emitted no signal, gave no clue to its presence. Even its low-noise propulsion system was difficult to detect, especially at its initial running depth of a hundred meters. Not until the torpedo was within a thousand meters of the target would Manilov activate its active sonar homing system.

He had another reason to like the SET-16. He had fired dozens of them in training, and by now he understood each foible of the torpedo. As with every primitive weapon, the trick was to get close. Very close.

They were eight kilometers from the *Reagan*. Close enough for a shot. He didn't want to rush and miss. A torpedo meandering through the midst of a battle group only meant quick and certain death for the submarine.

All these years he had waited. Another twenty minutes didn't matter. The *Reagan* was coming to them.

No one in the submarine's control room was speaking. Borodin and Keretzky were hunched intently over their consoles, filtering and refining their data. Popov, the former dissident and newly promoted executive officer, was supervising the planesman, monitoring the boat's progress.

Manilov felt a surge of pride. It was just as he had always imagined actual undersea warfare. They were creeping into the heart of the enemy's fleet. The danger was more real and immediate than any submariner had faced since World War II.

The doubts of yesterday had evaporated, as if the dead Ilychin had taken the crew's fears with him. The men were ready for whatever happened. True Russians. They had assigned their lives and fortunes to fate.

The minutes ticked by. Everything depended on the *Reagan*'s adhering to the original point of intended movement, which they had received, via Al-Fasr, over twelve hours ago. Since then the *Mourmetz* had been unable to extend its antenna to receive or transmit any new information.

Manilov was concerned. What if the weather had caused a change? What if a new operating plan had been ordered? What if—

Remain focused, he ordered himself. *No more what-ifs.*

He could see by the MVU-110 display that the largest acoustic mass—it had to be the *Reagan*—was still coming toward them. It meant that the ship's point of intended movement had not changed, at least not yet.

Ten minutes.

He had delayed the last and most critical decision of the mission. He could fire torpedoes from this depth, ninety meters down, aiming on the *Reagan*'s passive sonar return and using the MVU-110 to calculate the firing solution. At a close enough range, the kill probability was acceptable.

Or he could be more certain. He could ascend to periscope depth, obtain a positive visual bearing and range on his target—and raise the kill probability by several percent.

He would also raise to a hundred percent the chances that they would be located.

Manilov turned away from the console for a moment and massaged his temples with his fingertips. He didn't need to calculate the odds again. During the first few minutes after the sub hunters obtained a track on his periscope, their initial search area would be tiny. But if they were denied a precise starting point, the area to be searched swelled exponentially. With each passing minute, the submarine's radius of movement expanded.

Safety or certainty? It was the submariner's dilemma.

Manilov's dream of destiny was thundering in his Russian soul like an ancient refrain. How long had he waited for this moment? Had he come this close so that he could take the safe course? Miss the target, then run like a fox fleeing from hounds?

Five minutes. The *Reagan*'s course was unchanged. The acoustic mass was still coming toward them.

"Ascend to thirty meters," he ordered in a quiet voice.

Every pair of eyes in the control room swung toward him.

"Ascend?" asked Popov.

"You heard correctly," said Manilov. "Thirty meters. When we're stabilized in firing range, we rise to periscope depth."

Popov was staring at him. So were Borodin and Keretzky. They understood the decision he had just made. Manilov looked at each of them, a gentle smile on his face. They could refuse to follow his orders and there was nothing he could do about it. After this moment, nothing else mattered.

Seconds ticked past. A silence as heavy as the grave hung over the control room.

"Aye, Captain," answered Popov, breaking the spell. "Ascend to thirty meters."

CHAPTER EIGHTEEN

TARGET REAGAN

Gulf of Aden
0920, Thursday, 20 June

"Range?"

"Six thousand meters, Captain. No change."

Manilov peered at the console and nodded. The waiting was over. It was as close as the *Reagan* would come on its present course, passing them broadside, then opening the distance again as it cruised to the southwest.

"Ready tubes one, two, three, four."

"Tubes one, two, three, four loaded and ready."

Theoretically, two torpedoes were enough. If he could get two into the hull of the *Reagan*, he had a chance to sink her. He would fire a salvo of four, fanning them to account for any evasive maneuvering the giant ship might attempt. The remaining two tubes—the *Mourmetz* had six available—he would save for defense while the fast-loader replenished the first four tubes.

The *Mourmetz*'s survival depended on the magnitude of surprise. If they detected his periscope on their radar—

and he was certain they would—he might fend off incoming destroyers with his remaining torpedoes. Antiship missiles would be better, but those were left behind in Vladivostok.

Without doubt, aircraft would come after them too. For that he had a solution. "Igla batteries on standby," he ordered.

"Aye, sir. Already done."

The Igla SA-N-10 was a short-range, heat-seeking anti-aircraft missile that could be launched from beneath the surface. With only three of the missiles on the *Mourmetz,* Manilov knew he couldn't wage a sea-air battle with the sub-hunting aircraft. But the enemy wouldn't know how few he had. When they saw one of the vicious little killer missiles bursting from the sea, it might hold the helicopters and S-3 Vikings at bay long enough for the *Mourmetz* to break out of the search envelope.

Manilov felt the eyes of his crewmen on him. He saw no rancor, no hostility, just determination and faith. For this tiny speck in time, the lives of Yevgeny Manilov and his fellow submariners were intertwined.

"Gentlemen," he said, "I'd like you to know it has been a privilege to serve with you. Remember that we are Russians. We will fight with honor."

"Aye, aye, Captain," said the executive officer. Each man in the control room nodded in agreement.

"Ascend to periscope depth."

Petty Officer Third Class Wanda Rainey, the nineteen-year-old radar operator in the *Arkansas*'s Combat Information Center, was the first to see it. Fresh from the Navy's "A" school, she had arrived on the Aegis cruiser two months ago.

"Contact, bearing 290, range seven thousand yards," Rainey called out.

The watch supervisor, Lt. Cmdr. Walt Finney, walked over and stood behind her. "Track?"

"Track 2672," she said, reading the number that appeared on her screen.

"Link it to flag ops on the *Reagan,*" said Finney.

"I was just about to— Whoops." She peered intently at the console. "It's gone."

Finney leaned closer, also peering into the display. "Damn!"

"Just like the one the other day. Four sweeps, then nothing. No course, no speed."

Finney shook his head. "Here we go again. We spend the rest of the day chasing another damn ghost—a whale or some piece of floating junk."

"Do you still want me to link it over to flag ops?"

"Wait a sec." He continued to watch the screen, just in case the contact reappeared. Like most antisubmarine warfare officers, he knew you could get yourself branded as a hipshot if you were too quick to jump on spurious targets, sending ships and airplanes running off after shadows. With experience and a cool head, you evaluated these things. You made a judgment call before you called in the hounds.

Half a minute later, he was still evaluating when the sonar operator called out, "Sonar contact, screws in the water, bearing 310, range—" The operator's voice went up an octave. "Oh, man! It's a . . . it's a torpedo! Range five thousand yards. No . . . make that *two* torpedoes!"

As he called out the contacts, his voice rising in pitch, he punched a mushroom-shaped button that sent an alert to the combat information rooms of every vessel in the battle group.

Finney ran to the sonar console. "What the fuck is going on?"

"Three torpedoes!" yelled the sonarman. "No, goddammit, we got four now! Four torpedoes in the water, Mr. Finney. Looks like two hundred down, bearing 305, four thousand yards inbound."

Finney felt the hair stand up on his arms and neck. He knew the information on the sonar screen was being repeated on a similar screen in flag plot in the *Reagan*.

This is a drill, he thought. It had to be some kind of stupid damned exercise to see if all this gee-whiz shit really worked. No one had fired a real torpedo at an American ship for over fifty years.

"Bearings 300, 290, 280, range three thousand to five thousand yards," called out the sonarman. "All tracking on *Reagan*."

Finney could see it now on the screen. The computer-enhanced display made the sonar returns look like pulsing yellow worms. They were in trail, diverging in about a five-degree spread.

All moving at forty knots toward USS *Ronald Reagan*.

Finney turned to the tactical display, checking the disposition of the battle group. The *Reagan* was nestled in the middle of the formation like a mother hen surrounded by her chicks. On her starboard beam were the two screening destroyers, *O'Hara* and *Royal*. On the far side, cruising off the carrier's port beam, was the ammunition ship *Baywater*. Two miles in trail was Finney's own ship, the Aegis cruiser *Arkansas*.

The torpedoes were on a path that would take them between the lead destroyer, USS *Royal*, and the trailing vessel, USS *O'Hara*. Every ship in the battle group was maneuvering now, responding to the torpedo alerts.

"The decoys are deploying," reported the sonar operator. He pressed his finger against the display, leaving an oily print. Finney could see the sonar echoes of the decoys as they spilled into the wake of each warship.

This is no goddamn drill, he thought. With morbid fascination he stared at the pulses on the display. Real ships, real torpedoes. It didn't make sense. Who the hell would be firing torpedoes?

Reagan was in a hard turn to starboard. Both *O'Hara* and *Royal* were making their own tight turns to starboard inside the massive ship's radius. On the screen the decoys were casting a large acoustic clutter behind each ship.

The torpedoes were ignoring the decoys.

"Two thousand yards and closing," called out the sonar operator.

Rear Adm. Langhorne Fletcher kept his eyes riveted on Claire. As she told him what she had heard in San'a, his eyes steadily narrowed. The features of his lean face seemed to harden.

The four of them—Fletcher and Claire, Boyce and Maxwell—sat at the small table in the admiral's stateroom, directly below the flag bridge.

"Ms. Phillips, you're quite sure that your contact, Mr.—"

"Maloney."

"You're sure he mentioned Mr. Babcock by name?"

"Yes, sir. Several times."

"And you are certain that he—"

Fletcher stopped. A drink skittered across the glass table. The ship was leaning hard to the port side.

Fletcher's telephone was ringing. While the others at his table watched, he snatched the phone up, listened for a moment, then said, "I'm on my way."

Heading for the door, he grabbed his float coat survival vest. "Thank you, Ms. Phillips. Your story has cleared up several issues for me. Now all of you get to your stations. The *Reagan* is about to go to general quarters."

He dashed out of the compartment, feet pounding on the steps as he ascended the ladder to the flag bridge.

The voice of the bosun's mate boomed over the public ad-

dress system: "General quarters! General quarters! All
hands, man your battle stations. This is not a drill."

As Fletcher stormed into the flag bridge, he saw that
everyone in the space—Vitale, Morse, the flag chief yeoman—was staring at the tactical display on the bulkhead.

He looked at the display and said, "Oh, shit."

The torpedo tracks were pulsing yellow on the screen.
They were close, diverging at separate angles toward the
Reagan in a fan-shaped pattern. The first two were sliding
off behind the carrier's stern. The second two torpedoes
were aimed amidships.

Fletcher realized again that a hundred-thousand-ton aircraft carrier didn't dodge and weave like a destroyer. Not
even a cruiser, which was the largest vessel he had commanded, could elude forty-knot homing torpedoes.

The torpedoes must have been fired at close range. And
they weren't going for the decoys, which meant they were
still in an inactive guidance mode.

Not much longer, he knew.

Instinctively he looked out at the whitecapped sea for the
distinguishing white wakes. He knew that they didn't really
look like that. These fish were almost surely running deep,
invisible from the surface. Not until the last few seconds of
their run would they arc upward to explode into the hull of
their target.

A blur of impressions sped across Fletcher's mind. Something had gone horribly wrong, and it was just coming to
him what it was. The traditional military chain of command
had been severed. Instead of reporting directly to his superiors—Fifth Fleet, CincLant, the Chief of Naval Operations—
Fletcher had been receiving orders from a civilian official.
Worse, he had not reported the circumstances to the officers
above him.

It was a classic mistake—one that had been committed before with tragic consequences.

Torpedoes were homing in on the USS *Reagan,* and the dismal thought occurred to Fletcher that it was his fault. In his great vanity and hubris, he had taken leave of his judgment. He had allowed his command authority to be suborned by—

The door to the flag bridge burst open. A white-faced Whitney Babcock entered the compartment as the first torpedo struck the *Reagan.*

CHAPTER NINETEEN

THE HUNTERS

Gulf of Aden
1003, Thursday, June 20

The dull *whump* rumbled up from somewhere in the bowels of the ship. Five seconds later, another *whump,* this one closer, more pronounced. It came from the starboard side, somewhere amidships. The *Reagan* shuddered from the muffled explosion.

Fletcher gripped the handhold on the bulkhead and stared at the display. "That's two. Where are—"

"Missed," said Vitale, pointing at the display. "The last two just missed the rudder."

Klaxons blared. Over the public address came the bosun's mate's voice again: "Torpedo impact, fourth deck aft and amidships! Away all damage control teams. Set condition Zebra."

Fletcher slid into his tall padded chair and picked up his sound powered telephone. "CIC, flag. Do you have a lock on the sub?"

"Yes, sir," came the voice of the Combat Information

Center duty officer. "*O'Hara* has a contact and is on the way with *Royal* backing up. We're launching Seahawks, and they're getting a sonobuoy screen down."

"I want that sonofabitch blown out of the water."

"We're doing our best, Admiral."

Fletcher put down the microphone. He saw Babcock staring at him.

"This is crazy," said Babcock. "Who . . . who would torpedo the *Reagan*?" All trace of color was gone from his face.

"You tell me."

"What do you mean?"

"While you were playing geopolitics with a terrorist, he was setting us up for a torpedo shot. It was a sucker play, Mr. Babcock." Fletcher spat the words out.

"That's absurd."

"Is it? Why else has he been yanking us around, holding off an air strike to rescue our marines?"

"Watch your tongue, Admiral. I'm the one who put you in this job and I'll—"

He stopped when he saw the look on Fletcher's face. Fletcher was staring at something over his shoulder, out the port side of the flag bridge.

An orange fireball was mushrooming skyward. Above the fireball rose an oily dark cloud. Flaming debris spurted like roman candles from the inferno.

It took six seconds for the concussion to reach the *Reagan*.

The blast hammered the stormproof windows of the flag bridge. Down below, men and equipment were swept across the open flight deck, tumbling over the fantail, into the catwalks, over the side. Masts ripped from their moorings on the island, crashing down to the deck below. A Seahawk helicopter, just lifting from the fantail, flipped into a vertical bank and plummeted into the water.

"Jesus," said Guido Vitale, looking up in shock. "What the hell was that?"

"The *Baywater*," said Fletcher. "The ammunition ship. It took one of the torpedoes that was meant for us."

Horrified, Fletcher stared at the carnage one and a half miles off the *Reagan*'s aft port quarter. The stricken ship was blown in half. The severed stern of the *Baywater* was already sliding into the sea, flames leaping from the shattered structure. The forward half was low in the water, burning fiercely. As Fletcher watched, an explosion boiled up from the hull. Another black mushroom belched into the sky.

Guido Vitale made a sign of the cross. "God help them."

Fletcher stared at Babcock. "God help us all."

"Fast contact, Captain. A hundred and fifty degrees, three thousand meters. A destroyer, by the screw noise."

"Course and speed?"

"Twenty knots, accelerating, turning to an intercept bearing."

One of the escort destroyers, thought Manilov. *No surprise.* After a possible periscope echo, then a salvo of torpedoes, they were coming with all their knives drawn. They would never stop hunting the submarine that torpedoed their battle group.

"Forward five knots, descend to eighty meters."

"Aye, Captain."

Manilov had always wondered how it would feel at this moment. Never in his years of naval service had he actually fired a shot in anger. Now, not one but *four* shots. Three had found targets.

It was as sweet as he could have hoped.

At least two torpedoes had impacted the *Reagan*. No secondary explosions, which was unfortunate. He could only hope now that the two-hundred-kilogram warheads had sufficiently ruptured the carrier's hull, destroying its watertight integrity. Even sweeter would be an explosion in one of the ship's reactor spaces, setting off a nuclear calamity that would force them to scuttle the ship.

But the sweetest moment—the kind that submarine skippers enjoyed in their wildest fantasies—was the explosion of the escort vessel. The magnitude of the blast was enough to nearly rupture the ears of the sonar operator. The hull of the *Mourmetz* had trembled from the blast, causing the crew in the control room to break their silence and cheer at the top of their lungs.

"More screw noise, Captain. Another destroyer. And something else . . . I think an aircraft. A helicopter . . . yes, definitely a helicopter."

Manilov made a quick calculation. With the destroyer's fast closing speed, they would merge in four minutes, presuming the destroyer had a reasonable fix on the submarine's last position. The helo would be overhead at approximately the same time. Each, he knew, carried Mark 46 or Mark 50 antisubmarine torpedoes.

The *Mourmetz* had only minutes left to live.

"Ready tubes five and six. Reload the first four."

He saw Popov and Borodin look at each other and nod. *Good,* thought Manilov. *Let them know how Russian submariners fight.*

"Tubes five and six ready, Captain."

"Stand by." He leaned over the combat computer operator's console. "Do we have a firing solution on the destroyer?"

"Almost. It will be difficult with the target head-on."

"Compute a solution for the trailing destroyer. We'll put one up both their snouts."

"Aye, Captain. It is not precise, just the passive return."

"I understand. It's our only option."

Manilov studied the display for another ten seconds, choosing his moment. "Fire five."

"Fire five," Popov responded.

The *Mourmetz* shuddered as the 2,220-kilogram weapon burst from the number five tube.

Manilov did another quick check of the display. "Fire six."

"Aye, fire six."

Another shudder. The sound of the exiting torpedo filled the interior of the *Mourmetz*.

"The aircraft, Captain. Coming closer. It will fly directly over us."

"How many?"

"Just one is all I am detecting."

"Ready the missile battery."

"Ready with Igla one, sir."

Manilov had no idea whether the Igla missiles even worked. The SAM battery had been a retrofit on the Kilo-class submarines and was never tested before the *Mourmetz* was sold to the Iranians. No matter. If fate allowed the missiles to function today, then they would.

He waited until he was sure the helicopter was within the killing envelope of the short-range Igla. The trick was not to wait too long. The helicopter would launch its torpedo.

"Stand by . . . Fire!"

He heard a rumbling noise, the sound of the compressed air blowing the weapon free of its battery in the sail. Then the gurgling sound of the missile ascending to the surface.

"Ahead five knots, course a hundred and sixty-five degrees, maintain eighty meters."

The warrant officer looked up at him. "Captain, that course will take us directly beneath the enemy aircraft carrier."

"Precisely."

The first SH-60B Seahawk—call sign Blister Eleven—was on a mission of vengeance. The pilot and his crew had barely escaped the blast from the exploding *Baywater*. His squadron mates in Blister Ten—the second SH-60B that launched ten seconds behind them—had been smashed like a cheap toy into the sea behind the *Reagan*.

The ATO—the airborne tactical officer in the helicopter—had already loaded the fix from the disappeared periscope sighting into his mission computer, then correlated the information with the recorded tracks of the four torpedoes, datalinked from the *Arkansas*.

While the helicopter accelerated low over the water, he saw it—*Yes!*—the sub-tracking solution on his situational display. He knew where the sonofabitch was. Computers were really pretty cool gadgets.

For the pilot of the Seahawk, it was coming down to a race between him and the destroyer. He could see *O'Hara* leaving a wake like a speedboat as it sliced through the water. Somebody was going to kill the submarine and he was damned well going to make sure it was Blister Eleven.

Making a good 120 knots, the helicopter skimmed over the top of the *O'Hara* on the same course—330 degrees—headed for the sub's position. According to the ATO's inertial navigation computer, the sub was exactly one mile straight ahead.

The ATO wanted to pin him first with a pattern of sonobuoys. They'd make a high-speed pass, drop the sonobuoys, then swing around while the ATO tightened the noose on the sub. Then they'd put the Mark 50 in the water.

The sub was dead meat.

Then he saw something peculiar. It lasted for only a second—while he was looking straight down. It was deep, maybe a hundred feet down, leaving a thin bubbly stream behind it. *Shit! Not another fucking torpedo—*

His thoughts were cut short by the warning from the *O'Hara*: "Blister Eleven, SAM in the air! You're targeted, Blister!"

For an instant the Seahawk pilot was confused. *SAM? No way.* He had just seen a freaking *torpedo* in the water. What the hell was this about a SAM?

Because he had already overflown the submarine's last position, the pilot didn't see the geyser that erupted from the sea behind him. Nor did he see the trail of fire from the missile as its rocket motor ignited and propelled it toward its target.

"Flares! Flares!" yelled the ATO over the intercom, aware of the danger.

It was the right call—but too late. The decoy illuminators had just begun streaming behind the Seahawk as the heat-seeking Igla missile boresighted the helicopter's left turbine exhaust pipe.

The sensor operator, seated at his console behind the ATO, was the first to know. He felt the lurch, heard the shriek of tortured machinery. He looked up in time to see the left turbine engine of the Sikorsky explode, taking away the overhead cabin section. To his horror, the whole structure was ripping upward through the big whirling rotor blades.

The mortally wounded helicopter rolled over in a sickening death dive. Tumbling end over end, the Sikorsky plunged 150 feet into the Arabian Sea, barely making a splash before it disappeared beneath the waves.

Alerted by sonar to the torpedoes, both destroyers were spewing out acoustic decoys in a trail behind them. On the bridge of the *O'Hara,* the captain ordered a violent evasive turn, then swung the narrow bow of the destroyer back toward the oncoming torpedo. He glimpsed the thin white wake as the torpedo sped twenty yards past his port beam.

Farther behind and with more time to evade, the captain of the *Royal* simply took a thirty-degree offset course, putting several hundred yards between his destroyer and the path of the enemy torpedo.

The *Royal* churned directly to the spot where the Seahawk had crashed, checking for any sign of survivors. The *O'Hara* continued at flank speed toward the presumed position of the enemy submarine. Loaded in her tubes and ready to fire were two Mark 50 lightweight anti-submarine torpedoes.

But the *O'Hara*'s sonar operator no longer had an active contact. Nor did the antisubmarine warfare technicians on the *Royal*. Or the cruiser *Arkansas*. Without a positive sonar ID on the Kilo class, it was too dangerous to launch a homing torpedo. The same torpedo could home in on a friendly vessel.

Within minutes three more destroyers had joined the search. Two additional Seahawks arrived with MAD gear and sonobuoy dispensers. A forest of sonobuoys was soon bobbing on the water, providing acoustic cross-bearings for the sub hunters.

But the contact was lost. The submarine had vanished.

The damage reports, relayed from the *Reagan*'s captain, were coming in faster than Fletcher and his staff could process them. Four enlisted sailors and five officers, including the group operations officer, were busy on the sound-powered telephones.

"Damage control teams are still getting the inner hull plug in place in the aft machinery room bulkhead."

"Flooding in the turbine rooms is contained. All six compartments are sealed, and the plug should be in place within an hour."

"Situation now stable amidships fourth deck. Firefighters report the machinery room blaze is under control."

"Three men overboard still missing, and five picked up by the destroyer *Crockett*."

"*Reagan*'s engineering officer reports number four steam turbine and propeller inoperative."

"*Joplin* has finished taking all survivors from *Baywater* aboard."

At this, Fletcher turned to Vitale. "How many?"

"Only eighteen, several of them critical. A hundred-ten missing and presumed lost in the explosion, including Commander Borden, the skipper."

Fletcher felt a pall of gloom descend over him as the enormity of the loss of the ammunition ship and its crew sank in. In a single flash, the lives of over a hundred men and women had been snuffed like a light. Not since World War II had an American vessel suffered such damage from hostile action.

Fletcher didn't want to think of the outcry in the press and in Washington. The Gulf of Aden had turned into a killing ground.

Still on the prowl was a killer submarine.

"Update on the sub plot?"

"Nothing new," said Vitale. "No new contacts. Our guy, whoever he is, has either bugged out without being detected, or he's in deep hiding."

"Waiting for his next shot," said Fletcher.

"That's possible, but it would be suicide. As soon as he makes a sound or takes a peek with the scope, they're gonna be all over him like a cheap suit. We've got more sub-hunting equipment on station than we had in Desert Storm. We even have P-3s on the way down from Masirah in Oman."

"What about the SSNs?"

"SUBLANT has ordered the *Bremerton* to rejoin the battle group ASAP. They're on their way out of the Red Sea, clearing Bab el Mandeb—the strait at the end of the Red Sea—in about an hour. On station by nightfall. *Tulsa* is on its way from Diego Garcia and won't get here until late tomorrow."

Fletcher nodded. *Bremerton* and *Tulsa* were *Los Angeles*–class nuclear attack submarines whose specialty was hunting other subs. For most operations, a carrier battle group had at least one and usually two attack submarines assigned. Because of the *Reagan*'s unscheduled departure from Dubai, the battle group had assembled without the immediate company of an attack submarine. At the time, Fletcher hadn't been concerned. He was on his way to engage third-world guerillas in Yemen, not undersea enemies.

Another bitter lesson, he reflected. One of many. When the battle of Yemen was dissected and analyzed by military strategists, it would be declared one of the Navy's most egregiously arrogant blunders. Unfortunately, the name of Langhorne Fletcher would be forever linked to the blunder.

"COMFIVE wants to know our status and intentions, Admiral."

"Stand by," Fletcher said. He picked up the direct line to the captain's bridge. "Sticks, this is BG."

"Go, Admiral," came the voice of Sticks Stickney.

"I know you're up to your butt in alligators. A quick yes or no. Can *Reagan* maintain station?"

"If the DC team gets the plug in the inner hull, yes, sir. I should have that nailed down in the next fifteen minutes. We won't be a hundred percent, but we can operate."

"How about air ops?"

"With only three turbines and the damaged hull, engineering can't give me more than about twenty knots. That restricts our aircraft weights for launch and recovery. And there's another problem. When the turbine was hit, we lost steam to the waist catapults. We're down to the two bow cats."

"But we could launch a strike if we had to?"

A pause. "Technically, yes. CAG will have a problem with only two catapults. He might have a bigger problem if we can't give him enough wind over the deck to launch the bombers."

Fletcher considered. The carrier wasn't sinking, despite

the two torpedoes she had taken. Like all *Nimitz*-class carriers, *Reagan* had been constructed with a double-bottomed hull. The idea was that the outer hull would absorb the damage of a torpedo attack while the inner hull maintained watertight integrity. Until today, the design had never been tested in combat.

"Okay, Sticks. Get back to me with the damage control report."

"Aye, aye, sir."

As Fletcher hung up the phone, he felt Babcock watching him from across the room. For a moment the two men exchanged looks. Fletcher yelled to the yeoman across the room: "Call the Air Wing Commander. I need him up here on the double."

He caught Babcock's surprised look. *He looks worried.* Whitney Babcock looked like a man who was losing control.

CHAPTER TWENTY

METAMORPHOSIS

Gulf of Aden
1045, Thursday, 20 June

Something has changed.

Boyce couldn't put his finger on it, but he sensed it the moment the marine sentry let them onto the flag bridge. It wasn't the same Rear Adm. Langhorne Fletcher.

Boyce brought Maxwell with him, not only as a current authority about the ground situation in Yemen, but for a backup. For sure, there would be another of these tedious goddamned arguments with Fletcher and Babcock.

He felt the tension in the flag compartment. Babcock was standing in the corner, wearing a petulant look. Fletcher was in his high padded leather chair that afforded a panoramic view of the flight deck and the sea beyond.

"Who are we at war with, Admiral?" asked Boyce.

"Al-Fasr for one, and now with the owner of the submarine who torpedoed us."

"Do we know who that is?"

"SUBLANT's running a check on every diesel/electric in

service. Ruling out the Brits and Israelis, it comes down to only a few possible players. The Russians are already screaming innocence, although they won't deny that it could be one of their export boats, maybe even a Russian crew."

"I suppose you've considered the possibility that it's the same guy we've been fighting in Yemen."

Fletcher nodded. "It's been considered, and that's why I sent for you. How soon can the air wing launch a strike in support of an amphibious assault?"

At this, a spluttering sound came from Whitney Babcock. He strode across the room. "Admiral, this hasn't been discussed with me yet. There are national security implications here, and you don't have the authority to initiate a military strike without consulting me."

Fletcher picked up a sheet of paper from his console. "Remember this? These are my orders from the Commander of the Fifth Fleet, endorsed by the Commander in Chief, Atlantic, authorizing the local commander—that's me, by the way—to use the all the forces in my command to ensure the recovery of our personnel in Yemen."

"Those are contingency orders. I'll remind you, Admiral, that more is at stake here than the immediate rescue of the marines."

Fascinated, Boyce watched the exchange. This wasn't the same Fletcher. The old Fletcher was a spineless toady who had sucked his way up the promotional ladder.

The admiral swiveled his chair away from Babcock and faced Boyce. "Captain Stickney reports that the *Reagan* has only the bow catapults available. He also says that he can only give us about twenty knots forward. How much of a problem does that give you?"

Boyce thought a second, then deferred to Maxwell.

"The forward speed is no problem for the Hornets as long we have wind," said Maxwell. "Ten knots will do.

With only two cats, it'll take longer to get the jets launched. We can do it."

"I concur," said Boyce.

Fletcher said, "The senior marine commander on the *Saipan* says he can have his assault force ready to lift in ninety minutes. How long will it take to do the load-out for the strike package, CAG?"

"We're ready. I gave the go-ahead this morning."

Fletcher raised an eyebrow. "Without getting a tasking order from the battle group commander?"

"I was, ah, anticipating the order, sir. The jets are fueled, ordnance loaded, crews assigned and briefed. All we need is a final weather and intel update."

Babcock looked like he was choking on something. "Admiral, we need to speak in private."

"Later." Fletcher waved him away and turned to Vitale. "Signal COMFIVE and all CVBG commands that the *Reagan* battle group will maintain station. We'll activate the Bravo op plan at"—he glanced at his watch—"twelve-thirty. It's now T minus ninety-eight minutes."

"Admiral Fletcher!" Babcock's voice was swelling with indignation. "I'm giving you an order. You will defer the strike until I've had a chance to consult with Washington."

Fletcher swiveled in his chair to face Babcock. "About what, Mr. Babcock? About the marines we abandoned while you negotiated with Al-Fasr? About the hundred and ten Navy men who perished on the *Baywater* while we cruised out here like a sitting duck? About how your negotiating partner lured us into Yemen so he could shoot down our jets and kill our people? It's time I talked to Washington also."

Babcock glowered at Fletcher. "You are now several levels out of your depth. I'll remind you that this is a complicated and sensitive diplomatic situation. This has implications that your puny little military mind obviously does not understand."

"The one thing my puny mind understands is that we have to get our people out of Yemen. While we're doing it, I don't mind if Boyce and Maxwell here bomb the living shit out of your friend Al-Fasr."

"This is preposterous. You are violating the President's explicit instructions." Babcock headed for the door. "I'll put a stop to this. You'll be removed from command of the *Reagan* battle group."

Fletcher raised a hand and motioned for one of the marines stationed inside the flag bridge. The sergeant strode briskly to the admiral's chair, carrying his M16A2 combat rifle.

"Take that man into custody, Sergeant."

The marine gave him a curt nod. "Yes, sir."

"Keep him confined in a space with no phone, no computer, no communication devices."

"What?" spluttered Babcock. "You're going to lose those stars, Admiral."

The sergeant was joined by another marine, a burly African-American corporal. They seized each of Babcock's arms.

"You can't do this!" Babcock yelled back at Fletcher as the marines led him out of the compartment.

"Looks like he just did," observed Maxwell.

The watertight door clunked shut behind them. For several seconds no one spoke. The flag bridge was silent as a tomb. Every man in the compartment was staring at Fletcher.

He glanced at his watch. "T minus ninety-four," he said. "What the hell are you all standing around for?"

For another few seconds, Boyce studied Fletcher, seeing something in the man's lean, aristocratic features that he hadn't noticed before. Perhaps, he thought, because it hadn't been there.

"Aye, aye, sir," He gave the admiral a smart salute.

B. J. Johnson stormed though the front door of the ready room. Heels hammering on the steel deck, she marched directly to the coffee mess at the back of the room where Claire was talking to Maxwell. She was no longer wearing the sling on her left arm.

"Someone's made a mistake," she said to Maxwell, ignoring Claire. "I've been assigned as squadron duty officer."

"What's the problem?" said Maxwell.

"I should be on the schedule for the air strike."

"You're still medically grounded."

"The flight surgeon says I'm okay. I don't have to be grounded."

"The flight surgeon is not the commanding officer. I say you're still grounded."

B.J.'s face reddened. "Why?"

"Because you've been shot down once." Maxwell kept his voice low. "What do you think they'll do if you're shot down again?"

Her eyes flashed. "You were shot down. What will they do to you?"

"I'm a man. It's different."

It was the wrong thing to say. B.J. turned livid. "So that's it. I'm not flying this strike because I'm a woman?"

Maxwell looked like he was suffering a migraine. "This is not a gender thing. I need eight fully capable pilots for the strike, no more. You're not one of them for a simple reason: You've been wounded."

"It was you who wounded me!"

Maxwell's headache was worsening. B.J. had the attention of everyone in the room.

He leaned close to her and said in a low voice, "Listen up,

Lieutenant. I am the commanding officer. I have decided that you will not be on the schedule. Period. Knock off the bitching and do your job."

B.J. started to protest again, then caught herself. "Yes, sir." She gave Maxwell and Claire one last baleful look, then stomped back toward the duty officer's desk.

Claire waited until she was out of range. "I think she's angry."

"She wants to fly."

Claire shook her head, still watching B.J. at the far end of the room. "No. It's more than that."

Maxwell was giving her a wary look. "What are you talking about?"

"No wonder they call you Brick. It's perfectly obvious," she said. "The girl is in love with you."

CHAPTER TWENTY-ONE

BATTLE JOINED

Al Hazir, Yemen
1230, Thursday, 20 June

Gritti listened to the sharp exchanges of automatic fire, trying to distinguish the staccato sound of M249 SAWs—Squad Automatic Weapons—from the intermittent crackle of the Kalashnikovs. The smoke blanket was drifting southward, still obscuring the hillside where his three fire teams had penetrated the *Sherji* positions.

He motioned to Master Sergeant Plunkett. "Who's firing the SAWs?"

Plunkett knelt next to Gritti. "The first fire team. Corporal Ricci reports a clean hit, maybe twenty *Sherji* down."

"Pull 'em back, set up again a hundred yards north. What's going on with second and third?"

"Nothing. They're still under the smoke, no enemy contact."

Before Gritti could answer, he heard the muffled bark from the fifty-caliber Barrett sniper rifle. It meant the snipers were finding targets. If they could spread a little fear and confusion, the *Sherji*'s interest in overrunning the perimeter might be dampened. And if the fire teams were successful in ambushing the advancing enemy, the marines still had a chance of holding out until darkness.

He heard another rapid exchange of automatic fire, this time more AK-47 than SAW. That was a bad sign. The bastards were shooting back, probably at real targets. The advantage of surprise hadn't lasted long.

From beneath the smoke blanket came a long burst of M249 fire. "That's third fire team," said Plunkett, listening to the brittle sound of the automatic gun. "Hitting the right flank of the main force."

Gritti nodded and pointed with his hand toward the hillside. "The smoke's drifting to the east." They had only a few more minutes before the fire teams were exposed. "Advance the next three fire teams past the perimeter. We have to bottle them up while we've still got cover."

It was a hell of a gamble. He would have half his available marines outside the perimeter, dispersed *inside* the enemy's advancing troops. He was counting on the *Sherji*'s being unprepared for a counterattack.

Another long rattle of automatic fire came from the hillside, answered by a crackle of individual bursts.

"D team's not answering, Colonel. A is under fire. B is pinned down, in the open now. They say the *Sherji* are moving up maybe a battalion-sized force, going straight for the perimeter."

"Have we got more smoke?"

"No, sir. We used everything we had."

"Okay, we'll try to pincer them, put teams on either side." He saw Plunkett's dubious look. "Well? Damn it, Master Sergeant, speak up if you've got a better idea."

"No better idea. I was wondering how long you think we can hold out before . . ." He left the thought unfinished.

"Before we run up the white flag?"

Plunkett nodded.

Gritti peered back out at the hillside. Long wisps of smoke were drifting eastward, leaving the terrain naked and exposed. He heard another sharp exchange of automatic fire. It wouldn't take much, he thought. If he just had another company, he could chase these assholes right back to their hooches.

But he didn't. So what was he trying to prove? Was he prepared to sacrifice fifty brave young men to demonstrate that they could die like marines?

He felt Plunkett looking at him. "When we can't hold out any longer, Master Sergeant. Until then we fight."

"Runner One-one," came the voice of Guido Vitale. "You're cleared to push."

Maxwell acknowledged. He and his first flight of Hornets were cleared inbound to the target area.

"No joy from Boomer," said Vitale. "We think it's his batteries. Since you won't have forward air control from the ground, the Cobras will mark targets."

"Runner One-one copies."

Without a forward air controller in position, spotting targets would be tough. The FAC was inbound to the target area, aboard one of the CH-53Es in the assault force. Until he was set up, they depended on what the Cobra pilot spotted. And on what they saw from their own cockpits.

The battle line ran roughly east to west. From the previous strike, Maxwell had already gotten a look at the marine perimeter. The toughest job was distinguishing the *Sherji* positions from the friendlies.

He had three divisions, four Hornets to a division. Each jet carried twelve M20 Rockeye canisters, as well as a standard load of AIM-9 and AIM-120 air-to-air missiles and a full load of twenty millimeter. They no longer had an altitude floor. They could come in as low as they needed.

He punched his elapsed timer and rolled the Hornet into a turn toward the target area. Thirty seconds behind him, his wingman, Pearly Gates, would push. Every thirty seconds, another Hornet would head for the target. A steady rain of cluster bombs was on its way to support the marines.

He hoped they were still there.

Armor.

Gritti felt a chill run through him. It was the news he feared most.

Plunkett confirmed it. "Yes, sir. Three light AVs. A team just reported contact. They're coming out of cover and heading up the hill."

Gritti ran his hand over the stubble on his jaw, feeling the fatigue, resisting the despair that hung over him. If the tanks reached the perimeter, it was all over. With armor running interference for the *Sherji,* they would roll over the marines' position on the hill.

A fully equipped marine unit would have an antitank platoon with TOW missiles—tube launched, optically tracked, wire-guided weapons that could convert tanks to scrap metal. But he had come with a TRAP team whose single mission was the rescue of downed pilots. For that purpose they had grenades, M203 grenade launchers, and a handful of mortars. Useful weapons against infantry; damned near useless against tanks.

"We pick a fire zone where the tanks have to pass. We'll use what's left of the mortars and grenade launchers. It's our only shot."

Plunkett nodded and began barking the instructions. In midsentence he stopped. "Too late, Colonel. They're already here."

So they were. Gritti could see them, a column of three armored vehicles, charging out of cover three hundred yards away. A rooster tail of dirt spewed up behind each vehicle.

"Ready with the grenade launchers. Maybe we can slow them down while we get the forward fire teams back."

While Plunkett passed the new orders, Gritti's mind was racing, trying to come up with a new plan. It no longer made sense to stand and defend an indefensible position. They would have to fall back, retreat through terrain the tanks couldn't handle. But he couldn't abandon the fire teams who were already behind the enemy's front positions. The *Sherji* would hunt them down like wild game.

Shit! Some commander he was. Why hadn't he anticipated the tanks? Why hadn't the goddamned wind stayed calm so the smoke would last? His TRAP team was about to be converted into a dozen isolated fire teams.

On top of everything else, his radio—the piece-of-shit PRC-117 UHF that was supposed to keep him satellite-linked with his commanders—was dead as a rock. The batteries were drained.

Gritti turned his attention again to the oncoming tanks. The first was winding its way down a terraced hillside. Trotting along in its wake was a platoon-sized group of *Sherji,* carrying their AK-47s. The vehicles would be in firing range in another fifty yards. When they were close enough—

Boom! Boom! Boom! The earth around the tank erupted in plumes of dirt. The tank exploded.

Gritti stared in astonishment. It took his fatigued mind several seconds to understand. Then he saw the twin tailpipes, the canted vertical stabilizers of a jet swooping low over the destroyed tank.

Half a minute later, more explosions.

Boom! Boom! Boom! The earth erupted ten feet in front of the second tank.

As the tank veered around the destroyed lead vehicle, a bomb took out the third tank. An oily ball of fire mushroomed upward from the destroyed tank.

Another twin-finned fighter swept overhead. One after the other, long-nosed, stubby-winged F/A-18s raked the *Sherji* positions with cluster bombs. As Gritti watched, the surviving tank backed up, reversed course, and was clanking at high speed toward the canopy cover from which it had emerged.

Another near-miss. A bomb hit three feet from the tank's left side, kicking it sideways, destroying its left track. Seconds later the hatch flew open. The crippled tank's three-man crew bailed out and ran pell-mell across the exposed hillside. Twenty yards from the low scrub brush, they were cut down by a hail of automatic fire.

"That's Corporal Brady's team earning their pay," said Plunkett, watching the action with his glasses.

"Get the fire teams back to the perimeter," Gritti ordered. "They have to get out of the way of the bombers."

While Plunkett issued the instructions, Gritti heard something else—a familiar beating noise above the din of the explosions and the roar of the jets.

Rotor blades. Whopping, thrashing the air, coming from the south. A beautiful sound.

Gritti and Plunkett looked at each other. Each wore a two-day stubble of beard. A layer of grime and camo paint covered their faces. Their eyes were red-rimmed with fatigue and stress.

"Master Sergeant," Gritti said, "it appears that the cavalry may be on its way."

"About damn time, sir."

The beat of the rotor blades swelled in intensity. A pair of Whiskey Cobras popped over the southern ridgeline, their noses low, the chin-mounted rotary cannons swiveling from side to side looking for targets. A second pair appeared behind them. As the Cobras swept over the marines' perimeter, the brittle roar of the high-velocity cannon drowned out the other battle noises. From the lead Cobra's inboard pylon a salvo of 2.75-inch rockets screeched toward a gun position in the trees. A geyser of flame and debris gushed upward from the foliage.

A deeper throbbing sound pounded on Gritti's eardrums. Behind another pair of protective Whiskey Cobras appeared the CH-53E Super Stallions. Three of the cargo helicopters were hauling swing loads—fighting vehicles suspended in slings beneath the aircraft.

Gritti tried to count the helos. He couldn't. They kept coming, one wave behind the other.

"Jesus," said Plunkett, staring at the apparition. "It looks like *Apocalypse Now.*"

Gritti nodded. He could feel the throb of the blades all the way up through the soles of his boots. Marines were fast-roping out of the hovering craft. The Stallions with the swing loads were lowering the heavy vehicles to the earth.

So far, Gritti observed, no SAMs. No fireballs from destroyed helicopters. No mortars being lobbed into the perimeter. The heavy guns of the *Sherji* had fallen silent. He liked the way this was going.

His ambush teams were making their way back. The first wave of the assault force was entering the southern perimeter. Gritti heard the deep chuffing of diesel engines, and seconds later a pair of LAV-25s—light armored vehicles—rumbled over the ridgeline and into the perimeter.

In trail behind the two light tanks appeared an HMMWV Hummer. As Gritti rose to his feet, the Hummer rolled across the clearing and ground to a halt.

From the right seat of the vehicle emerged Lt. Col. Aubrey Hewlitt, Gritti's executive officer and second-in-command of the 43rd Marine Expeditionary Unit. He wore perfectly starched desert-camo BDUs, a sidearm, and the ubiquitous Fritz helmet.

Hewlitt peered at Gritti, unsure of what he was seeing.

"What the hell are you staring at?" said Gritti.

Recognizing his boss's voice, Hewlitt stared. "Sorry, Colonel." He stared for another second. "If you'll pardon my saying so, sir, you look like shit."

It was too good to last, thought Maxwell. *Something always happened that you didn't expect.*

Now it was happening. "Runner One-one, pop-up contact! Snap vector, bearing 345, twenty, low, in the weeds."

The warning came from the E-2C Hawkeye—the turboprop airborne early warning aircraft—deployed in an orbit twenty miles south of the Yemeni coastline.

Fulcrums again? From where? Had they somehow gotten across the Red Sea from Eritrea or Chad? How did they arrive undetected?

They didn't, he decided. They would have been picked up by the Hawkeye. These guys were locals.

"Bogeys bearing 330, fifteen, weeds."

Maxwell still had no ID on them. *Bogeys or bandits?* Bogeys were unidentified, while bandits were bona fide, no-shit hostiles. They *had* to be bandits if they were coming in low from the north.

If they waited any longer for an ID, it would be too late. They were already within missile range.

"Runner flight, jettison stores," Maxwell called on the tactical frequency. He hit the emergency jettison button and felt a *whump* through the Hornet's airframe as his remaining Rockeye containers and the centerline external fuel tank were punched away. The Super Hornet was no longer a lumbering bomber. It was a slick-winged fighter.

They were low, still pulling up from a pass on the *Sherji* positions. Above and behind were Leroi Jones and Flash Gordon, about to roll in on ground targets.

The bogeys were coming in on the deck, fifteen miles away, head-on. The merge would come in less than a minute.

"Radar air-to-air." Maxwell switched his APG-73 radar from bombing mode to air-to-air. Within a few sweeps of the radar, he saw an EID—electronic identification—on the incoming bogey. It was what he expected—a MiG-29.

Fulcrum.

He looked again. No, not just one bogey. *Damn it, there are three more.* "Four bandits, twelve o'clock, ten miles low," called the controller in the Hawkeye, confirming Maxwell's radar display.

His RWR shrieked a high-pitched warbling sound. He was being targeted by a Russian Slotback radar.

"Runner One-one spiked at twelve, defending!" he called, rolling his Hornet and pulling hard. He hoped Pearly was staying with him. "Runner One-two, press!" he called, giving the tactical lead to Pearly.

A classic setup. The MiGs were getting the first shot. His best chance to defeat the missile—he guessed that it was a radar-guided Alamo—was chaff, a cloud of radar-decoying aluminum foil.

Rolling back to the left, he saw it. Coming up at him, trailing a wisp of gray smoke, the missile was flying a classic pursuit curve. Toward Maxwell's jet.

"Brick, break left!" Pearly Gates's voice was urgent. "Bandit ten o'clock low."

Maxwell swung his head—and there it was, the cobralike shape of the lead MiG-29 silhouetted against the landscape. The MiG was in a climbing turn toward him.

But he had a more immediate problem—the incoming Alamo. The missile was in a maximum-rate turn, arcing upward.

Another barrel roll to the left, pulling hard, seven Gs. The missile was closing on him, curving toward his tail.

Whoosh.

Straining under the heavy G load, he watched the Alamo sizzling past his tail, then felt the concussion as the proximity fuse exploded the warhead a hundred yards behind him.

How close? Maxwell braced, waiting for the same sickening sensation of two days before—loss of control, warning lights, engine fire.

"You okay, Brick?" asked Pearly Gates.

"I think so. Everything is still working."

"Runner Two, Fox Three on the lead group trailer."

"Take him. I've got the leader engaged."

"Roger. Yo-yo. Runner One-one engaged defensive with the leader." Pearly was on his own while Maxwell fought the lead Fulcrum.

"Runner One-three and -four have the trailers," called Leroi Jones, leading the second section of Hornets. "We're sorted."

Maneuvering to defeat the Alamo had cost him airspeed. The lead MiG's nose was pointed well inside Maxwell's turn radius, gaining a precious angle on him.

The fighters passed, a hundred yards apart. As the desert-colored MiG swept past, Maxwell glimpsed the yellow helmet, a visored face watching him. Puffs of vapor were spilling off the MiG's wings from the high G load.

Who is this guy? What was with the yellow helmet?

Was it Al-Fasr?

As the MiG passed behind his shoulder, Maxwell swung his head, keeping the fighter in sight. He hauled the nose up, up, then rolled toward the MiG.

The MiG's nose came up, countering Maxwell. Climbing,

the two fighters pulled back toward each other. Again they crossed, noses high.

Now what? Maxwell asked himself. In a one-vee-one with a MiG-29, there was no way out. The aging Russian fighter was as fast as a Hornet. If you tried to bug out, the MiG had a free shot at your tail.

Now he was in a turning fight with a Fulcrum. And the guy flying it was matching the Hornet move for move. Definitely not your average undertrained and demoralized MiG pilot who just wanted to save his ass.

It had to be Al-Fasr.

CHAPTER TWENTY-TWO

THE TROUBLE WITH SAM

North Central Yemen
1305, Thursday, 20 June

"Splash One!" called Pearly Gates.

It was the brevity signal for an aerial kill. Pearly Gates watched his AIM-120 radar-guided missile slam into the right intake of the second MiG-29. The fighter split in half, spewing debris and pieces from the shattered airframe. Exactly one second later, the main fuel cell erupted in an orange fireball. From five hundred feet, the flaming wreckage tumbled to the floor of the desert.

Where were the trailers? Pearly picked them up on his situational display, then went outside again for a visual ID.

There. He saw the dark shapes of the two trailing MiGs a mile behind the destroyed fighter, fast and low in a combat spread.

He heard Leroi Jones call, "Runner One-three and -four have the trailers locked."

Okay, the trailers were covered. But that left Brick and the lead MiG still in a furball somewhere.

"Runner Two blind on One," Pearly called, declaring that he didn't have Maxwell in sight.

"One's blind on you, engaged neutral," Maxwell answered.

Pearly called the Hawkeye. "Battle-ax, Runner Two. Vector for Runner One-one."

"Runner One-one is ten miles, merged plot," answered the controller in the Hawkeye.

"Runner One-two inbound." Pearly reefed the Hornet's nose around in a climbing turn, switching his scan from outside back to the APG-73 radar.

Then he saw the two blips—Maxwell's Hornet and the MiG-29. The blips were nearly superimposed.

Another AIM-120 missile shot was out of the question. They were too close together. The autonomously guided missile was as likely to home in on Maxwell as the MiG.

Maybe a heat-seeking Sidewinder, which was a "fire and forget" weapon. He'd wait until he had a clear shot.

In the next second, Pearly's blood ran cold.

"Burner six! Burner six hot!" It was Ironclaw, the EA-6B Prowler, reporting an SA-6 surface-to-air missile.

At the same time Pearly heard the warbling sound from his RWR. The SAM was airborne—locked on Pearly's Hornet.

He saw it, bursting into the hazy sky like a fire-tailed comet. He hit the chaff-dispenser button on his throttle, releasing a trail of the finely cut aluminum foil into the wake of his jet.

"Runner One-two spiked, defending," he yelled on the radio, declaring that he was leaving the fight. "Shit, it's an SA-6."

He rolled perpendicular to the missile and punched his chaff program dispenser. *Make it maneuver. Make it break lock. Out-turn the sonofabitch.* He pulled the Hornet's nose down, seeing the rugged terrain of Yemen fill up his wind-screen.

By modern standards, the Russian-built SA-6 wasn't a highly sophisticated missile, but it was still deadly. Pearly guessed that the radar-guided weapon was smart enough not to be fooled by chaff or the electronic jamming being provided by the Prowler.

He was right. It was coming up in a corkscrew pattern, constantly adjusting its flight path to stay locked onto Pearly's Hornet.

As the missile came nearer, Pearly yanked the Hornet into an orthogonal roll—a high-G, square-cornered maneuver—using the maximum G load the Hornet's fly-by-wire control system would allow.The missile followed. Still accelerating. Still tracking him.

Pearly's heart hammered in his chest. The goddamn missile was like a hunter from hell. He could see the nose of the thing pulling lead, making tiny directional changes as it homed in on Pearly's jet.

Coming closer. So close now he could see the control fins on the tail. Any second now, it would detonate. Pearly saw the missile coming for him.

Wait, he told himself. *Wait until . . .*

Now. He jammed the stick hard into the corner, completing the last right-angle corner of the roll.

He heard the dull moan of the rocket engine as the SAM zoomed past him. Not close enough to detonate the proximity fuse.

Peering over his shoulder, he saw the missile wobbling in a ballistic arc. Without a target, the SAM was flying an unguided descent back toward the earth.

He had escaped. But just barely.

Pearly eased back on the stick, leveling the Hornet at only two hundred feet above the terrain. For the first time since he saw the SAM, he resumed breathing. The feeling of relief flowed over him like a warm bath.

But only for a few seconds. The feeling was rapidly replaced by a fresh emotion: rage. *Those ragheads tried to take me out with that goddamn rocket!*

The anger swelled in Pearly Gates as another thought took hold of him. *They're still down there, the bastards! Loading up another one to shoot at us.*

He heard the Hawkeye calling: "Runner Two, status check. Do you have battle damage?"

Pearly's left thumb went to the mike button to acknowledge. Then he removed it.

"Runner Two, do you read Battle-ax? Answer up."

He didn't answer. Instead, his fingers went to the stores page on his multipurpose display. He had no air-to-ground weapons with which to fight the SAM. Except one. He selected A/G GUN.

Gritti sat in the Hummer and stifled a yawn. Jesus, a short nap would be heaven. He'd never been so tired in his life.

But he couldn't sleep now.

Hewlitt was giving him a worried look. "Maybe you'd better chill out, Gus. You can keep the Hummer and run the operation with—"

"Fuck that! I've been fighting this asshole for three days. Do you think I'm gonna miss the last hour of the battle?"

"Just thought I'd ask."

The sounds of the skirmish across the valley had abated. The *Sherji* had put up a brief fight when the marines broke out of the perimeter, trying to defend what was left of their armor and artillery. With the Whiskey Cobras and a flight of Hornets spewing high explosives on them, they quickly ran out of enthusiasm.

"How many prisoners?" Gritti asked.

"Over a hundred. Those that couldn't haul ass quick enough."

Gritti could see them squatting in the clearing, guarded by a couple of marines. They looked less like soldiers than frightened tribesmen. Two intel specialists, with the help of a linguist, were pumping them for information about the Al-Fasr complex and the remaining *Sherji* force.

"Casualties?"

"One, a gunny in Delta company. A 7.62 round in the calf. He's already been evacuated along with the wounded from the TRAP team."

Gritti realized he had already asked that question. He removed his helmet and massaged his temples with his fingertips. Shit, he was tired. He was starting to forget stuff.

Darkness was less than three hours away, and he had no intention of spending another night in Yemen. But even more than the impending nightfall, he had another worry. At any time he expected to receive the order to withdraw. Before that happened, he intended to be inside Al-Fasr's compound.

Pearly kept the Hornet low, a hundred feet above the deck, paralleling the ridge. The high ridge protruded from the scruffy terrain like the spine of a dragon. In tactical language this was called "terrain masking"—using topographic features like the ridge to obstruct the view of air defense radar.

As he skimmed the undulating terrain, a thought nagged at him: *I'm going to catch hell for this. Maxwell is gonna kick my ass from here to Bahrain.*

Pilots weren't supposed to go after a SAM site by themselves, and certainly not with guns. It was the business of the EA-6B Prowlers or another package of F/A-18s to hammer the sites with HARM missiles. The HARM—high-speed antiradiation missile—homed in on the briefest of emissions from a fire control radar. Best of all, it could be fired from a safe standoff distance.

He put the thought out of his mind. He was a man on a mission. Like all fighter pilots, he hated SAMs and the evil bastards who fired them. Enemy fighter pilots he could regard as equals—warriors with whom he shared a code of battle. But the sneaky little shits who fired missiles at you were like rattlesnakes in the weeds.

Five miles. Almost to the pullup point. He needed at least three miles to pop up, acquire the target, and roll in. The site was concealed in a patch of trees at the end of a high, twisting ridgeline.

Nudging the throttles forward, he watched the airspeed notch over five hundred knots. He wanted lots of energy when he popped up.

At this speed and altitude, Pearly's view amounted to a narrow cone of vision directly ahead. On either side, the terrain unrolled in a brownish blur. He had to concentrate, gently moving the stick to keep the Hornet just above the earth. One second's lapse, and he would be a grease spot in the desert.

Still no RWR warning. Either the fire controllers weren't picking him up yet—or they had hauled ass. The launcher and fire control radar were mounted on tracked vehicles. He prayed that they hadn't yanked up their gear and headed for cover.

Three miles. Time to unmask.

He pulled the Hornet up hard, grunting under the four-G load. With the nose thirty degrees above the horizon on his HUD, he peered through the canopy at the drab brown Yemeni landscape, looking for the SAM site.

Nothing. Where was the goddamn missile site?

The warbling sharpened in pitch. They were getting a lock. Any second now he would see the flaming telephone pole streaking toward him. *Where is the fucking site . . . ?*

Over there! He had been off by a couple of miles. Farther to the west, beyond the ridge line, pointing like a monolith through the canopy of trees and camouflage net. Moving, swiveling on its self-propelled launch chassis.

Toward him.

Rolling inverted, Pearly hauled the Hornet's nose back through the horizon. He shoved the throttles full forward.

He guessed the range was two miles, maybe less. The warbling RWR changed pitch, telling him that the acquisition radar was locking onto him. The thought flashed through his mind that he perhaps should have let the HARM shooters do the job.

Too late. The long tapered nose of the missile was swinging toward him. Pearly and the SA-6 were both committed.

Diving at a shallow angle, the Hornet gathered speed quickly. Five hundred knots. Five-twenty.

He could see the site clearly. The missile was dark brown, nearly twenty feet long, slender and menacing. Another missile was nestled next to it, ready to fire. He remembered the intel details about the SA-6. Labeled "Gainful" by NATO, it had been around since the 1970s and ravaged Israeli jets during the Yom Kippur war.

The SA-6 was aimed directly at him. The warbling sound became frantic in his RWR.

Smoke was billowing from around the self-propelled launcher. *The thing is launching!*

He squeezed the trigger.

Brrrrrraaaaappppp. The first burst hit the earth twenty yards short, kicking up a storm of dirt and rocks.

The second caught the missile as it cleared the launcher. The high-explosive shells ripped through the missile's cylindrical body.

The missile's warhead detonated.

Twenty-millimeter cannon fire continued raining down on the SAM site. The second missile, still on the launcher, exploded. In succession, each missile in the stockpile exploded. Smoke and orange flame gushed into the sky above the site.

Pearly squeezed his eyes shut as the Hornet punched through the cloud of debris.

He gave his engine display a quick glance. Temperatures, RPMs, fuel flows still okay. No damage.

As he cranked around to make another firing pass on the missile battery, he saw that it wasn't necessary. The self-propelled launcher was a smoldering hulk. A thirty-yard-wide hole had been cleared by the explosions of the missiles. The radar and fire control vehicles looked like shattered toys.

For the first time in several minutes, he became aware of the persistent voice in his earphones. "Runner One-two, do you read Battle-Ax? Are you on frequency, Runner One-two?"

"Go ahead, Battle-Ax."

"Where have you been? We thought we lost you. We were calling a hot burner six in your sector, but it's just gone cold."

Pearly gazed down at the blackened ruin of the SA-6 battery. "I confirm that, Battle-Ax. The burner six is cold."

CHAPTER TWENTY-THREE

EYE OF THE NEEDLE

North Central Yemen
1315, Thursday, 20 June

A gun kill.

With his left hand, Al-Fasr punched the arm switch for the Gsh-301 thirty-millimeter cannon. It was the most primitive of air-to-air weapons—and the most satisfying. Nothing matched the rattling, visceral satisfaction of a gun kill. Modern weapons like the radar-guided Alamo and the heat-seeking Archer missile were efficient killers, but for him the big rotary cannon mounted in the Fulcrum's left wing root was the weapon of choice.

He rolled the MiG into another high scissors, hauling the nose back toward the opposing Hornet. Sweat stung his eyes as he fought to keep the enemy in sight. The high G forces caused perspiration to ooze from beneath the skullcap of his helmet.

He guessed that this was the Hornet flight leader, probably a senior officer. He was flying the F/A-18 with surprising skill. Al-Fasr wondered if it was someone he knew from the old Red Flag competitions. He hoped so. This would be a symbolic kill, just as the assassination of the two admirals had been symbolic.

Just as the sinking of the *Reagan* would have been symbolic.

The carrier was still afloat. That much he knew. That the ship could still operate was a mystery to him. Somehow they were able to contain the damage and launch fighters.

The thought made him wonder again—what happened to Manilov? Since the torpedo attack, he had heard nothing more about the Russian captain or the fate of the *Ilia Mourmetz*. Perhaps he was maneuvering for a second attack.

He put it out of his mind. That phase of the plan was finished. He had deluded that posturing fool, Babcock, into believing that Yemen would become an American puppet state, a source of cheap oil. Assuming all went according to plans, after today the United States would have no more stomach for military adventures on the Arabian peninsula. Especially not after almost losing their most prized warship.

As the ruler of Yemen, he would be regarded as an equal by the Arab world. By the Americans, of course, he would be hated. And feared.

He felt the MiG lurch in the jetwash of the Hornet as they crossed flight paths again. He glimpsed once more the pilot peering at him. Time was critical. He was taking a great gamble going one-vee-one—one fighter versus one fighter—against a Hornet. He couldn't expect support from his three other mercenary pilots. They were expendables who would probably not be alive in five more minutes. He had to kill this Hornet quickly before others joined the fight.

The Hornet was pitching up again, rolling. Al-Fasr

matched the maneuver, pitching and rolling into him, gaining a tiny increment of advantage, and—

What happened? Al-Fasr blinked, then craned his head from side to side in the cockpit. Something was terribly wrong.

The Hornet. It had vanished.

They called it a bunt, and it was the most brutal of maneuvers.

Maxwell shoved the stick full forward. The Hornet's nose punched down, transitioning instantly from positive Gs to negative.

His helmet thunked into the Plexiglas canopy. His vision became a blurry red, and he felt himself jammed upward against his harness fittings.

With the jet pitching downward, he pushed the stick into the right forward corner, rolled away to the right, then again yanked back on the stick. The sudden positive G load slammed him back hard into his seat.

He strained to peer over his left shoulder. The Fulcrum pilot had lost sight of him, at least for a critical second. The MiG was still rolling left, belly to him, searching for the missing Hornet.

Maxwell hauled the nose up and around in a high-G barrel roll. Coming through the roll, he saw exactly what he had hoped for—the underside and tail of the MiG-29.

His fingers went to the select button for the AIM-9—a heat-seeking Sidewinder. The range was close, less than a thousand yards. He uncaged the missile's seeker head and heard the low growl indicating that the missile was tracking the heat of the Fulcrum's jet exhausts. The mottled brown paint scheme of the Fulcrum swelled in his HUD.

He squeezed the trigger.

The Sidewinder leaped off the rail on the Hornet's starboard wing tip, trailing a thin gray wisp of smoke.

The MiG pilot realized the danger. A stream of decoy flares appeared behind the Fulcrum. The jet abruptly rolled inverted and pitched downward.

Maxwell couldn't believe it. They were only six thousand feet above the terrain. The Fulcrum pilot was executing a split-S—pulling his nose into a vertical dive, flying the bottom half of a loop.

The sudden maneuver—and the short range—were too much for the Sidewinder. The missile whizzed past the tail of the diving Fulcrum, then flew aimlessly off into the clear sky.

Maxwell watched the MiG escape the missile. This pilot was either very lucky or very good. Both, probably. Only one MiG pilot in this part of the world fit that description.

It had to be Al-Fasr.

He hesitated, watching the MiG-29 dive at the earth. It was suicide.

He rolled the Hornet inverted and followed the MiG.

Seven Gs. It was the best he could do without stalling the wing. To stall would ensure that he made a smoking hole in the earth below.

Al-Fasr kept a steady pressure on the stick, watching the brown landscape fill up the fighter's windscreen. The pullout would be low, dangerously low.

He had dodged the missile. How had the Hornet pilot gained the advantage? Whoever it was behind him was not the average U.S. Navy fighter pilot—the kind Al-Fasr used to humiliate back in the old days. The kind he had scraped off on the ridge during the Red Flag games.

The altimeter was unwinding in a blur. The nose of the Fulcrum was coming through the vertical while the hard earth of Yemen rose up to meet him.

He grunted against the grayout effect of the sustained Gs.

His vision was tunneling—narrowing to a thin channel of awareness. Dimly he sensed the ground rushing up at him.

Through the gray veil of his remaining vision he searched the ground—and glimpsed what he wanted. *There!* The valley.

He nudged the Fulcrum's nose to the right, aiming for the notch in the earth. He grunted harder, pressing his diaphragm against his guts in the effort to maintain consciousness.

The valley opened up under the nose of the jet. He was bottoming out of the split-S. On either side he sensed the walls of the chasm speeding past in a brown blur.

The jet was level. With the G-load lifting from him, his vision returned.

Where was the Hornet?

He rolled the MiG into a knife-edge bank and peered over his shoulder. He hoped to see an oily black mushroom of smoke marking the death site of the Hornet.

No smoke. Instead, a dull gray frontal silhouette, three kilometers behind him—an F/A-18 Super Hornet.

He slammed his fist against the padded glareshield. *The smug, arrogant American bastard!* Al-Fasr sucked hard on his oxygen, held his breath a second, forced himself to be calm.

Think. You know the terrain; he doesn't. Kill him like you killed that fool in the Red Flag exercise.

He knew where he was. The valley was a relic from an antediluvian period when Yemen had flowing rivers and green hills. Now it was a brownish ravine that wound northward into the barren high desert. Within a few kilometers, the valley deepened and widened into a twisting canyon.

Yes, that was it. The canyon.

This is crazy, thought Maxwell. It was also dangerous as hell.

The canyon twisted one way, then the other, sometimes making ninety-degree turns. Towering rock formations sprang up, looking like monuments from the Stone Age.

Sweat poured from his helmet as he weaved and dodged, staying on the Fulcrum's tail. The MiG was flitting like an insect across the display in the HUD. He had the Sidewinder seeker head uncaged, tracking the Fulcrum's tailpipes. The low acquisition growl would swell in his earphones, then cease as the MiG vanished around a corner of the canyon.

A female voice barked at him: "Bingo! Bingo!" It was Bitchin' Betty, the aural warning. Bingo meant that he was fuel critical. He would have to refuel from a tanker or he wouldn't make it back to the ship. A prolonged duel with the MiG would exhaust his reserve fuel and he'd be forced to punch out.

The thought of another ejection over Yemen filled Maxwell with dread.

They were no more than a hundred feet above the floor of the canyon. It occurred to him that Al-Fasr knew where he was going.

And Maxwell didn't. *This is stupid. He's setting you up. He's going to plant you into a canyon wall.*

The MiG rolled into a hard right bank. A second later it disappeared around the corner of the canyon. Maxwell rolled the Hornet into a vertical bank and followed the MiG around the corner.

The MiG was gone.

Suddenly he saw why. The canyon made a zigzag turn back to the left. Ahead, the far wall of the canyon rose in front of him, approaching at a speed of four hundred knots. He could see sprigs of scrub brush and dwarf trees protruding from the slanting wall.

He wrenched the stick to the left and pulled hard. The acceleration jammed him down into the seat as the jet wheeled into a maximum-G turn to the left.

Bzzzzttt. Bzzzztt. Bzzzzt. It sounded like the croak of a cicada. He could feel it through the airframe of the jet—and he knew what it was.

The Hornet was clipping the trees on the slope of the canyon wall.

The buzzing noise abruptly ceased.

Ahead Maxwell could see the canyon straightening out, then bending back to the right. The MiG was still there, low and fast.

The MiG rolled into another bank, knifing into the next turn. Maxwell's heart was pounding from the near-miss with the canyon wall. He nudged the throttles forward.

The canyon made a gradual turn back to the east. Vertical clusters of sandstone jumped up at him as he skimmed the deck. Both jets were weaving through the canyon, each dodging the rock formations that rose from the floor like primordial monoliths.

Again the MiG made a sharp right bank and disappeared around a sheer precipice. Maxwell wheeled the Hornet around the same corner—and his heart nearly stopped.

Across the canyon stretched a natural stone bridge. The opening looked like the eye of a needle. It was high, a hundred feet or more, but too narrow for the Hornet's wingspan.

He glimpsed Al-Fasr's MiG-29 disappearing through the eye of the needle in a vertical bank.

In a millisecond the realization flashed through Maxwell's mind: *This is what he was waiting for.*

Instinct took over. As the narrow passage rushed at him, he reacted. He snapped the Hornet into a knife-edge bank. Into the eye of the needle.

CHAPTER TWENTY-FOUR

THE COMPOUND

North Central Yemen
1320, Thursday, 20 June

Maxwell squeezed his eyes shut, waiting for the impact.

In the next instant the Hornet was through the eye of the needle, in the clear. He rolled the wings level and peered around. Ahead, the canyon opened into a broad valley. No more rock formations, no more bridges.

The MiG was gone.

Maxwell's eyes flicked to the radar display. Where was the Fulcrum? No return. No blip, no target where the MiG-29 should have been.

He looked outside again, scanning the terrain. Had the Fulcrum hit the ground? Crashed against the slope of the valley?

He saw nothing.

An alarm was going off in Maxwell's head. When he was visible, Al-Fasr was a dangerous adversary. Invisible, he was deadly. The old fighter pilot's maxim came to Maxwell's mind—Lose sight, lose the fight.

He had lost sight. The eye of the needle was another Al-Fasr surprise. Now he was defensive again.

Something alerted him—a flicker of light, a momentary shadow in the cockpit.

He tilted his head back and peered straight up through the Plexiglas.

Directly above him—the Fulcrum. It looked like a bat, wings swept back almost to the tail, inverted, diving on him like a predator.

Suddenly he understood. Passing through the eye of the needle, Al-Fasr had flicked the MiG's wings level and pulled straight up into a loop. From six thousand feet, he was sweeping back down on the Hornet's tail.

Maxwell hauled the nose of the F/A-18 up in a tight Immelmann, the upper half of a loop. As his nose passed through vertical, he saw the MiG-29 countering him. The jets passed canopy to canopy, pulling hard into each other.

Another vertical scissors. This time there would be no exit.

They crossed again, and Maxwell got a good look at the yellow helmet, the oxygen-masked figure staring at him. *This is the guy who killed Josh Dunn. The guy who tried to sink the* Reagan.

He nudged the stick back, coaxing the Hornet through a maximum-performance loop. With each sweep of the vertical scissors, he was gaining a tiny advantage on the MiG.

The scissors was depleting the energy of both fighters. By the third opposing pass, they were bottoming out only a few hundred feet above the terrain. In tiny increments, Maxwell was inching his way behind the MiG.

Another vertical scissors. As Maxwell completed the loop, he brought the nose of the Hornet to bear on the Fulcrum. The Sidewinder's acquisition tone warbled in his earphones. He squeezed the trigger.

The AIM-9 missile streaked toward its target.

Again the MiG pilot sensed imminent danger. He snapped the Fulcrum into a barrel roll to the left, spewing a trail of flares to decoy the missile.

Maxwell rolled with him, staying high and outside. Keeping his eye on the MiG, he rocked back his air-to-air weapons selector to A/A GUN. With grudging admiration he watched the MiG execute a roll, its nose coming down, pulling hard as the jet dived close to the earth.

The Sidewinder flew to the trail of flares, briefly wobbled as its guidance system sorted out the decoys, then went again for the big tailpipes of the Fulcrum. Too late, the missile overshot the hard-turning MiG and impacted the base of a ridge.

Maxwell watched the MiG, still in a knife-edge bank, slicing toward the earth. The Fulcrum was close to the terrain, skimming the scrub brush along the ridgeline. Vapor puffs spilled off the wings as the pilot pulled the nose up.

The right wing clipped the top of the ridge. A geyser of dirt and debris erupted from the earth.

Maxwell skimmed low over the disintegrating MiG. As he pulled up in a climbing reversal, he glimpsed the hulk of the shattered fighter caroming across the desert, shedding pieces. Over his shoulder he glimpsed what he had been praying for—an orange fireball.

When he swept back again over the blazing wreckage, he saw that nothing was left of the Fulcrum, just smoking fragments and debris. Fires were burning along the slope of the valley where hunks of the fighter had landed.

His eyes scanned the landscape, looking for a chute, any sign that the pilot had escaped.

Nothing.

The MiG pilot—he prayed that it was Al-Fasr—was dead.

This was the moment he had been waiting for since the day in Dubai when they had killed Josh Dunn. He had wanted revenge, and here it was.

He had expected that when this moment came, he would be feeling something—pride, relief, exultation. He should be hearing trumpets and choirs of avenging angels. Down in his gut he should be feeling a grim satisfaction.

No such emotion was rising up in him. Josh Dunn was gone. So were the sailors and marines and pilots killed by Jamal Al-Fasr and his terrorists. Nothing would change that.

Revenge wasn't sweet, he thought. It was empty.

A glance at the EFD—engine fuel display—returned him to the present. The totalizer indicated nine-hundred pounds remaining. Less than ten minutes flying time.

He wouldn't make it out of Yemen.

Gritti listened to the reports on the PRC-90. On either side—east and west—of the complex he had landed two companies of marines. They were applying a pincers on the *Sherji* who were dug in outside the old BP compound. The Cobras were raking them with 2.75 rockets and rotary cannons.

He removed the steel-rimmed spectacles and took a look through his field glasses. A few scattered pockets of *Sherji* were still resisting. "What the hell are they fighting for?"

Hewlitt, who was given to philosophizing, offered a theory: "It's a macho thing. These are mountain men, an ancient Islamic warrior clan. They may not feel like dying, but they have to prove that they're not afraid to. Once that's established, they'll pack it in."

"They'd better start packing," grumbled Gritti. "They're wasting my time and ordnance."

The *Sherji*'s western-flank defenders had already gotten a

close-up look at the pair of LAV-25 light tanks rumbling toward their line and reached a pragmatic decision. A white flag was flying over their position. Slowly, each of the hundred and fifty fighters rose from cover and began stacking AK-47s and machine guns.

While a squad took charge of the prisoners, the tanks charged into the complex, followed by an infantry company. Under fire from three sides, the defenders on the eastern flank quickly reached the same conclusion as their western comrades. One by one, they laid down their arms, making a show of placing their hands on their heads.

In the command Hummer, Gritti and Hewlitt rolled into the compound on the heels of the advancing marines. After transmitting a situation update on the satellite UHF radio, Gritti climbed out and looked around.

A hard-surfaced gravel road ran between two rows of tin-roofed buildings. At the end of the road, on either side, swelled half a dozen earth-covered mounds, each large enough, Gritti supposed, to store vehicles and supplies.

Inside the complex, between two of the buildings, over two hundred *Sherji* were kneeling in a cluster while marine intelligence specialists and the linguist went through the group. Gritti could see the prisoners nodding agreeably and pointing to various features in the compound.

He turned to Hewlitt. "Anyone report seeing Al-Fasr?"

"They claim he's flying one of the MiGs."

Gritti watched the advance fire teams cautiously entering the complex of tin-roofed buildings. "What about mines and booby traps?"

"The clearing squad is working the area. The captured *Sherji* all swear that it's clean. Nothing planted."

Gritti nodded toward the kneeling prisoners. "Do they understand how extremely pissed off I'm going to be if any of my marines step on a mine?"

"I told them you will cut off their balls with a bayonet."

At this, Gritti had to grin. "Tell 'em that's just for starters."

"Runner One-one is fuel critical. I need a tanker now." Maxwell tried to suppress the urgency in his voice.

"Roger, Runner One-one," answered the controller in the Hawkeye. "Texaco tanker is on Bravo station. Can you make it to him?"

"Negative. I've got six minutes left. Maybe less." His totalizer was indicating seven hundred pounds. At such a low quantity, the indication could be off by several hundred pounds.

The controller didn't answer for several seconds. Maxwell knew he was conferring with the tanker pilot and the Air Warfare Commander in the *Reagan*. Finally the controller came back. "We can't join you with the tanker in time, Runner One-one. He's too far from you."

"Okay, then give me vectors to a runway. Any runway."

Another long silence. After half a minute the controller said, "Sorry, Runner One-one. Closest suitable would be San'a. That's more than ten minutes' flying time."

Maxwell didn't argue. Whether or not he could make the San'a airport was irrelevant. He knew the United States Navy didn't want one of its Super Hornets dropping into the capital of the country they'd just finished attacking.

"Okay, give me a vector to a safe ejection area."

"Copy, Runner. Take a heading of 110 and climb to ten thousand. We're alerting the SAR helo now."

Maxwell felt his stomach churning. Another damned ejection over Yemen. It had to be some kind of record. Using the ejection seat of a jet fighter was, by definition, a violent and dangerous way to exit an airplane. He'd gotten away with it once, and that was as much luck as he deserved.

He nudged the nose of the jet upward and started the turn to the southeast. He mentally reviewed the ejection procedures: squawk emergency; cabin pressure ram/dump; shoulder harness locked . . .

His thoughts were interrupted by a transmission. "Runner One-one, do you read Boomer?"

It was a new, croaky voice. Maxwell had to think for a second. "Is that you, Gus?"

"Affirmative. I hear that you're gonna punch out of another government-issue airplane. That's kind of wasteful, isn't it?"

"I'm open to suggestions."

"I've got one, Runner. How about a ten-thousand-foot runway?"

As runways go, it was neither wide—only about seventy-five feet—nor straight. It had a few gentle twists, undulating across the high desert like the path of a snake. The British had constructed the road half a century ago. Al-Fasr had resurfaced it, added gravel, and turned it into a runway for fighters.

"If those MiG jockeys could fly off this road," said Gritti on the tac frequency, "it should be a piece of cake for you squid tailhookers."

Against the drab bleakness of the desert, the road was nearly invisible. Not until he was close—lower than two hundred feet above the ground—did he get a clear view of the surface.

It was rough.

Landing a $40-million fighter on a surface that you wouldn't drive a new truck on was an unnatural act. He flared the jet—another unnatural act for a pilot accustomed to slamming down on a carrier—and eased the Hornet's wheels onto the narrow road.

Scrunch. Scrunch. The landing gear bit into gravel.

Maxwell held his breath as the full weight of the jet settled onto the road. For several seconds he remained tense, waiting to see if the road surface would support the twenty-ton F/A-18.

It did. He snatched both throttles to OFF.

Unlike the MiG-29, the F/A-18 was intended for the sterile runways and flight decks of the U.S. Navy. The Hornet's F414 engines self-destructed at the first whiff of a foreign object in their intakes.

While the engine RPMs slowly wound down, Maxwell steered the Hornet along the gently twisting road. In the eerie quiet outside the cockpit, he could hear the tires crunching through the loose gravel.

Ahead, a Hummer was parked at the roadside. As Maxwell brought the fighter to a smooth stop, he opened the canopy.

The cool mountain air swept through the cockpit. His flight suit was soaked with perspiration. He removed his helmet and let the dry wind blow over him.

Before he shut off the switches, he glanced at his engine fuel display. The totalizer indicated two hundred pounds. Less than two minutes' worth.

An officer with a dirt-streaked face and disheveled BDUs dismounted from the Hummer and strolled over to the side of the cockpit. "Welcome to Al-Fasr International Airport."

"Hey, Gus, has anyone told you that you look like shit?"

He followed Gritti into the tin building.

"Look at this," said Gritti. He was standing in the middle of the large room. An array of electronic devices lined two entire walls. "Radios, scanners, monitors, SatComm— you name it. Enough gear in this room to run a country. The entire complex is networked with computers, all fed by that jumbo server over in the corner." Gritti shook his head. "Incredible, when you consider that most of the peasants out here have never even seen a television."

He moved from rack to rack, peering at each device. He stopped in front of a black-paneled console. "This is pure gold. You know what it is?"

Maxwell leaned close. "Looks like some kind of disc player."

"An optical data storage unit. A damn big one. I'll bet this thing holds more secrets than the Kremlin." He turned to Hewlitt. "Make sure that sucker leaves with us."

Gritti checked his watch again. "We have to be airborne by dusk. Let's check the rest of this joint out."

They walked through each of the buildings, finding more communications equipment. In the last of the tin-roofed structures, they discovered a bank of file cabinets. "More goodies," said Gritti. He called for a squad of marines to load the cabinets into one of the Super Stallions.

At the northern end of the complex, six earth-covered mounds rose twenty feet above the ground. A hard-surfaced ramp sloped downward to the entrance of each mound.

Gritti went down the ramp of the first mound and opened the sliding overhead door. A light came on automatically, illuminating a cavernous space beneath the ground. The space was empty.

They walked inside, peering around at the concrete-reinforced walls and ceiling. The interior of the mound was even larger than it appeared from the outside.

"Guess what they kept in here," Gritti said.

Maxwell nodded. "So this is it." He looked at the gray-painted tug vehicle in the back of the space; then he walked over to the wall where a collection of hoses and tools was hanging. "The mystery MiG base."

"It didn't show up in the TARPS photos you guys took," said Gritti. "Even the recon satellite missed it."

Maxwell was shaking his head. "Another intelligence breakdown. They kept telling us the MiGs came from Eritrea or Chad."

"All Al-Fasr had to do was come roaring out these bunkers, take off on the road, and he was on you like a dirty shirt."

Maxwell kept looking at the empty bunker. Something kept nagging at him. The MiG base should have been obvious, but it went undetected.

Why?

CHAPTER TWENTY-FIVE

SPY CATCHER

USS Ronald Reagan
Gulf of Aden
1815, Thursday, 20 June

Maxwell counted six destroyers weaving in a crisscross pattern across the Gulf. A squadron of sub-hunting helicopters was working fore and aft of the *Reagan* as the carrier cruised eastward into the Arabian Sea. Several miles away, two P-3 Orion patrol planes were skimming the ocean ahead of the battle group.

At the far end of the conference table sat Admiral Fletcher. Next to him sat Captain Stickney, and on the opposite side Spook Morse and Guido Vitale. Col. Gus Gritti, haggard and shaking from fatigue, had given his account of the campaign, then gone to bed, promising to rejoin them in the morning.

Fletcher looked directly at Maxwell. "What makes you so sure it was Al-Fasr?"

"I'm a fighter pilot. I saw the way he flew, the fact that he was in the lead, the tactics he used."

"Was there any chance that he could have survived the crash?" asked Fletcher. "Could he have ejected?"

"Not likely," said Maxwell. "It would have to have happened in a split second before the MiG exploded."

"I haven't seen the HUD tape yet," said Boyce. The Hornet's cockpit video recorder taped everything the pilot saw through the heads-up display. "Let's have a look."

Maxwell reached into the zippered leg pocket of his flight suit and pulled out a cassette. "It was running the whole time." He handed the tape to Morse, who inserted it in the VCR mounted behind the conference table.

The flickering, grainy image shot through the windscreen of Maxwell's Hornet appeared on the wall-mounted screen. Morse fast-forwarded the picture until the shape of a MiG-29 flitted into the HUD's field of view. "That was the first engagement," said Maxwell. "I took an AIM-9 shot, but he beat it."

They watched the view change to the narrow walls of the canyon. Maxwell was chasing the MiG through the narrow ravine.

"Jesus," muttered Boyce. "It looks like a video game."

Suddenly the canyon bridge—the eye of the needle—appeared in the HUD. They saw the MiG roll up on its side and vanish through the hole.

The HUD view abruptly tilted sideways, and the eye of the needle zipped past the camera.

Several audible gasps came from around the table. "You're either crazy as a bedbug," said Boyce, "or you're the world's hottest fighter pilot."

For the next several seconds, the MiG was gone from the HUD view. When it appeared again, it was in a high scissors, diving again toward the ground.

A SHOOT message appeared in the HUD. "That's when I took the second AIM-9 shot," said Maxwell.

The gray smoke trail of a missile could be seen aiming toward the rolling MiG. The missile exploded into the earth just behind the hard-turning MiG-29.

Again the MiG vanished from the screen. Not until several seconds later, after the Hornet had completed a reversal turn, did the terrain reappear. Scattered pockets of smoke and flame marked the crash site of the Fulcrum.

Morse pushed the STOP button. "The impact with the ground was out of the HUD's field of view," he said.

None of the officers at the table spoke.

Finally Fletcher rose. "Gentlemen, if the man flying that MiG was Al-Fasr, then this unholy war is over. The marine unit has finished culling all the intelligence material from the terrorist base and the complex has been destroyed. I will report to CNO and the Joint Chiefs that our campaign in Yemen is concluded and all our personnel have been extracted. The *Reagan* has suffered major battle damage and will be heading through the Strait of Hormuz to Bahrain."

"What about the submarine threat, Admiral?" Boyce asked. "Do you have a fix on him?"

"I wish we did. SUBLANT has tagged the sub—a Project 636 boat named *Ilia Mourmetz*—the only Kilo class unaccounted for in this part of the world. It was sold to Iran, but it seems that it never arrived."

"So who's crewing it?" Boyce asked. "Who put the torpedoes into us?"

"Best guess is the Russian crew that was supposed to be delivering the boat to Iran and who most likely were bought out by Al-Fasr. The Russian government has been very forthcoming with data about the sub and the crew, mainly because they don't want us to think they did it."

"Where's the sub now?"

"We don't know. The ASW commander in the *Arkansas* is certain that it's no longer in our periphery."

"If they don't know where he is, how do they know he's not just waiting somewhere to take another shot?"

Vitale pointed to the window. "Look out there. What you're seeing is the biggest sub hunt in modern history. When that Kilo boat so much as turns a blade—and he'll have to very soon—they're going to kill him."

"How'd he get away after firing his torpedoes?"

The operations officer just shook his head. "One of the dirty little secrets about antisubmarine warfare is that the old diesel/electrics, which we gave up years ago, by the way, are the stealthiest boats in the world. The sub skipper is either brilliant or incredibly lucky. He took an obsolete submarine and a mercenary crew and managed to get inside the most powerful battle group in the world."

"And then escape," added Boyce.

"Maybe there's a lesson in this," said Fletcher. He walked around from the end of the table and gazed out the window. "Our technology and our tactics evolved during the Cold War to battle the Soviet Union. Somewhere along the way we forgot how to fight an enemy like Al-Fasr with old-fashioned weapons."

"Sort of like getting knifed when you thought you were in a gunfight," Boyce said.

"Something like that. A lot of mistakes were made in this campaign." Fletcher stood with his hands clasped behind him, his back to the group at the table. "Most of them mine."

A hush fell over the room. Morse was doodling on a notepad. Vitale's mouth was half open. Stickney looked mesmerized. They were all watching Fletcher.

"The biggest mistake," Fletcher went on, "was in letting the military chain of command be subverted by outside influences. That was *my* error. It's one I will carry responsibility for to my grave."

The silence hung in the compartment like a shroud. None

of them had ever heard a flag officer bare his soul as Fletcher was doing.

"When they convene my court-martial," said Fletcher, "I will testify that it was my overweening ambition and my acquiescence to . . ." He paused, and everyone waited for him to mention Babcock, but he didn't. Instead he said, ". . . my inappropriate deference to a non-military official."

He turned and looked at them. "You all have brilliant careers ahead of you. I want you to remember what happened here so that you don't have to repeat it. It seems that we go through something like this every generation or so—a short-circuit in our military leadership. It happened in Vietnam, with politicians determining our targets. In Iran with the mismanaged hostage rescue. It happened in Lebanon when officials in Washington presumed to manage an air strike against the Syrians."

Fletcher went back to his seat. "And history will show that it happened in Yemen."

Stickney was the first to speak up. "Admiral, may I ask the status of Mr. Babcock? The last I heard, he was—"

"In his quarters." Fletcher glanced at his watch. "Within the hour, he will be flown off to Dubai, and then be on his way back to Washington, where, no doubt, he will arrange for me to be relieved of this command."

Maxwell caught the sardonic note in Fletcher's voice. It was odd, he thought. In the past two days he had actually come to like the white-haired admiral—the same Fletcher whom he had written off as an empty suit. At the eleventh hour the admiral had reached deep inside himself and found a source of inner steel. The tragedy of Langhorne Fletcher was that it happened too late.

"You're dismissed, gentlemen," Fletcher said. "You have my thanks for a job well done."

As the officers headed for the door, he added, "Commander Maxwell, before you leave, may I have a word with you?"

The SCIF—Sensitive Compartmental Information Facility—was located amidships, down in the spaces of the *Reagan*'s surface plot, called Alpha Sierra. Two marine sentries guarded the entrance. The bulkheads of the compartment were specially treated and padded to prevent bugging or passive emissions monitoring.

At his worktable inside the SCIF, FBI agent Adam Korchek tilted back in his steel desk chair and rubbed his eyes. He hated this place—the claustrophobic sterility of the windowless compartment, halide lamps glaring from the overhead, the drab gray furniture. One bulkhead was lined with tape reels and disc players. Across the compartment six cryptologists, linguists, and intelligence analysts were laboring at their consoles.

For the past thirteen hours Korchek and Dick Mosely, the CIA officer who specialized in Arab terrorist organizations, had been analyzing the transcribed material that the marines had brought from Al-Fasr's base compound. Most of the data was encrypted, which took time to decode and translate.

It was hard work, but by the time he'd worked through the third stack of transcriptions—the data from the optical storage unit in the Al-Fasr compound—Korchek knew he had struck pay dirt. He now had half a dozen recorded Sat-Comm conversations between Al-Fasr and someone who was obviously in an influential position. Though the official's name was never explicitly used, it was clear in the transcription that he and Al-Fasr were more than well acquainted.

As he sifted through the piles of transcriptions, something still troubled Korchek. There were these snippets of encrypted one-way transmissions and received messages.

Some were clearly intended for a clandestine warship, relaying information and points of intended movement of the *Reagan* and its battle group. From the content of the messages, Korchek deduced that they were intended for a submarine, presumably the Kilo-class boat that had attacked the carrier.

Were these from the same source as the SatComm exchanges?

By his nature and experience, Korchek was a cynical man. He had no wife, no immediate family except for a pair of brothers in Chicago whom he despised. His early years in law enforcement had imbued him with a distrust of his fellow man, and it was this trait that had served him best in the field of counterintelligence. Like a bloodhound, Korchek had a knack for sniffing out the tiniest whiff of perfidy.

Now he was sniffing. He didn't have the scent yet, but he knew that he was getting close.

Korchek returned to his piles of transcriptions. For another two hours he pored over them, puzzling out the meaning of the tiny encrypted snippets, looking for a pattern.

Suddenly it jumped off the page, jolting him like a hot spark. *Of course!* Korchek sat upright in the chair, staring at the piles of transcribed messages. It made perfect sense. Nothing solid, nothing provable, at least not yet. But he had the scent clearly in his nostrils.

He rose and went over to the watch officer, a pudgy lieutenant commander in khakis. He gave the officer a pink memo sheet with a handwritten name on it. "Download the background investigation file on this man. For my eyes only."

The watch officer looked annoyed. "Is this urgent?" he said. "I'm pretty busy getting—"

"Do you want me to get the operations officer on the line? Just fucking do it and quit wasting time."

The watch officer was not accustomed to being insulted by civilians. He glowered at Korchek for a second. Grudgingly, he picked up the pink sheet and read it.

A look of shock passed over his face. Nodding his head in amazement, he swung his chair around to his desk keyboard and began typing in the file download order.

Fletcher's eyes bored into him. "Why didn't you tell me that your father was Harlan Maxwell?"

Maxwell was taken aback. "Ah, it wasn't relevant, Admiral. I don't bring up my father's name in connection with my own career."

Fletcher nodded. "Knowing you as I do now, I understand. It so happens I'm well acquainted with your father. Served under him when he had the Second Fleet. He was a very good officer, a hard man to work for sometimes, rather blunt and fixed in his opinions. But you always knew where you stood with Harlan Maxwell. Sort of like you, I suspect."

Maxwell kept his silence, wondering where this was going.

Fletcher pulled an envelope from his shirt pocket. "This came in on the Athena net the day before yesterday. It seems that your father was worried and wanted to know if you were okay. I didn't answer, because at the time you weren't okay. You had been shot down in Yemen."

Maxwell felt an old familiar emptiness as he listened to Fletcher. How long had it been? More than two years since he and his father had communicated, and then only to exchange terse Christmas greetings. It had been that way for most of his adult life, this discordant relationship. The elder Maxwell could never stop being the Admiral—the senior presence in his life. He could never stop being the rebellious son.

Now the Admiral was worried about his son.

"I'm probably violating a confidence by telling you this," Fletcher said. "In his note, Harlan asked me not to let you know. But I find it troubling, such a disconnect between father and son."

Disconnect. There was an understatement, thought Maxwell. He and his father had been disconnected since the day Sam—that was before he received the call sign "Brick"—announced that he had declined his appointment to the U.S. Naval Academy.

His father, an academy grad and the son and grandson of academy alumni, was apoplectic. The chill lasted until Sam graduated from Rensselaer and took his commission in the U.S. Navy.

The next major rift occurred when Brick, then a test pilot, left active Navy duty to become an astronaut. To his father, it was a breach of tradition. Maxwells were seagoing naval officers, not space cowboys.

No one, however, stood taller or prouder in the viewing area than Harlan Maxwell on the day his son lifted off in the shuttle *Atlantis*. It was his first flight into space and, as it turned out, his last, which caused the next rift between the Maxwells.

His father had not spoken to him since he had resigned from NASA.

"My father and I don't see eye to eye," Brick heard himself saying.

"I never had a son, just daughters," said Fletcher. "But I know something about trying to live up to someone else's expectations. My own father was an admiral, you know."

Maxwell nodded. He knew that he liked Fletcher.

"I'm going to answer Harlan's letter," Fletcher said. "You know what I'm going to say?"

Maxwell shook his head.

"I'm going to tell him that if I had a son like you, I would be the proudest man in the world. If he doesn't immediately sit down and tell you he loves you, he doesn't deserve to be a father."

Maxwell didn't know what to say. Old emotions were whirling around inside him like a storm. "Sir, I don't—"

"Do the same thing. Go write a letter to your old man. Tell him you love him. Trust me, son; he wants to hear that more than anything."

Maxwell fought back a well of tears. He nodded and said, "Yes, sir. I'll do that."

CHAPTER TWENTY-SIX

DESTINY

Gulf of Aden
1905, Thursday, 20 June

"Range increasing on the primary target, Captain."

Manilov looked at the technician on the sonar console. "Bearing and distance?"

"Zero-eight-five degrees, 5,200 meters on the primary. The two trailing targets, same bearing, 3,500 meters."

Manilov acknowledged with a headshake. The battle group was moving away to the east. He had managed to stymie the searchers by concealing the *Mourmetz* directly beneath the huge mass of the aircraft carrier, then transitioning to a totally silent operating mode. For over six hours they had been concealed here, emitting no signal, registering no audible sound. The boat was only partially stable, and he had been compelled to use his crew for balance, moving them fore and aft, to help maintain the *Mourmetz*'s attitude.

In every direction he could hear the sub hunters scouring the Gulf of Aden. They had failed to find the *Ilia Mourmetz*. Now he could strike again.

Five thousand meters was still a suitable range for the SET-16 torpedo. He would not ascend to periscope depth. From where they were, at a depth of 210 meters, he would fire a salvo of four torpedoes.

Perhaps it would be enough to kill the *Reagan*. If he was lucky, he would strike a vital organ of the carrier.

"What are your intentions, Captain?"

Manilov glanced up at his executive officer, Dimitri Popov. The young officer had proven himself to be a capable second-in-command. With his cool, unruffled composure during the tense hours of combat, he had earned the respect of the men.

All his crew, even the lowest-ranking enlisted seamen, had discharged their duties honorably. Since they had entered the Gulf of Aden, he himself had acquired a feeling for these men that was very much like familial love. In their crisp, unswerving response to his orders, he knew that they respected him.

Even in his most bizarre fantasies, he could not have imagined a sweeter finish to an otherwise dreary career. The epic adventure they had undertaken was the stuff of Russian fables. He and his gallant young crew had sailed into the teeth of an impossibly powerful foe. They had kept their appointment with destiny.

Popov was waiting for an answer.

"I think we should complete our mission, Mr. Popov."

The executive officer's expression didn't change. "The men will follow your orders, whatever you decide, Captain."

"And you, Mr. Popov?"

Popov brought his heels together with a click. "I am at your command, sir."

Manilov nodded, touched by the display of loyalty. He gazed around the control compartment at the tense young faces—Antonin, Popov, Borodin, Keretsky—the eager warrants, the conscripted sailors. Each trusted him with his life.

Each had his own soaring hopes, aspirations, dreams of the future. Many had left young wives and infant children back in Mother Russia.

They had a right to live.

For the first time since their voyage began, Manilov's sense of ultimate destiny was tempered by another emotion. It nibbled at him now, buzzing in his brain like a gnat.

They trust you with their lives.

The men had done everything he had asked of them. More, actually. None had volunteered for a suicide mission. They were mercenaries, not martyrs. They had taken unthinkable risks, completed their assigned mission with skill and daring. It was not their fault the damned obsolete SET-16 torpedoes had failed to kill the *Reagan,* not their doing that the hull of the carrier had been constructed to resist conventional warheads.

Ah, if the *Mourmetz*'s torpedoes had been tipped with nuclear warheads, it would have been a different story. The invincible *Reagan* would be vaporized in a cloud of steam.

"Fifty-four hundred meters, Captain, range increasing. We still have a valid firing solution."

Four more torpedoes. He could expect at least two to strike the primary target. And then what? The damned ship still might not sink. The antisubmarine force hovering around the *Reagan* would pounce like a pack of jackals. The *Mourmetz* would be doomed.

So be it. It's your destiny.

Perhaps. But was it theirs? Did he have the right to take them with him into eternity—all in pursuit of some mystical Russian fate?

No.

He barked out the order: "Forward five knots, come starboard to 170 degrees. Maintain 220 meters."

Every head in the control compartment swung toward him.

"The torpedo tubes are loaded and ready, Captain," said Popov.

"Seal them. The war is over for us. We're departing the area."

A buzz of whispered conversation spread through the control compartment. He could see jubilation on their faces. *The war is over for us.*

"May I ask where we're heading, sir?" Popov asked. His eyes were shining.

"Around the horn, down the east coast of Africa. Near Mombasa. That is our best escape route. We'll pick the exact spot after we've established contact ashore."

Beyond that, he had no idea. They would have to scuttle the *Mourmetz,* which would be painful for him. They had no choice. The boat was about to become the object of the greatest submarine hunt—

"Aircraft overhead," called out Borodin from his console. Then, seconds later, "Sonobuoys in the water."

Silence filled the control compartment. Manilov rushed over to Borodin's display.

"Contact," the sonar technician called out. "They're pinging us!"

"Depth 250 meters," Manilov ordered. "Slow to three knots, left 090 degrees."

"It's a large aircraft," Borodin reported. "Four engines, turboprop."

Manilov frowned. A P-3 Orion. That was troubling. Probably from one of their bases in the Persian Gulf. The P-3 carried a crew of twelve or so, and had the most sophisticated airborne sub-tracking system in the world.

His options were limited. He could stop forward motion and remain motionless here beneath the thermal layer, adrift in the depths like a suspended carcass. Their survival would depend on the sonar-deflecting anechoic tiles on the *Mourmetz*'s hull. Or he could turn and try to slip out of the search area, returning to the littoral waters off the Yemeni coastline. Or he could run for the rocky shoreline of Socotra, the island twenty miles south in the Arabian Sea.

He didn't like any of the choices. The P-3 was just the advance scout. Within minutes, the entire antisubmarine force of the *Reagan* battle group would join the hunt.

The thought struck Manilov that he could still fire his torpedoes. The *Reagan* was still within range. The source of the torpedoes would be instantly clear. The subhunters would have a positive location on the *Mourmetz*.

Again he thought of his gallant young crew. No, he decided. They deserved to live.

"MAD, MAD, MAD!" called out the petty officer running the magnetic anomaly-detection gear. He stabbed the position lock key on his panel, fixing the exact location of the contact in the Orion's inertial guidance navigational computer.

Lt. Chip Weyrhauser, the twenty-eight-year-old P-3 plane commander, felt a surge of excitement. A MAD contact! The long stinger on the tail of the P-3—the MAD boom—was ancient technology in antisubmarine warfare equipment. Its only usefulness was when you passed directly over the magnetic field of a submerged boat.

As they had just done.

It had to be the Kilo.

He knew that the TACCO—tactical coordination officer—Lt. Jethro Williams, was already on the horn back to the ASW commander aboard USS *Arkansas*. They were datalinked to the command center, and the commander was seeing everything the TACCO saw.

Weyrhauser couldn't believe his luck. He had been about to pack it in, declare minimum fuel, and head back to Masirah, their island base off Oman. For six hours they had been sweeping this piece of ocean, coming up with nothing.

Weyrhauser had often regretted choosing patrol planes instead of carrier-based fighters. He thought it would be cushy duty. Patrol plane pilots got to live in neat shore-based quarters—Hawaii or California or Spain—flying big four-engined turboprops, which gave you a good résumé for an airline job. What he hadn't counted on was the tedium of these god-awful long patrols, the endless search patterns for submarines that, in most cases, got away. Even when you caught them, it was anticlimactic because you never did anything about it. Nobody had sunk an enemy submarine for over half a century.

That's about to change.

They had the Kilo locked up. Or close, anyway. All they needed was an active lock with the sonobuoys. And clearance to shoot.

The notion made Weyrhauser giddy. This was the renegade sub that had already stuck two fish into the *Reagan.* The crew who nailed this boat would be the greatest heroes since Dolittle raided Tokyo.

"Steer right, 290 degrees," called the TACCO.

Weyrhauser complied, bending the P-3 around in a hard right turn back to the northwest. He was flying the patrol plane by hand, not willing to use the autopilot down this low. They were skimming the water at only a hundred feet altitude, going nearly two hundred knots.

They were flying a box pattern, laying a wall of sonobuoys at each side of the box. Sonobuoys were floating sonar signaling devices that transmitted their returns back to the P-3's mission computer. These were the advanced DIFAR models—directional frequency and ranging—with microphones that could be lowered to listen at preselected depths.

The TACCO selected the array of sonobuoys on his console display, then let the computer automatically eject them from the tubes.

"Contact! Contact!" called out the number two sensor operator.

The TACCO noted the plot, then ordered another right turn. "Roll out 105 degrees. Shit, we're losing him again!"

It was a bitch trying to pick out the muted hush of a submarine from the gurgling clamor of the ocean. Out here they had not only the sounds of a dozen other ships, but the waves beating the rocks over at Socotra and on the Yemeni coast.

"Getting him again," said the TACCO. "He's turning. Come left ten degrees . . . hold it there." Then, ten seconds later, "Contact!"

Weyrhauser could feel the charged atmosphere inside the P-3. They were close, very close. He could almost smell the adrenaline in the cabin of the Orion.

"Are we weapons free?" he called to Williams on the intercom.

"Negative," the TACCO came back. "Weapons locked. We're waiting for clearance from Popeye." Popeye was the call sign for the antisubmarine warfare commander, a Navy captain stationed aboard the Aegis cruiser *Arkansas.*

Weyrhauser chafed at the restriction, even though he knew the reason. There was at least one other submarine in these waters—the *Bremerton,* the nuclear attack boat that had joined the hunt for the killer sub.

But, goddammit, they were being too cautious. The commander on the *Arkansas* was seeing the same thing the TACCO saw. No way could this be an American nuke boat. Only one kind of submarine in the world emitted that distinctive seven-bladed screw signature—a Russian Kilo class.

Weyrhauser could barely contain himself. While the brass dithered, this Ivan was getting away.

Eight thousand yards was a good range for the Mark 50 torpedo. The torpedo would make its own passive search for the submarine. When it acquired the target, the seeker would go to active pinging. After that, the submarine was dead meat.

"MAD, MAD!" cried out the operator at his panel.

The sub was directly beneath them.

The TACCO again fixed the position in the navigational computer. "Got him, turning south, heading for Socotra."

"Check our weapons status again," Weyrhauser ordered.

A quarter minute passed. "Got it!" Jethro Williams said over the intercom. "Weapons free."

Weyrhauser felt a shiver of excitement run through him. They were about to make history.

He received another heading change from Williams. This time they would fly a mile-long, wings-level pass directly along the axis of the submarine's last two plotted positions.

"Bomb bay doors open," Weyrhauser ordered.

It was a calculated gamble, turning south and running for it. Manilov knew he was risking everything on the chance that the P-3 would lose its lock on the *Mourmetz* before the other aircraft and ships showed up. He would be outside the net of sonobuoys before they could reestablish the contact.

Only twenty miles. If he reached Socotra, they might escape. In the undersea wilderness off the island's shore, sonar echoes were strewn like chaff in the wind. The submarine would be undetectable.

Did he make the right decision?

Strange, he thought. Never before had he questioned his own judgment. His objective had always been clear: Kill the enemy. To that end, every decision he made, each order he gave, was like the subliminal moves of a fencer. Thrust and parry. Act and react. Yevgeny Manilov possessed an unwavering confidence in his ability.

But something had changed. His single-minded obsession with sinking the *Reagan* was replaced by a different imperative: He wanted to live. More than that, he wanted his crew to live.

A rivulet of perspiration found its way past his brow, dripping off his nose and splashing onto the chart before him. His palms were damp. He felt a dryness in his throat.

Should he have remained in place? In deep water, beneath the thermal layer, the *Mourmetz* might have stayed undetected by the sub-hunting patrol plane.

Perhaps. It was a decision he couldn't undo. Now they would live or die with it.

The earlier jubilation in the control compartment was gone. The crew wore expressions of grim determination. Borodin stared at the console of the MGK-400EM digital sonar. Popov busied himself scribbling on a notepad, ignoring the chirping pings of the sonobuoys.

Then another sound. A deeper, more sinister noise.

"Torpedo in the water!" shouted Borodin.

Each head in the control compartment swung to the sonar operator. "Bearing 025, seven thousand meters," the sonar operator announced. "Forty knots, passive searching."

Manilov's thoughts raced ahead. It had to be a Mark 46 or a Mark 50. In either case, the torpedo would conduct its own private little search until it located a target within its programmed radius. Then it went into active sonar tracking and homed in like a killer angel.

He thought about firing another Igla, taking out the patrol plane. It was too late. Firing the missile would only betray their exact position.

"Ascend to fifty meters, steer 205 degrees. Ahead full."

He saw Popov looking at him questioningly. "We're putting our stern to the torpedo?"

"We're buying time," said Manilov. "We'll run until he goes active. Then we make noise near the surface, turn and try to decoy it."

Popov was still staring at him. It was contrary to the textbook Russian Navy tactic, which favored turning *toward* an incoming torpedo, making it overshoot. Manilov had never believed in the tactic.

Did he make the right decision?

There it was again. The doubt.

"Decoys, Captain?"

Manilov shook his head. "Not yet. Not until he goes active."

The submarine tilted upward, ascending rapidly. Through the hull they could hear the sound of the torpedo's high-speed screw.

"Three thousand meters," Borodin called.

Then a new sound: rapid, relentless, high-frequency pinging. It sounded like the chirping of a maniacal insect.

"Active sonar!" Borodin yelled. "We're targeted."

In the mission computer display he saw the digital symbol of the torpedo with a flashing circle around it. He was right. It was a Mark 50.

"Hard left, full rudder, 020 degrees."

"Aye, Captain."

"Decoys now."

Popov punched the switch for the decoy dispenser, spewing a trail of sonar-attracting decoys in the wake of the submarine.

At a speed of fifteen knots and accelerating, the *Mourmetz* sliced into the hard left turn. Manilov was gambling that the torpedo would sense the false mass of the decoys and continue straight for them.

By the time the submarine was halfway through the turn, Manilov knew it wasn't working.

The torpedo wasn't fooled.

The pinging reached a fanatical pitch. Manilov saw the flashing symbol on the display moving leftward, intercepting the submarine's new course.

"A thousand meters, closing," Borodin said. His voice was flat, without emotion.

Manilov nodded. He felt the eyes of his young crew watching him. Popov's lips were moving in a silent supplication. Borodin's face was solemn, resigned.

Manilov looked from one to the other, returning each man's questioning gaze. *They trusted you. They've placed their lives in your hands.*

He knew what he had to do. Rising from his console, he picked up his Russian Navy officer's cap and placed it on his head.

He turned to Popov. "Bow planes full up," he ordered. "Flank speed, emergency ascent."

Popov's mouth dropped open. "Ascent? Captain, the torpedo . . . it will—"

"I gave you an order, Mr. Popov. Emergency ascent!"

Popov nodded and turned to his console.

Manilov gripped the brass handhold at his station as the hull of the *Mourmetz* tilted upward. He heard the nearly silent hum of the propulsion system deepen to a noisy throb. *So much for stealthy running,* he thought. The *Mourmetz* had no more need for stealth.

"Thirty meters, ascending," called out Antonin in an unnaturally high voice. Manilov saw the digital depth gage unwinding in a blur.

In a forty-five degree ascent, the submarine was racing for the open sky.

"Twenty meters."

Most emergency ascents, in Manilov's experience, were showboat maneuvers. They were performed to impress bureaucrats and high-ranking officers and the media. In reality, bursting through the surface at such a speed and angle was guaranteed to inflict damage on antennae and planes and exterior running gear.

None of that mattered now.

Clinging to the brass handhold, Manilov kept his eye on the sonar display. The symbol of the incoming torpedo was blinking on the screen like a firefly. With each blink, it appeared closer to the symbol of the *Mourmetz*. The symbols were nearly merged.

Borodin saw it too. He glanced up at Manilov. Manilov just nodded.

In the next instant, he felt the bow of the *Ilia Mourmetz* shoot through the surface like an erupting geyser. He braced himself as the bow plunged back downward. He snatched the microphone from his console.

"Attention all hands, this is the captain. Stand by for torpedo damage. Prepare to—"

The torpedo smashed into the *Mourmetz*'s port side, just forward of the bow plane. The explosion ripped through the pressure hull, opening the submarine to a flood of seawater.

The control cabin went black. Manilov was flung against the bulkhead, smashing his head into a switch panel. He dropped to the deck, knocked senseless.

He was dimly aware of water sloshing over him. He saw the dim yellow emergency lights flicker, then come on.

Dazed, he struggled to his knees and looked around the compartment. In the flickering light, it looked like a scene from hell. The decks were awash. Torrents of seawater poured in through a ruptured bulkhead.

Antonin lay hunched over his panel. Blood gushed from a deep wound in his temple. Borodin was sprawled face-down on the flooded deck, looking lifeless. Keretzky was nowhere in sight.

Someone—he guessed that it was Popov—was standing on the ladder to the sail bridge. He was struggling to open the hatch.

Manilov staggered over to where Borodin lay. He pulled the young man upright, then dragged him toward the ladder.

Popov had the hatch open. A fresh torrent of seawater sloshed in on them.

Manilov shoved Borodin up to Popov. "Take him." His voice sounded tinny and distant. The explosion had rendered him nearly deaf.

He returned to the control compartment. Antonin was on his feet, bleeding profusely and looking confused. Manilov steered him to the ladder, then shoved him toward the hatch where Popov had stationed himself.

"They're getting out," Popov yelled down. "I can see the others escaping from the aft hatch."

Manilov nodded. At least half his crew, those in the aft compartments, would live. So would those in the forward section who survived the torpedo blast. He had made the right decision.

Twice more he returned, dragging Keretzky and then Chenin, one of the young enlisted men, to the hatch.

He made one more pass, looking for survivors. The compartment was waist deep in seawater. The hull was listing to port, the bow tilting downward. Manilov heard a long, creaking metallic noise, which he knew was a bulkhead giving way.

The *Ilia Mourmetz* was dying.

In the yellow light, he saw something, a dark round object, floating past him. It was his Russian Navy officer's cap. Manilov retrieved the cap, gave it a shake, then placed it squarely on his head.

In a thousand dreams, he had lived this moment. He stood as tall as he could in the shifting compartment. He was a Russian naval officer. This was his destiny.

The lights flickered again, then went out, pitching the compartment into blackness. With a final shudder, the *Ilia Mourmetz* rolled over and began its long descent to the bottom of the sea.

CHAPTER TWENTY-SEVEN

THE TAKEDOWN

USS Ronald Reagan
0755, Friday, 21 June

"This is preposterous," said Fletcher. "You're telling me that Commander Parsons is not the spy?"

Adam Korchek, on the secure phone in the SCIF, said, "He never was."

"How long have you known that?"

"Since I arrested him."

He heard a spluttering noise from Admiral Fletcher's end of the line. "You've got some explaining to do, Mr. Korchek. Without informing me, you went ahead and arrested an innocent man—"

"Knock it off, Admiral. I'm here to take down traitors, not play your silly little military etiquette games."

A long silent moment followed. Korchek knew he had thoroughly pissed off a senior naval officer. He didn't care.

When Fletcher again spoke, his voice was strained. "How did you know it wasn't Parsons?"

"Because the encrypted stuff I found on his computer

didn't originate there. The origin codes, which my software can trace, came from a different computer. It had to have been planted on Parsons's computer."

"Are you going to tell me whose computer it came from?"

"Are you sitting down?"

"Go ahead."

Korchek told him.

Several seconds of silence passed. "Oh, my God," he heard Fletcher say. "Inform me as soon as he's in custody."

"You'll be the first to know," Korchek said, and hung up.

From his battered leather briefcase he pulled out the Glock. After he'd checked the pistol, he shoved the clip back into the grip and slipped it into the holster in the small of his back. He could use the ship's security detail to make the actual arrest, but that wasn't his style. It would be like inviting someone else to finish off a piece of tail for you.

This was the part of the job that Korchek liked most. After the sleuthing, assembling the myriad pieces of the mosaic, zeroing in on the identity of your subject, then you got to take him down.

This was a big fish, and Korchek hoped the guilty scumbag would put up some resistance. Not a lot, just enough to make it sporting. That was the absolutely best part, when the perp saw that it was over and he tried to make a break. Then you could quite justifiably kick the shit out of him. Within limits, of course.

He waited until the two marine security guards showed up. They were waiting in the passageway outside the SCIF, in full combat gear, carrying their M16A2 carbines. That was all the firepower Korchek wanted for this job.

He had deliberately left the other three team members out of it. The two CIA types, Mosely and Grad, would immediately be on the line to their bosses back in spook headquarters, and the whole operation would then be micromanaged from Virginia. The other FBI agent, Bill Gould, was a trial

lawyer by training, and his shtick was to analyze the shit out
of everything before he ever made a move. By then the spy
could be in Patagonia.

This would be Adam Korchek's private little coup.

With the marines clumping along in trail, he left the SCIF
and ascended to the O-3 level. He knew the area well by
now. They passed the sign on the bulkhead that read OFFI-
CERS COUNTRY, and entered the warren of staterooms.

He looked up and down the passageway, then approached
the middle stateroom. He heard music—a modern jazz
piece—coming from inside.

Korchek slipped the Glock from the holster behind his
back. Holding the pistol at the ready, he paused to read the
placarded name on the door: COMMANDER O. B. "SPOOK"
MORSE, CVBG INTEL OFFICER.

The instant Morse turned the corner in the passageway, he
knew. They were already there. They'd gotten inside his
room.

A marine stood in the doorway, his back to him. How
many were inside? Who was it? That FBI attack dog, Korchek?

For sure it would be Korchek.

Another minute and he would have gotten to the room before them. His pistol—the Beretta nine millimeter—was
still in there. Now he was unarmed, no place to go, five hundred miles at sea.

A hunted man.

A spy.

For a fleeting instant he considered hitting the marine
from behind. He was a martial arts expert, skilled enough to
drop a man with a blow to the base of his skull. Then he'd
grab the carbine. Whoever was inside was probably searching the room. With the advantage of surprise, he'd be able to
kill them with the M16.

He dismissed the idea. Korchek was not a man to be taken by surprise. He was a cunning predator, waiting for him to do something stupid. Stupid ideas grew out of desperation. If he was to stay alive, he had to stop thinking like a desperate man.

This was the moment that Spook Morse knew would come someday. In his conscious mind he had deceived himself in a dozen ways, rationalizing that he was too intelligent, too careful, too experienced to be found out and captured.

Why had he taken such risks?

When he became acquainted with the cultivated Emirate Air Force colonel, Jamal Al-Fasr, during his assignment to the Fifth Fleet staff, it had seemed a mutually useful association. Al-Fasr would sometimes slip to him items about the Arab countries' defense initiatives and future weapons acquisitions. In turn, Morse would feed him innocuous tidbits about coalition force dispersal and fleet deployments. Never anything sensitive or highly classified. It was the sort of exchange intelligence officers practiced all the time.

Then, while Morse was still assigned to the fleet post in Bahrain, two events changed his life. The first was his wife's announcement that she was leaving him for a British RAF squadron leader with whom she'd been having an affair for two years. The second, which occurred almost simultaneously, was the Navy's decision to pass him over for promotion to captain.

It was too much to accept. He, Spook Morse, who should have risen to flag rank and, at the least, to command of the National Security Agency, would be forever relegated to menial staff posts.

Then Jamal Al-Fasr made him an offer he couldn't refuse.

He hadn't done it just for the money. It was something far greater than that. Justice. Honor. Revenge, even. He had been wronged and—*damn them to hell!*—they would pay.

The marine was backing out of the doorway.

For what seemed like an eternity, Morse and the marine stood in the passageway, twenty feet apart, exchanging gazes. The young man—he was white, about twenty years old—wore the standard Kevlar helmet, holding an M16 across his chest.

Staring at him.

Recognizing him.

Run. The command came from somewhere in the back of his brain, a primal directive. *Run! Run like an animal.*

Blindly, pell-mell, without direction, he sprinted down the passageway, around a corner to the left. Behind him he heard voices: "Mr. Korchek, it's him! He's heading for the hangar deck!"

The heavy clumping of boots echoed on steel bulk-heads—*whump whump whump*—pursuing him like beasts from hell.

He collided with two men—junior officers engaged in conversation at the door before the ladder down to the hangar deck. One of the men, a lieutenant said, "Hey! What do you think—"

He stiff-armed the man out of his way, shoving him against the bulkhead. He scrambled down the ladder. "Hey, you!" he heard the lieutenant yelling after him. "Come back here, asshole!"

Morse had no idea where he was running to. In theory, it was possible to disappear aboard an aircraft carrier like the *Reagan,* which had as many enclosures and spaces as a medium-sized city.

He reached the bottom of the ladder and bolted into the hangar bay. For a second he stood there, surveying the scene. The cavernous area was filled with aircraft, wings folded, fastened to the deck with tie-down chains. Tugs chugged across the deck, towing fifty-thousand-pound war-planes like semitrailers.

Again, the sound of boots. Coming from the ladder above.

He darted across the hangar deck, then caught his shin on a tie-down chain and went tumbling across the rough, non-skid surface of the deck. The chain ripped into his leg. Blood spurted from his torn trousers. Painfully he climbed to his feet and hobbled aft, in the direction of the fantail.

"Stop him!" someone yelled. "Stop that man! He's a fugitive."

At this, a husky young sailor in blue chambray working clothes stepped from under the wing of an F/A-18, blocking his path. The sailor grabbed for his arm.

He let the sailor set himself, allowing him to yank his arm. Suddenly he shot his right hand forward, heel extended with his full weight behind it, catching the sailor beneath the chin. The man's head snapped backward as if on a hinge, making a cracking sound. He toppled backward like a rag doll onto the hangar deck.

The sound of his pursuers grew louder. Boots pounding on the steel deck.

Run.

Running was difficult. His injured leg throbbed, and his breath came in short, hard rasps. *The Beretta.* Why hadn't he kept the pistol with him? He should have been ready for this. *Where to run?*

That way. Across the deck he saw daylight, clouds, an opaque sky and ocean. The elevator bay was open. The giant deck-edge elevator was used to transport jets between the flight deck and the big interior hangar deck. The elevator was topside now, flush with the flight deck. The great cavity in the side of the ship was open to the sea.

He ran toward the elevator bay. An EA-6B Prowler was tied down at the aft side of the open elevator well, and an F/A-18 on the forward side. His heart pounded. He fought the mounting sense of desperation that was seizing control of him.

At the deck edge Morse stopped, looking wildly around him. They were trotting toward him, thirty yards away. He recognized the burly, oily-faced Korchek, chuffing behind the two marines. He carried a pistol.

Morse was cornered. No place to hide, no options, not even a weapon . . .

He saw something—a locker mounted on the bulkhead behind him. Stenciled on the cover was

PYROTECHNIC SIGNALING DEVICES,

EMERGENCY USE ONLY.

He snatched the cover open. Inside the locker was a stack of night signaling flares, another stack of smoke flares, and a box of pencil flares that deck crew wore in their flotation vests.

A box was labeled VERY PISTOLS. He tore the box open. It contained three of the brass-colored pistols. Beside it was another box—STAR SHELLS.

The Very pistol had been around for over a century. It was a short-barreled device that fired a single large-caliber signaling cartridge.

He picked up one of the pistols. He snatched one of the star-shell cartridges and shoved it into the pistol.

Clutching the Very pistol close to him, he ran to the edge of the elevator bay. He stood at the deck edge, peering out at the open sea.

"Hold it right there!" The voice came from behind him.

He continued gazing toward the ocean. The dark rim of a land formation jutted from the distant horizon. The coast of Somalia? Perhaps the Yemeni island of Socotra, nestled in the Gulf of Aden. It meant the ship was heading eastward.

"Turn around with your hands on your head," he heard Korchek order. "The game's over."

Morse didn't respond. A strange sense of calm had come over him. The urgent, cornered-animal desperation was gone, replaced by a cool detachment. He was again in control. He was Spook Morse, master of espionage.

He turned to face his enemies. His hands came up with the Very pistol.

Boom! He was shocked at the heavy recoil of the gun. For an instant he caught the look of disbelief on Korchek's face. The star-shell signaling charge exploded in a blinding flash where the FBI agent's face had been.

He was dimly aware of the muzzle flashes from the two M16 combat rifles as the 5.56-millimeter bullets tore into him.

Within seconds, a crowd had gathered around the elevator bay.

"Medic!" someone yelled. "Get the medics here on the double!"

"No hurry," someone else said. "These guys ain't going nowhere."

The hangar deck officer, a lieutenant commander in a yellow jersey, charged across the hangar bay. He pushed his way into the crowd of sailors, wondering what was going on. From up in his control compartment he'd heard something that definitely sounded like gunfire. On *his* goddamned hangar deck.

Two marines stood there, wearing their combat gear. On the deck lay a man's body, some guy in civvies. Ten feet away, at the deck edge, was another body in officer's khakis.

The hangar deck officer pushed his way over to the civilian. He saw the guy's feet, wearing wing-tip cordovans. Someone had covered his head with a towel. A puddle of fluid was spreading on the deck around him.

"What the hell's going on?" the hangar deck officer demanded. Without waiting for a reply, he stooped over and removed the towel from the man's head.

His face was a molten mass of bloody protoplasm. The

stench of incinerated hair and flesh hit the officer in the gut like a hammer blow.

He recoiled from the sight. His hour-old lunch surged like lava from the depths of his stomach. He couldn't hold it. He staggered to the deck edge and leaned out over the rail, heaving his guts out.

After a minute of concentrated barfing, the officer turned from the rail and wiped his mouth with a handkerchief. Weakly, he walked over to the marines, making a heroic effort not to look at the faceless corpse in civvies.

"Okay, what happened?"

The senior marine, a corporal, told him.

The officer shook his head, his stomach still roiling.

He looked at the other body, the one in the officer's uniform. The dead man wore silver oak leaves on his collar. At least half a dozen rounds had been fired into him. He lay on his back, his eyes staring sightlessly out to sea.

The hangar deck officer recognized him from the wardroom. He was an intelligence officer, one of those prissy staff guys who never wasted his time conversing with the working stiffs. The guy was a mess.

Torpedoes, air strikes, now a shootout on his deck. It had been a hell of a day. "Fucking incredible," said the hangar deck officer.

CHAPTER TWENTY-EIGHT

STRAIT OF HORMUZ

USS Ronald Reagan
Arabian Sea
1145, Friday, 21 June

On the third ring, a voice answered. "Lieutenant Johnson."

"It's Claire Phillips. Would you be available for some conversation?"

A pause. Claire could sense the hostility over the phone. "The answer's still no," B. J. Johnson said. "No interview, no television exclusive of the amazing wounded girl pilot."

"That's not what it's about."

"What then?"

"Some girl talk. No business, no Navy stuff."

"Look, Ms. Phillips, I have a lot to—"

"Call me Claire. And I promise I won't keep you long."

Another hesitation. "For a few minutes. Where do you want to meet?"

"Your call."

"You know how to find the viewing gallery up behind the island? Vultures' row, they call it."

"I know it. See you in ten minutes."

She's very good looking, thought B.J., and the thought only made her angrier. Even in a shapeless jumpsuit and wearing minimal makeup, Claire Phillips was one of those women who could look like a fashion model even in a twenty-knot wind on the *Reagan*'s viewing deck.

"Okay," said B.J., "what did you want to talk about?"

"Just some personal stuff. What it's like being a woman in a man's world."

"I told you before, no interview."

Claire held her hands up. "See? No notepad, no recorder. You have my word that whatever we talk about won't go any farther."

"I gather you don't want me talking about what I saw this morning."

Claire tilted her head, looking at her. "What did you see this morning?"

"You and Commander Maxwell, alone in his room."

Claire nodded. "I think I'm getting the picture. And what do you think we were doing in his room?"

B.J. struggled to keep her voice neutral. "Seems obvious enough. I believe they call it shacking up."

"Would it make any difference if I told you we weren't doing that?"

For a moment, B.J. wasn't sure how to answer. She folded her arms over her chest and turned to the rail. "I really don't care, one way or the other."

"Yes, you do. Otherwise you wouldn't be so angry."

"I am *not* angry," she said, aware that the anger was spilling out of her like venom. "What you do together doesn't interest me in the slightest."

"Look, B.J., you can believe what you want. But you ought

to know that Sam Maxwell has more personal integrity than you're giving him credit for. He happens to care very much about his squadron and the example he sets for his officers."

B.J gnawed on her lower lip while she digested this statement. Whether she believed Claire Phillips or not, she suspected that this part was true. Brick Maxwell might be a misguided buffoon whose taste in women was zip, but he was an ethical guy. Especially when it concerned his squadron.

Still, the fury was bubbling up in her. As much as she hated it, she knew why. She was jealous, damn it.

"Are we finished talking?"

Claire nodded. "Sure, if you want. I'm sorry if I upset you. I just thought that . . . since we have so much in common, it would be nice if we could talk."

B.J. looked at her. "What is it we have in common?"

"Our jobs, for one thing. We both work in what is mostly a man's profession, and they don't like us for it. For every woman in a foreign press bureau, there are a hundred guys who think she ought to be home mending their socks. I know it's the same for you. Look around this ship. How many of you are there?"

B.J. didn't have to look around. Since the death of Spam Parker, she had been the only woman fighter pilot on the USS *Reagan*. Things might have gotten better lately, but she could still sense the same old women-aren't-warriors resentment.

"You know what they call us?" B.J. said.

"What?"

"Aliens." She had to smile as she said it. "It was supposed to be an insult, but I've gotten over that. I even had a picture of a little green extraterrestrial stenciled on my locker. Just to piss them off."

At this, Claire had a good laugh. "I love it. You're a trailblazer, and they don't know how to deal with it."

B.J. felt a tingle go through her. "Trailblazer?" She stared at Claire. "That's what Brick once said about . . . his wife. Did you know her?"

"I met her once, when I was doing a story at the cape. Now that I think about it, she was a lot like you. Same features, same size. She was smart, good-looking, and tough."

B.J. didn't reply. Claire Phillips's words were replaying in her mind. *She was a lot like you.* For a while she leaned against the rail, letting the warm sea wind blow through her hair. It explained a few things. Seven bullet holes, for example, in the body of the man who was holding the knife to her throat. Brick Maxwell was shooting the man who threatened his wife.

A lot like you.

She had come up here determined to dislike this woman. Claire Phillips was an adversary. One of those fluff-headed females whose looks and connections counted for more than talent and guts.

Wrong again.

"Look, Ms. Phillips, I ought to tell you—"

"Claire."

"Claire." B.J. cleared her throat and started over. "What I meant to say was . . . I'm sorry."

"Sorry? For what?"

"For being rude." She knew she was blurting the words, but she wanted to get it over. "For behaving like a jerk. I apologize."

There, she said it. Now she would get the hell out of there.

As she turned to leave, Claire touched her arm. "You're not wearing your sling."

"It wasn't much of a wound. Just a nick, really."

"I heard it was a close thing."

B.J. had to grin, thinking about it. "Hard to believe, isn't it? Brick Maxwell—a great pilot, but a really lousy shot."

The staccato beat of the whirling blades broke the morning stillness. The two helicopters—the AH-1W Whiskey

Cobra in the lead, trailed by the UH-1N Super Huey—skimmed the floor of the canyon, pulling up over the natural bridge that spanned the canyon.

Before them spread the valley. On the western slope rose a high ridge.

In the raised aft seat of the Cobra, the pilot glanced at his GPS coordinates again, then turned toward the ridge. Beyond the crest, he saw what they were looking for. The hillside was littered with debris, torn metal, destroyed machinery. In several places the slope was splotched with the black residue of an intense blaze.

After the Cobra completed a sweep, meeting no opposition, both choppers settled onto the sloping brown terrain.

A dozen men in combat gear spilled out of the Huey. A fire team armed with MP-5N submachine guns took the lead while the six men behind them fanned out, walking through the littered terrain, turning over and examining pieces of wreckage.

Fragments of the destroyed MiG-29 were strewn for half a mile. The officer in charge, marine Capt. Barry Weaver, snapped pictures with a Nikon digital while the others turned over hunks of metal, looking for clues.

"Over here, Captain," yelled Gunnery Sergeant Chavez. "Looks like part of the cockpit."

It was. There wasn't much left—the remnants of an instrument panel, part of a radio console. Weaver took several shots; then he turned the pieces over and took more. When he was finished, a Navy medical corpsman poked around, filling several plastic zip bags with samples and scrapings from the twisted metal.

They continued searching. The corpsman took more samples from likely hunks of wreckage. After half an hour, Weaver said, "That's it. We've seen enough of this place."

After the Whiskey Cobra did another periphery search, the Huey lifted off. The helicopters skimmed the ridge, heading eastward before making the turn toward the coast.

Weaver, standing between the two pilots in the Huey, saw it first—something metallic, glinting in the sand.

"There." He pointed down and to the right. "Check it out."

The pilot nodded and slewed the Huey around into a turn. While the Huey hovered fifteen feet over the spot, Weaver and two marine riflemen fast-roped down.

Even before he reached the object, Weaver knew what he was seeing. He pulled out the Nikon and began clicking.

It was evening, and they were taking one of their walks—promenades, Claire used to call them—on the flight deck. The *Reagan*'s warplanes looked like museum exhibits, all tied down, intakes and tailpipes plugged with protective covers.

"Sam, do you think we'll get married?"

He stopped and looked at her in surprise. It was another of those questions out of the blue. She'd been doing that a lot lately.

"What kind of a question is that?"

"A perfectly simple one." She kept his hand clasped in hers. "Do you or do you not think we'll get married?"

"I don't . . . I guess I really haven't given it that much thought . . ."

"That is impossible to believe. You say you love me, but you haven't thought about whether you want to marry me?"

"I didn't mean that." He sounded flustered, and he hated it. "Where'd this come from? Do you want to get married?"

She smiled. "Is that a proposal?"

"No. I mean . . . it's a question. It sounds like you're asking me if I want to get married."

"Well, do you?"

"I don't know. I mean, yes, but not yet."

"You mean yes, you want to get married, but no, you haven't made up your mind to do it."

He stopped and looked at her. "Did I say that?"

"More or less. I'm just helping you out."

"Is this how you interview people on your television reports?"

"No. Sometimes I have to get pushy." Then she laughed, which was his clue that she was yanking him around again.

For a while neither spoke, watching the brown coastline of Oman slide past the carrier's port side. A pair of Seahawk helicopters skimmed the water between the *Reagan* and the shoreline.

She took his arm. "How long will the *Reagan* be in Bahrain?"

"Long enough to patch the hull. Two or three weeks; then we'll head to the States so the ship can get a major refitting."

She seemed to be mulling over this information. "That means, if we're going to be together, I'll have to be in the United States."

"Until the *Reagan* deploys again. Wherever that might be."

"Sam, have you ever thought of another line of work?"

"No. Have you?"

"No." She waited a moment. "But I'm open to suggestions."

"Bandar Abbas," said Gritti, "on the starboard side."

Maxwell looked through the thick panes of the flag bridge. The *Reagan* was transiting the narrow Strait of Hormuz, returning to the Persian Gulf. He could make out shadowed outlines on the Iranian shore—buildings, cranes, docks.

"Do you think they've figured out what happened to their missing submarine?"

"I hope they paid cash for it," said Gritti.

It was five past eleven, and they were waiting for the admiral to appear for the 1100 meeting he had called. On the opposite side of the compartment, Red Boyce was staring thoughtfully in the direction of Iran, a half-gnawed cigar jutting from his jaw. Guido Vitale was on the phone with Stickney, who had promised to drop into the briefing as soon as they'd passed the strait. Cmdr. Ed Mulvaney, the *Reagan*'s XO, was standing in for Stickney.

Two of Boyce's other squadron skippers were there—Rico Flores of the VFA-34 Bluetails, and Gordo Gray, who had taken over the Tomcat squadron after the skipper, Burner Crump, was killed in Yemen. The two commanders were talking quietly by the coffeepot in the corner of the compartment.

Admiral Fletcher burst into the room, trailed by his aide, a baby-faced lieutenant named Wenck. "Sorry, gentlemen." He tossed his hat onto the plotting table. "I just got off the line with SECNAV and CNO." He went to the head of the conference table. "Seats, please."

Maxwell was struck again by the change in Fletcher. Even after the calamitous events in Yemen and the Gulf of Aden, he still managed to exude command authority. Perhaps, he mused, Fletcher was one of those officers like Grant or Eisenhower who metamorphosed into leaders in the heat of war.

"I've been instructed to warn all of you, and each of your subordinates, that everything that happened during this campaign is classified. We will have selective memories about the events of the past week."

The officers all nodded.

For your information," Fletcher went on, "when the *Reagan* drops anchor in Bahrain, I'll be immediately relieved of command. Until my successor shows up, Captain Stickney will be the acting Battle Group Commander."

This caused murmurs around the table. No one was surprised, especially after Fletcher had assumed full responsibility for the action in Yemen.

"I'm informed that there will not be a court-martial." He paused and looked around the table. "The truth is, I was rather looking forward to testifying about what happened out here. About who was taking orders from whom."

Fletcher let this sink in. The unwelcome presence of Whitney Babcock still pervaded the room.

"As it turns out, no one—not the Joint Chiefs, the Secretary of the Navy, certainly not the White House—wants the world to hear how our chain of command was short-circuited. So I will be let off with a letter of reprimand—and a peremptory retirement."

Boyce spoke up. "That's a coverup, Admiral. They just want to suppress the truth about the deal between Babcock and Al-Fasr."

"You said it, not me. There are other things they'd like to suppress. The spy on our battle group staff, for one."

At this, everyone's eyes went to the empty chair next to Fletcher—the seat usually occupied by Spook Morse.

Mulvaney asked, "Has anyone figured why Morse sold out to Al-Fasr?"

Guido Vitale spoke up. "The FBI is working on it. Morse became acquainted with Al-Fasr about four years ago, when he was on Fifth Fleet staff in Manama. I was there, and I remember that Spook was going through a bad time. His wife had left him, run off with some Brit she met playing tennis. About then he was passed over for promotion to captain, and he was bitter. More than bitter, as I remember. Spook had a dark side to him. That was probably when Al-Fasr got to him."

"He got his revenge," said Boyce. "Sucked us into Al-Fasr's trap."

"We still don't know how much damage Morse did," said Vitale. "We know that he gave our op plans away, and it was he who relayed our points of intended movement, which enabled Al-Fasr to position the submarine."

"Another lesson learned the hard way," Fletcher said. "We spent forty years learning how to beat Russian nuclear attack submarines. Then an obsolete diesel/electric boat sneaks into our battle group and damned near sinks us."

"What was the point?" asked Commander Mulvaney. "What was Al-Fasr trying to accomplish?"

"The same thing terrorists all want to accomplish," said Fletcher. "Revenge. An eye for an eye."

"This time it bit him in the ass," said Boyce. "Brick scraped him off on that ridge in Yemen."

Fletcher and Vitale exchanged glances. Fletcher nodded, and Vitale picked up a file folder. "Early this morning we inserted a marine recon team into the crash site of the MiG. They determined from the serial number that it was definitely the same one Al-Fasr was flying. They also searched the wreckage, looking for human remains that might be identifiable from the DNA. They didn't find anything—until they were airborne and egressing the area."

Vitale withdrew an eight-by-ten color photograph from the folder. "Then they found this."

He passed the photo around the table.

Maxwell peered at the object in the photo. A chill passed through him. He handed the photo to Boyce.

Boyce removed his cigar and stared at the photo. "Oh, shit."

"The ejection seat," said Admiral Fletcher. "Notice that it's been used. Successfully, according to the experts who analyzed this photo. It was found about a mile from the main crash site."

Maxwell's thoughts were already back in the late afternoon sky over Yemen. He could see the canyon, the eye of the needle, the shadow flitting over his canopy that saved his life. In his mind he relived the vertical scissors engagement, the energy-depleting maneuver that brought both their fighters perilously close to the earth. Pulling out of the dive, the older Fulcrum was unable to match the pullout radius of the F/A-18.

Al-Fasr's jet struck the ground. The wreckage was scattered over a square mile.

He couldn't have survived.

Or could he? Maxwell had not seen the final impact. His own jet had been pointed away, turning back to counter the scissoring MiG.

At the instant the Fulcrum scraped the ridge, the pilot, if his reactions were quick enough, might have realized his jet was doomed and pulled the ejection handle.

The Zvezda K-36 ejection seat was good, better perhaps than anyone else's. At the 1989 Paris Air Show, a Russian demo pilot ejected at 250 feet while his jet was in a vertical dive. He survived.

Maxwell placed the photograph back on the table. For a moment he stared out the window at the dark coastline passing on the starboard side.

"He's still out there," he said to no one in particular.

Claire needed a nap. The stress and fatigue of the past week were weighing on her like a leaden mantle.

When she let herself in the stateroom she noticed the thick manila envelope atop the foldout desk. She wondered who had placed it there. The room steward? He had a key for all the staterooms.

She kicked off her shoes, noticing again the gray sterility of the stateroom. If she had to spend any more time aboard Navy warships, she would decorate. Oriental carpets, some decent prints on the bulkheads, photographs for the desk. And she'd have music, not that stuff they played on the ship's entertainment channel for the teenage sailors. She would bring CDs of light classical and soft jazz like Sam had in his stateroom.

She popped open a warm Diet Coke and settled into the straight-backed desk chair. That was another thing she hated—this damned spartan furniture. She'd get a decent padded chair, one with a little fashion to it that she could get comfortable in and do some serious reading.

The manila envelope lay in front her. It was sealed, no address, no marking.

She ran her fingernail under the flap and opened it. The stack of paper was half an inch thick. Each page bore a copy of a stamp: SECRET. RESTRICTED DISTRIBUTION. She found nothing to indicate the source of the document.

Not until she was through the second page did she realize what she was reading. It was a transcription of some kind of message traffic. By the conversational dialogue, she guessed that the parties were communicating via a telephone or radio. She also guessed the identity of the speakers.

> *"You have not kept your word."*
> *"I gave my word that we would not retaliate after the air strike if you did not send in an assault force. But then you sent in an assault force."*
> *"That was not an assault. You already know that the marine team was sent in for no purpose except to retrieve the downed pilots. They had no other objective. Now the situation has become very complicated. The President has authorized a strike."*

Claire felt her skin prickle. The document in her hand was potent enough to destroy a political career. Perhaps an administration.

She read on.

> *"This can still be resolved. My agents in San'a report that they are almost ready to initiate the coup. When they give the signal, my troops will immediately seize the military headquarters and the government broadcasting station. We expect no resistance. I will control the Republic of Yemen."*
> *"That is good. What about our marines on the ground? They have to be lifted out."*
> *"Soon. It will be possible within a day or so."*

She lowered the sheaf of papers for a moment. Vince Maloney's words came back to her: *We protect his new gov-*

ernment from all his resentful Arab neighbors, and Yemen becomes an American colony. Does that make sense?

Yes, it made sense now. Vince had it right, and it had cost him his life.

Al-Fasr wanted Yemen, and someone in a high office was helping him get it. None of the material was date-stamped, which meant that authentication would be impossible. She couldn't prove anything. All she had was paper, copies of documents without attribution, nothing verifiable.

On a yellow legal pad, she drew a time line, beginning with the killings of Admiral Dunn and Admiral Mellon and Ambassador Halaby, connecting them with all the events in Yemen. Then she began overlaying them with the transcribed conversations.

When she was finished, she was sure. The connection was unmistakable. Even if the documents did not provide legal proof, the circumstantial evidence was overwhelming. The sequence of transcriptions matched the events perfectly.

An anonymous donor had just delivered to her the most explosive news story of her career.

Why?

As she thought more about it, the answer came to her, like the pieces of a mosaic. She knew who had sent the documents, and she understood what she was supposed to do with them.

Thank you, Admiral, Claire thought.

CHAPTER TWENTY-NINE

YELLOW RIBBONS

Washington, D.C.
1905, Thursday, 8 August

That bitch, thought Whitney Babcock.

He was into his third Scotch, no ice, when the special segment of *The Nightly Report* began. When the face of Claire Phillips appeared on the television screen, Babcock felt his headache intensifying. *I should have thrown her off the ship when I had the chance.*

He was alone in his Georgetown apartment. Outside, long shadows of evening covered the tree-lined street. Ten minutes into the program, during the first commercial break, his telephone rang. It was the line used by the White House staff.

"Are you watching?" asked Dan Summerville, White House Chief of Staff.

"I am."

"It's worse than we expected."

Babcock's eyes stayed riveted to the flickering screen. The break was over and the Phillips woman was back. The camera switched from her face to a map of Yemen. She was talking about a place called Al-Hazir.

"Why didn't someone stop it?" Babcock said. "One phone call from the White House to the television network would have squashed it."

"You still don't get it, do you, Whit? Do you really think the President would let himself get implicated in a scandal like this?"

Babcock remembered that he had never liked Summerville. He was the President's crony and longtime hatchetman.

"Scandal? That woman doesn't have anything—"

"She has the biggest terrorist story of the year. In a few minutes, you're going to see a recently retired two-star admiral give his version of what happened in Yemen."

"Fletcher?" Babcock's voice cracked. "He doesn't have a clue about what was going on."

"Keep watching. In front of eighty million viewers, he's going to say that someone colluded with a terrorist who killed two hundred Americans and torpedoed our mightiest aircraft carrier."

With a mounting sense of dread, Babcock was getting the picture. After the World Trade Center and Pentagon attacks, the American public was in no mood to hear about deals made with terrorists. Instead of blaming the Yemen debacle on the President, or the Battle Group Commander, or the Joint Chiefs, the administration had selected another scapegoat.

"I need to see the President right away," said Babcock. "I've got to talk to him."

"Forget it."

"Dan, please. This is my career on the line. I should at least have a chance to offer my resignation."

"That's not an option. You were fired at four o'clock this afternoon."

Babcock felt a fresh stab of pain emanating from somewhere behind his eyes. He took a long pull from the glass of Scotch. "Why wasn't I told?"

"You can read the President's statement in the paper tomorrow. But it won't be exactly what he said in private to the National Security Council."

Babcock hated to ask, but he had to know. "Uh, what did he say, exactly?"

"He was pretty explicit." Summerville paused, and Babcock could tell that he was enjoying himself. "He said—and I'm quoting verbatim here—'Inform that supercilious little prick that he is going to swing in the breeze. This administration will have nothing to do with him.' "

The words penetrated Babcock's brain like hammer blows. He wondered if the President really said that. Summerville was a sadistic bastard.

It didn't matter. He lowered the telephone and stared at the television. He could hear Summerville still talking. He had heard enough.

On the screen was the face of Langhorne Fletcher. He looked different out of uniform. He no longer had that avuncular image, but looked more like a rumpled academician. He was talking about chains of command and presumptive authority and deadly force. As Fletcher spoke, the image switched to a map of the Gulf of Aden.

Another image appeared. Babcock sat upright in his chair and stared at the screen. It was a still shot of a man on the bridge of a Navy vessel, grinning and looking like a young MacArthur in his starched khakis and aviator sunglasses. In the background, Babcock could hear the voices of Claire Phillips and Langhorne Fletcher.

They were talking about *him*.

". . . while the marines were under fire from terrorists, you say this National Security Council staff member, Whitney Babcock, refused to authorize the use of deadly force?"

Fletcher was nodding his head. "That's essentially correct."

"While at the same time he was communicating secretly with the terrorist leader?"

"Yes."

Claire Phillips looked thoughtful. "Admiral, wouldn't you call that an act of disloyalty?"

"No," said Fletcher. "I would call that an act of treason."

"If so, won't it lead to a congressional investigation of Mr. Babcock? An indictment, perhaps?"

"So I have been informed," said Fletcher. "I have offered the investigators my full cooperation."

At this, Babcock rose and walked away from the television. For a while he stared out the window. Washington was in the thrall of late summer. The canopy of foliage covered the sidewalk on either side of the street. In the deepening shadows he could see joggers and Rollerbladers and a couple pushing a pram.

He pulled open the drawer of the antique writing desk. The oiled .38 Smith & Wesson lay in its felt-lined box. It had five rounds in the cylinder.

He picked up the revolver, hefted it, peered into the muzzle. The pistol both fascinated and repulsed him. He had never actually fired the thing, though he had rehearsed it many times in his imagination.

It had been so close. Almost within his grasp. Yemen and its oil deposits and a new order in the Middle East. He would have been hailed as the rising star of global politics.

No more. He wouldn't appear on the cover of *Time* magazine as Whitney Babcock—warrior-statesman. Instead, he would forever be Whitney Babcock—traitor.

With that thought, he raised the pistol to his temple.

The USS *Reagan* headed into a fifteen-knot wind. It was a classic Virginia coastal summer morning—milk-hazy sky, the sea sparkling like a field of jewels.

On the forward flight deck, clouds of steam billowed over the parked warplanes, giving them a ghostly, preternatural appearance. Helmeted deck crewmen scuttled beneath the jets like crabs in a mist. The howl of a hundred jet engines resonated over the steel deck. One after the other, every ten seconds, fighters hurtled down the catapults.

Poised on the number one catapult, Maxwell shoved both throttles to the full-thrust detent. At the center of the deck, between the two catapults, he could see the shooter. One last look inside his cockpit—no warnings, no lights. He tilted his helmet against the headrest and gave the shooter a curt salute—the ready signal.

Two and one-half seconds later, he felt the acceleration ram him back in the seat. In his peripheral vision, the gray mass of the USS *Ronald Reagan* swept behind him.

It had taken nearly four weeks for the shipfitters to apply the temporary patch to the carrier's punctured outer hull. Escorted by a flotilla of protective vessels, which this time included two *Los Angeles*–class submarines, the *Reagan* passed through the Strait of Hormuz, around the shore of Yemen, northward through the Red Sea to the Suez, then westward beyond Gibraltar and into the Atlantic. The voyage took thirteen days.

Maxwell could see the shoreline of Virginia. After joining up with his fifteen Super Hornets of VFA-36 overhead the ship, he waited another ten minutes while all the squadrons of the air wing aligned themselves into a seventy-five-ship gaggle.

With CAG Boyce leading in a VFA-34 Bluetail Hornet, the massive formation swept over the beach below False Cape, then turned north toward the Oceana naval air station. Roaring low over the sprawling base, the armada passed in review.

It was a ritual of carrier aviation. At the end of a long cruise, the jets of a carrier air wing catapulted for the last time from their ship and flew home. Waiting ashore were wives, children, parents, lovers, well-wishers—and mourners. Not all who sailed on the *Reagan* were coming home.

Fifteen seconds apart, the jets screeched down on the concrete of Oceana's long runways. As Maxwell led his squadron to their assigned parking row, he noticed the hangar closest to the flight line. An entire side of the building was covered with a giant yellow ribbon. Then he saw the crowd—at least a thousand—gathered in front of the hangar. They were waving yellow ribbons. A valiant squad of shore patrolmen was trying to hold the crowd back.

As the pilots climbed out of the jets and started across the ramp, the crowd stopped waiting. They surged through the restraining ribbon. Children squealed, women yelled, and the pilots broke ranks and sprinted toward them.

The two groups melded together like a confluence of flooding streams. Women and kids and girlfriends were swept up, whirled and kissed and squeezed. Gallons of tears gushed down all their cheeks, held back during six months of separation and pain and worry.

Maxwell worked his way through the crowd. He knew no one was there to meet him. He had no wife, no children, no immediate family, at least none who bothered with such things. Claire was in Washington, tied up with the Babcock story.

How many homecomings like this had he been through? The Gulf War had been the mother of all homecomings. That was before Claire, before Debbie. His father, of course, had been away.

That was a lifetime ago. Now Debbie was gone. So was his father, at least in spirit. Claire had her own life. The world had changed.

When he'd nearly reached the hangar with the yellow ribbon hanging from the side, he looked back. The crowd resembled celebrants after a World Series victory: yellow ribbons, hugs, kisses, grinning faces everywhere. It was a special moment.

"Welcome home, sailor."

The voice came from behind him. He turned, and a smile spread over his face. "You're supposed to be in Washington."

Claire was clutching a yellow ribbon. Around her neck was the scarf he had bought for her in Dubai. The easterly breeze ruffled her chestnut hair, sweeping the thin linen skirt around her legs. Maxwell had never seen her look more beautiful.

"I told them I had something more important to do."

He took her in his arms, pressed her to him. He could think of nothing to say. For a long while he held her, closing his eyes against the bustle and the tumult of the crowd around them.

Finally he looked at her and said, "I love you, Claire."

She smiled. "Took you long enough. You said it without being coached."

"I'm a slow learner."

"It must run in the family."

He was looking at her, puzzling over her words, when he became aware of another presence: a tall figure, ramrod straight, familiar and formidable.

"I think she means me," said Vice Adm. Harlan Maxwell.

The deep voice triggered a flood of memories, good and bad. "Dad?"

The older man was clutching his own yellow ribbon. "If you and Claire would rather be alone . . . then I understand." He looked awkward, unsure of himself.

That was different, thought Brick. One thing Admiral Harlan Maxwell had never been was unsure of himself.

Brick thought for a second; then it came to him. He looked at Claire. "You brought him."

"It was your father's idea. He called last night and suggested it."

"I'm the one who's the slow learner," said the admiral. "I've been a damned fool. I almost lost you in Yemen, and I wouldn't have been able to live with myself if"—Harlan Maxwell's voice cracked, and he struggled to keep his composure—"if I hadn't told my son how . . . how proud I was of him. That I loved him."

Brick was stunned. He felt as though he were dreaming. For most of his life he had wanted to hear those words.

His father hugged him, then kissed him on the cheek. Through the cotton shirt Brick could feel the thin frame, the bony shoulders. His father was showing his age. The years had slipped away from them.

They had both been fools, thought Brick. Prideful and stubborn and wrong. They had a lot of catching up to do. This was as good a place as any to begin.

"I love you, Dad," he said.

The electrifying fiction debut of
A MILITARY WRITER WHO "TRANSPORTS
READERS INTO THE COCKPIT."
—San Diego Union–Tribune

Robert Gandt

WITH HOSTILE INTENT

A novel of modern-day dogfights
by a former Navy pilot

"Aerial flight scenes more thrilling than a
back-to-back showing of *Top Gun* and *Iron Eagle*, this
red-hot piece of military fiction is certain to keep
readers riveted."
—*Publishers Weekly*

"**A GREAT JOB!** The suspense builds, the
characters are believable, and the combat scenes are
excellent." —**Dale Brown**

AVAILABLE FROM SIGNET
0-451-20486-7

To order call: 1-800-788-6262